TO THE HAPPY FEW

TO THE HAPPY FEW

A story of
death, love, and loss
in the Sudan

Hume Horan

ELECTRIC CITY

My thanks and admiration go to Irene Petrlik, whose impeccable taste and numberless imaginative, incremental improvements to the book's design resulted in a product that commends itself to the eye and hand. To mind and heart? Alas—that remains the author's job.

I also thank Professor Martin Daly of the University of Tennessee at Chattanooga for the slide that became the cover illustration. He brilliantly caught one of the all-too-frequent moments in Sudan's long revolutionary history.

Finally, I thank Margery Boichel Thompson, who brought to my rough manuscript her editorial jeweler's eye. What does one call an infinite capacity for taking pains? Genius.

ELECTRIC CITY PRESS
6609 31st Street, N.W.
Washington, D.C. 20015

Limited edition

Printed in the United States of America on acid-free, recycled paper.

Library of Congress Catalog Card Number: 96-85793

ISBN 0-9653528-0-3

For those I love

CONTENTS

Souviens-toi de notre amour, et que l'image de ton cher compagnon ne te quitte pas.

— Stendahl, *Promenades dans Rome*

"I have often wondered why I kept going. . . . But I am a man and a man is responsible for himself."

— George Gaylord Simpson, *The Dechronization of Sam Magruder*

TO THE HAPPY FEW

EN ROUTE

1

Khartoum took us by surprise. One moment there was only the thin, green trace of the Nile on the Nubian Desert's grainy, light brown surface. But then, just as the Swiss Air DC-9 banked to begin its descent, there it was!—revealed by the shadows of late afternoon. The centerfold of a children's story. A pop-up book of a town. At noontime, what would one see? A minimalist landscape? Brown on brown? Khartoum's tan bricks would vanish into the desert all about.

I looked over at Marjorie. Her head was back against the seat. Her eyes were closed. She was taking deep breaths and patches of perspiration stood on her forehead and upper lip. Even her fine, light brown hair looked moist. Her freckled hand—it always reminded me of a child's—held tight to Brian's last letter. He was winding up his summer counselor's job coaching inner-city children in English and math. I could see his return address label: Brian Chamberlain, Upward Bound, St. Andrew's School, Middletown, DE. Lucky kid! I thought. The mid-Atlantic region—bicycling, tennis, sailing, sculling on Noxentown Pond. I pulled my mind back to our trip.

Marjorie disliked air travel, and our intermediate stop in Cairo hadn't changed her mind. Not a glimpse of the Pyramids; a *qibli*, a dust storm from the southeast, had blacked out the town. As soon as the plane doors opened, the dust—fine as aerosol—was all around us. It felt like graphite on our skins. The mobile air conditioner never showed up. We had to stay on board. And when Marjorie stepped out onto the landing of the stairs, a soldier on the ground shouted and motioned her back with his machine gun.

We had waited an hour. Two hours. The captain had walked back to explain and apologize: "There is nothing we can do. It is always like this here. The missing fuel truck. The procedures. The nothing ready. The Arabs call it the *nizam*—what we call 'red tape.' This time we are waiting for some VIP." Three hours: A commotion at planeside. *He* had arrived. Finally we'd taken off, heading south toward Upper Egypt and Sudan. "Upper" Egypt? The term described where the Nile's water was coming from—but somehow conflicted with my instinct, which said "up" must be "north"!

It was a comfortable, companionable moment. The stewardess had brought us each a glass of champagne and assorted canapes. I'd put my seat back and taken up *Tennis* magazine—there was an article about the greatest Wimbledons in history. The writer favored the 1992 championship when Agassi and McEnroe had so gloriously said "hello" and "good-bye" in the singles and doubles, respectively. I wasn't sure I agreed. What about the great Borg-McEnroe or Borg-Connors Wimbledons of the 1980s? I had time to reflect, there was no rush: I might do some serious reading—Stendhal's *Chroniques Italiennes* was there (a present from Marj) in the seat pocket in front of me. Or maybe I'd put on my Walkman, and listen to one of the greatest first-cut, first-singles ever, Crosby, Stills, and Nash's "Sweet Judy Blue Eyes."

Marj was reading her latest *Gourmet*. She looked over and touched my arm. With a smile she pointed to Stendhal: "That's my problem. You read *Chroniques Italiennes*, while I sit—my mouth watering for *Crostata di Crema e Cioccolatta*. Makes me want to get up and raid the galley! I should have brought a vegetarian cookbook, my *Enchanted Broccoli Forest*? When we get to Khartoum, those pounds gained on home leave . . . it's back to mortification of the flesh."

I'd reflected that Marj was always dieting, but as I looked over at her, I also thought that she—and I—had no cause to complain about the results.

It was at that moment we'd argued. Someone in the first class compartment had lit up a cigar. The aroma of the downstream smoke was sharp and penetrating inside the still-hot cabin.

Marj called the flight attendant who confirmed that cigars were forbidden on this flight. Marj asked to have the cigar put out. The woman vanished through the curtains into first class land, and the smoke continued to reach us. When Marj called a second time, the stewardess seemed embarrassed: "Yes," she said, "but it's the Sudanese Presidency minister, Minister al-Atrash. Perhaps one of you could speak with him?"

"Would you?" Marj had asked me.

"Why start a new tour by arguing with some local VIP?" I'd answered. "We'll be in Khartoum soon anyway."

"In a few hours, you mean? You don't care if meanwhile *I* feel sick? Your nose wasn't always so insensitive! Remember our visit to the art gallery in DC? And your remarks about the manager?"

"That was different—vintage B.O. and Drakar Noire, all fusing in a unique, prehistoric funk. The guy was a threat to the ozone layer, a violation of the atmospheric test ban treaty, a one-man weapon of mass destruction . . . "

I'd started to laugh at my own humor, but Marj cut me off: "You're just avoiding the issue. And getting carried away, too. *I'd* go and politely ask him to put out his cigar, and I bet he'd do so. But then you'd get mad and be a sulker." She shrugged, and turned back to her magazine. I felt bad. I hadn't handled the issue well. I half apologized. I was relieved when, after half an hour, the smoker had evidently finished his cigar.

We were lower now; I could make out the smudged outlines of the "Union Jack" street pattern Lord Kitchener had imposed on the city he conquered in 1898. My watch said 3:50 P.M. Only minutes to landing, I thought.

Once again, I took out the State Department's "Country Notes" on Sudan from my breast pocket. One of those relaxing "preparation rituals," like a tennis player bouncing a ball three times before a serve. The "Notes" were well marked up. I looked over the underlining: "Land area 967,491 square miles. . . . Largest country in Africa. . . . Population estimated 24 million in mid-1985. . . . More than one hundred languages, . . . Arabic the primary language of more than half. There are major non-Arab groups in Sudan's northeast, west and far north. Non-Muslim Africans predominate in the southern provinces. Dust storms common, . . . mean temperatures and daily maximums extremely high. . . . A primarily agricultural economy based on cotton, groundnuts, and sorghum. . . . Independence in 1956."

A jolt. We'd landed. A roar of reverse thrust; the seat belts tightened. The plane tilted—it seemed to be searching for something on the ground. We raced on, across what felt like rumble bumps. A bin banged open in the galley. From a seat in front came the sounds and smell of air sick. "Breathe through your mouth!" I ordered Marjorie. She'd been sponging with eau de cologne. Now she pressed the handkerchief against her nose. Her eyes were shut.

Even maximum reverse thrust seemed hardly to be slowing us down as we sped through the thin, superheated air outside. We passed

3

two parked Sudan Air Force C-130's. Their camouflage paint was lighter than ours. On their fuselage were Sudan's national markings—a bull's-eye of red, white, and black. Near them—same camouflage paint, same markings—two helicopters, French manufacture. A Puma and an Alouette. The Puma's door hung crookedly from a broken hinge, the Alouette, with a flat tire, was "down on the port side." Did its rotor blades have an especially forlorn droop? A derelict DC-3 angled blind engine housings toward the sky. In the background, prefab metal hangars stood, their bays open. Next to one stood a Saladin armored car. The military wing of the airport, I guessed, but not a uniform in sight.

"We made it kid," I said to Marjorie. "Terra firma."

But as we approached—then passed—the civilian terminal, I wasn't so sure. I glimpsed service vehicles and, for the first time, people. They appeared to be wading through water up to their knees—mirage effect, I realized.

I get a feeling of rebirth, almost reincarnation, every time we land at a new Foreign Service post. We're carried, sheltered, and nourished by this airplane-mother, our last link to the old life—the life of Safeways, the *Washington Post*, phones that work, maybe even a ballet at the Kennedy Center—and deposited, keyed up and a little apprehensive, at the start of a new one. We deplane to a new job, a new town, new friends. New chances to succeed, or *not* to succeed (in the Foreign Service one never "failed"). What would it be like, I wondered, being the embassy's deputy chief of mission?

I recalled our director general's lecturing us in Washington about the rough and smooth of a DCM's assignment: how we'd all been selected from the very top of our class. How for maybe two decades we'd faced new jobs, new bosses, new countries, and new languages every two to three years. Each time with success.

But just ahead of us now was the most hazardous "white water" of the Foreign Service rapids. As DCMs we were to be our ambassadors' "alter egos," their "right hands," their "main men." We'd coordinate, organize, and sometimes enforce. We'd run the embassy in the ambassador's absence. The job would test us for experience and management skill; it would also test for personal qualities: leadership, integrity, skill with people, loyalty (up and down).

The director general had laid out the odds: four out of ten DCMs succeeded and would eventually become ambassadors. He didn't have to tell us about the others. We'd all seen them, huddled together in the cafeteria—briefly escaping from their dead-end jobs. "Spent rockets!" "Wounded eagles!" Their topic of conversation? "We wuz contenders. We shoulda had another shot, only . . . "

The plane jerked to a halt on seemingly the last feet of apron. As it taxied back, through the window I could see the main terminal, about a hundred fifty yards away—two stories high, a balcony running the length of the building. All was cracked, stained, peeling. Had the sands just yielded to the archaeologists's spade? Middle Kingdom, circa 2100 B.C.? A piece of torn and faded cloth fluttered atop a flagpole. Probably the original one raised in 1956! The balcony was crowded, and some banners hung from the railing.

We passengers were told to remain in our seats until "His Excellency" had gotten off. Through the window, I saw a balding head, atop a thickset body, make its way through a reception committee and climb into a limousine, which disappeared in the direction of the airport terminal. We were among the last to deplane. Marj used the time to freshen her makeup and smooth her hair. As we stood in the aisle, she put her palms on the back of her hips and stretched. She caught me looking. Smiled.

"Curtain's going up. Our audience is waiting," I said, adding: "And watch out for those wobbly stairs. You don't want to hear for the next three years about 'how the Humpty Dumpties came to Khartoum.' Bad for the *bella figura!* And the *bella* bottom!" Another smile—our argument forgotten.

From the doorway, I could see a car from the airport authority drive up. Two Americans got out—one in a safari suit, carrying a radio in his hand. Security, for sure. Over by the terminal I could see a group of Americans gathered. Several official-looking cars. I looked carefully: none carried a flag. I'd wondered if the ambassador might have come out to meet us.

Whatever people say, a first impression counts. Those watching us deplane saw a couple in their late thirties. The wife: tall, fair-complected, with pleasant, regular features. Very little makeup. Her figure? Well proportioned, well filled out. Pretty legs, *I* always said—though with characteristic modesty Marj would say her ankles were "heavy." The husband: about six-one. A rangy 175 pounds. Straight, thick, medium-to-short brown hair. Parted on the right. No signs of blow-drying. Blue eyes. A thin face, already lined, with a little too much jaw. He carried a Dunlop tennis bag. In Washington, D.C., his tan wash-and-wear suit, the blue button-down, oxford-cloth shirt said "young professional." In Third World capitals, they said "U.S. Embassy."

I remarked: "They look like friendlies. Poor guys—braced for the new DCM. For them, it's like Carl Sagan and the 'first encounter with extraterrestrials.' Probably expecting a pair of BEMs—bug-eyed monsters! Here goes—*Toujours gai!*"

LANDFALL

2

Heat. The sort of heat that precedes martyrdom. From the top of the steps I thought of smoke and bonfires. St. Joan of Arc. I heard Marj gasp. Automatically, I reached back for her hand. We began (carefully) descending the stairs. When we reached the macadam, I felt we were walking on the sun.

"Mr. Chamberlain? Will Dawkins—political counselor. You're most welcome to Khartoum. And this is your regional security officer, Pete Valiant." We shook hands. I'd been right. He was the safari suit. Rugged, intelligent-looking.

Dawkins went on: "A warm welcome, you'll agree. I'm sorry. A lousy thing to say. You must feel you've stepped off at the Earth's core. But this is almost the hottest day of the year in the hottest capital in the world—47 degrees Celsius! That's 116 degrees Fahrenheit—in the shade! The ambassador regrets he couldn't come. But our expeditor will clear customs and immigration for you. He'll bring your bags, if they haven't already fused in the hold."

Dawkins spoke fast. The words tumbled over themselves. I'd heard he was a good Arabist and had served in several Arab and African countries. Medium height, receding dark hair. Alert and studious-looking. Like me, he was wearing a brown, summer-weight wash-and-wear suit.

The crowd began to chant. Dawkins explained: "They're saying 'Sahyuniyya Imberialiyya laa tukhawwif al Jamahiriyyah!' That is, 'Libya defies Zionism and Imperialism.' It's on the banners. Not in your honor," Dawkins added with a smile. "They're warming up for an arrival ceremony of some kind."

Valiant was looking the balcony over carefully. He shook his head. "Maggots! Let's go." The four of us squeezed into the airport car and drove to the terminal.

There weren't many people in the receiving line. No wives, either. A few stood out: The defense attaché. Government-issue: A full colonel, six-three, athletic, hair in a modified high-and-tight. Army. Next came the ambassador's special assistant, Jack Kirby: fortyish, Tony Lama boots, brown Levis, Navajo silver buckle, short-sleeved red plaid cotton shirt. His full black beard, squared off at the bottom, gave him a patriarchal look. Dawkins explained the economic counselor had been called to an important meeting at the Foreign Ministry. A junior officer was representing him. I reproached myself: I hadn't been listening to names.

An expeditor came up—I gave him our passport case with our tickets, passports, shot cards, and baggage stubs. I asked him to look for three brown suitcases with green woolen twine on the handles.

I caught Valiant's eye on Marj. He broke in: "I say we get these poor people off the tarmac and out of here—before the Chamberlains run back to the plane." (*There's* an observant colleague, I thought. I owe you one already.)

Kirby, the special assistant, was looking toward the diplomatic gate. His eyes were following a maroon Mercedes 300 that had just come onto the field and was speeding toward us. I heard him say to Valiant: "Are we about to be privileged by a vision of Young Lochinvar?"

"The Playboy of the Eastern World?" Valiant laughed.

The Mercedes stopped a few feet from us. I approved of the driver. He rolled out and quickly—but smoothly—came around to open the right rear door for his VIP. (At official arrivals, you don't want your driver to run; but also you don't want him to amble around the car while you just sit there—baffled by the door mechanism?)

Because of the sun's angle, the interior of the Mercedes was in shadow. A long, dark-trousered leg unfolded itself, then a long arm in a dark suit jacket followed, and then the rest of him. Something spiderish about that exit, I thought. Before us stood a Sudanese, in his early thirties? My height, but thinner. His navy blue suit was well tailored, in a European manner. The material suggested silk. (How does he dry clean it? I wondered.) The jacket was pinched in at the waist—on him, an inch or two higher than on most Americans.

Women, I imagined, would find his looks clean-cut, even handsome. Thin lips, straight nose. What I was to come to recognize as a Sudanese anomaly: dark skin, with Caucasian features. On each cheek were three vertical keloid scars—they marked him (as I knew from my area training at the State Department's Foreign Service Institute) as a chief of the powerful, western Sudanese *Fur* ethnic group. I could hear our professor saying: "The *Fur* are one of the dominant Sudanese tribal federations. An ordinary tribesman has one cut on each cheek; a clan leader, two; chiefs and their sons, three. Slave auxiliaries none—until elected to full tribal status."

Ignoring the other Americans, he came directly up to Marj and me: "Minister-Counselor and Mrs. Chamberlain, I presume?" A mid-Atlantic English accent, a smooth, well-inflected voice. My hand was firmly clasped by fingers at least an inch longer than mine. "Sa'eed al-Masri, chief of presidential *and* Foreign Ministry protocol—at your service. On behalf of my country and government let me welcome you to Sudan—and offer you, and your bride, a modest refreshment in the VIP lounge? Meanwhile, your administrative people can perhaps complete the formalities?" His glance seemed to take in the entire embassy group.

"Already taken care of, Excellency," replied Dawkins.

"No, no, no!" said al-Masri, "I'm no excellency, no ambassador—yet, that is. Just a simple protocol official, trying to do my pleasant duty by my American friends!" Turning to me: "Shall we take our first cup of Arab coffee together?"

I saw Marj hesitate. But with (what I fancied as) my subtle arm pressure, we moved with al-Masri toward the "VIP reception" area. I was pleased that my embassy colleagues, following Kirby's example, had fallen in behind me. It hadn't been at all clear, I thought, that al-Masri had included them in his invitation to coffee.

A gravel path led us to a small, cinder-block building with French doors. Inside, an overstuffed couch faced four overstuffed chairs around a coffee table of "Louis Farouk" design: wobbly, arthritic legs and peeling artificial gold leaf. On its surface, the Olympic logo run wild. Too many drinks. An international symbol for arrivals and departures? The oriental rug was worn and nondescript. Dust bunnies peeked out from behind the brown velvet slip covers.

At a gesture from Sa'eed, a waiter came up with demitasse cups of coffee. Another waiter brought glasses of water for chasers. No one, I noticed, touched the water. The coffee was extra sweet. After a couple of swallows, sandy lees began to strain through my teeth. A quick look showed that while the window air conditioner was set on "maximum," only noise and hot air came out. One had to speak loudly and clearly. The plush of the upholstery was molding itself intimately to my legs and buttocks. The couch springs were gone. I felt I was sitting in a sports car, watching al-Masri through the windshield. Marj was doing something modest with her legs and dress.

"Mr. Minister-Counselor," Sa'eed was saying to me, "this is your first visit to the Arab world? But the embassy informs us that you have already studied some Arabic at your Foreign Service Institute. I studied in your country, too. Five years. One year at one of your big East Coast schools, then four at Menlo University in California. I liked Menlo 'too much.' Ha, ha! They liked me so much, they even kept my degree! Ha, ha!"

As Sa'eed spoke, his hands were in constant motion. They wove complicated patterns in the air. His knees rose and fell, as if working some invisible brake-clutch combination. He looked cool, cheerfully animated.

He went on: "You will like Sudan. That is for certain. Everyone says the Sudanese are very friendly. You must visit all parts of our country, Mr. Chamberlain. Especially the south. They are still pagans but with some Christian bosses. They are doing better and better. America and Sudan have much in common, indeed. Many ethnic groups, fertile agricultural land; you have the great Mississippi; we have the Nile. But I talk too much. I neglect my guests. Mrs. Chamberlain, another coffee? One of these Oranginas?"

Marj laughed as she took a glass of an orange-colored drink. "You've been very kind to meet us Mr. al-Masri, and I know I'll soon get used to the heat. Washington can be hot, too, you know. But right now, I feel I could transfuse this fluid into my arm, as some tennis players do!"

Al-Masri nodded sympathetically. "Most understandable. Khartoum, you know, is the hottest capital in the world. We Sudanese are almost proud of that. But soon you'll be accustomed." He turned to me: "I shall let you all go. But I'll see you tomorrow, perhaps, at ten at the ministry? Yes? Also, apropos of tennis—am I correct in guessing you both play?" (Sa'eed pointed to my Dunlop bag.)

Marj shook her head: "I'm more of an indoor person, but Josh . . . "

"I like to play for recreation," I said, "and also it's a way to make friends."

"We must play someday. But consider me already your friend. Ha, Ha! My renewed best wishes. We shall see each other often—in more pleasant settings than this airport. Though I fear the airport will become something of a home to you, as it is to me."

The last words were lost in the sound of jet engines rising to a crescendo as an aircraft taxied up to the VIP lounge. Then silence. The inner door of the VIP lounge opened, and I saw—this time from the front—a thickset body begin to cross the lounge toward the exit. The man's hairline was receding, his complexion pockmarked. His right hand held a cigar. Sa'eed glanced up. A look of childlike merriment?—anticipation?—crossed his features. For that instant he looked no more than fifteen.

"Mr. Minister! Excellency!" he called out in a rather high-pitched voice. The man stopped, Sa'eed was on his feet. He'd crossed the room, shaken the man's hand, and was leading him toward us. Sa'eed's features were again under control. His expression was composed, straightforward. We all rose.

"Excellency," Sa'eed began, "may I introduce the new American minister-counselor, Mr. Chamberlain, and his wife. You already know, I believe, the other members of the American embassy. Mr. and Mrs. Chamberlain, this is His Excellency Salim al-Atrash, minister for Presidency affairs, and a most important man! He has just returned from Cairo. Perhaps you two traveled together?" The minister's handshake was limp, his greeting perfunctory. He was looking over my shoulder at the door.

Sa'eed seemed to intercept the look. "The minister," he explained to us, "is to receive a visiting delegation. I will join him. But you all will at least come with us to the door?" (Did I detect an undercurrent in Sa'eed's words and manner? The merest trace of malicious satisfaction?)

From the exit of the VIP lounge, we could see the aircraft doors just opening, the stairs were not yet in place. The plane was a big one: an Ilyushin Il-62, four engines, turbofans, a wingspread of almost 150 feet. The model had begun service in the mid-1960s. From my days in the U.S. Marine Corps I could even remember the NATO reporting name, "CLASSIC." Above the fuselage I could decipher—in green Arabic script—the words, *Jamahiriyyah Libiyya Arabiyyah*." The tail unit bore the rectangular fin flash of Libyan civil aviation.

"A friendship delegation, I understand, from our sister republic," Sa'eed remarked to me. (Was his voice a bit *too* bland, expressionless?) Al-Atrash's look of admonition seemed to slide off al-Masri's polished exterior.

It seemed time to go. I thanked my colleagues for coming out to meet me. A warm handshake from Sa'eed, a perfunctory one from al-Atrash, then Marj and I excused ourselves and went to our car. Pete Valiant "rode shotgun" in the front passenger seat. Jack Kirby asked to ride in the back with us.

My driver eased the doors shut with a sound like a vault closing. I half-expected to see him spin a combination dial.

I'd seen and ridden in such cars before. A fully armored, Chevrolet Impala. Its brown paint and conventional lines would have looked normal at a car wash. But just raise the hood, or try to open the door, or lower the windows. No Impala is pushed by a 450-horsepower, 4.8 cubic liter engine. No ordinary car doors do so much for the upper body of those that open and close them. It was amusing at diplomatic functions to see doormen give the handle an imperious tug. And then another. Finally, they'd have to plant their feet, and pull—like oarsmen. Only then would the door, grudgingly, start to move. The bulletproof windows were immovable, so the air-conditioning had better never fail. And the windows gave you headaches: to look out through a half-inch of security glass was like using someone else's prescription eyeglasses.

My first surprise: Pointing his finger directly across the runways, Valiant indicated a track leading to a secondary gate at the opposite side of the field. "Go!" he told the driver. The car started with a jerk. (It always would. I never met a Sudanese with compassion for the horseless carriage.) Glancing back, I saw Sa'eed watching us with astonishment. We were the lead car in a motorcade. Behind us came my follow car, then two other cars with my embassy colleagues.

I hoped their air-conditioning was working better than ours. Or maybe the five of us were too much for the car's system. The air from the VIP lounge was still with us—hot, dusty, and stale. Marj asked, "Is there no fresh air?" I shook my head and knocked my knuckles against the glass. The car had other peculiarities, I noticed: it had the suspension of an Afrika Korps half-track. We had to brace ourselves against the sides and each other. I told Marj: "Don't worry. They say you just can't overturn a car on a level road."

Kirby turned to Marj and me: "Let me explain," he said. "You're not being kidnapped, but we needed to avoid the terminal exit." (The front end plunged into an especially deep pothole. Like a ship shaking off a big wave, the hood seemed slowly to come up and we resumed headway. A few more turns, then—blessedly—the road smoothed out a little).

Speaking to Marj, Kirby went on, "It's just precautionary. We know some bad people are in town. For days they've been tailing the ambassador. We think they're Libyans or PLO, or both together. In the last twenty-four hours it's gotten worse in the lead-up to the Israeli's execution . . . "

I interrupted: "An *Israeli* was executed here?"

Kirby nodded: "At dawn today. The ambassador will want to talk some more about that. Also today, a really ugly letter—signed by no one we've ever heard of before. So the ambassador asks that you and Mrs. Chamberlain come to the Residence first. We need to talk."

"We're not going to our house?" asked Marj. "The way I probably look . . . !"

"Sorry, no, ma'am," replied Kirby. "But the ambassador asked me to give you both this letter to read en route to his residence."

The ambassador had written:

Dear Mr. and Mrs. Chamberlain:
You've already heard it from your new colleagues—but let me add my own warm welcome to Khartoum.

I wish I could have been at the airport to meet you. In our business, though, there are times when we must go out when we'd rather stay at home. There are also—more rarely—times we must stay at home, when we'd rather go out. As Jack Kirby will explain, this is one of those latter times.

A special greeting to Mrs. Chamberlain. We are all far from our native New England, but you'll find community life at Amembassy Khartoum in some ways like that of the towns we grew up in. No greens, no Civil War monuments, nor church spires, to be sure, but a close-knit community, where people help each other.

More talk later. Remember: showers, followed by iced tea—or something stronger—on the veranda are only minutes away.

With all good wishes,
Jonathan Farnsworth

Farnsworth signed his name "Jon" in a tight, orderly cursive.

"Thoughtful of the ambassador," I said to Kirby.

"He's a thoughtful, stylish sort of guy," Kirby replied, "and a complete pro. Best Arabist, maybe, in the Service. Gutsy. During the Jordanian civil war, our current DG was the new ambassador and Farnsworth was his political officer. Anyhow, Farnsworth rescued an embassy secretary who was caught in a PLO–Jordanian Army crossfire. Then he talked his way through PLO roadblocks back to the Embassy. The PLO thought he was Syrian. A year later, he and the secretary were married. Romantic, right?

"Toward the end of the war, King Husain sent an armored column to bring the new ambassador from the Embassy to the Palace. The ambassador took Farnsworth with him. It made a great photo in the papers—first time I think an ambassador literally had to fight his way to a credentials ceremony. After that, Farnsworth was launched. He was soon made DCM in Saudi Arabia, then on to his first ambassadorship. He likes excitement. When things are dull, he's a little broody. Hasn't really gotten over Mrs. Farnsworth's death; she died three years ago. But he doesn't get on people's cases. Hey! We're getting near the Residence."

Ahead was a roadblock: a candy-striped sawhorse, with several green-clad Sudanese soldiers standing guard. They carried German 7.62mm G-3s. One stepped out as we approached. When he saw our diplomatic plates, he waved us on.

Before us rose a circumferential wall—not much lower, or narrower, than the one which, Herodotus says, surrounded ancient Babylon. The wall enclosed the entire block. It was still daylight, but floodlights, set every ten yards along its top, shone down onto the footing of the wall. Between the wall and the street ran a line of whitewashed "flower boxes." Children of World War II's "dragon teeth," each box was solid concrete, ten feet long and five feet high. There was perhaps space for a man to walk between the "headers" of the boxes. Nothing larger, though, could pass through to the wall surface. In the middle of each box a shallow depression held a few spadefuls of earth and some dead lobelias. (The RSO lacks a green thumb, I thought.)

We drove straight at the gate, hardly slowing down. Like the wall, it was of Babylonish proportions. Or like something dropped off by Samson on his way home from Gath. I could see Marj stiffening and locking her knees. At the final instant the boom in front of the gate— a length of railroad track—lifted. Simultaneously, the wings of the gate swung apart, just letting the car slip through, then began to close behind us. I glimpsed three or four Sudanese on each side. They were leaning forward and digging hard with their feet—like football linemen at blocking practice.

Kirby smiled. "One of the few real successes of USG operations in Sudan. You should see Pete working these teams—like gun drill under Nelson. There are four gate teams, and each week there's a competition—the winning team gets a ten dollar bonus. That's good money here. Pete jokes about starting his own football league. But the idea is to give any bad guys the briefest possible glimpse as Bre'r Rabbit enters and leaves his brier patch."

The light brown stucco Residence was centered at the rear of the property. We drove along the right-hand wall to a parking area; I saw steps leading to a tiled veranda that encircled the building. Atop the stairs to one's right, a modernistic "Great Seal" was grouted into the wall. The main floor stood four or five feet above garden level. Just below the second-floor balcony, a flagpole jutted upwards at forty-five degrees. A crisp, new American flag moved slowly about in the late afternoon air currents.

As we stepped out of the car, I looked about me. We had entered a parklike lawn and garden. Its green, watered, shaded confines might have been twenty degrees cooler than the dusty, sun-baked street. Mature acacias, date palms, and neem trees dotted the lawn. The neem trees astonished me. They had the look and size of oaks.

An oasis in the heart of downtown Khartoum!

SUMMER AFTERNOON

3

Ambassador Farnsworth must have heard the gates open. He was coming down the steps, dressed in khaki slacks, blue short-sleeved sport shirt, moccasins, white athletic socks.

I liked the ambassador on sight. He was just above medium height. A thin face, aquiline features, he was handsome, in an austere, thin-lipped way. He actually looked older than his fifty-eight years. His graying hair was almost crew-cut; a tan seemed to deepen the vertical lines by his mouth and the radial lines at the corner of his eyes. He looked fit, strong in the arms and shoulders. During my briefings in the Bureau of African Affairs, I'd heard a lot about his early morning runs with the Marine Security Guards (MSGs); there had been jokes about building up my wind.

The ambassador came first to Marj. A father greeting a daughter? He took her hand in both of his. "Have you already heard people say 'Welcome to Khartoum?' Yes? No matter. This is the most sincere greeting of them all. But come . . . " We followed the ambassador up to the veranda.

"Abbas!" he called out. The French doors opened—and a Sudanese emerged. He was about six feet tall, but his loosely wrapped turban—a stork's nest among Middle Eastern turbans—gave him another six inches. He wore a white, long-staple-cotton gown. He looked columnar, prime ministerial, a caryatid on the move.

Abbas was carrying a long, dark blue box. He gave the box to Farnsworth, who removed the cover, returning it to Abbas, then presented the box to Marj. Inside, on a bed of tissue paper, lay a dozen long-stemmed yellow roses.

"Foreign Service life can be hard," said Farnsworth, "particularly in the Arab world, and even more so when one has to leave a child behind." ("How did he know?" I asked myself, "Why should he care?")

Marj looked at Farnsworth. She glanced down at the roses. Then up again at him. Her eyes were moist. After a moment she said: "I'm just overcome. Mr. Ambassador . . . your special thoughtfulness at this time . . . words come with great difficulty, but . . . " Another pause— then, smiling, she quickly took a step forward, put her hand on Farnsworth's shoulder, and—half woman, half daughter?—kissed him on each cheek. She shook hands with Abbas. Someone applauded.

A smile softened and brightened Farnsworth's features: "As Sudanese who study English at our Cultural Center learn to say, 'no need to thank.' You're hot and tired. Your bags are now upstairs. Why don't you change, and come down in half an hour or so. And I'll explain why you're not turning out the lights in your very own house right now."

A man and a woman, meanwhile, had come up to our group. The man was my height, but some thirty pounds heavier. It wasn't muscle. He had long sideburns, but wore his hair in a modified flattop. His yellow Chemise Lacoste was soaked through—so were his short, gray sweatpants. He wore high-top basketball shoes. The woman with him, I judged, was in her late twenties. Almost as tall as Marj. She looked slim but strong in a well-fitting, white tennis dress. She had a good tan. I especially noticed her legs. Long and well-proportioned. I didn't much notice her face. Dark blond hair—layered? Cut fairly short.

The ambassador was saying: "Joshua and Marjorie, this is my able staff assistant, Sally Tolson; she also plays tennis expertly. Her very wet partner has been trying to keep up with her. I'm glad I'm no tennis player. Anyway, he's Bryce Hilverding, one of our resident security experts. I mean just that—he lives here."

As the ambassador spoke, Sally watched us with a grave, almost appraising expression. She wasn't really pretty, I decided. Then she smiled. A nice, no, a *brilliant* smile. We shook hands. Hers felt strong and dry. Hilverding's? Like grabbing a fish under water.

The ambassador had a final introduction. "And this is Frank Greer, our junior political officer. Frank's here on his first tour—got a master's in political science at Northeastern." Greer shuffled forward, moving his body from side to side as he walked. An odd, spiky haircut could have come from a barber's college. It gave his big head a "pollarded" look, that is, cut short, yet bushy! His soiled brown seersucker suit fit like plastic wrapping—heat-shrunk; his shirt was mostly out of his trousers. He wore his wide belt low, like a hernia truss. He was fat—210?

220? But he also looked hard. His arms strained at his coat sleeves and hung awkwardly from massive sloping shoulders. *Bibendum?* The Michelin Man? I could imagine setting Mr. Greer down on the Residence lawn and seeing him burrow out of sight in minutes.

He took my hand—"Pleased to meetcha, Mr. DCM"—but he didn't release. He looked me in the eye. He squeezed. It was like something hydraulic. Worse, he'd gotten the angle on me, and there was nothing I could do. Just when things would have become embarrassing, he let go. He smiled. Big square teeth, with narrow spaces between them. I thought of *Zeralda's Ogre*, the wonderfully illustrated children's book.

"Welcome to Khartoum," he said.

The ambassador didn't seem to have noticed. To Hilverding and Tolson he said, "Why don't you change in the cabana, then join us on the veranda for a 'mini–country team' meeting. We've a lot to pass on to the Chamberlains. About half an hour then?"

We showered and changed fast. As we rejoined the group on the veranda, the ambassador was reading at a table under a beach umbrella. Sally Tolson was sitting between Greer and Hilverding. Greer was describing—for her benefit?—some exploit at the Marine House: "So this oil guy, some roughneck from Connel Oil, he'd been drinking. Said embassy people were 'pansies and wusses.' So I put a hundred bucks on myself. We arm wrestle. I started slow, even let him get a little bit of an angle. He was smiling, maybe seeing Ben Franklin smiling back at him. Then—on goes the afterburner. POW! Almost put his knuckles through the deck. An easy hundred! But he was a good guy. We had some more drinks, went out together after." Greer smiled. Hilverding laughed meaningfully.

Greer turned to Sally Tolson: "That Sa'eed friend of yours. You know he doesn't look like much, and he has this perfume on his hands—you smell it on your own hand after you shake with him. Maybe it comes from what he rubs on his hair. Georgia Peach? Dippity-Do?" Greer and Hilverding again laughed together.

Greer continued: "But he's strong. I mean I'd take him easy, but guys like that, pound for pound, you get so you can spot 'em even in street clothes."

Sally, in a patient, counselor's voice, said: "Frank, for the embassy's sake, please don't break Sa'eed's arm. Please don't even challenge him to an arm wrestle. We'll never again get a shipment cleared through customs. Your oil man must have been wandering in the jungles since World War II! By now, I thought all Africa knew of your little arm wrestling stunt."

Greer: "For your sake, Sally, I grant you his life."

The ambassador called us to order: "I wish I had better news for Josh, Marj, for the USA, in fact. But maybe you remember May 1980, when geologists observed an abscess on the west face of Mt. St. Helens—just days before the explosion? Well, the same kind of pressures are building up on the government of Sudan. Prime Minister Muntasser has tried to give Sudan what it hasn't had for a long while: democracy and prosperity. But what with radical challenges from Libya, PLO factions, and local extremists, he hasn't done either. He's barely surviving. And now, just this morning the GOS"—to Marj, Farnsworth added "Government of Sudan"—"hanged one of its Jewish citizens as an Israeli spy."

I broke in: "Jack mentioned something about that in the car, but . . . "

Farnsworth explained: "The man was caught last week entirely by a fluke. One of the secret police agents who had investigated our extraction of Ethiopian Jews back in 1984 and 1985 happened to recognize him. The government would have liked to hush up the entire matter. They have plenty of problems now without taking on Israel, the United States, and the human rights community. But the arresting officer was some sort of fanatic. He got the word out to his colleagues in the fringe media. Radicals here and elsewhere immediately saw their opportunity and acted quickly to make it impossible for the government to back away. They demanded Justice! Demanded that the death penalty against the 'Falasha conspirators,' still on the books after all these years, be carried out. And, leading the chant was Presidency Minister al-Atrash himself. Who then conveniently absents himself from the scene of the crime."

"Implausible denial?" spoke up Kirby.

"Right," the ambassador said, continuing: "Washington did all it could. There was even talk of a message from the pope. All too late. The GOS knew that the longer it delayed, the more pressure it would get from each side. So they decided to move fast—a quick trial, and a quick execution.

"Twice in the past forty-eight hours I've weighed in with the prime minister. I told him he truly stood at a watershed in his relations with the United States and the world. A death sentence was contrary to Sudan's interests; I implored him not to deliver himself and his country into the hands of the radicals."

Farnsworth sat back and sighed. "The worst development in the worst place at the worst time. The radicals now have the government where they want it. They've forced it to shed blood. There's no going back now. Washington's furious. And the Israelis? Their prime minister today announced to the Knesset that if the world is not safe for Jews it will not be safe for their enemies either."

Farnsworth paused again, then: "And tomorrow morning it's Muntasser's turn to run away and hide at some Arab conference in Alexandria! Just when there might be trouble at home!"

Then Farnsworth laughed. "But the day *did* have its lighter moment: After I saw the PM, our friend Sa'eed escorted me to the car. Looking all around to make sure no one could overhear, he almost whispered that 'like others in the Presidency,' he knew about this urgent and delicate issue and that, speaking personally, he wished he could help. I didn't know whether to laugh or cry—but I thanked him nicely. I said that while our relations were headed for an ice age, I hoped we'd still be seeing him socially."

"We shouldn't underestimate Sa'eed, Mr. Ambassador," Sally broke in. "He's a very complicated person. It must have been hard for the favorite son of a paramount chief of the Fur peoples to fly straight to college in the USA. Everything so different and all at once! No one cares who you are—except for the groupies at your school's international student center. Sa'eed picked up right away on that one. He went to the student center exactly once. What he told me was, 'It's where the Third World meets the Nerd World.' He's proud and perceptive. He understands power relationships. Besides, he can be fun, and he plays good tennis!" Sally ended with a laugh.

Ambassador Farnsworth seemed to smile: "The court thanks the witness for the defense." He continued: "My problem with Sa'eed is not his intentions; it's his priorities. There's his social life, his car, his tennis, then nothing, nothing, still nothing—then politics? Probably safer for a protocol official, anyway."

Farnsworth reflected a moment: "But you've a point. We may be too hard on al-Masri just because of his playboy lifestyle. There *have* been times when we needed him and he's been helpful." The ambassador laughed: "Remember our little problem last winter of Scotch on the docks?" To Marj and me he explained: "The embassy's liquor shipment came in marked 'Household Effects.' But the container was damaged and began to leak, and the Prohibition Police were having fits. Al-Masri got *that* all straightened out, and wished us a Merry Christmas!"

In a more serious tone, Farnsworth turned to me, saying, "However, we got an intelligence report today." He looked around. "Some, but not all of you are aware of what I'm talking about. This information must be strictly protected, but all our embassy people are involved. You have a right to know, and I have a duty to tell you.

"We've received an intercept from our National Security Agency that points specifically to Khartoum for the first time. As you know, Libyan communications security's much tighter ever since we bombed Qadhaafi in the 1980s. But the intercept—we picked it up on the microwave leg of the transmission—said only 'Team arriving Khartoum airport September 8. Play game soonest with Sudanese.' Obviously we're building up to something—and it's not athletic. Who'd ever come to Khartoum in the summer to play anything but dead? Even the rec site pool's like clam chowder."

Valiant interrupted, saying to us: "That's why we brought you here—and why the muscle in the garden." He pointed to the far right-hand corner of the lawn. Two marines stood there in flak vests and camouflage fatigues, "cammies." They each carried a 12-gauge riot gun—its folding metal stock, I knew, made it a beast to shoot. And when fitted with the antipersonnel choke—which made the shot pattern fan out horizontally—the recoil after five shots could almost leave the shooter disabled. But by then a wise crowd would have found urgent business elsewhere.

The ambassador turned to Kirby: "So, Jack, you were staking out the airport. See anything?"

Kirby stood up and stretched his legs. He said: "I went bird watching this afternoon, before the DCM and Mrs. Chamberlain came in. Looking for green-and-white Libyan jet birds, with green rectangular fin flashes. I'm sitting on the observation deck watching the demonstrators and having a lemonade, and guess who I see coming in on the DCM's flight? Dr. Salim al-Atrash, commander of the Presidential Guard and minister for Presidency affairs, a.k.a. 'The Red Dean.' "

"We call him that," Kirby explained, "because he used to be dean of the science faculty at Khartoum University. In the 1960s. Taught biology. He's a real biologist, studied in Cairo and Italy and even has a graduate degree in biology from Yale, a master's, but everyone here calls him 'Doctor.' Here in Khartoum, he got in trouble with some of his women students. But that may not be the main reason he left the university. Supposedly he was tiring of a narrow, scientific worldview. So he got religion, of sorts. Or invented one. Don't ask me to define it. Some hybrid between spiritualism, Khalil Gibran, and Karl Marx. Maybe Dawkins here could explain it better than I."

Dawkins made a face: "Ba'thism—yes, maybe even Arab Socialism, but not *Atrash-ism!*"

Kirby: "The Agency's psychiatrists have a theory that Third World scientists—at a certain point in life—can be suckers for 'a village idiot philosophy.' Long ago they may have abandoned their traditional beliefs; then, in middle age they feel a need for something to replace them. But since their education's been so narrow, they can end up with something really weird, undiscriminating. That's OK. Sudan's intellectuals are already so screwed up, one Arabic 'L. Ron Hubbard' more or less would just be lost in the crowd.

"But al-Atrash matters to us for two reasons: first, the prime minister psychologically and intellectually defers to him. A sort of empress/Rasputin relationship. That's why al-Muntasser gave him the Presidential Guard. Al-Muntasser loves to sit up at night with al-Atrash discussing 'the dialectic,' the 'cycles of world history,' and 'the exploitation of the spiritual East by the materialist, money-grubbing West.' Second, as you might have guessed, al-Atrash is no friend of ours. I think he hates us. *Cherchez* our screw-ups with the Sudanese government? Drain the pond? You'll often find our friend al-Atrash, sitting there on the bottom.

"But back to the airport: Twenty minutes after al-Atrash arrives, in come the Libyans. And there was al-Atrash hurrying out to meet them—but not before Sa'eed, our 'Mr.GQ Elegant,' practically drapes him over the Chamberlains. You could tell al-Masri was having some fun. All smiles. I thought al-Atrash might choke."

Farnsworth shook his head: "One of these days our boulevardier's going to snag his designer britches. Too blithe a spirit? Al-Atrash is a heavy."

"Just one last comment." Kirby pointed to the walkie-talkie on his hip. "On the secure radio I've heard that some fifty passengers got off that Ilyushin. Three were staff members of the Libyan People's Bureau—we knew them from before. Don't know why they'd been in Tripoli this time, though. The rest? All young males, military-looking. Also, a lot of diplomatic pouches." Kirby looked wistful: "Sorry. No x-rays or penetration. In the old days . . . "

"And that threatening letter from 'Abu Nar'?" the ambassador asked.

Turning to me, Kirby said: "It's the one I mentioned coming in from the airport." He went on: "Don't know anything about it or him, sir. Maybe a local agent? Cell leader? Some disgruntled student at the university? We're looking."

"Try to keep the Libyans under surveillance," said the ambassador. "And Jack, call the minister of interior—or his secretary. We have to protect our sources, but as a follow-up to my call on the PM, we can at least ask again for more security. And tell embassy people via the security net to 'watch the local TV news tonight.' Will they remember it's the 'stay indoors' code? Depend on it—someone will radio back and ask, 'Why? What program?' Let's also cable the counterterrorism office for another satellite phone. They've got the big budgets these days. Then tomorrow, at country team meeting, we'll review where we are."

The ambassador turned to Marj and me: "So that's why you may have to be my house guests for the next few days. With trouble out there, Pete and Jack and Bryce all agree this is the safest place for us high-risk types. The grounds are patrolled, and not even a tank could make it through the wall."

To the group: "Thank you all for coming over. Keep your heads down. And let's wish the Chamberlains a good night's sleep."

TOTAL ECLIPSE

4

After our colleagues left, Marj and I joined the ambassador for a light supper. He was charming. A fund of amusing stories—none with himself as hero or participant. Not once did we hear the narcotic, trance-inducing mantra: "When I was . . . " He drew Marj out on our previous assignments and what Brian was up to.

Later, during dessert and coffee, I was happy—a little proud even—to see how Marj in turn drew Farnsworth out. With the ambassador a widower, I knew that many of the hostess and community functions would devolve onto her—and that she'd enjoy them and do them well. Farnsworth parried questions about family, but spoke about his youth in Portsmouth, Rhode Island, army service in Germany as a draftee, then Harvard College and grad school on the GI Bill.

"Then I didn't know what I wanted to do. So like many young men—and in those times, a few women—I took the Foreign Service exam and passed. So I decided to give it a try. Just for a few years, you understand, then I'd return to teach in college or high school. The next thing I know, I'm sitting here in Khartoum speaking to the Chamberlains."

Marj laughed. "And in the meantime the colonies had become the United States of America! I've read Rip van Winkle, too, Mr. Ambassador." Then in a more serious voice, "Some other time, I'll have you tell me about those missing twenty or thirty years. But now, if you'd excuse me, I've got to finish unpacking and I know you'll want to talk."

The ambassador rose as Marj got up. She paused at the door and said to Farnsworth with emphasis, "Thanks for a nice welcome, a nice evening. And I'll always remember the roses."

The ambassador was silent for a moment after she left. Then he turned to me saying, "Well, here we are. The house all to ourselves— except for the Marine Guards, the security officer, and the ten-man Sudanese security detail. Not exactly the Foreign Service that I—or I'll bet you—first joined. But security's now a part of our lives. With Pete Valiant's help, we can report the news, and mostly stay out of it."

Taking a sip of coffee, Farnsworth added: "It's getting late, and we'll talk again, so just a few words about the Big Picture and how I see your job.

"I was of two minds about staying in Africa. This is my second African embassy and I'd also been offered an attractive ambassador- ship in Southeast Asia. But I chose Khartoum—a maximum hardship post. Why? Because with the Cold War over, this is where a high stakes game is still played."

Maybe I looked puzzled or astonished, because Farnsworth seemed to gather his thoughts before he went on: "You see, with Com- munism dead, I believe the greatest threat to our value system comes from Africa. That is, if Africa's future is mostly a series of Somalias, Liberias, and Zaires, can we still believe our founding principles are universal? If we find ourselves writing off an entire continent—an en- tire race—might we become more selfish and introverted? Less ideal- istic? Less committed to resolving our own domestic problems of race and ethnicity? I'm afraid we'd stop caring—and Africans might give up trying. That's why for our sake *and* Africa's, we have to tutor African countries with potential, like Sudan, to pass the development exam!"

Farnsworth continued: "I'm realistic—not optimistic. Many Afri- can nations are likely to fail."

"Why are you so pessimistic, sir?" I asked.

"Please call me Jon," the ambassador interjected, continuing: "Why am I *realistic*, you mean? Geography matters: The Sahara iso- lated black Africa from the traffic of peoples, technology, and ideas that moved about the Mediterranean and Eurasia; then internal geography further splintered the continent into subregions. There's the ecology— the climate and disease. Maybe Africa's ecology protected it better from colonialism than the New World's did. But Africa's ecology also posed for its peoples some mammoth obstacles to development. You were at the airport today; you know what I mean. And just to our south is the world's AIDS capital—Uganda."

Farnsworth stopped, as if to catch his breath. He smiled: "So much for 'AF 101' with Professor Farnsworth. I know I carry on! But bear with me just a little longer. As to your job, do you wonder why you—a Latin American expert—were chosen as DCM in an Afro-Arab post?"

"Yes, sir," I replied. "I've been mostly in Latin America. But I bid on Khartoum because it was a good job. Any FSO of my class wants to be a DCM—must become one—to make the Senior Foreign Service. Management's what the promotion panels look for. And Sudan had a lot going for it. A strategically key country—the back door to Egypt and the front door to Saudi Arabia. One of the largest aid programs in Africa, plus an insurgency in the south and a Libyan threat.

"It's where things are happening—and where post leadership, frankly, is well regarded. But that's why I asked for the job. Not why I got it."

Farnsworth said: "The answer, Joshua, is partly your record. I'd told the department I wanted a younger officer, on the move, not some experienced know-it-all who ran out of gas five years ago. I wanted someone who should be an ambassador himself some day.

"The department suggested some excellent men and women," Farnsworth went on. "You may have been the best—your corridor reputation was as good as your file. That's not the full reason, though. It may prove your good or ill fortune, but American history is my hobby. And how could I resist 'Joshua Lawrence Chamberlain,' the commander of the Second Maine? At Gettysburg the hero of Little Round Top, and winner of the Congressional Medal of Honor? A soldier often wounded, but who always, miraculously, recovered? And in later years, governor of Maine and president of Bowdoin College? Tell me—are you the third or the fourth?"

I laughed. "I'd be number four. I was named after my great-grandfather. We're both from Maine, but I went to Bates, not Bowdoin. We lived near Lewiston, and Bates had a better tennis program. They recruited me and offered me a partial scholarship. Mostly I use just 'Josh Chamberlain.' My father and his father, though, always used all three names."

Farnsworth smiled: "Just some final words about the job. A few things should be clear and understood early. I'll treat you, and expect you to act, as my alter ego. You and I are two people working at a single job: promoting and preserving the interests of the United States and its citizens. I have only a few management principles: I give trust and demand accountability. I don't mind bad news, but I don't like surprises. Take a principal role in embassy management, but don't crowd the line officers. Remember, you're not the embassy's Field Marshal for Political Affairs. You are the deputy chief of *mission*. And that means all agencies. Management? We talk too much about it. Maybe good for

Washington, D.C. But in the field people need a *leader*. Everyone's got their own style. Do what comes naturally. *Then* you'll seem genuine. Confident. People will sense that, and they'll follow you willingly. They also can tell right away if someone cares more for his own career than for their well-being.

"I do have one special request: the Marine Security Guards. They must be made part of our embassy family. It takes leadership and close bonding to keep up their efficiency and morale. The Moscow scandal—remember Sergeant Lonetree?—was a failure of embassy leadership, more than the failure of a couple of young Marines. I know you were a Marine yourself; so go to functions at the Marine house—and include some of the MSGs in your own. I go to the Marine House myself—but I don't stay too long. I hate to feel like a chaperon or wet blanket.

"What else? Yes—my office door is always open. Come in any time. Also, tomorrow, some of the wives will want to call on Mrs. Chamberlain. She's had a tough day. For both your sakes, I hope we won't be mured up in the residence too much longer. Roommates are fine in college—but we'll be together enough on the job."

Farnsworth paused and added: "This may sound very old-fashioned, and I certainly hope not presumptuous, but I have a hunch the post will be well served by the new DCM—*and* his wife. You should have an interesting tour of duty, Josh—but nothing, I hope, like that of the first Joshua Lawrence Chamberlain. Now go to bed and sleep well."

It was close to midnight. Marj had left a night light on. The suitcases, I noticed, were gone. Her things and mine were hanging or put away on shelves in our walk-in closet—basically a small, masonry-walled room off the bedroom.

As I undressed, I reflected that it had been a good day. We'd have fun in Khartoum, I was more sure than ever. True, Khartoum had some disadvantages: a lot of poverty, shaky public security, and heat! Heat pumped right up from the Inferno itself! But there seemed to be a nice embassy community—the ambassador was great, and he and Marj had hit it off well. In any close-knit hierarchy that was a definite career plus. And I'd heard the DCM's house was very comfortable—another plus.

In bed, I leaned over and gently gave Marj a kiss. She didn't stir.

My last thoughts were grateful ones: the bed was flat and hard, and the pillows soft.

Strange. Afterwards it seemed to me that, in my half sleep, I'd sensed the shots and *then* heard them.

There was a ripple of thuds against the side of the building, a slamming sound from our bathroom, as a round went through the louvered metal shutter. Fractionally later, I became aware of the pounding of a weapon on full automatic.

I knew the sound. As a second lieutenant of Marines, I used to hear it often during field training exercises—FTXs—at Quantico's infantry officer course. "Aggressor" company used the Russian AK-47 Kalashnikov assault rifle and other East Bloc weapons. The idea was for us to learn Soviet weaponry—Russia at the time was our main adversary, and radicals everywhere used mostly Russian hardware. The AK-47's rate of fire was much slower than our M16 A1. The difference between a 7.62 mm weapon firing at 100 rpm and one of 5.56 mm firing at 800. The AK's maximum effective range was only 300 meters. But against an area target like the Residence, a gunman could stand off another one or two hundred meters.

All this went through my mind as I half sat up and groped for my bearings in the darkness. Amazing what training will do.

It was habit also that made me reach over and jerk Marj's hand away from the bedside light.

"No light," I whispered urgently. Silly, I thought, who's to hear me? "Something's up. Maybe just some fool of a guard getting off some joy shots. Wait here." I slipped out of bed and headed for the hall door.

As I opened it, I saw a light come on in Bryce Hilverding's bedroom. Seconds later, a thunderclap of smoke and debris exploded into the upstairs corridor. I heard Marj scream. I ran back to the bed. "Down, quick!" I ordered. At a crouch, I half led, half pulled her to the closet. "Stay here until I look around. Someone's fired something at the Residence. I'm going to check with the ambassador. I'll be back quick as I can. Don't come out until I'm back. If there's any more shooting at the Residence, you'll be safe here."

In a half-crouch I went into the hallway. One of the Marines, riot gun at the ready, was coming up the stairs. I could make out the other standing at the bottom of the stairwell. Ambassador Farnsworth was with him. I called down: "Sir, I think Mr. Hilverding's room has been hit. Maybe an RPG-7. Nobody come up. Keep all the lights off. Perhaps someone should call the embassy on the land line. Get the nurse? The RSO, too. The Marines and the security detail should check the perimeter. Let me look around. I'll report back."

From the door of Hilverding's room, I surveyed the interior. The louvered shutters had been blown outward by the explosion. The smoke of the blast had mostly cleared. From the window opening, a faint glow suffused the room—the light pollution of any large town? Had Hilverding's turning on the light given the gunner the target he was looking for, I wondered? The high-explosive round hadn't much hurt the room's masonry walls. But the interior looked—I searched for a word—*trashed*.

On my knees I crawled forward a few feet. There was no sign of anyone. A few feet more—I made out a shape on the far side of the bed. It was—or had been—Hilverding. He was still intact. I remembered a Marine instructor saying, "The human body just naturally resists dismemberment." The natural tendency of the body, he said, was to absorb the shock—although sometimes (he added with gusto) the body parts themselves burst under hydrostatic pressure.

Hilverding was dead. His body lay half-seated against the wall. Its front had been scooped away—to form an aureole of blood and matter on the wall behind. His rib cage was deeply exposed. There was nothing definable about his head. It had a childish silhouette—and proceeded directly from his neck to his cranium. No chin, no jaw, no nose. On impulse I felt his wrist for a heartbeat. As quickly I pulled my hand back.

"Fool!" I thought. "Get a hold of yourself. Be calm. Be practical. You trained for this once!" The thought was remarkably steadying. It enabled me to look over the scene professionally, almost clinically. I felt my heart rate slow. I looked around the room again—taking it all in carefully.

I crawled backward out of the room—then went below to report to the ambassador. The light was on in his study. The heavy curtains had been pulled. He said, "We can talk here. No light escapes, and we're below the outside level of the walls."

I told him Hilverding was dead. For a moment he thought, then said: "We'll get to that. But first—is your wife all right? Bring her down right away to join us. And before you go up to her, go to my room, wash your hands, and put on some of my pajamas." Looking down, I could see the knees of my white cotton pajamas were like butcher's paper. My right hand also was red and sticky.

As it was, when I looked back in at our room, Marj was gone. I found her already downstairs, in her quilted bathrobe, talking to Farnsworth. She looked up: "Jon's told me . . . awful! Poor Hilverding. (She rose.) You two, and others, will have plenty to do. Is there any way I can be useful? Typing or anything else? I'll be in the guest bedroom across from the study door. If I can help in any way, you don't have to worry about waking me up."

The ambassador and I were a good crisis management team. We clicked. We caught Sally Tolson still at the Embassy. On secure radio we gave her the information for a set of cables back to Washington. The ambassador called the Presidency. Al-Muntasser was already gone, and the foreign minister was acting prime minister. He expressed shock and condolence. He'd see the ambassador at eight the next morning.

An "all call" message on the radio net told embassy people that there had been a rocket attack on the Residence; the ambassador and the DCM were unhurt; all personnel were told to stay at home until a further "all call" notice. Through Kirby, who was our liaison with State Security, a company of National Guardsmen appeared, and also a team of investigators. The consul came over—with a police escort. He sent a death notice to Hilverding's mother, his only next-of-kin.

Had we forgotten something? Maybe. We were to be reminded. It was early morning. Some four hours had passed since the murder. Farnsworth and I were still in the study. We noticed it simultaneously and looked at each other. There came to our ears, growing louder at first, and then more faint, the sound of a multiple-engine jet aircraft leaving Khartoum.

Farnsworth was still in his dressing gown. (Afterwards, he told me an ambassador should always keep one handy. Ambassadors were often called urgently from their beds. A nice bathrobe enabled them to be prompt, but decent.) "Do you suppose we've just been had?" he asked.

THE MORNING AFTER

5

Nothing travels faster than light. But bad news comes close. The next morning at 0600, with Big Ben's final, resonant toll, it reached us via "the main points of the news." Announcer Pippa Harben told the world: "The residence of the American ambassador in Khartoum has been shelled; one American official has been killed. Meanwhile, in Khartoum, one Abu Nar, 'the Father of Flame,' claimed responsibility for the attack in the name of the Islamic Sons of Karare. 'Karare' is the Sudanese name for the battle of Omdurman."

A glum beginning to a glum breakfast. The ambassador, RSO Valiant, Marj, and I huddled at one end of the black, lacquered dining room table—twenty feet of the River Styx. Hilverding's body had been taken away during the night. The ambassador and I had worked through the night; just before breakfast we'd showered and changed our clothes.

Marj claimed to have gotten some sleep the night before. She *looked* fresh and rested, I thought. She said she really wanted to go on with plans to meet other embassy wives. Maybe with a Marine escort? She thought that by following Foreign Service "arrival routine" she might help other wives "keep an even strain." Crises, she observed correctly, were hardest on those who didn't have anything to do.

Farnsworth and I left for the Chancery after breakfast with a Marine at the wheel of the ambassador's armored Cadillac. The ride gave me my first glimpse of downtown Khartoum. The town and its people looked tired. The roads were cratered, the sidewalks worn and buckled. Beneath the neem trees, on the scuffed and dusty public lawns, late sleepers? early nappers? lay scattered about like bundles of laundry. Building facades were of plain, brown brick—often quilted with many years' political posters.

"A good paperhanger could make his fortune here," said the ambassador, as we passed the university. "Will Dawkins often drops by to see what's playing, so to speak. It's like the marquee of a movie back home, or Democracy Wall. It's all up there in shorthand—communist, Ba'thist, pan-Arab, and Arab-socialist propaganda."

I remarked that many of the posters featured a turbaned, hollow-eyed face. "Dr. al-Mughraibiy," Pete responded. "The 'Supreme Guide' of the Islamists. A strong figure. We guess a radical one. No one really knows him. His people are a minority at the university but control the student senate. Shows what hard work, leadership, and maybe some foreign money can do."

We swept through downtown with *blitzkrieg* speed—and firepower. There were military escorts fore and aft, and sirens wailing, until we passed the roadblock at the Chancery. There we dropped our escorts, took a sharp left into an alley, then another left into the covered embassy parking lot. I watched the Chancery's gate drill with new appreciation.

The ambassador and I shared an office suite on the seventh floor. We entered a waiting room (work space for Sally Tolson and our two secretaries), which connected with the ambassador's office on one side and mine on the other.

Sally rose as we came in and followed the ambassador to his desk. Its surface looked as if she had been playing solitaire with cables. They lay in columns, one over the other—only the address blocks and subject headings showed. Some cables, I could see, were annotated. Others, had references attached. She and the consular officer clearly had worked through most of the night.

"You were here all night, Sally?" Looking over the cable traffic the ambassador said, "You did well."

I looked about me, as Farnsworth reviewed the traffic. His office was part work space, and part living room. A sitting area by the door, with three overstuffed chairs, a low, square coffee table, and a couch. I thought of the airport. No dust bunnies? No rings on the table? At the far end of the room stood the desk, flanked by the American and presidential flags. Behind the desk, forming an altarpiece, as it were, hung Farnsworth's current and four previous ambassadorial commissions, plus a large, signed portrait photo of the president of the United States and the ambassador shaking hands.

Farnsworth looked up from his work, caught my glance, and smiled. "Back home," he said, "I keep all these in the attic. But here, our visitors—our patients—find them reassuring. They figure we won't pull the wrong tooth."

Other walls were hung with 24" x 36" color enlargements of New England scenes, in the winter and fall. They'd been taken by Ambassador Farnsworth himself. On the bookshelves was a set of the American University Area Handbook Series, plus several ostrich eggs—upright on ebony annular stands.

There was, finally, a framed photograph of the ambassador and a pygmy hunter. In one hand, the hunter displayed his crossbow, quiver, and poisoned shafts. With the other, he held up his next meal: a howler monkey. The pygmy village—small, domed, leaf-covered huts—could be seen in the background. The photo dated from one of the ambassador's field trips, years ago, in Central Africa. I'd seen it before, on the cover of *State*, the department's official magazine.

I walked over to the framed photo to read an inscription. It was signed by the director general and read: "The staff of Amembassy Khartoum is looking forward with some anxiety to the arrival of Ambassador Farnsworth. They understand he is a hard taskmaster. The picture shows the ambassador at a previous post with his Deputy Chief of Mission. The DCM was six feet tall when he began to work with Ambassador Farnsworth. The ambassador is giving his DCM a cross, as a memento of the time they spent together. In the background can be seen what remains of the Embassy, after a meticulous inspection by Ambassador Farnsworth."

"I didn't think the department had a sense of humor," I laughed. Farnsworth pushed the stack of cables away. He answered: "It doesn't. But our director general does. He gave me that photo while swearing me in for Sudan."

Then turning to Sally: "No further instructions from the department?"

"No sir, just some language for a statement at the noon press briefing. They accepted your proposed language. I checked again with commo, just as you were coming in. Nothing in the queue."

"And what about the 'Karare' group we heard about on BBC?"

Sally answered: "Kirby says the information was handed to the news agencies right after the shooting. We've cabled the text of the statement to the department. It's in the pile there," Sally added, point-ing to the desk. "But there's nothing to say it's authentic. No one knows anything about 'Abu Nar' or his group."

"OK," Farnsworth said to both of us. "Take it as a good sign that the department remains silent. It means we've given them enough to chew on. Always, Josh, try to keep the initiative in our own hands. It's more easily done here than in Latin America—usually, no one cares much what happens in Africa. And with the seven-hour time differ-ence, we can get our messages to Washington while they're still asleep. Then Washington learns what we've done or plan to do.

"Remember," he went on, "the bureaucrats in D.C. will be glad to give us as much responsibility as we ask for. One condition: we'd better be right. But as Jack would say, 'No guts, no glory.' "

"Mr. Ambassador," Maryann, his secretary, said from the door, "you should leave for your eight o'clock meeting at the Foreign Minis-try. Deng's acting prime minister but hasn't moved over to the Pal-ace—too much Foreign Ministry business, al-Masri says."

"Pity," said the ambassador. "I'd hoped to show Josh the Presi-dential Palace. A real confection, architectural 'turkish delight.' One of the best architectural legacies of the Anglo-Egyptian Sudan; not even Lutyens in India built much better. Some other time."

Our motorcade launched itself from the Chancery lot. Pete Val-iant sat in the front passenger seat with a satchel of ordnance by his side. As Farnsworth took the right rear seat, I the left, he made a joke about "Pete carrying the nuclear codes." Sally sat between us, strad-dling the hump of the drive shaft.

The ambassador was talking about Foreign Minister Deng: "He's that rarity in Sudanese politics, a top-ranking official of southern Sudanese origin. That means pure African. Sudanese may speak a lot about their being an 'Afro-Arab' civilization, but since independence, anything important's been run by ethnic Arabs from the Khartoum-Wad Madani-Dongola 'Main Line.' Arabs are a minority in Sudan—30 or 40 percent at most. But they hold almost all the top jobs."

He went on: "Deng got his job because some smart Sudanese, including Prime Minister al-Muntasser, saw that with a black 'African' rebellion in the south, his 'Arab' government had better do something, show some respect for southerners and their traditions. Also, get Sudan back in the diplomatic game. The Sudanese have been condemned in just about every international forum except the Arab League—which on race issues could be the Ku Klux Klan International! Anyhow, the Sudanese couldn't have chosen better. Deng's one of the leaders of the Dinka nation, the biggest ethnic group in the south. *Never* use the word *tribe*! Sounds too colonial, a little patronizing. Like the word *native*. Deng's been ambassador to the O.A.U. and to the U.K. He has a Ph.D. from Columbia; his wife's American. Most important, he's honest and respected."

"But do the Arabs listen to him?" I asked.

The ambassador shrugged. "Good question. The PM knows his worth. The other Arab ministers? They put up with him. They remember their grandfathers raided Deng's people for slaves. No one's forgotten this—and the civil war keeps memories fresh. Remember, too, that full-blooded Sudanese *Arabs* are as rare as full-blooded Hawaiians. So most 'Arab' Sudanese really cling to their 'patent of nobility,' that fraction of lighter, Arab blood—a distillate?—as opposed to the black, heavy *African* crude!"

Sa'eed met us at the entrance of the ministry. He had on a black tie. Mourning? His dark suit was almost the twin of the one he wore yesterday. His linen shirt was immaculate. He shook hands with the ambassador, then me, then Sally.

"Together with all my fellow Sudanese," he said, "I am shocked, grieved, and outraged by the violence done to a guest. Please accept my condolences as an official and also as a friend of the United States and of the American community in Sudan." Gone was the playboy manner of yesterday; Sa'eed seemed a serious and distressed colleague. I was relieved he wasn't *always* the lightweight he'd appeared earlier. Protocol can be sensitive and one doesn't want to have to work with a fool.

Sa'eed was going on: "The acting prime minister will see you immediately. And," leaning forward, Sa'eed said quietly, "speaking confidentially, I think you will be somewhat pleased with what he has to say."

I was at home in the Foreign Ministry. From the outside, to an uncanny degree, the building resembled those of poorer Latin American countries. Decaying, nondescript modern. Within, the similarities were even greater. The same torn carpets, the same jagged nosing of the stair treads, the same elevators that, protesting all the way, hauled one up the shaft. Even the same breathless air conditioners that seemed to plug shell holes in the wall. Unhappy thought!

Then I had to smile. In the foreign minister's outer office hung

The Portrait. I would have recognized the prime minister's photo from my briefings, anyway. But at that angle, and that close to the ceiling—it could only be, as they say in Boston, "Himself." Photos of a similar type used to be seen in every *cuartel,* or barracks, republic south of the border. And always on the presidential chest, wide as the heavens, there sparkled a galaxy!—a universe!—of orders and decorations bestowed upon the *jefe,* often by his own adoring self. It is said that as a Latin American, or African or Arab, president increasingly dominates the political scene, his portrait—one of heaven's bright ornaments—begins its rise. Finally (barring sudden eclipse), it reaches an apogee, hard against the joint of wall and ceiling. But note: here man's earthly progress ends. Ceilings are still reserved for saints, angels, and God himself.

Deng came out of his office to meet us. Tall, attenuated, *thin* thin. Could that trunk really hold a full issue of vital organs, I wondered. Then, the way he moved, the way he spoke, from his first words, one felt a vitality. I noticed three V-shaped scars in the middle of his forehead. Dinka markings, I guessed.

Afterwards Sally drafted the cable on the meeting:

Secret
Action: Secstate Niact Immediate
Info: Amembassy Beirut
    Amembassy Cairo
    Amembassy London
    Amembassy Paris
    Amembassy Riyadh
    DOD
    USCENTCOM
    DOD for JCS
    Beirut limitel considered

Subj: ATTACK ON RESIDENCE—AMBASSADOR MEETS WITH ACTING PRIME MINISTER

1. Ambassador discussed the assassination of A/RSO Hilverding with acting PM Deng morning of September 9. Meeting lasted one hour. Ambassador was accompanied by DCM Chamberlain and staff assistant Tolson (notetaker).
2. Ambassador said he could not overstress the importance of the issue to U.S.-Sudanese relations. Governments were fully and totally responsible for the well-being of diplomatic guests. And because Sudan and the United States were so important to each other,

and because our sometimes strained bilateral relations had shown signs of improving, we considered the prompt apprehension and punishment of the criminals essential. After the deplorable execution of a supposed Israeli spy, the eyes of the world would be sharply focused on Sudan's justice. Ambassador said this was a time to speak frankly, not diplomatically.

3. Deng repeatedly stated his government's profound and sincere condolences. His government accepted full responsibility for the security of its official guests. The murder was repugnant to all Sudanese. It could only have been undertaken by elements bent on undermining Sudan's traditional good relations with the United States.

4. Deng, however, said he had progress to report. A military police patrol had heard the firing and intercepted the killers as they were leaving the Lawyers' Union Building, from which the attack against the Residence had been made. In an exchange of fire, all three criminals were killed. One policeman was wounded.

5. Deng provided Ambassador with copy of a communiqué that had been found on the body of one of the assassins. It began with a quotation from the Qur'an, chapter V, verse 54, that warns against Jews and Christians:

> Do not follow their lusts
> And beware of their tempting thee away from
> Any part of what God hath revealed to thee.

6. The name at the bottom of the communiqué—a certain 'Abu Nar,' i.e., 'the father of flame,' was unknown to the Security Directorate.

7. Ambassador noted the arrival in Sudan yesterday of a nonscheduled Libyan flight, a flight which took off again only hours after the attack in which Mr. Hilverding had lost his life. Might there be a Libyan connection?

8. Deng replied that at this stage nothing should be assumed or excluded. But to him the communiqué's religious, fundamentalist tone did not sound Libyan. Deng refused to speculate on possibility—raised by RSO Valiant—that radical Islamists might have had a hand. Nor would he be drawn out on a role for Palestinian extremists.

9. Ambassador and Deng will keep in close touch.

10. All Americans are safe. Ambassador will address them this A.M. on an all-call. We plan to permit renewed movement about town starting tomorrow. School will reopen under tight security. Morale is steady and holding.

Farnsworth

As the ambassador came out of the ministry, the path was blocked by a crowd of safari suits, Australian military surplus hats, and tangles of loops, flaps, pouches, and buttons—the foreign press corps. The Sudan News Agency (SUNA) correspondent, dressed in ragged gray pants and blue shirt, stood off to one side, in the shade. I thought of Lord Kitchener's reaction in such a situation. After Omdurman, the press was waiting outside Kitchener's tent for him to make a statement. When the time came, he stalked through them, saying only: "Get out of my way, you drunken swabs!"

One of the correspondents stepped forward. Pete Valiant moved as if to intervene, but Farnsworth shook his head.

"Mr. Ambassador," the correspondent almost shouted into his portable microphone. "Heinz. *Die Zeit,* Is it true they've caught the murderers?"

"OK," Farnsworth began, "This is for the record."

Tape recorders flashed out like sabers.

"For the record," the ambassador repeated, "I told the foreign minister that we must move heaven and that other place—the only one that's hotter than Sudan—to get to the bottom of the Hilverding assassination and deal with *all* the culprits. I'll let the Sudanese government describe the latest developments. But I can hardly believe that any true Sudanese, any citizen of this great and hospitable country, Sudan, would murder a guest and a friend." Farnsworth paused.

A correspondent said: "We've just seen Dr. al-Atrash, the minister for Presidency affairs. He told us—(the correspondent flipped through his notebook, then began to read): 'Sudan regrets any incident involves injury to a foreigner; it would be unhistorical, however, entirely to dissociate violence today from that of the Western . . .'"

Farnsworth cut him off: "I'm glad the minister deplores the Hilverding murder; I look forward to working with him to solve a crime that all decent men must abhor."

A third correspondent called out: "We've heard claims the Libyans are behind this. Others say the PLO or Muslim fundamentalists are to blame. What's your view?"

The ambassador looked toward his questioner: "The great French medievalist, Marc Bloch, wrote just before the Nazis shot him, 'In history, as elsewhere, the causes are not to be assumed. They are to be looked for.' There's your answer. And that's what we'll do."

As we drove away, Sally Tolson looked over at Farnsworth: "The Sudanese will like that part about 'no Sudanese would have committed such a crime.' "

"Sometimes flattery is better at giving one the upper hand than pounding on the table; and we mustn't close any doors prematurely, Sally," the ambassador replied. "We mustn't block the Sudanese from ourselves by emotional statements—no matter what 'Dr. Trash' says. We want them on our side in this investigation. You never know what might turn up. Is a Libyan hand stirring the water?"

After a moment he added: "Sally, how would you sum up the meeting? I think Josh, here, would like your views, too."

Sally seemed nonplussed. "You want *my* views of the meeting?"

"Yes, indeed," said Farnsworth. "That's how *I* learn, and how *you* develop judgment. A wise boss once said to me, 'Good judgment comes from experience, and experience comes from bad judgment.' Into the batting box, Ms. Tolson."

Sally began—slowly at first, then picking up speed: "I thought Deng was nervous and ill at ease. I'd bet he doesn't know anything more about the case than we do. How convenient that the three assassins were all killed—and that they had on their persons an incriminating document that *didn't* seem to point to Libya."

"Do you think they're the killers?" asked Farnsworth.

"Could well be," Sally answered. "But they might only be the tip of the iceberg. And as the investigation goes on, how much information will the police and army share with Deng? A southerner? Their lines are more likely to run to the Prime Ministry and to al-Atrash. Poor Deng may wonder, regardless of what al-Muntasser may have said, just how hard the government will try to break the case. I bet the prime minister won't hurry home. Instead, he'll hope this hot potato may cool as he continues with his foreign travels. Look for an extension, a side trip to Bermuda, even? Meanwhile, I'll bet he's relieved that a southerner just now is sitting on the prime ministerial hot seat. He knows we wouldn't come down as hard on him as we would on an Arab PM."

"Bingo!" said Farnsworth. "After you report the straight facts, do a separate cable—LIMDIS—giving those comments. Let Josh see the draft."

We drove back to the Embassy at a moderate pace. No sirens this time; I guess the RSO thought no one would take us on frontally and in broad daylight. Valiant sat quietly, his eyes scanning the road. Occasionally, he'd make a quiet remark. A word from the bridge to the engine room, so to speak. I admired how he did it. It didn't seem at all like back-seat driving.

"Slow up a little," Pete said, "don't let them box you in. Drop back some, now let the follow car block for us in the circle . . . that big pot hole . . . buffalo wallow. Nice. *LOOK OUT!*"

From the left of the car, two children dashed across the road in front of us. The Marine jerked the wheel to the right. The car rode up over the sidewalk. The worn-down curb was more like a ramp to our security tires and suspension. We missed a tree. Slewed back into the street. The boys were gone.

The Marine driver and Valiant had been wearing their safety belts. They'd easily taken the g's of the turn. But in the rear, all was confusion. The ambassador had kept his seat, but Sally and I had been thrown into the leg space behind the armored front seat. It was surprisingly difficult to get out. Sally's face was only inches from mine. A smooth complexion, just the beginning of smile lines by her cheek bones. My right arm was around her—my hand pressed between her arm and her side. I pulled it away. Her body felt thin, firm, muscular.

Valiant looked back over the seat. "You're a fast worker, indeed, Mr. Chamberlain," he said.

With the ambassador helping, Sally regained her seat. Awkwardly, I followed. She tugged her skirt back down to her knees. She laughed. Again, I noticed nice, even teeth. Did she blush?

To the driver, Valiant said: "Well done. Quick reactions; driving in Khartoum is tough. But the important thing here is *never, never lose control!*"

SMALLTOWN, U.S.A.

6

"How can people back home understand the life we lead?" I asked myself one morning, as I arrived at work to begin my introductory rounds of the embassy and its people.

I recalled that often when on home leave good friends would say: "What an interesting life you have! You must tell us all about it!" And how after a few minutes their eyes would unfocus, and they'd find a way to shift the topic back into familiar channels. Their last vacation. Their next vacation. The children. Once, my college roommate even got up to turn on the TV as I was talking. He half explained, half apologized: "Just want to see the score." I've learned to choose my audiences, and to keep my answers short—knowing that "the Foreign Service" to most Americans suggests the mercenaries France used to fight its colonial wars.

My toughest audience, however, was my in-laws. I'd always had trouble explaining the Foreign Service to them. Was it their "white-gray" Boston world? A point of view that reached from Beacon Hill only as far as . . . Martha's Vineyard? Maybe Nantucket? Or maybe they just never *wanted* to understand. I always seemed to end up trying to justify or apologize. Once Marj's father had come right out and asked: "Isn't life in the U.S.A. good enough for you?" The words that came to me—patriotism, public service, sheer curiosity, a taste for adventure, plus the occasional spice of danger—to him would have seemed perverse, immature, self-indulgent. Incomprehensible.

To Marj's parents, the Hilverding assassination would almost be expected. It would confirm all their admonitions. Had *I* been the victim, I could imagine Marj's father holding forth at his Beacon Street club: "Many's the time I told that young man to come home." I could almost hear his reedy, disapproving tones.

Hilverding's death hit us hard—even harder than would have a neighbor's murder back home. Back home, Americans may live in neighborhoods—but they leave them to go their different ways to different jobs. But Foreign Service people, when we're in the Third World, drop back a generation or more; we live and work in "village" communities. We live in a peculiar, storybook world. The world of Mom and Dad, Dick and Jane, and their dog Spot. There are no poor, no unemployed, few handicapped, and no chronically ill among us.

Except for visits by the occasional grandparent over the holidays, we're mostly young or middle-aged. We tend to get along well, partly because interpersonal relations—as in a military unit—are not random, but aligned with our community's official structure and purpose; and also because Foreign Service people tend to be both imaginative *and* pragmatic. Because our lives are so mobile, and the settings often exotic, we have to be adaptable, open, inquisitive—but for the same reasons we have to be conventional, and level-headed. I once asked a class of junior officers who, in fiction, would be their ideal Foreign Service officer. The class wag suggested "Captain Ahab." The winner (rightfully) was Alice-in-Wonderland.

The ambassador began my introduction to the post by walking with me across Abdul Latif Street—from where we looked up at the drab "projects" facade of the Embassy.

Pointing upwards, Jonathan said, "In architecture, Josh, form should promote function. Good function results from good form, they say. Could the reverse ever be true? Could the shortcomings of our diplomacy be linked to our bland, chicken-coop of a headquarters in Washington? Are we producing foreign policy and practitioners by Perdue Chickens, Inc.?"

I laughed and asked: "And what does our Chancery architecture produce?"

Jonathan answered: "Nervous breakdowns, or ingenious survivors."

The Chancery—the embassy office building—was a converted apartment house. Its seven stories teetered between their natural desire to collapse, and our administrative section's efforts (as the ambassador said), "to keep the drunk on his feet." The building wasn't strong enough. The upper stories couldn't safely support our vault room, so an external scaffolding had been added. Balconies were off limits. Not for fear of snipers, but because only a dash of cement held them to the building facade. Any day they might "calve off" onto the traffic jams below.

Pete Valiant lamented the building's shallow setback. We were only twenty feet from the curb, while the State Department's Bureau of Diplomatic Security (DS) preferred at least a hundred.

"A truck bomb attack," Pete remarked, "with gas-cylinder enhanced explosives—the kind that killed our Marines in Beirut"—he raised his hand to his lips and blew—"like a dandelion puff."

As Farnsworth had said, I met "ingenious survivors"—Pete Valiant, for one. My good impression of him at the airport had been correct. He was popular and respected. He'd also been in the Marines, an MSG in Tehran, and done a stint with DEA before joining the Foreign Service. "Cultivate him," said Farnsworth, "first, because he's a good officer—period. *Never* listen to those who would rate one Foreign Service function above another. But second, cultivate him because he's got one of the genuinely hardest jobs in the mission. Pete's just right. He's serious, but doesn't run around with a rat in his teeth and his hair on fire."

Another "survivor" of note was our CIA station chief, Jack Kirby. Jack was "declared." This meant that a few key Sudanese officials with whom we maintained an intelligence liaison knew of his identity and functions. But Farnsworth respected Jack's good sense and service-mindedness.

"Jack," the ambassador remarked to me, "isn't one of those CIA types who feels he 'must back into the limelight.' He's also good about demythologizing his work. He meets with all the new officers, *and* their wives, and explains his work to them. It's his way, he says, of having them on his side when the talk at receptions turns to 'let's spot the spook.'

"Just a few more comments on Kirby and his people. Remember this: His men and women, especially those who aren't declared, have a second work day that begins when ours, no matter how long, is ending. The life can be tough on a couple. Little public recognition for the principal and none for the spouse. And the Agency's single women employees don't have it any easier. Then, just wait until our spy retires and tries to find another job! Vague, watery CVs. Employers wonder in which federal institution our applicant had been serving. Lorton?

Marion? Getting warm! So make a special effort to show appreciation. Recognition. It's deserved. *The Agency people are our Jesuits.* You might say they take a special, supplementary vow of obedience to Uncle Sam. And, to get back to management, spend a little time, and you'll be repaid by better relations with the Agency."

But we weren't all survivors. I met the economic counselor, Bill Gray. He had a Ph.D. and had taught economics at a small northeastern college before joining the service. He was now approaching retirement after a career spent mostly in Washington. For his final tour, he'd asked for Europe, and his fixed, dour look seemed to show how he felt about Washington's answer. Bill worked behind a closed door. His "I-love-me" wall was a photographer's gallery. Picture after picture of Bill with former bosses or visiting VIPs. There were few comments, however, mostly just signatures. Bill's fingernails were bitten to the quick. His hair was slicked down. "One of the last Wildroot cream oil men," I reflected. He looked out at the world—suspiciously? apprehensively?—through steel-rimmed glasses. I thought of Bernard Goetz.

Late in the morning, Pete took me on a physical security tour of other embassy properties. We drove past the airport and the al-Riyadh quarter to the Manshiyya and Blue Nile subdistricts. Not far from the river, we drove along a low, whitewashed, cinder-block wall and stopped at a gate: "The rec site," Pete announced.

A pleasant surprise awaited me. The recreation site sloped back from a thirty-foot retaining wall along the Blue Nile. The landscape was flat on the other side. I remembered my land-navigation from the U.S.M.C.: "One's distance to the horizon is equal to the square root of one's altitude or elevation." I was looking out five or six miles. I counted eight mosques opposite me. Their tall, pointed, clustered minarets gave the opposing bank a strangely space-age look. The Arab League's Cape Kennedy? Upstream, lines of squat, neolithic-looking structures gave off smoke. These, Pete explained, were brick kilns. They cooked brick day and night and were manned exclusively by black Sudanese from the South.

He went on: "We're about three miles upstream from where the Blue and White Niles meet at Khartoum. The Blue starts in Ethiopia. It's fast and pretty clean. You can swim in it. It delivers about 70 percent of the water in the Nile. In the winter, during the rainy season in

43

Ethiopia, the river rises twenty or thirty feet. That's why we're standing on this piece of Maginot Line."

I asked Pete about the White Nile.

He replied: "A great book, by Alan Moorehead. But an awful river. The White Nile's 'the mother of all waterborne diseases.' It enters Sudan near Juba, in Equatoria, coming from Uganda. In Juba, they say that on a calm night, if you listen hard, you can *hear* the viruses mutating. But now, the rest of the site."

Moving back from the fence atop the retaining wall, we crossed a well-tended lawn to a patio/dance floor, and a two-story modern, air-conditioned clubhouse. Beyond it, through an arcade, I could see a pool and four clay tennis courts.

"Tennis your game, they say?" remarked Valiant.

"I played a little in college."

"How good?"

"OK for Bates. We played NCAA Division III schools: Bowdoin, Amherst, Middlebury. Each year we'd get stomped by Harvard. Went to the U.K. one summer for some exhibition matches. The high point of my career: I beat the Welsh champion."

"You'll probably be asked to play by Mr. Bogosian," said Pete. "He's a wealthy Sudanese-Armenian. Has family in Europe and the U.S.A. He's a good friend of the embassy. A real gentleman. And a tennis fan. His grass court, they say, is better than Center Court at Wimbledon."

I replied: "I've only played on grass once—while I was in the U.K. It's nice. Like a good carpet. Makes you feel rich."

Pete and I drove home for lunch. Two days after the Hilverding murder, Marj and I had moved into our own house, with security aplenty. Military guards at the front and back gates, plus a squad in the garden. I was glad to be out of the ambassador's residence. The thought of what had happened upstairs still made Marj uncomfortable. And settling in, I thought, would be helpful to us both. Give Marj a sense of place and lots to do, and give me a chance, over casual lunches, to begin to size up our colleagues—and they me.

It *was* a nice house, I thought, as Pete and I walked through the gate and down a short path to our front door. Tall mango trees, a beautiful lawn—and behind the house, a small, but usable pool. Inside, even as we stood in the lobby, I could see that Marj (and the houseboy) had been hard at work. The windows were spotless. There were flowers on the tables, some knickknacks and family photos were on display. The furniture had somehow been rearranged to make the room look larger and more hospitable. The wood shone. I smelled lemon oil. By the couch lay an Arab-looking rug that not been there in the morning.

I heard Marj call: "You're home! Listen!" Piano music greeted us. Around the corner, Marj was sitting at the keyboard of the residence's "Baby" Baldwin.

She looked up at us smiling. "How wonderful to have one's own piano overseas! Never before! Listen."

She composed her face into a grim look. Then began to play—something discordant? Once or twice she struck the keyboard with her fists.

"Sound familiar?" she asked me. I shook my head.

"Silly! *Our* song! Charles Wuorinen, Piano Variations. It's part of what I played for my recital at Mother and Dad's the night we met."

To Pete: "He'd just been commissioned in the Marine Corps; a friend of ours brought him over. Josh was still in uniform. He looked so good! Afterwards he said he really admired my playing. Invited me to the Boston Symphony the next night. He made a lot of good comments—that was before I knew he was tone deaf. The comments were all from theater programs he'd gotten earlier! But in a week we were married and off to Quantico! My parents have never gotten over it. That was as far as Josh ever got with good music. As for me, tennis gives me blisters, and languages, stage fright. But now listen to this. Even you, Josh, will like it."

Cheerful sound began cascading from the piano, Marj's shoulders swung from side to side, her shoulder-length brown hair bouncing lightly. After a minute, her eyes still on the keyboard, she said: "George Gershwin, *Girl Crazy;* imagine, almost seventy years ago. Now this . . . " And she swung into? *I knew this one!* "Scott Joplin! 'Maple Leaf Rag'!" Marj stopped: "Maybe there's hope for the lieutenant after all! Let's have lunch."

Lunch was just the three of us. Frank Greer didn't show up, and Pete's wife was in the States having their first baby. Marj was cheerful: she'd loved the flower market—exotic blooms from gardens along the Nile; the rug had come from the airport duty-free shop. A bargain.

Our houseboy brought us peanut soup, a Sudanese staple, with home-baked rolls. What coffee is to Brazil, the peanut is to Sudan. It was in everything. Peanuts were drunk—in soup; eaten—roasted or boiled; cooked with—as peanut oil. Folk healers conjured with it. The flagging or aging Sudanese male swore by it. Arabs even called the peanut *fuul sudaniy*, 'the Sudanese bean.' After soup, came grilled Nile perch steaks. The Nile perch was big. It could weigh two hundred pounds or more. Its flesh was firm, dry, meaty. The perch was served with rice—sprinkled with peanuts, pine nuts, and almonds.

The food was delicious. I reflected that for all her gentle ways, Marjorie was no softie as a household manager. She kept a sharp eye on the books, yet everywhere our servants had liked and tried to please her.

Pete asked Marj how the move into the new house was going. "I'm surprised, frankly," he commented. "You look so well established. None of that living-out-of-a-suitcase look."

Marj answered, "The move's alright. One gets pretty good at setting up one's tent in this business. The airfreight came in good shape; it was here waiting. And I always bring along personal things to help make us and our guests feel more at home. Once we moved in the winter, I left out some of our woolens in favor of Christmas decorations!" She went on: "The house and garden are great—except that the guards lie around with half their clothes off. And they're always bothering the cook for food. Doesn't their government do *anything* for them?"

Seeing Pete's expression, she nodded: "Silly question. But on the clothes—could you talk to them?"

Pete answered: "I'll try to stop the lying around. It's a problem all the time for you and the ambassador. The houses just aren't built for private, within-the-wall police forces—just the opposite. I'll try on the mooching from the kitchen, too, though that'll be harder."

As dessert was brought to the table, Pete exclaimed: "What is this marvel!" (I'd never seen it before.)

Matter-of-factly Marj answered: "Just an old family favorite. I call it *Crostata di Crema e Cioccolata.*" She caught my eye. Smiled. Pete had a large second helping. Then the houseboy brought us Arab coffee.

"You're lucky in your servants," said Pete. "You've got good houseboys, and your cook/head boy, Mustafa, is one of the best in Khartoum."

I reflected how lucky we were to have Mustafa. He was in his sixties and had worked for several of my predecessors. He was dignified, yet warm and friendly. He was thin, but not frail. Each day he bicycled the six kilometers to our house—and back at night. He was pious, as one might have guessed from the *zabib*, a sort of Muslim stigmata, on his forehead. Over the years, by frequent prostrations, a callosity can form on the forehead of a pious Muslim. Mustafa never made a display of his religion, however. But every evening, after bringing Marj and me our drinks, he'd quietly excuse himself. Then he'd go to the back lawn and lead the Muslims in our household—security guards, too—in prayer.

I once asked the head of the security detail about Mustafa.

"Sayyid Mustafa very good man," he replied. "Holy man. Family all holy men. Islamic holy man must work *and* pray. Sayyid Mustafa work for you. Pray with us. He pray for you and Madame and your son in America, too. He even pray for black Christian houseboys! Angel stand right by Mustafa. Carry his prayers each night to God in heaven."

There was harmony between Mustafa and the houseboys—all of whom were black southern Sudanese. They willingly helped the older man with some of the heavy work in the kitchen. And in his own way, Mustafa looked out for *them*. Recently, one of the houseboys hadn't shown up for work in the morning. The police, we learned, had rounded up several thousand supposedly vagrant southerners in a sweep (the infamous *kasha*) through Khartoum. Most would be packed into cattle cars or army trucks and sent back South.

Mustafa had gotten on his bicycle and ridden to the *markaz*—police headquarters. An hour later he and the houseboy were back at work.

Afterwards, the houseboy swore to me it was a miracle: "Excellency. This Mustafa like Saint Peter. Or like the angel. He come in the jailyard. The Arabs they all bow. Run this way and that way looking for me. They tell me, 'You go now with your friend. You are very lucky southerner.' Truly, they not really say 'southerner.' They use other, very bad word. They say *abid*. That mean 'slave' in Arabic. Mustafa not like other Arabs. I almost kiss him hand."

I looked at my watch. Time to go. I looked over at Valiant. "Ready for the office—for a full in-box and what Kirby calls 'the postlunch dip'?"

As we all rose from the table, Marj said: "I'll help keep you awake—at least until you get to your car." She went directly to the piano bench and began to play.

An easy one: "Funiculi funicula!" I called out.

For a moment she stopped: "The lieutenant's right—and doesn't know it. Rimsky-Korsakov, 1880! Neapolitan Song. It's really a duet—'funiculi funicula' is part of it."

The playing started again. Stiff-legged, swinging my arms, toy soldier fashion, I marched toward the door, as Pete fell in behind me.

OUR FRIENDS AND NEIGHBORS

7

The dust had risen again by the time we got to the Chancery. The ambassador was looking out of the windows in the outer office. The Mylar shatterproof lamination on the inside of the windows admitted a mustardish, stained-glass light. Clayton, my secretary, was pouring us all coffee.

The ambassador raised his cup and, in mock-oratorical tones, said: "I address you, my fellow crewmen, from beneath the waves of the Yellow Sea. Before us, through the viewports, lies the ocean floor, half seen. Here, the forms of crumbling buildings, there, a palimpsest of streets. Those other shapes—once upon a time, cars and buses? But all is still. What cataclysm has overwhelmed this once great city? A fish swims by!

"But—Maryann, Clayton, Sally, Joshua," the ambassador continued, looking at us, "this is no latter-day Atlantis. It is Khartoum. In the middle of a *hubuub*, in the hot season." He turned into his office. "But come on in, Josh; bring your coffee, and let's talk."

Farnsworth took an armchair by the telephone. I sat by him on the couch. "A further word about personnel," he said. "An ambassador sets the tone at post; the DCM is key to implementing it. To the junior officers and the specialists an ambassador can seem remote. Clouds and lightning on the mountain top. But you'll be able to reach out more easily. You'll review many of their efficiency reports. Be a 'big brother' to the younger officers. Everyone needs a role model. Actually, 'hero' is a better word—too bad it's out of style. Be cheerful: was it Marshal Lyautey who said *gaiety* was needed to be a good officer? Walk around. Get to know people in their offices. Bring them into your own office regularly—work with them on their drafting and on oral presentations. Suggest readings."

The ambassador went on: "Take them with you on calls and field trips. I do that myself. Share your thinking with them. But ask for their opinions first. Remember my question in the car to Sally? They all have brains—the exams see to that. Our job is to make sure they exercise them.

"One thing more: you'll meet Ward Kapecka and Frank Greer." At this Farnsworth paused, then went on in a noncommittal tone: "At some point, give me your thinking on them. They're both on their second assignment. Still probationers under the new personnel act. Greer's a little defensive. Has a bit of an attitude. But he can be effective in his own way." Farnsworth smiled to himself: "When Greer was running the motor pool, the wives came to him complaining about the drivers' B.O. Greer told the drivers once to wear deodorant. The complaints kept coming. So he called them in again—and came to the meeting wearing a gas mask! Result: problem solved. And somehow the drivers didn't take offense. Found it funny. Greer tested high on the Foreign Service exam, too. See what polish he'll take. Kapecka? I've heard Bill Gray thinks he's a brilliant economist.

"Also, there's Sally Tolson. Nice girl. First tour. A B.A. from the University of Pennsylvania, then taught French and German at some private school in the east. Also coached tennis. Then joined the Peace Corps. Served in Cameroon. Next came a Peace Corps cadre job in Gabon. She started here a year ago and did very well in the consular section. She's talented and writes well. Has a capacity for apparently unlimited hard work. But how can I say it—I think she lives more inside her own mind than others do. She may need to project more. Since you're a tennis player, too, maybe use that to draw her out?"

Farnsworth rose and walked over to his desk. "Let me look at the cable traffic. I hear you're scheduled for a little talk with Mr. Greer. Don't be too hard on him, but it *is* for his own good. And then we'll do the staff meeting."

I was scheduled to counsel Frank Greer about protocol. I understood that his current boss, Dawkins, had previously spoken to him, but without effect. There had been his nonappearance at my lunch and, I'd heard, a habit of arriving late and leaving early at representational functions.

I went down to the political section to talk to Greer. I could have had him sent in, but it always seemed more person-to-person if I went myself either to praise or to "counsel." I also believed a boss should deliver "constructive criticism" in the open. He shouldn't shoot, so to speak, from behind a prepared position—like his own desk.

Just inside the entrance to the political section, I stopped to look over the Post Library. Some new fascicles of *The Encyclopedia of Islam* caught my eye. As I took one down and leafed through it, I could overhear Frank and Will talking in Frank's office.

Suddenly Frank's voice rose: "And did you know, Will, I've been memorizing parts of the Holy Koran?"

Will's voice (pleased, eager): "That's terrific, Frank. Arabs are really pleased when one of us shows some interest in their cul . . . "

Frank snorted, cleared his throat, and spat. "That's the first verse!" he boomed triumphantly. "Now verse number two." And began to snort again.

I walked in. Frank looked astonished. Swallowed. Will covered his face with his hands.

I tried to give nothing away. "Could I have a moment with Frank?" I asked.

On Frank's coffee table lay several Post Library books. They even had markers in them. Then on the wall, I noticed a 10" x 12" framed black-and-white photo. It showed an athletic group. The men were of differing sizes, but all of the same basic shape. "A weight-lifting squad?" I guessed out loud.

"That's right," Frank answered. "The AAU New England championships from my last year in grad school. I won the light-heavy division. Snatched 285 and clean-and-jerked 390. Total 675 pounds. Still my Personal Best."

"Did you ever use steroids?" I asked curiously.

"Honestly, no. Sure, they'll give results, but they'll ruin you, too. Oh, if it'd been my career—football, maybe—I guess I'd have done it, but pro ball never really interested me. Though a couple of scouts called me. They thought I was strong enough and maybe fast enough to try out at halfback—did forty yards in about four point five seconds."

Greer was looking open, animated. He went on: "I always liked the honesty of weight lifting. No cheating. No disputed calls. No instant replays. The judges could be anyone in the audience. No excuses. Either you get the weight up or you don't. Most people don't understand the *completeness* of weight lifting. It's got everything 'slow motion' sports have got—just squeezed into a split second. Strength is just 'for openers.' You need speed, concentration, coordination, and balance. Otherwise, you try to 'fast-forward' a fifth of a ton of iron—that bar can KILL you. And it's a real amateur sport. No one ever got rich lifting."

"What about bodybuilders?" I asked.

For a moment Greer looked irritated. Then amused. "Pathetic guys," he answered. "Something's seriously wrong. They start by lopping the legs off their sweatpants. Then their sweatshirts—they hack the necklines wider and deeper. Then as they start bulking up, the guys'll go sleeveless, wax their chests, grease up their bodies, starve!" A long, thoughtful look down at his waistline: "I always had trouble making weight. I guess maybe I'd be a little over right now."

Greer went on: "Weight lifters don't like to work out with body-builders. Those prettyboys, they can't lift *shit*! I'm not being prejudiced, but a lot are gay. Two different cultures. One's a sport, the other just fashion. Somewhere I read: 'Bodybuilders *become* their costumes.' But you're not here 'to talk smack'?"

I nodded. "Frank," I asked, "did the department brief your class on protocol while you were in orientation?"

At mention of the word "protocol," Greer's body language contracted. He leaned away from me, back pressed into the chair. He dropped his chin towards his chest.

"I'm sorry about lunch," he said. "I was working on a crash project for Dawkins, and it all just slipped my mind. But in general, I guess I don't just get as tied up in protocol as some people do in the Foreign Service. Some really go in for that stuff, I guess. In my basic class they handed out something—honestly, I could hardly believe some of what I read. I figured it was some mistake. Really medieval. I figured it came from some monastery's cartulary! Should have been written in Latin! On vellum! Only thing left out was the ambassador's *droit de seigneur.*" Mimicking a nagging feminine tone, Greer recited: "Arrive early, get your instructions, mix with the foreign guests, don't talk to your friends."

"Can you see a reason for any of these guidelines?" I asked.

Frank's chin dropped a further degree or two closer to his chest: "I suppose it's a way to pump information out of people at a party—if that's what we`re supposed to be doing in Sudan. But most don't know much, or just want to eat and drink, or don't speak much English. Doesn't seem worth it. And it seems a little sneaky—inviting people not because you like them but just because you want to get information from them. If I'd wanted to do that, I could've worked for Kirby's people."

I thought for a moment, then said: "Frank, let me try to explain. Up to now you've lived in a university world. Your success or failure depended only on grades—not your degree of socialization in an organization's culture. But out of school, believe me, most people make their impact, get ahead, by how they deal with people. That's true of banks, law firms, and even of the *politics* of a university. We're not unique that way. You'll find Foreign Service work is mostly dealing with people—and sometimes dealing with them at parties. Maybe you don't like the social guidelines. But they're not arbitrary. They help us get the maximum information, the maximum benefit out of each social function. We're like traders—and representational functions are *our* stock or commodities exchange."

Greer was silent for a moment. When he spoke, he sounded still unpersuaded: "OK. But what about those frankly absurd rules about the right-hand corner of the couch belonging to the highest-ranking person, or why he gets on the plane last and all that precedence stuff?" Frank was beginning to breathe hard.

I said: "Let me try to explain protocol this way: When you drive a car, you follow the rules of the road. Correct? Why? Because that's how you avoid traffic accidents. It's the same for us. The officials we deal with may come from different cultures—but every official has a doubly inflated ego: once for himself, and secondly for his country. So I ask you: how does one avoid needlessly giving offense? *By protocol.* Protocol is our lubricant and our traffic cop. It minimizes friction. It keeps us all driving on the same side of the road. We avoid fender-benders. Does that sound reasonable?"

Greer watched me silently. So I went on: "There are always things that one at first may not like about an organization. Isn't it better, though, not to assume that one's colleagues are fools or stuffed shirts? Give them a chance. Don't fight the problem. And remember, when you meet with our businessmen or foreign officials, these people are looking at a representative of the United States of America. We're not formal here in Khartoum the way they might be in a European capital"—I hesitated, took a look at Greer's shapeless, stained seersucker, then went on—"but in matters of dress, you might consider their expectations."

Immediately, I could tell Greer was offended. Somehow, I hadn't reached him—or he hadn't really tried to listen. I reproached myself. Had I been too direct about his appearance?

"Is that all?" he asked stiffly.

"Yes," I answered. "Except that Marjorie and I hope to see you some other time at our house. But I guess we'd better head for the staff meeting."

Staff meetings were held three times a week. The conference room looked like the African gallery of a small-town museum, a landfill of unwanted bric-a-brac, the moraine of embassy field trips. Martin and Osa Johnson's den?

The walls were hung with spears: throwing and stabbing swords, both long and short; hippopotamus-hide shields: the round and the oblong models—with iron-hard, finely wrinkled surfaces. There was a confabulation of drums, *balafons*, or hollowed-out logs used for drumming, and one-stringed Arab violins. Leopard skins. There was also a *kurbaj*, the infamous Sudanese hippopotamus-hide whip, used by cattle drovers, but formerly also the slavers' tool. The *kurbaj* always drew a comment, especially from junior officers. These trip mementoes gave the room an atmosphere: adventurous to some, gamy to others.

How would the ambassador manage his staff meetings? Staff meetings—their frequency, composition, length, and management—told a lot about our Foreign Service, a post, and its boss. Farnsworth didn't like "the mendicant approach." He didn't like going around the room "collecting alms." Instead, he asked his officers always to think of what they'd done that was important or of general interest—then call Maryann or Clayton and get on the agenda. Agendas, Farnsworth thought, helped focus discussion. They helped keep a meeting on track; they discouraged meandering beyond the allotted forty-five minutes.

Today's agenda had four items:

1. Hilverding investigation (S/A Kirby and RSO Valiant).
2. F-5e program—termination? (DATT).
3. The state of the economy—Quarterly Report (ECON)
4. Report on trip to the west (Kapecka/Greer)

I entered the conference room with Farnsworth just behind me. All rose and remained standing until he had taken his seat at the head of the conference table. Involuntarily, I glanced over to Frank Greer, as I sat down at Jon's right; Frank seemed to avoid my gaze.

The ambassador began by remarking that the Sudan government, it seemed, had made no progress on the Hilverding investigation. Turning to Valiant, he asked: "Pete, did you meet yesterday with the minister of the interior?"

"No sir," Pete answered. "I waited in his office for an hour. They filled me up with tea. Then his deputy came and said the minister had been detained at the Police Academy in Wad Madani. Said he was sure the minister would call me as soon as he got back. Fat chance! I tell you, they're looking to bury this one. Two more weeks, and we'll be entering the 'hurt look' phase of the investigation. Or, 'How can you do this to me, when I want only to be your friend?'

"It comes down to this, sir," Valiant concluded: "They're more afraid of the Libyans and the radicals than they are of us. They feel they got the killers—pure luck! Then they pray every night that nothing more turns up. Because then they might have to do something. And if something *did* turn up, Deng might be the last to know."

"You're right, I think," said Farnsworth. "I tell you, Pete, as soon as the prime minister returns, I'll go ruin his day."

The meeting moved on. The defense attaché reminded us that three years ago Sudan had received five F-5e's, as a first step toward a squadron of twelve. Two were soon lost to rebel fire in the south. The remaining aircraft were lost yesterday while participating in a parade in Juba. The lead pilot had done a flyover, ending with a rollout. Only he'd rolled out, then down, into the middle of Juba. The two other pilots had followed him closely—into the ground. At least fifty people were dead.

Gray found this funny. He chuckled: "Looks like our Military Training Mission's worked itself out of a job! Well done! Maybe we needn't have bombed Libya after all! We could have offered an MTT instead!"

The defense attaché reddened. He leaned forward as if to say something—checked himself—then sat back.

Gray was on next. He looked up from his pad—the top sheet was webbed over with tight little penciled doodles.

"Mr. Ambassador, I know this subject isn't on the agenda, but I thought I'd mention it as of general interest. It could also affect post morale."

"Go ahead Bill," replied the ambassador. "We're always glad for your suggestions about how something so important to us all can be improved." Was there a dryness in Farnsworth's voice? Gray went on: "Last night I joined one of our colleagues at a very nice informal gathering he gave at his house. Just us embassy Americans. Good company and really good food. So I asked our host . . ."

I broke in: "Bill, you're talking about Jack's party out near the Nile last night?"

The frown lines above the bridge of Gray's noise deepened.

"Yes," he said, not looking toward me, and continued: "There were deep-fried butterfly shrimp, some good French cheeses, also some wines from California and the Yakima Valley vineyards. I was thinking, Mr. Ambassador, that it would be a real boost to morale if such commodities could be available to all people at post—maybe when the items come in, they could be stocked at the commissary, for instance." Gray looked around the room for support.

Kirby looked pointedly at me. He raised an eyebrow. Then rolled his eyes upwards. The gesture did not escape Gray. "Mr. Ambassador, I must . . . " he began. Speaking over him, Kirby said, "Come on, Bill, lighten up."

The ambassador's voice blandly cut through: "If we all talk at once, we can finish in half the time." Pause. Farnsworth looked at Kirby and Gray. He remarked: "Bill, that's an interesting suggestion. What do you say to that, Jack?"

"Yessir," said Kirby, "those were my shrimp and wine that Bill's talking about. And I'm glad he enjoyed them. And I wish I could do more to share what I have. But my station's only got a C-12. We don't have a C-130, as some people seem to think. Here are the facts: Every quarter we have to take the bird to Jidda for servicing. We stock up from the Air Force commissary there. Each of our families gets twenty pounds—most of the return cargo, you know, is in classified pouches. Security equipment, commo gear, and stuff like that. But as I said, we try to share."

The ambassador let the silence draw itself out. He seemed to be communing with the photographs of previous ambassadors looking down from the wall. I felt a lot of eyes were on Gray.

Then the ambassador said: "Years and years ago, as a PFC, I learned that if you were in the motor pool, you usually rode, not walked, to maneuvers. And at night you could usually sleep in a truck. Maybe you could even wangle an ambulance. No sleeping on the ground, anyway. And if you were in Medical Company, and you needed a shot to get back on the social trail—no questions asked. Nothing in your file." Farnsworth paused. He looked again around the room: "Am I making myself clear?"

Then his voice sharpened: "So if some want shrimp flown in from Jidda, or more recent videos than we get from State, they should have signed up with Jack's people years ago. And if some want to go camping in a well-equipped desert patrol vehicle—maybe the Marines can still use a few more good men. And so it goes. In brief—be kind—be forebearing with each other. We're a long way from home. Share when you can. Don't be dogs in the manger.

"You force me to share two wise sayings with you. First, there's the university president's guidance to his deans at fund-raising time: 'Gentlemen, every tub must stand on its own bottom.' Second, there are the immortal words of Edward Everett Hale: 'Look up, not down, look out, not in, look forward, not back, and—lend a hand.' Jack, your party was a nice thought. Now, Bill, do you have an economic report for us?" I heard a gentle emphasis on the words, "economic report."

"Yessir," Gray replied. He picked up his notes and tilted the limbs of his glasses up so he could look down at his papers then up at us over the rims. I thought of those tropical fishes that could focus both above and below the water.

Gray began. "For the past quarter my economic section has conducted parametric studies of Sudanese utility-maximizing consumption decisions, applying the discount function known as Herrnstein's matching law. We've discovered the discount curves are all hyperbolic." Looking up, Gray explained: "More bowed, that is, than an exponential curve would be. Aggregate behavior, it seems, is determined by nonconvex technologies. We have found Pareto-rankable disequilibria to exist, however, wherever Arrow-Debreu assumptions are violated."

Unobtrusively, I looked around me. The defense attaché looked puzzled and angry. Gray's little put-down still rankled? Dawkins looked amused. Kirby's eyes were half-closed; but Ward Kapecka, the junior economic officer, caught my eye. Kapecka always had an Ichabod Crane look to him. His sallow complexion and seal-beam glasses suggested a youth holed up in the library stacks. But now his slight moustache (that clung to a pronounced overbite) almost quivered with animation. He raised his hand. A little breathlessly he asked: "Isn't it true though, sir, that a too-wide acceptance of the ROCOA approach could inhibit our further development of a general taxonomy of trade-off processes? By using the two best RA models of the I-C nexus, or even bivariate regression, we'd be able to establish the different saliences and weights of a Euclidean distance preference rule?"

Gray beamed. "Precisely, Ward. I couldn't have put it better myself. In fact, those were just some of the points I was leading up to. Perhaps it would be appropriate to paraphrase for our noneconomist friends here (was Gray looking toward the DATT again?) the arguments for applying Pareto set theory to Sudan. If applicable, I'm confident we'd be led to conclude that . . ."

Farnsworth cut in: "To conclude that all complimentarities are local, and that Bayesian equilibria, plus the structure of aggregate fluctuations, suggest that Sudan is in deep economic trouble and sinking fast. Right?"

"Er, yes, quite, Mr. Ambassador," a nonplussed Gray finally got out.

The DATT laughed. Dawkins, I noticed, had bent over to tie his shoe. Kirby's eyes were still half-closed, but he looked to be slipping into a very pleasant daydream.

The ambassador continued evenly: "Bill, that was a highly professional piece of analysis—as always. I look forward to seeing it in despatch form. Now let's learn about the *real* Sudan. Ward and Frank will tell us what lies beyond the Great White Way of Abdul Lateef Street."

The ambassador looked toward Greer and Kapecka: "Your trip to el-Obeid was worthwhile, I hope? A few more shields and we'll have even the ceiling covered. Then Pete here will be happy. How was my friend the Vice-Governor?"

Greer and Kapecka looked at each other.

The silence continued.

Kapecka finally replied: "Really sorry, sir, I don't know how the item got onto your agenda. I thought I'd told the front office that we'd had to cancel at the last minute." He looked at Sally Tolson. Reproachfully?

"A pity," said Farnsworth. "How come?"

Another pause. Kapecka reluctantly went on: "I hate to point the finger, but Frank overslept. He was supposed to come by for me. Finally, I called his house, but by the time we got to the airport, the UNDP flight was already gone."

The ambassador looked at Greer, who reddened.

"I set the alarm alright, but either it didn't go off or I slept through it. I might have been pretty . . . tired. Got to bed late and it's been quite a week in our section."

Farnsworth rolled a pencil between his fingers. He thought a minute, then said: "In other words, 'no excuse.' I believe in redemption, however. I've just gotten an invitation from the al-Hilla Youth and Sports society. They are giving a pageant in the town of Hagar al-Salaya, west of the Jabal Awliya dam. A cycle of Furi folk dances, followed by dinner and other cultural attractions. It's been said no one can bear to watch a folk dance more than twenty minutes, and the shortest folk dance ever takes thirty. I disagree: in my experience, folk dances don't become excruciating until thirty minutes are up—until then, they're simply boring.

"Hagar al-Salaya is the capital of Sudan's sheep and goat country. It's also where our friend Sa'eed comes from. You'll be served the usual sheeps' eyes and stuffed, steamed intestines. Also 'FGS'—that is, 'funny green stuff.' What's in it? Don't ask. Finally, there's some sort of raw horror reserved for especially honored guests. We'll call right away and let the shaikhs know you're coming. Maybe you could make a cultural offering yourselves? Take some USA flag pins and key rings with you. Also some USIS presentation books—but look them over first. Make sure none of the illustrations will shock or offend. If you leave right now, you can be there for dinner. Enjoy. Anything else?"

Greer asked, "Can we take an embassy carryall? The road could be hard on our personal vehicles."

"Certainly," replied the ambassador. "And we'll hear from you at our next meeting." We all rose as he left the room.

Afterwards, I asked Valiant for his impressions of Kapecka and Greer. He was blunt, as usual: "They're the same—twins, really—one's a brownnoser and the other's a shithead. The only difference is a matter of depth perception."

BOY SCOUTS ALL

8

That afternoon, I was sitting with Maryann and Clayton. They had a nice office, I thought. They needed it, considering the time they spent there—and the drab world outside. The walls were decorated with photos of Sudan. One of Omdurman Plain filled much of the north wall. It was my least favorite. An ominous, darkening, blood-red scene—taken at sunset. The desert landscape radiated heat and violence. One thought of the battle of Omdurman, where more than twelve thousand Sudanese were killed, as against only twenty-eight British dead.

On the facing wall hung a temperate idyll—a softly lit, green and gold dawn at a teak plantation in the Imatong mountains. They were near Juba in the province of Equatoria, in the far south of Sudan. But they rose to ten thousand feet; their microclimate was like spring in the Pacific Northwest. The middle wall showed prodigiously muscled Nuban wrestlers—their nearly nude bodies painted in Miro-like colors and patterns.

Clayton resembled an ancient Greek oracle. She sat on her three-wheeled secretarial chair, shrouded in an inscrutable cloud of cigarillo smoke. We were drawing up a guest list for a representational dinner the ambassador was planning to give for a visiting UN official. Easy-sounding, but in reality a labor-intensive, frustrating chore. Who went well with whom? Who would bring out his wife—if others brought theirs? If they didn't? Before whom could you or other guests drink our smuggled alcohol? Clayton claimed doing guest lists was like working out a complex problem of organic chemistry!

When the guest list had been assembled, then the real work began. You called, you sent a follow-up, and then, if possible, you went by the person's office on the day of the function to underline once more how much your and the ambassador's happiness—in this and the next world—depended on his (or her) coming that evening. Dawkins wryly recalled the director of political affairs had once not shown up for dinner. The next day when asked why, he'd told Dawkins: "I wasn't hungry." The ambassador was better than most about sharing in the phone calls and follow-ups, but the planning and follow-through for official functions remained one of my (and the secretaries') least favorite jobs.

Accordingly, I was surprised but glad for a break when RSO Pete Valiant called. Would I come down for a fitting?

"A fitting? You're serious?"

He was. Arranged on his office couch were a number of official-looking boxes. Above the couch, former President Bush smiled at me and shook hands with Pete. I looked inquiringly at Pete. "One of your satisfied customers?"

"He's a great gentleman," Pete said. "I was on his security detail for two years. I don't care about what politicians or historians will say about him. I'm not knocking the Clintons, either. But he was great to work for, and Mrs. Bush, too. I'll never forget one night at Kennebunkport. A big storm was tearing at the sea wall. I was in one of the guardhouses when I hear a knock on the door. It was the President of the USA, in pajamas and a raincoat, bringing me a mug of coffee and a piece of fresh apple pie that Mrs. Bush had just baked! But to work."

At this Pete opened one of the boxes. He took out—a waistcoat.

The truth dawned: "A bulletproof vest?"

Valiant laughed. "You mean 'a ballistic vest,' or 'soft body armor.' You're right. But it's not what you saw in *The Godfather*. No walking sandbag. These are the light, summer-weight variety. Almost seersucker. In the old days these vests weighed thirty pounds minimum. Didn't do much good, either. But now, thanks to a Dupont plastic fiber, we're in a better situation. Cut twenty off the weight. And lots more stopping power against handgun rounds. The vests come in four weights. Four levels of ballistic protection. This baby here's the top of the line." He lifted up one of the vests. "It'll stop a slug from a .357 Magnum at six feet. You'll feel you've been doing about a thousand sit-ups. But better than looking like a human doughnut."

Pete continued: "We can fit the happy customer in all sizes 34 to 52. Only we don't do alterations. 42 long?"

I took off my coat and slipped the vest on. Valiant closed it over the shoulders and sides with velcro snaps. "OK over the chest," he said. It seemed to weigh a lot more than ten pounds.

Valiant read out loud from a manual: "This ballistic vest offers you protection with style and good looks. Used by diplomats, government executives, and detectives, it has saved countless lives. Its Kevlar panels offer protection up to class II+, including 9mm machine gun fire. Still further degrees of protection are available with additional panels. Waterproof, it offers its wearers the warmth of a 100 percent wool sweater. Ideal for travel to troubled parts of the world."

"Warm enough?" Valiant asked. "Could you also use a ballistic raincoat—only twenty-five pounds? You could tuck a teargas canister into its pocket. Here it is: a little gizmo that shoots a stream of chloroacetophenome twenty-five feet. Hit a person anywhere, and it's sidewalk pizza delivery time!"

"Very funny, Pete. Get me out of this. When do you expect me to wear this, if ever?"

"You keep it." Pete replied. "At least while you're in Khartoum. I hope you don't have to wear it often—hope you'll have some warning when you should wear it. That'll be my job. But keep it handy. You never know—if things get worse, and you have to go to National Days. It's like big game hunting. The bad guys know that at dusk their quarry must come down to these particular watering holes in the diplomatic jungle. They stake you out, and 'bang!'"

Pete made as if to shoulder a rifle and shoot at something below him.

"That's how the PLO got Cleo Noel and Curt Moore," he went on, "at a Saudi embassy reception. So when you and Mrs. Chamberlain go to one of these parties, look around. Stay alert. Terrorist attacks are the most disorienting and terrifying if you haven't thought one through and considered your probable reactions. Think how you'd leave in a hurry if something funny starts to happen. And if it does—go over the wall. Take some other exit. Don't stand on pride. Don't play the tourist. Don't rubberneck to see what's going on. Don't wait to collect two hundred dollars. Leave. Also, if Jack or I get any intelligence through our channels, you'll know. And if I say wear the vest—please, please, do it. Remember what General Patton said: 'Make the *other* poor bastard die for *his* country.' Let *me* worry about your security, and *you* focus on your job."

"Don't worry, Pete. You're the doctor. I'll wear the vest when you tell me to. Who knows? It might even prevent illness, like my malaria suppressants."

"Thanks," said Valiant, in a relieved tone of voice. "Just one more stop. Go see the gunny. Sometimes you're going to have to carry."

"Carry?"

"Yeah. A sidearm," Valiant slipped his hand along his waist, brushing his coat jacket back. A smooth gesture. Nestled on his hip was a revolver.

"Thirty-eight caliber, model 54. Just barely enough for the job. You must have qualified with something in the Marines?"

"Yes. The grandaddy of them all. The Colt .45 automatic. Seventy years old pretty much. Even shot Expert."

"See what the gunny can fix you up with. No, better: see what he *can't* fix you up with. With our armory, Eisenhower could reenact June 6, 1944."

Gunnery Sergeant Poe—a black, originally from Atlanta—came to attention as I entered. I put him at ease. Then as I told him why I'd come, he beamed. He looked like a lawyer who'd just gotten a lucrative referral.

He also looked all Marine: five-foot ten, barrel-chested, waspwaisted. Sergeant Poe held the regional physical fitness (P.F.T.) "gofor-broke" record. A perfect P.F.T. score was three hundred. But when the Marines went "for broke," they got additional points for performances beyond "perfect." Like the decathlon. The gunny easily got better-than-perfect scores on the run (three miles in eighteen minutes), and the sit-ups (seventy-nine in two minutes). But above all, he excelled in pull-ups. "Perfect" was twenty—with "kips," a sort of swinging jerk, allowed. The gunny did *his* from a dead hang. He'd done fifty—for a combined total of 487 points. What with prodigious upper body development, he wore size "large" cammie blouses, and size "small" pants. On his chest was an impressive "rack" of ribbons. I recognized the Bronze Star with a "V" for valor, and Desert Shield and Desert Storm campaign ribbons. I also noted gold jump wings and a silver scuba "bubble."

"Were you in recon, Sergeant Poe?" I asked. "You were a jumper, too? Military free fall and all that?"

"Yessir," he replied, "First Force Recon at Camp Pendleton. You know how it is"—in a semirap beat he went on—"devil dog, parafrog, air-insertible, water submersible, MRE-eatable. No sky too high, no bar too far." He laughed.

In a more serious tone, he added: "But you've come to the right place, sir." Taking out a jailer's cluster of keys, he unlocked a door in the wall of his office. Within was a small room. A familiar odor of solvent, oil, and canvas webbing filled the air. I looked in.

The walls of the room were stacked chest-high with olive drab ammo boxes. On their cover, I could read the stencil: "cal .30 Ball ammunition." Other boxes, reinforced by wooden slats and steel-banded, carried the stencils for antipersonnel hand grenades: "H.E." and "W.P."—"high explosive," and "white phosphorous"—"Willie Pete," I remembered. A weapons rack carried half a dozen riot guns. Another rack carried my old standby, the M16 A1. (I guessed the A2, less liable to jamming, was going to regular units.) An anthology of pistols and revolvers hung on the walls: a Luger, a Beretta, several S&W .357 Magnums, and maybe a dozen Colt .45s—the military version. I also saw an H&K submachine gun. No Uzis though.

"That's fine, gunny," I said, "but where is the 155 mm self-propelled field artillery? Already checked out of your library? And no tactical nuclear weapons? Victims of the nonproliferation treaty, maybe?" Sergeant Poe gave a pleased laugh.

"Marines been a long time collecting, sir. Never know what you'll need, you scrounge what you can. Did real well during our last naval visit to Port Sudan. And when the Corps moved to the Beretta, lots of .45s to be had. But you're looking for something to carry? Now the RSO, he carries a little State Department .38 *five* shooter. Two-inch barrel. Can't hit anything with that, 'less you hit him with it like a club! Give me a long gun any time. Nothing like the M16, sir. That bullet, she leaves the muzzle like a turpentine cat, 3200 fps, wobbles all the way. Splash right into the bad boys. And close up, you just switch to auto—'group therapy' we call it."

"Gunny, thanks," I replied, "but I'll stick to what I can carry—that means a handgun. And what I know—that means this here." I picked up one of the .45s. It was an old U.S. Army Colt Model 1911A1. I eased the slide back. With my thumbnail I reflected some light up the barrel. A smooth, dull gray light shone back from the "lands." The weapon was spotless.

"You pass inspection, gunny."

"Tools of the trade, sir. Clean 'em all every week. And shoot 'em almost every month. Maybe you'd like to come out on the range with us someday, sir."

"Count on me, gunny. That'll be a pleasure." I balanced the .45 in my hand. It felt comfortable and familiar. Was there a transfer of learning from tennis to handguns? Strong wrists and good hand-eye coordination? Whatever the case, I'd always shot well—but even better with the .45 than the M16. The difference between being on the borderline between "expert" and "sharpshooter" and qualifying as "high expert." With the .45, I felt I was placing the round where my index finger and eye pointed—without exactly aiming. Once when I'd shot 'for record' the instructor had said with astonishment in his voice: "Sir— you just blew the asshole right out of that target!" "Uncle Sam's Metamusil, Sergeant," I'd responded, holding up the .45.

To Sergeant Poe I said, "I'll take this one, Gunny. You have a holster?"

"No way to carry that on your hip, sir, and the whole world don't see. But we have one shoulder holster. A lot of straps. But do the job. For a right hand draw?"

"That's right."

The gunny chambered a round. Then he loaded a clip into the magazine, and checked the safety. He put the weapon in a small orange diplomatic pouch bag. Added two more magazines, and a cleaning kit. He dumped the holster and straps in last.

"That's all?" I asked. "No steel pot? No C-rations?"

"Now it's MREs—Meals-Ready-To-Eat. But come to think of it, sir, a man can always use backup."

He took my tennis bag (I preferred it to an attaché case) and indicated I should follow him into his armory. It only took a moment.

"Send 'em to hell, sir," I heard him say as I walked out the door.

Maryann smiled when I returned to the executive suite with my packages. "I see Pete Valiant's Khartoum outlet is having a sale today. What? No necktie? No sword canes? Oh, and the ambassador wants to see you."

"Thanks, Moneypenny," I said. Maryann's robust, full-throated laugh followed me into the ambassador's office.

Farnsworth looked up from a note he was writing. He saw the box and bag I was carrying. "Ready for your safari?" he asked. "Elephant gun by Holland and Holland? Food by Fortnum and Mason?"

The ambassador put down his Mont Blanc pen. I noticed his fingers were inky—but he refused to sign letters or to write thank-you notes with ballpoint or felt-tipped pens. "Hitch your horse by the door, pardner, and park your hardware there." He pointed to a coatrack, came out from behind his desk, and motioned me to sit down.

"Two things, Josh: First, more trouble from Salim al-Atrash. He's denounced the Joint Distribution Committee this morning. You know, the interembassy group that coordinates donor relief efforts in the South? Al-Atrash said he had proof that our private voluntary organizations were corrupting local governments, violating Sudanese sovereignty, and secretly helping the rebels. He's seized the Nile Safari 707 that was ferrying relief supplies south—I hear the army's now using it to move ammunition. The British ambassador is chairman of our committee this month. He tried to call al-Atrash to protest. The minister wouldn't even come to the phone. Southerners will be enraged. As for us Western donors, how can we justify continuing help to a government that's at war with its own civilian population?

"Second, I got a personal note early this afternoon from the foreign minister. In it, he says he assumes I've heard the speech of Minister al-Atrash about relief operations in the south. Then he goes on to say he would like to meet with one of us at his house tomorrow evening at six. The meeting's to be strictly private. Because you're still new—unidentified—he thinks perhaps it could be easier for you to move inconspicuously about town. It sounds as if he really doesn't want any security cavalcade pulling up before his door. I've just written him saying you'd be there."

"Anything more about why he wants to see one of us?"

"Only that he wanted to talk about some further developments, internal *and* external, that concerned him and that he thought would concern us."

"Could be almost anything."

"Yes, with al-Atrash in the picture, almost anything *bad*. I hesitate to say this, but when you go, leave your follow car and guards. Also, I wouldn't take your armored sedan. Both cars are too well known here. Aim for safety in the unexpected. And have Pete Valiant drive you in one of our other sedans. Jack Kirby can give you one of his cars with regular plates. You'll need a notetaker, also. Maybe Tolson."

Pete and I agreed that he'd drive by the house to pick me up at about 5:30 P.M. Then we'd go get Sally Tolson. As I feared, he said I should wear "the vest."

"But the heat! And what will Sally wear? You got a vest for her? What could be more safe than an unannounced visit to the foreign minister's, for Pete's sake." I stopped. We both laughed. "I mean, for heaven's sake, Pete."

"Ms. Tolson will wear a vest. You will be armed. I will wear a vest, and I will be armed. I will sit in the car. You will see me fast if anything happens. You will keep your eyes and ears open. I hope the evening will be boring as hell. I hope the mosquitoes in the garden bite your ankles to the bone. I hope the Fonmin only wants to complain that our consul won't give visas to all of his tribal brothers so they can travel to the U.S. and vanish into the woodwork. I hope we all live to be a hundred. And that Qadhaafi dies of AIDS. But as my dad would say, 'Hope's a good companion, but a poor guide.' So just think of me as your resident paranoid. I'll see you tomorrow. And *carry*."

All that afternoon and the next morning I found myself looking forward to the meeting with Foreign Minister Deng. Clearly an interesting man. And—I admitted to myself—the thought of going off as a sort of walking "arms and armor" exhibit was novel, even a little exciting. I decided I'd surprise Marj—get my gear all on then appear as "Josh Chamberlain, Federal Marshal."

The afternoon of the meeting, as I stood in front of the mirror, I realized that getting into the vest was easier said than done. I felt like a high-school senior, wrestling with a real bow tie before his first prom. The vest was not meant to be put on single-handedly. It came in two panels, fore and aft. They were fastened about the body with a multitude of velcro snaps. I'd hike the panels more or less into position with one hand, and quickly try to close the snaps with the other. But the panels would always shift. Whatever I did, the effect was that of a shirt with the upper buttons in the lower buttonholes. I could see why, to suit up, knights had needed squires.

Marj walked in as I was struggling. "What are you wearing!" she exclaimed. "Is that a bulletproof vest? My God! Why?"

My heart sank. "It's a ballistic vest, Marj," I explained. "No one calls them 'bulletproof' vests any more. Several of us at the embassy have them. Pete Valiant says there are times that we should wear them, strictly as a precautionary measure, of course."

"Pete Valiant? And he's always seemed a little less paranoid and dense than most of those security types! I bet he'll have you carrying a gun next!"

Her eyes fell on the holster and its tangle of leather straps.

She caught her breath: "I don't know what's going on, but could I remind you that you are a *Foreign Service officer*, not a Marine platoon leader any longer. Is there something you haven't told me? Would you have told me? Should I be looking for false moustaches, maybe? A wig? Because if it's a kind of stunt, dressing up like . . . Clint Eastwood, I'd appreciate your putting your fancy dress away. I don't even like those things in the house."

I tried to explain to Marj my plans for the evening. I felt miserable—about five years old. Marj interrupted: "I don't care what the ambassador or the foreign minister says. Let them get together any time they want. That's what receptions are for. I've never pried in your business, and maybe I sound 'just like a woman.' But this is different. Hilverding's dead. Will he be the last? And I don't like sneaky surprises. If there's risk, you should tell me, we're in this together, whether it involves just you or both of us. Remember what the ambassador said the night we arrived. Something about *our* right to know and *his* duty to tell us?"

It didn't get much better. Our discussion ended with Marj, still unpersuaded, silently going off to her sewing room—a bedroom converted to that purpose.

But time was getting on. Back to my one-armed paperhanger routine with the vest. I settled for a sloppy fit. Downstairs, I stopped by the kitchen to tell Mustafa that I would not be back for dinner. He was on the back terrace.

For a moment I thought I'd caught him at his prayers. That would have been strange. He always let me know in advance—if I was around—that he was going to pray. And he'd always pray on the back lawn. Then I noticed that he wasn't kneeling as if in prayer. He was sitting back on his heels, his toes pointed behind him. His eyes were fixed on a brass bowl on the ground—it appeared full of water. Some kind of water divination? I started to back out, and my movement must have caught his eye. He rose in a smooth motion. (How does he do it at that age? I wondered. It wouldn't be easy even for me.)

"Sorry to disturb you, Mustafa, but I'm going out and won't be back for dinner. Mrs. Chamberlain will have something later."

Mustafa nodded. Then said: "*Al-mustashar* (the DCM) will be careful; it will be all right. But must be quick and careful. *Laazim jiddan* (very necessary). And must carry this." From the pocket of his *thawb*, Mustafa drew out a small leather pouch, which he pressed into my hand with both of his. It was about an inch and a half square. It was not full; rather, flat and soft. A shiny white cowrie shell was fastened to the outside of the pouch, which was sewn shut with coarse-looking fibers. From its neck hung two thin leather thongs, each about eighteen inches long.

"Tie to leg, *fakhd*" (Mustafa slapped his thigh), "or arm" (he grasped his bicep), "or around neck" (he made a one-handed strangling motion).

"What do you mean, Mustafa. This is very nice, but why are you doing it? And what does it mean?"

"*Riih abyadh*—White Wind—here." He pointed to the pouch. "*Riih ahmar*, Red Wind, very bad. Red Wind there, outside, where you go. With Abu Nar." Mustafa waved an arm to encompass the entire world beyond the compound wall. "I see in bowl," he pointed behind him. "You carry *riih abyadh*? *Laazim jiddan*," he repeated in an urgent voice.

The gate guard rang the doorbell. The front door was ajar. He called in, "Mr. Valiant here, sah!"

"Mustafa!" I said sharply, "what do you mean about 'Abu Nar' and this 'Red Wind?' "

Mustafa looked at me impassively. He answered: "Cannot speak of Abu Nar. He 'Father of Fire.' Not speak of 'Red Wind.' But must carry *ta'widh*. Safer."

Did my frustration show in my voice? Urgently, I asked: "Mustafa, who *can* talk about this . . . person?"

Mustafa remained silent a moment. Then said: "Maybe no Sudanese, maybe Supreme Guide. Don't know."

The gate guard rang again. I said: "I still don't know what you mean, Mustafa, we'll have to talk some more. But I'll take your—your?"

"Called *ta'widh*. Very good. Power little like King Sulaiman. God make him wise, give him power over angels, and spirits, and *djinn*. Carry all time. *Ta'widh* closed with elephant hair. Very strong inside. Never never open *ta'widh*."

"If you say so, Mustafa. But I've got to go. We'll talk later. I'll just put it in my pocket, OK?"

As I walked off, Mustafa called after me: "Pocket good, leg, neck, arm better!"

A DARKENING GARDEN

9

Pete Valiant was at the back door in a cream-colored Peugeot of recent vintage. I walked around to the passenger side. The license plates, I noticed were "civilian," meaning they were white and simply showed numbers and a Khartoum prefix, an Arabic "KH." By contrast, the license plates the Foreign Ministry issued to embassies had a diagonal red stripe and carried the phrase *Hay'a Siyassiyah*, meaning "Diplomatic Corps." I got into the car. Immediately I felt the upper edge of the security vest ride up and press against my voice box. I coughed. My waistline, filled out by the vest, tightened painfully. The shoulders of my jacket seemed to be around my ears.

"You look fairly scary," Pete said. "The Hunchback of Notre Dame maybe, after a growth spurt?" I looked over at him. Pete didn't look very comfortable either. I answered, "It must be the light but I can now see the stitches all over your face, Pete; and can I maybe tighten up the bolts for you on either side of your neck?"

From our house to Sally's, in Khartoum 2, was only fifteen minutes. It could have been five but for the potholes and closed-off streets. No one knew why streets were closed off then left that way. There was never a sign of repaving or other work in progress.

I'd not seen Sally's villa before. In Khartoum "villa" didn't mean the cliffside palazzo of the orange juice king of Southern California. It just meant "house." Sally's had the usual plain iron gate, set in a brick-and-plaster, shoulder-high wall; behind it rose a line of acacia trees. (The *acacia senegal*—known in Sudan as *khashab*—is the source of one of Sudan's main exports, the gum arabic that goes into candies, especially jelly beans.)

I followed a tiled walk to a tiled porch and pressed the front doorbell. In a moment, an Eritrean maid opened the inside door; then, looking shyly at the ground, she pushed the screen door open and indicated I should come in. On a very good stereo the Dallin-Woodward-Fahey trio (Wow!) was singing:

> Once in a lifetime comes another,
> All you're looking for.
> Where will I find my perfect lover?
> Waited so long, for someone like you.

I knew the song—country, bluegrass, pop rock were my long suit. The song was also one of Brian's favorites—one of the songs he played over and over again when he was back from school.

Sally wasn't around. Might she be having the same problems suiting up that I'd had? I looked around the room—a small house, by embassy standards. A narrow entrance hallway led directly to what looked like the kitchen. Off the hallway were several doors that would be to the bathroom or bedrooms. An archway led to the combined living-dining room just to my left.

The furniture had once been good, but now was very worn. I guessed it had been handed down the diplomatic 'food chain' over the years as new furniture came in. Sally's Akai stereo was mounted in a cabinet in the living room; music came from several directions. There must have been two hundred CDs on the shelf above the amplifier. I recognized some of my own and Brian's favorites: Emmy Lou Harris, Alabama, Bruce Hornsby, and Hal Ketchum.

Looking at the bookshelf, I saw a good collection of French and German books. Goethe's *Gedichte*, three or four Stendhal novels, the Pleiade edition of *A la Recherche du Temps Perdu*, also Mann's *Der Zauberberg*. The bottom shelf, though, confused me: all westerns. There was founding father Owen Wister's *The Virginian*, and Rex Beach's *The Spoilers*—I hadn't read either one—but also some I knew: Louis L'Amour's *Silver Canyon*, plus at least ten Max Brands and several by (as I remembered) the ever-predictable William McLeod Raine.

Cameroon looked down from the walls: wooden masks of animal

and human (?) faces. Clearly, none were pleased with what they saw. I looked at them more closely, then drew back. They gave off a spicy, smoky, disagreeable, conference room odor. On the coffee table were several glossy magazines: *Natural History, Smithsonian, Seattle.* The walls were almost bare.

Lionel Richie intoned, "Stuck on you . . ."

"I'm sorry, Mr. Chamberlain, really sorry. I hope we won't be too late for the minister." It was Sally. She was wearing a safari-type shirt, with a khaki skirt. And no doubt about it—she also had on a ballistic vest. It gave her that upper body look one sees in otherwise delicate-looking female gymnasts. Her hair hung straight—still wet from a shower. I could see the collar and shoulders of her shirt were damp.

She added: "The darn thing, though, isn't meant to be put on single-handed. I know now why Scarlett O'Hara needed help in getting dressed."

I laughed. "No problem on the time. I had a chance to look at your books and tapes. Nice collections. I like this, too." I pointed to a framed poem on the wall. The text was written out in graceful Spencerian script. I admired the slant, shading, and line quality. Looking at the last verse of the poem, I read silently to myself:

I'm close by you; however far you be,
You're always near;
The sun doth sink, now stars come out for me,
O wish you were here!

I turned to Sally and, trying to speak clearly, recited:

Ich bin bei dir, du seist auch noch so ferne,
Du bist mir nah!
Die Sonne sinkt, bald leuchten mir die Sterne.
O warst du da!

"Goethe. *Nahe des Geliebten.* Right?"

Sally looked astonished. "How did you know?"

"I served my first tour in Germany—didn't I tell you? Studied German at FSI before I went out; worked at it while in Frankfurt. Still do. Sorry about the accent. But it's a pretty well-known poem. Good translation. Whose?"

Sally smiled. "Actually," she said, "my own—in Cameroon. Should we be off?"

"OK. I can't wait to see the minister's face as he sees us shuffling and shouldering our way up to his door. Straight from *The Planet of the Apes!*"

She laughed. "I'm glad I haven't looked at myself in a mirror. After showering—played some tennis with Sa'eed—I was combing my hair, when I heard you at the door. I threw on the vest, put on my safari suit, and came down."

"As a matter of fact, Sally," I said, "you still look healthy, wholesome, and cheerful."

"High praise, Mr. Chamberlain," she answered, turning off the stereo.

I felt a little embarrassed. "Call me Josh?"

Strictly speaking, Minister Deng did not occupy a house. His quarters covered an area of about a city block. Somewhere on the property was a house. We could see its upper stories above the wall and through the trees. They looked shabby—slats were missing from the wooden louvers at the window openings. A scaffolding rose to the top floor. On the scaffold, overalled workmen were plastering or painting.

As we rounded the block, we passed several gates. In front of each, a squad of security guards stood, or sat, or lay back against the neem trees. All were Nilotics—that is, southern Sudanese from the minister's own region, the ethnically "African" provinces of Bahr el-Ghazal and Upper Nile. I thought: "They look as if they've just raided Sergeant Poe's locker, or the conference room. Each one's got a different weapon."

We stopped the car before the gate that seemed most directly before the house. Pete rolled down the window. He called to one of the guards: "American embassy—we have an appointment to see the minister." No response. Pete said again: "We are here to see the minister." Another guard came forward.

"See Chief Deng?" he asked.

"That's right," Pete replied. "We're from the American embassy. The minister is expecting us."

As they were speaking, I couldn't take my eyes off the guard's forehead. Starting just above the bridge of his nose, and rising into his hairline, narrow ridges of keloid scars ran across his forehead from one temple to the other. It looked like a roast beef that had been boned, sliced, then reassembled. What a "rite of passage!" I thought. The pain!

The guard seemed to understand Pete. He left us and went inside by a flanking door at the gate. We waited. And waited. The remaining guards on duty paid no attention to us. The motor began to overheat. Peter turned it off, and we rolled down the windows. The heat reached in greedily for us. I sweated. I didn't feel like talking to Pete or to Sally. I felt like stripping to the waist—taking a shower. I thought of swimming in the Gulf of Maine.

The guard reappeared at the side gate. He waved for us to follow him in.

"I'll wait in the car," said Pete. "It looks OK. A lot of guards around. But still—remember what I said. Be careful. You can tell me later how I was a foolish old woman."

My impressions of the compound from the outside had been correct. The minister didn't occupy a house. He lived in a neighborhood. We wound our way along a hard-packed earth track, past shoulder-high dividers of woven raffia palm mats.

"Very modern," said Sally in a low voice. "See? All the inside space is modularized—just like the offices in New State."

The sounds of family life and communal smells—food, bodies, inadequate sanitation—were all around us. Small, naked children peeked out from beaded curtains that hung across the entrances to some living quarters. I liked the name South Americans used for such curtains, *lagrimas de San Pedro*—Saint Peter's tears.

A chicken ran across our path. An African mother, bent low, one hand holding up her roomy *thawb*, ran after it. They both disappeared around a bend in the path. The sounds of squawking receded.

We continued to follow our guide—here and there the corrugated iron roofs of the huts almost met from either side, creating a tunnel effect. But the path did not seem to be leading us any closer to the house. Its grayish-blue bulk seemed to revolve about us, as we continued our circumambulation of—what could I call it?—the minister's village?

The path came to a dead end. But pushing aside a section of matting, our guard showed us into a garden. We were in front of the house— huge, rambling, verandaed, decaying. In the middle of the lawn, several folding wooden chairs had been set up around a small wooden table. The guard pointed to the chairs; without waiting to see whether we sat or not, he went into the house.

It was only minutes before Minister Deng came out. He looked cool and elegant in white linen slacks and a cotton *batik* sport shirt.

"My good friends! Mr. Chamberlain, how nice to meet you! Nice of you to come! A pleasure again to see Ambassador Farnsworth's assistant, Miss . . . "

"Miss Tolson," I inserted.

"Please, Miss Tolson, Mr. Chamberlain, won't you have a seat? We can serve you refreshments in just a minute. Some hot tea? Or would you prefer a cold drink? A gin and tonic, perhaps? I'm sorry my wife is not here to help serve you. But at this time of year you'll find as many Sudanese in London as in Khartoum!"

Sally looked to take her cue from me. I yearned for a gin and tonic—but "business first." Firmly, I said, "We'd love some tea, Mr. Minister."

"Of course. Right away. You won't mind if I have a gin and tonic, I hope? The sun is over the yardarm, as our British friends would say. And it's so hot today."

I glanced at Sally—apologetically? She seemed to be amused by the steno pad and pen in her lap. I noticed she was sitting as women do—knees and ankles together, legs slightly angled to one side. Tanned, pretty legs.

By the time the tea came, I could feel my chair legs settling at an awkward angle into the lawn. The mosquitoes had begun *their* happy hour—feeding frenzy?—between my shoe tops and trouser cuffs. Rubbing my ankles together did no good. The buzzing only grew higher pitched, more angry. Were the mosquitoes beginning to attack the seat of my pants? "Get a hold of your imagination, Chamberlain," I said to myself. "But how could you have been such a dope—forgotten to put on Deet?" The mosquitoes didn't seem to be bothering Sally, though, I noticed. Nor the minister.

As a houseboy poured the tea, then served up plates of pound cake with currants in it, Deng quickly finished his G&T. He smacked his lips. He asked for another. "Make sure there's lots of ice *and* a fresh lime," he specified. Sally smiled at me—caustically?—over the edge of her steaming cup.

With a second drink in hand, Deng said, "I appreciate Ambassador Farnsworth's sending his right-hand staff (he looked over at Sally) in answer to my request. No one, I assume, saw you come?"

I explained to Deng that the ambassador's secretary had received his request and that only the ambassador, our security officer, and ourselves knew of the evening's engagement. "We borrowed a 'sterile' car from Mr. Kirby," I added, "but even he doesn't know the reason why."

"A good man, your Mr. Kirby," said Deng. "You may want to share my remarks with him, too, but in the first instance what I have to say, is for the ambassador and for you, and for Washington, D.C."

Deng continued: "I worry about my country. Not the civil war in the South. Not the collapsing economy—the $11 *billion* debt and a 225 percent debt service ratio, our official paper trading for four cents on the dollar. These problems have been with us for years. We Sudanese can take it. Besides, what African country has ever collapsed—vanished—because it neglected IMF advice? Or the World Bank's? 'Brush your teeth. Floss your gums. Eat much fiber . . .' And the war? *I* worry about it. My nation—the Nilotic Sudanese of the South—are the ones who suffer most. But the government in Khartoum doesn't worry at all. It only cares about what happens in the Arab areas: Khartoum, Wad Medani, Dongola."

Deng added: "What I worry about is something that can *end* my country. You look astonished, Mr. Chamberlain?"

I confessed to Deng I found it hard to imagine how Africa's largest nation—that for decades had endured every sort of natural and man-made calamity, could be facing even greater danger.

"Our country is large," Deng went on, "but fractured and fragile. Its fabric is tired by corruption, war, economic decline. It lacks solidity. The government's power base has been narrowing steadily for years, even in the Arab areas. You know what the infrastructure is like! Even here in Khartoum! And consider the railroads—they have ten times the employees they did at independence—but carry only one-tenth the freight they did then! Economists would say their efficiency has declined by a factor of one hundred. And there are other examples."

Deng took a long sip, then said: "So I worry that this vast region is susceptible to what your Wall Street people might call a highly leveraged stock takeover. Or what in London the bobbies would call a smash-and-grab."

"But Mr. Minister," I interjected, "from where could such a challenge come? If the country is so fractured, doesn't this fracturing also apply to the very groups who might aspire to power?"

"I'm not talking about domestic groups, Mr. Chamberlain," Deng replied, "or at least not entirely. I'll be frank. I'm talking in the first place about the Libyans. Remember: they tried to seize power once before, in 1976. They failed because our former dictator—for all his great vices—was lucky and brave. I believe they are thinking of trying to do so again. The prize is considerable: Qadhaafi's *Jamahiriyah* triples in size. Qadhaafi outflanks Egypt. He can blackmail Saudi Arabia and menace the flow of Nile water to Egypt. Chad falls into place? A new radical African Empire springs up to threaten your interests—even in a post–Cold War world!

"So what I called you over for, even more specifically, is this: You are always watching the Libyans here. Your CIA gets some information from sources here and in Tripoli. I'm sure you also get good photos of what Qadhaafi is moving across the desert and over our western borders. But what you perhaps don't know—can't photograph—is who is on Libya's side here? And how does this information so far stay secret? A successful coup in Sudan would be like a demolition. Demolition involves an explosive. It also involves a detonator. It's this detonator that I want to speak to you about, share my thoughts—as a Sudanese tribesman, as well as a Ph.D.—on the matter."

I asked, "Would this detonator have anything to do with internal figures—maybe even with a recent speech by a certain individual who attacked the private voluntary agencies?"

The air in the garden from the start had seemed close. At my last words, a particularly strong whiff of latrine crossed the lawn. Deng looked apologetic. He explained: "This was not always my house. It belongs to the government. All senior officials are given one. One of the perks of office—until you lose your job, that is. Then your successor suddenly shows up at the door—as if by magic—to make sure you don't take out any of the furnishings!

"We moved in the week I was named foreign minister. The first of my fellow tribesmen showed up our first evening. I couldn't turn him away. Then more came. Then still more. Like the African folk tale 'Why the Sun and Moon Live in the Sky.' I'll tell it to you sometime. But then came sanitation problems. Over in the corner, there, is a very modern privy. One of your Peace Corps volunteers, in fact, gave me the plan and helped to supervise the construction. At night, though, no one wants to walk to the corner of the garden. And the little children . . .

"Have some?" The minister offered a bowl of peanuts. We declined. He took a handful. (I refrained from telling him we'd refused because Sudanese harvest methods caused a buildup in the nuts of a chemical, aflatoxin, that caused liver disease and cancer.)

I saw the minister looking to his right. "*Kammaltum al-mashruu?*" (I gathered he was asking "Was the project done?")

I looked over. Three painters were walking across the lawn in our direction. They were the ones I'd seen working on the scaffolding as we drove up. They carried buckets in their hands. Their coveralls were dirty, but not threadbare. The men looked more Arab, I thought, than African. (In Sudan's society you quickly become sensitive to slight variations in skin coloring.) One painter was walking in front; he was older— maybe in his mid-forties. The two behind, I noticed, walked in step with him. One had a little hitch in his gait. Their shoes looked new. The painters stopped some ten feet away.

Minister Deng said, a little impatiently: "*Ihna masghuuliyn, ashuufak bukra.* (We're busy. I'll see you tomorrow)."

No answer. Instead the lead painter put his right hand into the paint bucket, as if reaching for a brush. His hand came out with a revolver. The barrel had a stovepipe look. "It's silenced!" I thought.

The pistol swung upwards on an arm that was almost fully extended—like a signal barrier. The arm stabilized. The report was simultaneous. A sharp expulsion of air. It sounded like a broom handle being laid across a pillow, hard. The round took Deng in the middle of the forehead. His head snapped back in whiplash. He started to fall backwards. The second round took him just below the left cheek. The top of his skull gave way.

The pistol started to swivel toward me. I seemed to be looking right down the barrel. "The lead-in for a James Bond movie," I thought. Incredible how the mind works. I saw the tip of the gunman's tongue showing between his lips. He looked intent, as if working out a math problem.

Sally screamed. She threw her teacup in the man's face. He flinched. The gun coughed again. Something snapped past my ear. Finally, I moved. I rolled out of the chair, pulling for my gun. Another report. Something hit me in the ribs. Then a third shot. A punch to the solar plexus this time. I saw the man take a step towards me. He held the gun now with both hands. He was aiming down at me. Sally was shouting something. Peanuts filled the air. The heavy glass peanut bowl hit him in the shoulder. Another shot. Another miss.

Finally, my gun was out. I thumbed off the safety. Nothing fancy, I thought, center of the body mass, it's no silhouette.

I got off my first round. It sounded like a cannon going off. Heck— it *was* a cannon! The round took him near the belt buckle. It bent him over and threw him back. He fell. Another one—into the chest cavity. I slammed a third after it. The bullet nudged him. I looked for the "assistant painters." They were running away across the garden—they were carrying pistols, but seemed unnerved by someone who was shooting back. I was getting into the rhythm of the thing. Again, I aimed and fired. A long shot but, I knew, a good one. The weapon seemed to aim itself—I felt almost surprised as it went off. One man skidded forward on his face, lay still. The other, with the gimp, vanished down one of the alleys of the minister's "village."

Pandemonium. In seconds the garden began to fill up with alarmed guardsmen, bewildered tribal elders, ululating women, screaming children. Pete—thank heavens—was among the first to enter the garden from the maze.

One look seemed to tell him what he needed to know. Almost at his feet lay the silenced revolver. In one motion, with his left hand, he drew out his pocket handkerchief and with it scooped the revolver up.

"Let's get the fuck out of here," he said. He grabbed Sally's arm and started back the way he'd come. As we headed for the car, our white faces seemed somehow to help clear a way for us.

At the car I asked: "Shouldn't we wait for the police or an investigation?"

Pete answered: "To hell with the investigation. Deng's dead. I want you both alive and where you'll be safe. Get in—FAST!" Sally got in front, I climbed into the back seat. "Fasten your seat belts!" Pete ordered. "Lock the doors!"

Pete drove fast and expertly. In and out of traffic. He didn't worry this time about bumps and potholes. Somehow the seatbelts held. Between jolts I told him what had happened. And how Sally had bought me enough time to get my gun out.

"Where are you taking us, Pete?" I asked.

"Ambassador's residence. It's the closest. Good security. Good communications. You better figure on staying there awhile. I'll go get Mrs. Chamberlain. I'll see about getting some of your things, too, Sally."

"But why not our residences?"

"Deng's dead. Looks very professional. People you want to take seriously. They know you can identify them. They will know who you are—we can assume they'll find out where you live. 'Try, try again' and all that. Also, they've got a score to settle."

Pete glanced to his right: "Quite a voice you've got there, Sally. Almost drowned out the gunshots. You know, I'm so proud of you I could almost bust."

She smiled. "You know, Pete, you sound just a teeny bit chauvinist."

As Pete spoke it dawned on me. I could see Deng's head opening up like a jar of strawberry preserves. I looked at Sally. I felt almost teary. An irrational reaction. Shock.

I broke in: "My God! What can I say! 'I'll always be grateful'? 'I'll never forget this'? Yes. But to have to be reminded by Pete. I'm such an ass!" I leaned forward and took Sally's left hand—she was holding onto the seat back. I added, slowly, and a little unsteadily: *Thank you, Sally, for saving my life.* And forgive me for just sitting here until now. It was like looking down the Lincoln Tunnel when he turned his gun on me! If you hadn't hit him with your tea cup, and then the peanut bowl—thrown his aim off, stopped those head shots . . . "

Sally looked back at me and smiled. Before she could answer, Pete broke in: "Looks like the ambassador's got himself some room-mates again!"

Less than two hours later, while working by the study window at the Residence, I heard—then saw—Marj arrive with Pete, driven by one of the Marines. Two of the houseboys went to the car; one opened her door, then together they unloaded our bags.

I'd tried to make the packing easy for Marj. I told her we wouldn't need any of our airfreight—just the items we'd brought in our hand and checked luggage. I could see she'd brought my tennis raquets, as I'd asked. But there was something forlorn, I thought, about the sight of Marj following our three suitcases—still with the green wool yarn on the handles—into the house. She and Pete and the Marine were in the living room as I came out to meet her.

Pete and I had agreed it would be better first to get Marj to the Residence—*then* describe just what had happened that afternoon. Pete was just to say we'd gotten a report that made a temporary shift to the Residence advisable.

The lance corporal's face brightened when he saw me. "Way to go, sir! *Two* confirmed kills! OK!"

From Marj's expression—and Pete's—I guessed she was hearing this news for the first time.

SECOND DEMARCHE

10

Another gloomy breakfast around the Residence's long, black lacquered table. A bier? Something to be laid out on? The ambassador and Pete had coffee; Sally, Marj, and I had tea. Boxes of Wheaties, Raisin Bran, and Cheerios had been set out. But no one was eating. Sally and I had worked through most of the night. The separate reports we'd done on Deng's murder, when put together, were almost of novel length. Marj, I knew, hadn't gotten much sleep either. We waited for the news. The time was just short of 0400 GMT—6 A.M. in Khartoum.

We'd called Washington on the secure phone the night before. Gave them an oral report of Deng's killing and said that a full, detailed report would follow. For once, Washington was speechless. Farnsworth had told them he didn't need any instructions—he knew just what he would say to the prime minister the next morning. Then he'd hung up.

Sa'eed al-Masri had called to say the prime minister was flying back to Sudan that night; immediately after his arrival the cabinet would meet in emergency session. The PM would not be available until the following day. Al-Masri was apologetic. How about a morning meeting? Farnsworth said we'd be at the People's Palace at opening of business. We had some important information for him. Sa'eed said we could count on "1000 percent cooperation" from the government; the prime minister, Sa'eed was sure, would be available at the time the ambassador had proposed.

Sa'eed asked to speak to me. He congratulated me on my "providential" escape. "God and His angels were watching over you!"

That same evening, Jack Kirby had brought over his collection of "beauty queens." "No bathing suit shots," he'd apologized. Speaking more seriously, he said he could understand if I didn't want to dwell on the assassination just now. But follow-up was important while memories were still fresh. Had I gotten a good look at the men in Deng's garden? Did I think I could identify them in real life? From pictures?

"A good look? Two of them—no. But the shooter? Did I get a look at him? Yeah. Him I'll never forget. I could spot him in a satellite photo. Of the top of his head—in a crowd! Let's see those beauty queens!"

"I'm not going to tell you anything about these photos," Jack began. "Some are for real. Some maybe for control. Just look—you don't have to buy—sound like a rug merchant? But image the men carefully. Then stop from time to time. Don't let the edges of your memory get blunt through overuse. Sharpen them up now and then. And concentrate on the shooter. From what you say, he must have been something special. A craftsman. Way above the backup he had with him."

Sally and I must have looked at two hundred photos—spread across the living room floor. The quality varied. Some looked more like fingerprints. Others could have been taken by Karsh or Avedon. Most subjects seemed to be in their twenties or thirties. Mediterranean-looking. Almost all had moustaches. Nothing.

"You sure none of these beauties will fill the bill? You really sure? Look again." Jack sounded discouraged. But I was sure. So was Sally.

"Well," he said in a resigned tone of voice, "let's have a last try." Gathering up the first collection, he then laid out another packet of photos. Forty or fifty perhaps. I looked them over. To one side of the pattern was a grouping of five or six photos—the subjects looked a little bit older than the average. I felt a nervous tingling as the first photo caught my eye. The feeling persisted with the second—and the third. Then one more. "He's it!" I shouted.

Jack got down on his knees and turned the photo over. He looked at the name. Then showed the photo to Sally. She thought it was the man, too.

"But I wasn't looking at him so much as for things to throw. And yelling for help," she added.

"You really sure?" he asked me in a quizzical tone.

"Jack, would you believe me if I told you I know what my mother looked like? What my father looked like? What Brian looks like? He's it."

"Jesus," said Kirby. "I can't believe it. If what you say is true—Jackpot! Holy Mother of God."

"Who is it, Jack?" said the ambassador. "If we're going to see the PM in the morning, a positive ID would help. And a copy of that photo."

"Yessir. Here's how it is. I put this photo (Kirby held up the one in his hand) in with several close look-alikes. Josh, I gotta tell you. I was pretty sure none of the first batch would test 'seropositive.' But I wanted to try out your memory. After all, Arabs twenty to forty years old can have some similarities."

"I *told* you, Jack. He's it. But who is he?"

"OK. His name is—was—Abdul Raziq 'Umayyir. Forty-seven years old. Born in Haifa. And—hold onto your seats—he was the ring-leader of the eight-man PLO unit that murdered Ambassador Cleo Noel and his deputy, Curt Moore. Remember? The PLO killed them in Khartoum, back in 1973. As disgusting as the Klinghoffer case. Five of the eight were arrested, convicted, and then exported to Egypt—which held them a while. 'Umayyyir somehow avoided the dragnet. Maybe with Libyan help? But now he had a big name in terrorist circles. Re-spect. Arafat loved him. Even sent him the next year to New York under an alias as part of the PLO delegation! We found out later. The terrorists have their assets, even in the United States. And the Arabs wonder that we closed the PLO's offices in Washington!

"Anyway, all the bad guys wanted to hire 'Umayyir—better than that slob Carlos, the Farouk of terrorists. Reliable, no swelled head. Kept his mouth shut. No particular vices—not a homo. Liked women. But what he liked best was killing."

"Jack, did you know this man was in Sudan?" asked the ambassador.

"Sort of—we knew he'd been here. And now I'd guess he and his men came in on that Libyan flight that al-Atrash and the rest of us met. No wonder the good doctor seemed cool! 'Umayyir's been traveling between Tripoli and Khartoum, and now Gaza. There was a story of tension brewing betwen him and Arafat. Did 'Umayyir want more money? An organization of his own? We don't know for sure. He's come here, though, at least three times. On political work, not as a shooter—at least not until now. He'd see government officials, including the minister for Presidency affairs, 'Dr. Trash.' "

"Hard to believe," said Marj, "that he was seeing *government* offi-cials."

"Not that hard," answered Kirby. "See, by now 'Umayyir wasn't just a soldier. He was moving up. A vice-president type. Maybe thinking of switching firms. Or even starting out on his own. But we knew that, now and then, he liked to walk down the aisles, check the stock, talk to the cashiers. Keep his hand in, you know?

"And listen to this, Josh—'Umayyir was good with all sorts of weapons—but he had one preferred M.O.: *head shots.* Like he was following the advice of one of our own kooks—Gordon Liddy! Arafat called 'Umayyir 'my brain surgeon.' That's why I thought of him right away when you told me how they dinged Deng. Sorry. It's just a way of talking. But if you're right, Josh—and frankly, I think you are—I'm looking at Sheriff Pat Garrett who's just put down Billy the Kid. What you just did for Cleo and Curt is a lot more than our government's ever done! And I want to shake your hand, old buddy." Jack did just that.

0700 hours. Big Ben tolled his dirge. Donne's lines, "Ask not for whom the bell tolls" went through my mind, as I glanced at my watch and Pippa began her morning necrology.

Such a nice voice, I thought, for such gloomy news. Why not have a Wicked Witch of the West announcer for the bad news? And give Pippa the births, the marriages, the tennis championships? How would *I* feel—off to BBC's Bush House every day at 3 or 4 A.M., in the London drizzle, to ruin the world's breakfast with my rotten news!

Today's winning entry came from Jerusalem. A bomb had gone off in a school bus, killing eight Israeli children and wounding many more. Hamas and several other terrorist groups disputed credit for "the heroic assault."

Sudan was runner-up: "The foreign minister of Sudan, Dr. Immanuel Deng," Pippa read, "has been shot dead in his Khartoum residence. Prime Minister al-Muntasser has called his cabinet into emergency session. A certain Abu Nar has claimed responsibility for the killing in the name of the 'Islamic Sons of Karare.' Abu Nar's communiqué states that Minister Deng was 'executed' for conspiring with the United States against Arab and Islamic interests in Sudan. The same group recently claimed responsibility for the killing of an American embassy official in Khartoum. In Washington, the Department of State deplores the killing as 'another example of cowardly, mindless terrorism.'"

Farnsworth jammed his finger down on the "STOP/OFF" button. He commented wryly—bitterly?—"The State Department 'deplores,' it 'condemns.' M.E.G.O—that's short for 'my eyes glaze over.' Well, today's another day. Let's go to work."

I had a surprise as I came down the residence steps to the car. Mustafa was standing next to his bicycle. "He looks so . . . shaikh-ly . . . so noble," I thought.

I shook his hand. "Hello, Mustafa, nice to see you. I think Mrs. Chamberlain and I will be here at the Residence for a few days at least. Do you think our houseboys could help out here? The ambassador's servants will have a lot to do." (I'd thought this over carefully and knew there wouldn't be a problem. The contract guards could watch our residence; and Mustafa was the uncle of the ambassador's chief "boy" and the acknowledged "dean" of servants in our American community. And then Marj just seemed to like having him around.)

"*Wa law* (of course), *Saaidiy*. We all here already. Stay all time. Help Mrs. Chamberlain." A pause. "*Alhamdilla 'assalama!* (God be praised for your safety!)"

"Thanks, Mustafa, I was very lucky. Say a prayer for us."

Mustafa looked anxious. "Have *ta'widh?*"" (He made a motion as if to strap something to his arm).

"I guess it's upstairs in my other coat, Mustafa, but . . . "

"Must wear *ta'widh*. Or carry *ta'widh*. Please. For Mrs. Chamberlain. For self. *Laazim jiddan*."

So of course I did as he asked. "It's done its job so far," I said to myself.

I had another surprise at the office. As we walked into the Chancery from the motor pool—past the security bollards and through the narrow entrance in the blast/crash wall—the Marine security guards were lined up in formation. They were in their "Class A's." Sergeant Poe called out: "D-e-etachment, 'tehn-hut! Preee-sent *ahms*!" They all saluted.

"Detachment ready for inspection, sir!" he said.

For the second time in twenty-four hours I felt a choking in my throat. Slowly, I walked down the line. Coming to the end, I turned to Sergeant Poe: "Lookin' good. Gunny. Why don't you and your men try for embassy duty? You might just make it. Might even *really* luck out and be sent to Khartoum."

"Sir," said Poe, "the Detachment asks the lieutenant's pardon for inviting him to go to the ranges sometime with us. We respectfully ask if the lieutenant will sometimes invite *us* to go to the ranges with *him*."

"Gunny" I said, "you want to see a strong man cry?"

As the ambassador and I rode up in the elevator, he said, "What happened in Deng's garden made quite an impression on the Marines. They asked me—through Pete—if they could do something special for you. I thought it would be good for their morale. I told them I didn't think you'd mind a little ceremony."

We drove to the Presidency for the ambassador's 8 A.M. meeting: the ambassador, myself, Sally, and Pete Valiant.

From a block away, I could see that Farnsworth hadn't exaggerated. The Presidential Palace—also called 'The People's Palace'—*did* look like Turkish Delight. It had no sharp edges. It was snow-white, entirely made of brick, plastered then whitewashed. No stone or cement. Even the window moldings and the pilasters that decorated its facade were of carefully shaped and carved brick. The basic structure, Farnsworth said, had been built by the Egyptians as their headquarters in 1821 and been substantially replaced by today's palace.

The palace sat hard by the river. A two-lane road passed directly in front of its square, flat-topped portico. The ambassador's limousine, flying its small American flag, drew up before the double doors of the entrance. An honor guard saluted as Farnsworth descended from his car. I looked them over. African Sudanese. Such height! Such uniforms! Even Field Marshal Herbert, Lord Kitchener, would have approved. Farnsworth acknowledged their salute and led me around the car to look at the river.

"To the right there," he said, pointing out towards the Nile, "you see a discoloration in the water. It seems to start just south of what looks like an island. See? A dark current blending with a grayish one? That's the confluence of the White and Blue Niles. You've seen the Blue Nile; it runs past our recreation site. The White Nile gets its name because it's slow, sandy, and muddy. The hunt for the Nile's source was the Grail, so to speak, of nineteenth century explorers. Sometime you should read about the Victorian explorers in this area: Gordon of Khartoum, Sir Samuel and Lady Baker, Stanley, and of course Livingstone. Incredible people. No self-doubt. Like bulldozers. Almost indestructible."

The ambassador looked at his watch. "Almost class time. Let's go see H.E. But just a quick look at the ground floor first."

It seemed we'd stepped into the Metropolitan Museum's collection of Arms and Armor—Eastern Division. Every sort of Arab and Ottoman edged weapon hung on the wall. Axes, swords, daggers, spears. Even combinations of the above. Chain mail. Helmets. Hauberks. In Western castles one might see such weapons displayed in floriate clusters—Windsor, for instance. But here they stood in racks and stands. In business-like formations. One could imagine any moment the guard turning out, each man grabbing a weapon and running to his post. We passed under an inward-curving pair of elephant tusks. They were even larger than those flanking the entrance to the American Museum of Natural History's Akeley Gallery. More guns. More daggers.

Farnsworth drew my attention in particular to two items. One was an elephant gun. A *two*-gauge elephant gun. Eight feet tall. Really a small cannon. It could be fired from a boat or from land. But only with the help of a miniature caisson. Second, was a small brass plaque, ten feet above the ground, in the southwest corner of the lobby. Its brass surface, badly in need of polish, bore a simple inscription: "Gen. Charles Gordon, January 25, 1885." Tradition had it that here, where a staircase once led to the second floor, "Chinese" Gordon bravely met death fighting the Mahdi's soldiers. General Garnet Wolseley's relief column was only two day's away.

"But on to present crises," said Farnsworth. A spiral staircase took us to a porch on the second floor, from which we had a good view of the palace gardens. Sa'eed al-Masri was waiting for us.

"Mr. Ambassador! Joshua! Sally!" He shook all our hands. "Mr. Valiant, I believe? Yes, I noted your name in the embassy's report. An awful, awful, event. The only good thing is your providential escape. When I think . . . Poor Deng. Such a decent fellow. A great blow to national unity, the spirit of reconciliation. If only more southerners were like him. But please have a seat in the 'Vice President Bush' room. It's here Mr. Bush met with your embassy people during his important visit in March 1985. The prime minister will be with you in a jiffy."

It was no jiffy. We had tea. We had coffee. We had Jordan almonds. We had dates, dried almost to a plastic consistency by the sun. We even had peanuts—aflatoxin! We had lots of time to appreciate the attractive blue-white decor of the "Bush Room." Farnsworth mentioned that Presidency Minister al-Atrash had personally taken a hand in the room's design and decoration. "He fancies himself something of a Renaissance man," the ambassador commented.

It was more than an hour before the prime minister's door finally opened. Trooping out, single file, were the minister of defense, the minister of interior, the minister of finance, the minister of petroleum. None looked our way.

"Do you get that pariah feeling, Josh?" Farnsworth asked. "Do our schoolmates avoid the eye of those summoned before the head-master?"

A last person came out of the meeting, head high—it was the ambassador of the Libyan *Jamahiriyyah*. He looked over at us. Nodded. Smiled. Pete Valiant whispered: "He looks like he's just swallowed the canary."

"The prime minister will see you now," announced Sa'eed.

"So that's what they call the canary," Pete added in a louder whisper.

We walked past Sudanese television and print photographers. Sa'eed presented us to the PM, then shooed the newsmen out.

Prime Minister al-Muntasser was a true son of the Nile valley. Tall, broad-shouldered, slim-waisted, he had the look—the silhouette— of the Pharaohs from wall paintings in the Valley of the Kings. In pro-file, you half expected to see not one, but *two*, large almond-shaped eyes fixed on you. The prime minister was not alone. With him was Minister al-Atrash. The prime minister shook hands warmly. Al-Atrash's handshake was perfunctory. He seemed to be looking at the mantel-piece beyond us.

After what we diplomats call "the usual courtesies," al-Muntasser came to the point: "This is a dark day for Sudan, Mr. Ambassador. Minister Deng was—what do you call it?—a linchpin. He helped hold things in Sudan together. He will be missed. Badly, I fear. But I hope that with your cooperation we can dispel some of the troubling obscu-rity about his death."

Turning to me: "You, Mr. Chamberlain, have only been in Sudan a few weeks—but, for sure, an active few weeks. Would you explain to me, please, why you went to see my friend Immanuel Deng? And tell me also how he . . . met his end?"

As I spoke, I could tell the prime minister was less than enchanted with my visiting Deng. And there was nothing less than malevolence about the expression of al-Atrash. When I cited my last words to Deng— about the speech criticizing the PVOs, al-Atrash broke in. "Mr. Prime Minister! Is nothing sacred? Is everything grist for the grinding West-ern propaganda mill—even the death of our poor colleague Deng? We should not listen to this obviously concocted account."

Farnsworth raised a hand: "Mr. Prime Minister, unless this dis-cussion immediately takes a different tone, I am returning to my office.

Some crossword puzzles there deserve my attention more than listening—"

"We have been under much tension, Mr. Ambassador," the prime minister interjected in a conciliatory tone. "Let us continue to work together in a cooperative manner *and* spirit," he concluded, looking at us all, al-Atrash included.

Al-Muntasser came back to me: "*You* say, Mr. Chamberlain, that Deng invited you to tea. I'm sure this is so—I cannot imagine that you three, who knew him not at all, would otherwise have invited yourselves to his house. But please, can you explain why, if he had such a concern for 'the future of Sudan,' he would not share it with me, his friend and prime minister? He knew I was one of his principal cabinet supporters. Maybe he thought you, as a Westerner, as a fellow Christian, might be more sympathetic?"

"Mr. Prime Minister, I could not begin to guess why Minister Deng especially wanted to see someone from the embassy. I only know he thought there was some danger threatening the country from a source that, unfortunately, he never got to mention. Libya, or maybe the PLO, seemed to have something to do with it."

Al-Atrash cleared his throat explosively—al-Muntasser made a pacifying hand gesture to him. "Curiouser and curiouser," said al-Muntasser. Then: "Tell me. Mr. Chamberlain, are you not a Marine Corps officer? And are they not all formidable shots? Are these the usual qualities of a diplomat? May I even ask if, by chance, you have left earlier posts—shall we say after 'shortened' assignments?"

"Mr. Prime Minister," Farnsworth again broke in, "if you want to talk about the assassination of Dr. Deng, fine. If you want to talk about the investigation of Mr. Hilverding's murder, that's fine, too. But we're not even going to try to blow away the smoke barrage that the so-called Libyan ambassador just laid down. In all honesty, I must tell you that this issue is, to borrow language from the PLO, 'a cloud on the horizon that might either pass away or develop into a real storm.' Further, I believe the Libyans are somehow behind the Deng murder, just as I believe they were involved with that of Hilverding. Deng had something on them—if only he had lived."

Al-Atrash was not to be restrained. He said: "Ah, yes—if only he had not liked gin and tonics so much. He might then have given *Lieutenant* Chamberlain the rest of his story. They're like your American Indians, though, our southerners. They and their alcohol. Their mental faculties perhaps a bit uncritical, maybe even credulous? How *some people* (pause) would play upon his concerns about Libya! Wasn't your

Mr. Kirby a good friend of his? Do you know, by the way, what the initials 'CIA' stand for?"

We looked at each other. Archly, al-Atrash explained, "Catholic Irish Alcoholic!" He went on: "Such stories your Mr. Kirby purveys! 'Caravans of arms!' 'Secret installations!' John Buchan, or Erskine Childers, could not have done better. *The Riddle of the Sands* should perhaps have been a Sudanese story instead? But (soulfully), as they say, *De morituri . . .*"

Farnsworth: "Or, as they also say, 'Blame the dead.' "

Al-Muntasser smiled pacifically. "Mr. Ambassador, your remarks—I will not call them accusations against Colonel Qadhaafi—are surely unfounded. I received a personal communication this morning from the colonel. He expressed sincere condolences for Minister Deng's death. A special emissary will come to attend the funeral. The emissary will express again the colonel's deep sorrow and that of the Libyan people. Further, Colonel Qadhaafi gave me his solemn word that Libya had nothing to do with the death of Minister Deng; it stands ready to cooperate fully with us to solve the case. In addition, Libya will contribute a month's supply of oil to Sudan in Deng's name.

"Another point." Al-Muntasser paused for effect. "You should know that some nonsouthern elements are claiming Deng was conspiring with the United States to separate the South from Sudan. And that the United States would set up military bases in the new nation to seize Sudan's oil, control East Africa, and oppose the spread of Islamic fundamentalism."

Farnsworth: "Are you speaking of further communiqués from 'Abu Nar'? Who is he? Does anyone know?"

Al-Muntasser almost flushed. "Not that at all. We are looking into that story. We should have something soon. No, it's some other things." Al-Muntasser, for the first and only time in the meeting, seemed at a loss.

At this point, al-Atrash spoke: "My belief, Mr. Prime Minister, is that this 'Abu Nar' is an opportunistic troublemaker, or worse (looking hard at Farnsworth), and when we find him . . . "

Farnsworth opened a legal-sized Manila envelope he had with him. "Speaking of 'other things,' " he said, "here are some examples." He took out a picture of 'Umayyir. He continued: "Mr. Prime Minister, Joshua has positively identified the killer of Minister Deng. Ms. Tolson agrees. We've not been able to identify the others, but the killer himself was one Abdul Raziq 'Umayyir. He was one of the murderers of Cleo Noel and Curt Moore and a notorious contract killer for Yasser

Arafat and for Qadhaafi. Moreover, Interpol has just confirmed that the fingerprints on the silenced revolver we picked up at the scene were 'Umayyir's."

Al-Muntasser watched us all closely. He bent forward to take the photo. "Interesting. *I've* never seen this man before. Mr. Minister?" Al-Muntasser handed al-Atrash the picture. Did the minister pause? But he shook his head.

Al-Muntasser: "May I speak frankly?"

"The franker the better," said Farnsworth.

"All right. *You* say someone called 'Umayyir killed our minister with a silenced revolver. You say you have it, and of course, it has 'Umayyir's fingerprints on it. I don't doubt that for a minute. But— where is 'Umayyir? Where (he paused as if savoring his next words) is the *corpus delicti*?" Al-Muntasser released the Latin phrase almost sensuously, like a breath of good cigar smoke.

We looked at each other.

"You mean you don't know?" asked al-Muntasser. "I will tell you. Some people collected *two* bodies last night from the Deng residence. Minutes after the killing. They told the household they were from the Islamic Red Crescent Society. They took the bodies away. But the Red Crescent authorities know nothing. As for a silenced weapon, the only weapon the police found at the site was a .45 caliber automatic. Four shots had been fired. I suspect it may bear Mr. Chamberlain's fingerprints. A muddy trail, wouldn't you say?"

I admitted I'd holstered the weapon carelessly as we fled Deng's garden. The pistol had fallen out as we ran.

Al-Muntasser again picked up the photo of 'Umayyir. He waved it about: "And how can I be sure this is 'Umayyir?" He turned it toward us saying: "Maybe just one of your swarthy movie stars with baboon faces and big, wet lips?"

To me: "Mr. Chamberlain: you seem to be an event-making man. I know your embassy will provide us with your version of last night's events. We'll undertake our own investigation. We would appreciate your cooperating. Be glad—*I* was—that our police inform me Dr. Deng was killed by a 9 mm revolver round, not by a .45. For the time being, though, we will say only that poor Deng was killed by 'an assailant or assailants unknown.' I suggest your embassy avoid any comment at all—even about your being in the vicinity of Deng's house when he was shot."

Al-Muntasser continued in the tone of a college professor lecturing to an introductory class in economics: "In addition, I ask you to relax. You are welcome in my country. We have good, important relations with the United States of America. You give us much aid. We are properly grateful. You give us much advice, too. I want you to continue to be welcome in my country. It is good for both our sakes. So I ask only two things: First, please be quiet and careful. Second, perhaps you and your friends (he looked at Pete and Sally) should make a trip outside of Khartoum. See some other part of my great country. We are as big as the United States east of the Mississippi, don't you know? Perhaps you'd like to see Juba? Westerners are always liking to visit their 'southern Christian brothers.' "

Al-Muntasser found this very funny. He repeated: "Your southern Christian brothers, one might say your 'SCBs'! Almost a toxic chemical sound, eh?

"Some day," he continued, "you must speak to my friend Dr. al-Mughraibiy about them. He's one of our leading politicians and MPs. He fancies himself quite an expert on the South. Just don't mention him to southerners. Indeed, why not go to Juba? But if you do, remember, please don't kill anyone! (Chuckle)."

The meeting ended with al-Muntasser in a seemingly relaxed and cheerful mood.

UPRISINGS

11

"You guys would like Juba," said Pete, looking at Sally and at me. "Mrs. Chamberlain would like it. Everyone does. Juba makes Americans feel very appreciated. They like us there. It's really poor. Makes you glad to be an American; makes *northern* Sudanese feel like *they're* Americans! Nice in other ways, too. Nobody pays attention to Muslim religious law. You can get booze: Gold Tusker Kenyan beer. There's no cutting off of hands and feet for robbery. But I mustn't spoil it for you, mustn't say too much. Just remember, you're in Africa. Ooh la la! Native dances! Those *National Geographic* beauty queens!" Pete ran his hands down along his sides. He swayed his hips suggestively. Made a few mincing dance steps across the floor. Maryann, Clayton, and Sally laughed.

I saw the ambassador standing in the doorway of his office. "*Andale!*" he exclaimed. Pete stopped short. More feminine laughter.

Farnsworth asked Sally, Pete, and me to come in. He wanted to talk to us about the prime minister's Juba trip "suggestion."

"It's partly a matter of cooling off for a little while," Farnsworth said. "Al-Muntasser associates you with two, for him, very embarrassing experiences. He doesn't dare P.N.G. you. There are no grounds, and we give him too much economic assistance. Also, that would highlight his government's failure to protect us *or* Deng. But so much for why al-Muntasser wants you out of town. More important, from our point of view, is that Pete thinks there may be a security angle."

I looked at Pete questioningly.

"Could be," he said. "So the PM doesn't like you. I wouldn't sweat *that*. That's a diplomatic problem. For you and the ambassador. But I used to work up drug cases for DEA in Miami. Rule no. 1: If you had a witness, keep him safe. No witness, no case. I knew it. The crooks knew it. I had a star witness disappear once. Afterwards, one of the drug lords—a sort of Abu Nidal of the Miami underworld—says to me: 'I hear your star witness just got himself a change of venue.' 'Where to?' I ask. 'King Neptune's court,' he says."

"Is it that serious here, Pete?" asked Farnsworth.

"Dunno, sir. But Josh here's made 'em look bad. He smoked, I mean *killed*, Yasser Arafat's main man. I think if Josh and Sally spent maybe a week out of town, even a couple of days, we might have something more. Kirby's putting out a lot of heat on this case. And that man has *beaucoup* assets. If I were Yasser or the Libyans, I'd start worrying. I'd get out the word, 'either you clean up your mess, *or else*.' "

"What's your feeling about this, Josh?" asked the ambassador. "Remember, there's an alternative. A perfectly acceptable one, too. You could be direct transferred to Washington. It would be, I assure you, to a first-rate job. No one would reproach you or blame you for leaving, much less yourself, I hope. You're an adult. I don't think you'd stick around here out of political macho. Why not talk to Marjorie, and then do what you're both comfortable with? And don't forget Brian. So think about it for a day or so?"

"I think I know already what the answer will be. But as you say, I'll talk things over with Marj."

It didn't look, though, as if I'd be consulting with Marj that afternoon. Sergeant Poe came in to say there was trouble in town: "North-South trouble, Blue-versus-Gray trouble, Arab-African trouble. The 'brothers' are restless," he concluded.

Going to the window, I looked down over the neighboring buildings. Across from the Chancery was Cairo University's Khartoum branch; right next to it were the barracks of the Khartoum riot police. The juxtaposition was no accident.

In the Arab world, universities are sometimes open—more often closed. In Khartoum, at the moment, they were still closed for the summer term. But in Arab countries, there's always work for the riot police. I could see them boarding their trucks. The enlisted men carried shields, helmets, clubs, side arms, gas masks, and tear-gas grenades. The officers carried gas masks, radios, side arms, and submachine guns. As each truck was loaded, it would speed out the gate and take up position on a side street—waiting for a call to action.

"Pete," said the ambassador, "send out an all-call telling our people to stay off the streets; the American School should stand fast; send the same word to our business community through the warden system. Josh, we'll have a look from the roof. Gunny, get your binoculars and bring them along."

We went up two flights of stairs to the unused eighth floor—just TDY quarters and a security trapdoor to the roof. The gunny climbed up another half flight of stairs—took out his mammoth key ring. One, two, three deadbolts. He put his back to the door and lifted. He grunted. A blade of light entered the stairwell. I pushed too. We braced the door open.

"Watch out for the antennas, sir," said the gunny. "Some are carrying a lot of volts."

The ambassador and I approached the edge of the building. The railing wall had been hardened and raised. Around its top, a half-inch steel slab raised the barrier to head height. The slab was pierced every five feet or so by observation slits.

I felt excited—but hoped it didn't show. I felt as I had in college before a tough match—but one that I knew I was prepared for. Everything we could have done had been done. I'd gone over the emergency and evacuation plan with the Marines and the different sections of the embassy. I could see why physiologists said explorers, sky divers, and practitioners of other risky professions were simply addicted to their own adrenalin. Something told me that today's reporting might get wide readership back in the department. Never a bad thing! I looked over the barrier. Game time?

To the north of the Embassy was the Nile, the ministries, and the People's Palace. To the south, the shantytowns of the industrial area, and Hilla al Jadeedah, where most of Khartoum's southerners lived. The Embassy and the university buildings tended to funnel traffic between these axes. If trouble was coming, our seats, I guessed, were on the fifty-yard line.

The police were now visible. They had come out of their alleys to take up positions at the entrance to a traffic circle three blocks to the south. Police trucks were helping to close off the road. Oily smoke—from burning vehicles?—could be seen curling up from the Hilla quarter. Far to the left, we could see—and hear—a choking black mass of demonstrators. It was slowly working its way toward the police barrier.

"Josh," said the ambassador, "get a couple of officers out on the street. Tell them to be careful. They should avoid the conflict areas, but report by radio on nearby parts of town. A look around the Presidency itself might be interesting. A reporting chance maybe for Ward Kapecka and Frank Greer."

I went back to my office and asked Clayton to call in Kapecka and Greer. Sally looked up from an open drawer in the ambassador's safe: "A mission for 'the Twins?' A double suicide, maybe?"

"Sally," I responded, "aren't you a little tough on your colleagues? Was it really just 'accidental' that Frank and Ward's field trip was left on the agenda? And that the ambassador then sent them off to Hagar al-Salaya?"

Sally smiled inscrutably. "Whatever. Ward ate something that didn't like him; he's been throwing up all morning. About to crash? Bleed out? Ebola fever maybe? If you're lucky, you can hear him just down the hall—singing into the porcelain mike!" She smiled a satisfied smile and added, "But, you don't win 'em all! Our Polyphemus's fine. Loved the food. I bet he ate a whole sheep—fur, guts, horns, and all. Came back even fatter.

"Not to be unfair," Sally went on, "Kapecka's gross; Frank's only rude. See them eat in the Snack Bar together? They do it in time, aerobically. Holding their forks like daggers! And at the rec site? They never swim or play anything. Just lie there, drinking beer, watching us women play tennis. Once in a while Frank flops out of his chair and does about a thousand push-ups. Then Ward tries pathetically to imitate him. Looks like a cockroach mating. Then they both drink more beer. Frank never shows it—except around his waist. But poor Ward— by 5 P.M. he's wobbly. And at dances—Frank palms you, but Ward!" Sally gave a shudder and walked back to her Wang work station.

I heard the elevator door in the hallway open. The voices of Kapecka and Greer reached us. I called them both in. Kapecka did look drained. Greer? As robust as ever. Did I only imagine it? Or were there really still tracks of lamb grease around his mouth, and what were those *new* spots on his long-suffering seersucker? Would the chrysalis Greer one day just burst out of its confines, revealing some new, monstrous order of being?

"Ward, Frank," I said, "the ambassador and I've been up on the roof. There's a demonstration coming up Abdul Lateef Street. The riot police are blocking. We don't think there's much else going on in town, but we'd like to get a couple of radios, drive around, take a look—away from the areas of confrontation."

Greer smiled, showing all his big teeth. I thought of a clam-shell digger. He nodded his big head. "Sounds good! Can I pick up some hardware from the gunny's warehouse? A .45, maybe? A Taser? Some

Mace? Anyone gets in the way, and"—Greer drove a meaty fist into his palm—"Pow!"

"Uh, that's not exactly what I had in mind, Frank," I said. Kapecka was distressed and angry. "I resent Dawkins going out of channels and over my head," he said.

"What do you mean?" I asked. "I don't understand."

"Well," said Kapecka, "this morning, Dawkins suggested that since Frank wasn't in yet (a reproachful look at Greer), I might like to do some 'voluntary political reporting.' *He wanted me to go out of the building, look around some!* Can you beat that? Those guys out there'd have me screaming falsetto before I cleared the gate! I turned Dawkins down COLD. Reminded him that Mr. Gray was expecting me to get onto the annual minerals report," Kapecka finished a little smugly.

Clayton came in. "Mr. Dawkins would like to see you for a minute, sir."

Will came in with a map rolled up in his hand. He looked hot and dusty. "Sorry, Josh," he said, noticing Ward and Kapecka. "Don't mean to break in."

"No problem, Will," I replied. "Just talking to Ward and Frank here about scouting out the disturbances."

"Oh, yeah?" replied Will noncommitally. "Ward and I talked about that earlier. Meanwhile, *I've* done a little looking. Here's what's happening." Unfolding the street map of Khartoum, he showed us some of what we'd seen from the roof. "The rioters are getting a lot of reinforcements—there's organization behind them. Agents of the Sudan People's Liberation Army—the S.P.L.A.? Anyhow, people are walking, driving, even being trucked in—from other black neighborhoods out along the Nile. Nasser extension, from as far out as Gerief West, you know, where the kiln-workers all live? Hard men. What I'm saying is that the demonstration's not spontaneous. It's organized, looks determined. I predict big trouble."

The street sounds became louder. Even through the safety glass they became more distinct. As they drew closer they seemed to drop an octave.

"Let's go back up to the roof, Will. I've just one phone call to make. You two, Ward and Frank, wait right here."

I called the general services officer: "Remember the E&E supplies that came in last week? The 250 cases of MREs, hams, vegetables, fruits, and juices we got? That's right. Yeah. There *was* a lot of damage—blown tins, breakage. Well, I've got a volunteer to move and inventory the shipment. You say the A/C's broken? You're right—hot and dirty, but *someone*'s gotta do it. Ward will be right down."

To Kapecka I said: "I guess the minerals report will have to wait. Any questions?"

Silence. Kapecka looked balefully at Dawkins.

I turned to Greer. "Frank, I know the admin section will need someone to monitor the E&E net—there's a lot of traffic to be sent and received. Not glamorous? But important. You can learn how a community works under pressure. Any questions? Thank you."

From the doorway I heard: "Fuckin' . . . " Greer?

To Dawkins I said: "Well done. I value initiative in an officer."

Back on the roof, we could see that pressure was building fast against the police lines. The street—really an avenue—south of the circle was jammed with a chanting black mass. There must have been twenty to thirty thousand southerners in sight—and maybe as many more around the bend behind them. The police were laying down tear gas. But in that jam-up, there was no chance of the crowd dispersing. The front ranks coughed and choked. But there was no place for them to go. Now and again a gas canister would be thrown back.

I passed down word through the gunny that all embassy people should have their gas masks handy. Thank heavens, I reflected, we had plenty of them! There would not be a repeat of what happened at Embassy Islamabad. There, the rioters broke into the ground floor of the Chancery. The police never showed up. So the Marines flooded the area with tear gas—and the ventilation system sucked the gas into the safe havens. There were masks only for about one in four. It was "women and children first," just like the Titanic.

More gas. It enraged the mob. The demonstrators charged forward. And fell back. Charged again. The police line bent, but held. More gas. Another charge—the police line bent, sprang a leak. The leak became a torrent. A second line of riot police ran forward from our end of the circle. Demonstrators swirled around their edges. Through the binoculars one could see the police clubbing frantically. The demonstrators fought back with bricks, rubble, and steel rebars from construction sites. I thought: plenty of *these* in downtown Khartoum. No chance the demonstrators would run out of ammo.

Something knocked the police captain down. His men rescued him. They pulled him out of the hands of a dozen southerners. The officer got to his feet, unslinging his submachine gun. We heard a whole clip fired into the crowd. "Snap, crackle, pop!" The mob fell back. But only for a moment. Then it charged. I suddenly understood the meaning of "like a wounded buffalo."

The police line crumbled. It was the Johnstown Flood. We saw policemen go down. Demonstrators were threshing them with clubs and iron bars. Here and there a machete flashed. The remaining police were running away. Riot shields, clubs, helmets—all abandoned.

Even from our height, we could hear the "flip flop, flop flip" of policemen's boots as they ran past the Embassy. Coming up behind them, we could hear a muted, angry lowing. Some of it in rhythm. In waves. That was the crowd—the sound of rough surf on a pebbly beach.

As the rioters moved up the street, we could make out their chants. One went, "*A-a-a-rab: Kharab!*" Another, "*Damm al-Arab ilak Deng!*" "Down with Arabs!" "Arab blood for you, oh Deng!" Then, triumphantly, they began to sing.

I turned unbelievingly to Will: "Please tell me I'm not *really* hearing them sing 'Onward, Christian Soldiers'?"

"That's right. You're not. What they're singing, in Dinka, is the southern rebel anthem. John Garang decided his people needed an anthem; so, like a good missionary boy, he chose his favorite hymn. The lyrics, though, are John's own. The usual 'up with socialism, down with capitalism. Proletariat of the World, unite!' "

"Interesting. How do you say 'proletariat' in Dinka?"

"Listen," responded Will. "I think it's 'prooletarioot.' "

The mob was approaching the Embassy. The building was as buttoned up as we could make it. The metal screen *and* the metal shutters had been lowered and locked over the entrance. All windows were solidly barred; heavy iron cages—grouted into the building wall—protected the air-conditioners. Would-be infiltrators couldn't pull them out and climb in through the holes. We had enough food, water, tear gas, and ammo to withstand a siege.

As the mob's outrunners reached us, a squad of seven or eight, wearing yellow armbands, took up positions in front of and around the Embassy. They had no firearms, but instead carried a kind of axe—a broad metal head, on a longish wooden handle. The handles were decorated with alternating bands of black and bright red. Some of the axe heads had a sticky, maroon look. Similar axes were brandished here and there in the crowd.

"The official weapon-symbol of the S.P.L.A," explained Will. "A nasty weapon in a fight. Also, itself an anti-Arab political statement. Arabs always go for sword symbols, see? So the southerners choose axes."

I saw the squad members wave the other demonstrators by. None were allowed into the low, walled enclosure between the Chancery facade and the blast wall alongside the street.

Hoping to see better, I climbed a stool and looked down over the building edge. One of the—what could I call them? festival organizers?—saw me. He called to his fellow squad members. They all looked up, smiled, and waved. Then very ostentatiously, one made the sign of the cross, and gave me a "thumbs up" sign. They waved again and went back to "directing traffic."

From up the street—toward the river—other sounds could be heard. Heavy diesel motors changing gears. Metal pads rotating against concrete and macadam. I looked to my right and saw—just turning the corner—two of the Presidency's 48-ton, M-60 tanks. As they completed their turn and lined up with Abdul Lateef Street, two more appeared. Behind the tanks, and on either side, several platoons of the Presidential Guard came jogging. Red berets bobbing and swaying together. Like poppies—"In Flanders Field," I thought.

The tanks and infantry paused, then began to advance slowly toward the rioters.

The group organism that was the crowd wavered. A part of it began to fall back. Other parts broke off and took shelter in the university buildings along both sides of the street. The main body kept moving forward slowly toward the tanks and infantry. The demonstrators shouted. Shook their fists.

The tanks weren't buttoned up. Their commanders stood chest-high in the turrets. I saw them unlimbering their coaxial turret machine guns. The infantry took up a protective formation in front of the tanks, and the machine guns began to fire down the street. Short bursts of five or six rounds each. At first the gunners fired over the heads of the crowd. More cries of defiance. The crowd continued its advance, until not more than three hundred yards separated the tanks from the demonstrators.

Next—a signal from one tank commander to the other. A shouted acknowledgement. This time, the machine guns began a slow traverse across the face of the crowd. Still in controlled five- or six-round bursts. There was a syncopation to the sound. One gunner seemed to pick up the beat from the other. The jam session proceeded.

The results were deadly. But not violent. Demonstrators in the front ranks stumbled, then, as if overcome by sleep, slumped to the ground. Several put their hands out to the side, as if trying to break their fall. The street was soon littered with black, raggedly dressed bodies.

Under the lash of the tanks' machine guns, the mob shifted into reverse. Panic seized the demonstrators. They fled back along the avenue, often over one another. As the street cleared, I guessed as many had died in the crush as from the gunfire. Our yellow-armband detail had long vanished.

But it wasn't quite over. From the roof of the College of Arabic Literature—a handsome, red sandstone building, with window frames still smoke-blackened from demonstrations of two years before—petrol bombs arced downwards. Most fell short. But some didn't. The outside of one of the two lead tanks was ablaze. The driver buttoned up. He gunned his machine down the street out of range. No question of trying to avoid the dead and wounded in the street. A petrol bomb landed *inside* the turret of the second tank. The crew scrambled out, rolled on the ground, clothes afire.

The two reserve tanks in the file swung their 106 mm cannons toward the building. At that proximity they had to elevate the barrels to the maximum. "Holy shit!" I exclaimed to Dawkins. "Watch this—like the Russians in Berlin in 1956, I'll bet."

The two tanks fired almost simultaneously. The surrounding buildings magnified the sound of the explosion. I reflected, civilians can't imagine how loud cannon fire is—and why one of the most disorienting aspects of the modern battlefield is *noise*. The detonations were corporeal. Punishing. The tanks rocked back on their treads from the recoil. The side and upper story of the Literature College seemed to swell. Then—in slow motion—to pour down onto the street.

"Everyone keep your heads down!" I shouted. "They're going to fire again. Don't let those gunners mistake us for rioters. I hope to God they see the flag in front of the Embassy!" Amazingly, it still hung—undisturbed by the demonstrators. (I remembered bearing down with Pete about always having a crisp, clean, unmistakably *American* flag flying on the Chancery staff.)

To Will I said, "Can you imagine what one of those rounds would do to Pete's shiny, new Public Access Control project in the lobby?"

The gunners *had* seen the flag. And with two more rounds, the opposition ended. (I thought, only the most determined civilians—like the Russians in the streets of Stalingrad—can face tanks with just Molotov cocktails!)

The iron watchdogs of the Presidency put their gears into reverse and crept back to their kennels.

By nightfall, military ambulances had evacuated the wounded. After them, flatbed trucks came rolling slowly down the street, accompanied by military work parties. Meat wagons. As the trucks passed, members of the detail would flip the dead aboard—they got good at it after awhile. Got into the rhythm. Like sanitation workers in Washington, D.C., disposing of the trash each Monday morning.

The ambassador, Sally, and I got back to the Residence—through empty streets—at 10 P.M. The trip had still taken longer than normal—we'd had to pass through two checkpoints, each manned by tense, northern Sudanese soldiers. Farnsworth had flown his flag. We'd driven slowly, carefully, defensively.

Mustafa was waiting for me. He told me: "Madame she eat. Go to bed. Want see Excellency upstairs."

Marj was asleep in bed, with the light on. She opened her eyes as I came in.

I sat down on the edge of the bed and began to talk. It was the first time we'd had, I realized, just to sit and talk since Deng's murder. I felt keyed up. "It was like the movie," I said, "*The Longest Day!* You probably heard the crowd. You sure must have heard the tanks shelling the university buildings! What a . . . "

Marj threw back the bedclothes. For a moment, she sat on the edge of the bed, then walked over to the armchair. She sat down, leaned back. I waited for her to say something more. Silence. She looked at me. Under the nightgown, I could make out the form of her full breasts—the way she sat, the thin nightgown material hung straight from her nipples. I could tell she was also wearing some of her skimpy Victoria's Secret panties. I used to kid her about the name.

I looked—the release from the pressures of the day. I thought, maybe . . .? But I decided I should share with Marj more of my experiences, first.

So I began to tell her of the day's events. I filled her in on details—beyond the sketchy outlines we had broadcast every few hours on the E&E net. I'd done the day's wrap-up-analysis cable—a NIACT IMMEDIATE. It had been a good piece of work. Farnsworth had complimented me on it. I'd also sent her parents and Brian word through the desk officer at State, saying we were fine, in no danger, and would call whenever the international lines opened. Last, I said the ambassador and Pete thought we maybe should go to Juba for a week or two, travel around the south. See some teak plantations, call on regional governors . . . I came to a stop.

Marj still said nothing. Had she been listening?

Then: "I'm glad you're still alive" were her first words. She went on: "Sounds like you had a really exciting day. Maybe now you have a few minutes to listen to me? I . . . I feel I'll just burst if I don't talk to someone. Just me and the servants in this house . . ."

"I wish you would, Marj," I replied. "I know these must have been awful days for you. You know, it's really easier for those of us who are on the active end of things. Our minds are taken up with what we're doing. As you've said, times like these are hardest on dependents. It's natural for you to worry."

"Worry?" Marj said, with a forced smile. "Worry about what? That my husband's risking his life for the second time in three or four days? While I hear artillery fire from the Chancery, and you don't call or radio? While this Abu Nar maybe prepares another murderous plot, and drafts another boastful communiqué? While we hide below decks in the ambassador's fortress—this, this 'Führer bunker.' What? Me worry?"

"Aw, come on Marj . . ."

"No. That's just it. I won't 'aw, come on.' How I hate that expression! The last-ditch male wheedle. And do you think I can't see how you're looking at me? In a minute you'll make a move to get me into bed with you. I'll turn you down—and it'll be, 'Aw, come on, Marj . . .' and you'll be mad." Marj got up, went into the bathroom, and came out wearing her housecoat.

"Maybe *now* we can talk. Listen, Josh—and for once, stop thinking only about . . . that. I know what you want. Always the same thing—all the time. That look on your face. Wolfman as the moon comes up. But do you know or care what *I* want? I want you to be professional, to be prudent. I want you to stop playing platoon leader with the Marines."

I mentally cursed the lance corporal, and kicked myself for telling her about the Marines meeting me at the Embassy. I tried again: "Marj, we've got to be serious. Maybe I get distracted. But something big is going on in Sudan. The Libyans for sure are involved. Maybe Muslim extremists, too. I told you what Deng said—it can really matter for the United States. Washington's reading everything we put out. About half of the department's noon briefing yesterday was a rewrite of our cable traffic. And they haven't even digested today's take yet. This is how careers are made. How Farnsworth made *his* mark. He's counting on me—on you and me. Tonight, he and I . . ."

Marj cut in: "That's right. Stay up all night with your precious Jonathan. Do you hear yourself? It's 'Jon this' and 'Jon that' You're even aping some of his mannerisms! The way he wipes his lower lip with his hand sometimes after speaking. *He* doesn't have anyone to worry about—or to worry about him. So just focus on that all-important career! Even if it kills you!"

She went on. I thought of the tank treads that afternoon grinding over dead and wounded rioters.

"The trouble with you, Josh, is you're always working hard at some *thing*—not people. Your job, languages, sports."

I started to say something, when Marj raised her voice: "There's more. Remember when we joined the Foreign Service? 'We'll be a team, Marj,' you said. A team all right. You up on the coach seat, me down there between the traces. I run your household, raise your son, manage a dinner for the USG. And I've done it all darned well.

"But do you ever really talk to me? All the other wives know what's going on in the office. None of us have much by way of careers. Not possible in the Foreign Service. But they at least get *companionship*. You make me feel—look—stupid. The times people mention something and I've never heard of it! And I have to pretend I have, and hope to pick it up as we go along."

"But, Marj . . ."

"Just keep listening, Josh. Just a little more. Are you *hearing* me? Are we really a team? Or am I just your admin assistant? A sort of female Mustafa? You're almost killed, and when you call, it's 'and don't forget to pack the tennis racquets'! With Brian gone, I can tell you it's lonely. Yes, lonely. I can spend only so much time at the piano, sewing clothes, and walking behind the houseboys. You know I love animals— but we don't even have a pet. 'Too much trouble to move from one country to the other,' you say. There's no one to talk to when you're at the office. OK.

"But it's the same when you're not in the office. Then you're always working at one of your obsessions! Why not work at keeping up your marriage? You only care for me . . . in *that* way. It's like an obsession. None of the other wives . . . I'm just your convenience, your 'Judy Doll'! What did they call it in *Hill Street Blues*? Your 'squeeze'?"

I broke in: "Aw, c—Jesus, Marj! You're being really unfair. I know this has been an awful time for you. OK. That's just why I want you to go to Juba with me. It's nice. It's really different. So, please. *Please* think about going. The A.I.D. compound there is modern and comfortable. We can swim, tour the area—have a real vacation—relax. You'll feel better, then, afterwards we can talk. You need a change."

"You're right about *that*, anyhow," said Marj. "This house—it's like that horrible hotel of Stephen King's! The painters were back today.

For the upstairs bedroom. They said to me: 'We maybe have to dig out the plaster; the spots keep coming through.' And that loud hillbilly music down the hall, where the staff assistant stays."

"Sally Tolson's music?"

"Yes. All the time. Haven't you noticed? As soon as she comes in, on goes the boom-box. Like *Boys in the 'hood!* You know I like all kinds of music, but loud country and bluegrass *all the time?* People are entitled to a little peace and quiet. At home at least. Couldn't you ask her to turn it down?"

"Gee, Marj, I hate to do that. We all have to unwind some way."

"See! That's what I mean! You'll do anything for anyone else. What *they* want is fine. And they tell me what a wonderful person you are. I wish they could see you at home. *I* ask you to do one little thing— that minister's smoking, or Sally's music—and it's, 'Gee, Marj.' "

"Aw, I do try to help. I handle the household accounts, balance the books, do the taxes, keep in touch with our broker. I sold our Virginia house, bought the new one in D.C., arranged the financing . . . "

Marj shot back: "Well, goody for you, Mr. Wonderful. Is that too much to ask, I wonder?"

I had no answer. "Good night, Marj. I think I'll go to the study and write Brian a letter." I knew I sounded stuffy.

Sitting in the study, I thought about what Marj had said. Was I too focused? Sure, I was ambitious. But never in a calculating or underhanded way. To be honest, I'd never felt myself to be in personal competition with colleagues—the Foreign Service wasn't like sports. I'd always figured that I was fairly good, and that if I worked hard at each job, I'd do well. I remembered a boss who'd said, "Amazing! The luckiest people I know are those who work hardest!"

Was I selfish? I guessed I *was* happiest when things went my way— and maybe I *did* take Marj for granted. Did I speak with her the way I did with friends in the office? Maybe not. But was it wrong for me to assume—unspokenly—that she'd make her contribution to our marriage, just as she could assume I'd make mine?

I thought again of Marj in her nightgown and found myself listening to a song. Was it for the second time? It was coming from Sally's room. A pretty song. But loud, I admitted to myself. After a moment I got up and hesitantly knocked on her door.

It opened. Sally had on a kind of heavy Moroccan caftan. Her feet were bare. The light from behind her created a halo effect with the edges of her hair. Someone was singing:

Listen to the tears roll,
Down my face as she turns to go . . .

"Excuse me, Sally. But I was in the study and heard that really pretty song. Whose is it?" The singer continued:

I'll do my time,
Oh! Keepin' you off my mind,
But there're moments that I find,
I'm not feelin' so strong.

"You like it?" she asked. "I'm sorry, is it too loud?"

"No. Not at all. Well, maybe just a little. But it's pretty, and I wondered . . . "

She smiled. What a smile, I thought yet again.

"It's called 'Mandolin Rain,' " she replied. "By Bruce Hornsby and the Range. From their album, *The Way It Is*. Old but good. I bet Brian would like it, Josh."

I felt slightly foolish as I said good night and went back to the study. I was sorry, in a way, I'd asked. "That makes two bad exits in one night," I said to myself. Also, the music stopped right after I heard her close her door.

I thought of Sally's smiling.

I shook my head as if to clear it, and began my letter to Brian. I always enjoyed letter writing. I knew I wrote good letters. I suspected, though, that Brian sometimes didn't get beyond the 'check–no check' stage of reading them. When I finished, I enclosed a nice check—and told him to try to find a cassette by Bruce Hornsby.

"THE WAY YOU HOLD MY HAND..."

12

0700 again. BBC didn't keep us waiting. But this morning, John Stone read the bad news. It didn't sound so bad, actually, with a man reading it: "Four teachers and a dozen students have been killed as rebel soldiers attacked a missionary boarding school in Zaire's Shaba province. A Sri Lankan airliner bound for Singapore has exploded with fifty passengers aboard. The World Health Organization reports the dramatic spread of a new virulent strain of the HIV-2 AIDS virus in West Africa." (He makes it sound as though the Dow Jones average had just gone up, I said to myself.)

Stone reached us. He read: "Sudan: Violent clashes between ethnic southerners and security forces in the Sudanese capital, Khartoum, have left scores dead and wounded. The clashes followed protests by Khartoum's black African population against the recent killing of Sudan's foreign minister, Dr. Immanuel Deng, a noted black leader. The violence is considered the most serious challenge to date to the democratic government of Prime Minister al-Muntasser. The prime minister has appealed for all parties to respect law and order; a curfew has been declared."

"At least there's no mention of 'Mr. Nar' today and his something-or-other-Karare front," Sally remarked.

That was coming.

When we got to the chancery, Will Dawkins was sitting in the outer office. Clayton had gotten him some coffee. The day's Arabic language papers lay folded on the couch next to him.

"'Morning, Will," I said. "You heard BBC today? 'Violent ethnic clashes' and all that?"

"I heard their 0600 Arabic broadcast," he replied. "I get *my* bad news from Muna Rashid. But I've got some follow-up for you and the ambassador." He looked down at the Arab papers.

"You all come on in," said Farnsworth.

Dawkins laid his papers out on the ambassador's coffee table.

"Bad news?" Farnsworth queried.

Dawkins hesitated and smiled. "You'll have to judge—no, not altogether bad news. There's this." And Will opened one of the papers to the back page.

Half of the page was devoted to a photograph—indubitably of Frank Greer. But what a Frank Greer! A Frank Greer in a pair of skimpy Speedo shorts, and a string T-shirt with a crescent of letters "AAU." Skinny calves, huge thighs, a barrel-like trunk, led the eye up to columnar arms which supported, post-and-lintel fashion, a barbell. The barbell looked heavy. You could see it bending up in the middle—a row of forty-five-pound disks on either side. Frank's face looked like nothing human. The body? I'd seen similar shapes floating over the Macy's Thanksgiving Day parade.

"Where's the cape?" I asked.

Dawkins laughed. "I'd already heard about Frank's trip from Arab friends. They said he came down in the carryall and brought his weight bench and free weights with him. Asked for some time at the folk festival, and a little privacy in setting things up. I suppose they expected the usual: you know, a speech, book presentations, photos. I'm told the head man almost keeled over when the curtain parted and there was Frank . . . two hundred kilos of muscle in a one kilo wrapper!

"Frank started off with smaller weights and asked some of the audience to lift along with him. Good response. A couple of Nuban wrestlers came up and did well. It looked like a draw when Frank and the last Nuban both cleaned and jerked something like 275. My friend said Frank was shaking his head, rubbing his hands together, looking nervous. Then he showed he'd just been playing cat-and-mouse. Like his arm wrestling stunt.

"He asked the crowd if he should try 300. 'Yes! Yes!' He got the 300 up. Same for 325, and 350, and 375, and finally—400! Frank's personal best. He says he's never had an audience like it. The place was going wild. And on his last lift, Frank brought down the house—literally. He got the 400 pounds up—then dropped them. The bar and weights went right through the floor. End of program. No folk dancing. Nuban wrestlers adjourned. Much cheering."

Will looked at the paper. "The story's all here. About the most positive thing I've seen written on the USA since I've come to Sudan. They call him the American Giant, *al-Amriikiy al-'imlaaq*, and *Shimshun*—you can guess which Biblical person that is. And I hear half the shaikhs in the area now want Frank for a son-in-law!"

Sally remarked blandly, "Maybe Frank has a great future after all—in a traveling Sudanese circus?"

The ambassador looked over at me. He smiled: "Tell Greer to write up his trip report—and send it to *STATE* magazine. They ought to publish it, the pictures, too. Something different for the staff meeting. Not bad. But you've some other news, Will?" Farnsworth added.

"Afraid so," was the reply. "This morning I went by the university to check the sloganeering and billboards. They read like publishers' blurbs on dust jackets. There was a big notice from—guess whom?"

"Abu Nar?"

"Yep. Here's what he says: The poster starts with the phrase 'an open letter.' Then comes a headline: '*ameerikiyyah shu'ubiyya.*' That means the United Sates is a modern *shu'ubist* power, meaning anti-Islamic. The *shu'ubiyyah* was a political-cultural movement in early Islam; it opposed Arab claims to precedence in Islam. Nowadays—in this part of the world—the term just means 'anti-Arab.' Among Arabs, the best name-calling always goes back to religion or history. Anyhow, our friend goes on (Will translated as he read): 'Oppose the clear conspiracy of the imperialist embassy,' and, 'High American embassy officials behind bloody secessionist attempts in Khartoum.' "

Dawkins continued: "There are three or four more lines of the same stuff. But the newspapers are interesting, too. The headlines just mention the 'unfortunate incidents' (*hawaadith mu'sifa*). But three of them—the Islamic '*al-Risala*' and two of the so-called 'independents'— also carry statements by this 'Abu Nar.' Same as I saw at the university.

"They also claim you were on the roof of the Embassy directing the rioters, singing hymns with them. The Marine guards are supposed to have thrown Molotov cocktails and grenades down at the policemen who were trying to restore order. Abu Nar ends by rhetorically asking if 'the people' should not demand an apology from the 'imperious,' or 'arbitrary'—the word can go either way—embassy, and the prompt recall of its so-called *maz'uumiyn*—diplomats."

"When Pete Valiant hears this," I said, "he'll have us filling sand bags and digging bomb shelters—scenes from *Hope and Glory*."

"Sounds, too, as if someone's got a good pipeline into the embassy," Dawkins added. "Could be any one of a dozen Foreign Service Nationals. But listen now, the best is yet to come. The Libyan mouthpiece *al-Buq*—literally means *The Trumpet*—has an editorial. I'll skip the opening movements. Nothing new. But just listen to the finale."

Translating, Dawkins read: "What are the noble sons and daughters of the martyr masses to do before these Yankee wiles and incessant provocations? Did a thousand champions and *championesses*—"

He looked up: "That's the word, *batalaat*—but don't ask me, or any Sudanese for that matter, who they were." He went back to his translating: " . . . pour out their sacred blood to throw off the British yoke meekly to accept the American one? To the American eagle we say, 'Remove your diseased eaglets from our nest—your agent ambassador and his mercenary Marine mastiff—or else the hand of the people will reach out in righteous anger. They shall be swept away by Abu Nar and the Red Wind.

"Two points," commented Dawkins: "First, it's been a long, long time since any Sudanese paper threatened a diplomat. Our FSNs say not since '85, when President Nimeiry fell. A lot came out then about our ambassador and the airlift of Falasha Jews to Israel. That's also when the communicator here got shot—probably by Libyans, though we never found out.

"But back to the papers. Mostly they know just how loud to bark. And mostly we can listen and say 'it's only the wind.' Or as the Arabs say, *'al kalb yinbah, al jamal yamshi'*—figuratively, 'the dogs bark, the caravan moves on.' But this here's different. A threat, an incitation, anyhow.

"And second, I'll be darned if I know what the references to 'Abu Nar,' or 'the Red Wind' mean! I asked our FSNs. They were pretty fuzzy. Uncomfortable. Embarrassed. Like something in the family you don't want to talk about? Crazy Uncle Charlie's in the attic? Something like that? Josh, you're looking funny."

I told Will that Mustafa had tried to say that 'the Red Wind' was something really bad. But what, I couldn't make out. A Maoist fringe group? A gang of religious fanatics? I didn't mention the *Juju?*—*Wanga?*—*Gris-gris?*—that Mustafa had given me. I was darned if I'd tell Dawkins I had carried it a couple of times, or that at this very moment it lay in my tennis bag.

Farnsworth was angry. "Will, make an appointment for us to see the acting FonMin to protest this article. Do an *aide mémoire*, also, to leave with him. We'll make the point that the United States is foremost in defending freedom of the press. But this newspaper article incites to violence. Shouting 'Fire!' in a crowded theater's different. And Will, put in something about an embassy person being shot the last time something like this appeared in the press."

The ambassador went on: "I'll also ask the PAO to take a copy of the *aide mémoire* over to the minister of information. I won't take you, Josh, this time," Farnsworth added, "because the demarche concerns you directly. You'll be represented by counsel, so to speak."

Maryann appeared in the doorway. "Sir," she said, "pardon me, but Mr. Kirby wonders if he could see you and Josh in 'the Bubble.'"

I never liked meetings in the Bubble. Thanks to our commtechs, we were fairly sure the executive suite was "clean." But for really sensitive discussions, when sources and methods were involved—the lives of people, that is—we used our soundproof room, the Bubble, a.k.a. the Meat Locker. The air exchanger emitted a constant roaring noise. And as if to do penance for all its nonfunctional cousins in Sudan, it worked so well that the room temperature quickly dropped to the 60s; I'd find myself sitting on my icy fingers—a victim of "Raynaud's phenomenon"?

Jack was last in. He spun the lock shut and moved to take his seat. Cold air washed over us. A roaring noise. Here we sit, I thought to myself, in Jacques Cousteau's underwater laboratory, or Dr. Beebe's bathyscaphe, far below the surface of the Caribbean. Unimaginable pressures—a leak would rip through us like a bullet. I thought of 'Umayyir . . . Change the channel to . . . Marj leaning back in her nightgown, Sally's slim brown legs . . .

Looking at Kirby, I reflected no one would ever place him as hailing from anywhere but the Southwest. (He came from New Mexico, to be precise). It wasn't just his prospector's beard, or silver belt buckle, or the boots. And it wasn't his accent. He could sound—if he wanted to—as if he'd never done anything in life but neuter bulls and dehorn calves. But with a bachelor's from Georgetown and a J.D. from Notre Dame, Jack could also sound like a New York investment banker. More even than dress or accent, I decided, what pegged Jack as a westerner was *how he moved*. Hard to describe. But he *consumed* more space than an easterner. And vastly more than a European. He seemed to swim into a room—he was big—but not *that* big, you thought. Yet people would stand back, as if to take in a really large object.

Jack opened a folder. He took out two crudely printed notices: one in English and one in Arabic. From where I sat I could see, even upside down, that the English notice was signed "Abu Nar." I couldn't restrain myself.

"Well done, Jack," I said. "Looks like you've got the goods, or some goods, anyway, on the bastards."

Jack paused. "Mr. Ambassador," he said slowly, "early this morning I was counting the hours to my next promotion. Or maybe assignment as station chief/London. Instead (he nodded at the papers), I reflect again on the vanity of wishful thinking.

"You can imagine, Mr. Ambassador," he went on, "how Langley's been at me. Messages slugged 'Personal' from the DDO, secure phone calls—I've mentioned some to you. Langley can't believe, what with our assets in Sudan, we haven't yet pouched them Abu Nar's balls, in dry ice, to be served creamed on toast for the DCI's breakfast. The DDO said to me: 'Jack—you're just doing a dick dance out there!' His very words!"

Kirby's tempo quickened: "Then last night, we got a break, I thought. One of our unilaterals in Interior said they had a lead into the Karare front and Abu Nar. He claimed to have names, addresses. It was going to cost, though. So we paid. And he got us these documents here as a "first installment." He promised more. They looked good. But twenty years of intelligence work have put a dent in my trust in human nature. This morning, early, I had our man polygraphed. It was all garbage! He knew we had a hard-on for Abu Nar—so he thought he'd just jerk us off. He made up these documents in the ministry print shop. Soon, we'd have had the complete works of Abu Nar. Historians could have put them side by side on their shelves with the *Hitler Diaries*."

Farnsworth asked: "Do you suppose all the other Abu Nar messages were fabrications, too? Your agent—ex-agent?—could easily have gotten at the ministry the sort of information Abu Nar's been putting into his 'letters.' What I wonder is, could we have been barking up the wrong tree all along? Have *all* these manifestos been cooked up in the ministry print shop?"

"Nossir," Jack answered. "The one area where our source tested 'true' was when he claimed that the papers he'd given us were the first of their kind. He says the ministry thinks there really is something out there behind the Hilverding and Deng murders. They guess it's probably Libya, or maybe the extreme Muslims. But it's all just conjecture, really."

Looking glum, Jack digressed: "That's one trouble with the end of the Cold War. The world's terror underground is crawling with unemployed high-skilled spooks. One former Soviet *rezident* even put an ad in *Le Monde!* The market in spies is like the arms market; you can pretty much get anything you want, if you've got the funds."

"But does your source have anything to say about this 'Red Wind' the Libyan paper mentions?" the ambassador asked.

"Not much. His grandparents used to tell him to be good, or else the Red Wind would get him. Something like a bogeyman?"

"Sounds to me," said Farnsworth, "we're dealing with some aspect of folk culture. The issue may be broader than Libya. But how? And in which way? Keep looking, Jack. And keep that ice chest handy."

Kirby looked puzzled.

"For those prairie oysters, of course," Farnsworth explained. Turning toward me, he added: "But one thing's for sure: Joshua, you and Marjorie and Sally Tolson will leave tomorrow for area familiarization in Equatoria. You can go on the A.I.D. plane's regular run. I'm afraid I'll have to keep Pete here. I don't care what al-Muntasser suggested. We need our RSO. But down there you'll be safe from the Red Wind— or whatever.

"And Juba should be pleasant, too. I had a wonderful visit last year in mid-January. That's the best season. This time of year, it may be a little wet, but after Khartoum, green and wet may look good. Like Paradise, in fact. Also, our A.I.D. compound's nice. Take your tennis racquets. Forget Khartoum for awhile. The military governor—he's Arab, of course—was a little stiff. He gave me some books on Islam. Hardly best sellers down there. But the other officials were pleasant enough. You'll like the southerners, and their dances," the ambassador concluded smiling.

Maryann buzzed from outside the airlock. On the intercom, she told the ambassador that the acting foreign minister could see him right away.

The ambassador finished one last piece of business. "Joshua," he said, "your Marine friends are distressed you're going. I assured them it was just temporary. They asked if they could invite you and Marj over tonight for drinks, snacks, and maybe a little music. They're really talking about a mini–happy hour. I asked Pete. He thought State Security would provide cover. And after what the post's been through, he thought people needed to let off some steam. So I told the Marines OK—but to keep it to twenty or thirty *invited* guests. You haven't seen the Marine House yet? A nice villa. Not luxury, but nice."

As we returned to the outer office, Frank Greer came in behind us. In his hand were some draft cables to be cleared. Sally looked him over and said: "There was sure a lot of you on the society page, Frank.

And about the dance tonight at the Marines'—maybe I could get someone to fix you up with a nice blind date."

"Yeah, who?" said Frank.

"Jane Goodall," came Sally's reply.

Greer laughed good-naturedly. "Just you wait and see!"

Sally insisted on the last word: "Diane Fossey might have been
even better. Too bad. You know, the gorilla lady." But she said it with a
smile.

I went home to tell Marj of our travel plans. The news seemed not to
displease her. Marj wondered how long we'd be gone. A week or ten
days, I figured. What would she wear? Pushing my luck, I replied: "As
little as possible." She gave me a look—but not an unfriendly one? I
sensed a clearer, more relaxed atmosphere between Marj and me. I
asked if Mustafa was at work. It was his day off. My questions about
Abu Nar and the Red Wind would have to wait.

I hadn't mentioned to Marj the new threats in the local Arabic
newspapers, though. If she learned of them, I knew she'd reproach me
for holding the information back. Thinking back on our argument, I
thought I was still right *never* to take home my own, or other people's
troubles—if there was nothing Marj could do about them. When fellow officers spoke of "sharing" post news with a spouse, I suspected
"sharing" often meant just gossip and a raking-over of others' foibles
and misfortunes.

The Marine House was on Street 16, off Shari'a Sinnaat in Khartoum
2. One couldn't mistake either the street or the house. Pete had been
as good as his word: Street 16 had a roadblock at each end. A police
sergeant stopped us. He checked the plates. He looked in. When he
saw Marj—and me—he stepped back, saluted, and waved us on. There
were perhaps fifteen cars in front of the Marine House. But not too
close. A line of bollards, each three feet apart and linked by a heavy
chain, stood five yards out into the street from the Marine House wall.

The bollards extended two houses past the Marine House in either direction. (Pete told me the neighbors complained they couldn't park. He had answered that the barriers had the OK of the chief of police and that, while they might be a nuisance, a truck bomb would be worse.)

One of the Marines, a lance corporal, was checking invitations at the gate. "Evening ma'am, welcome to your Marine House. Welcome home, sir," he saluted.

The Marines had a nice house for entertaining. The downstairs was basically one large room. You came into what was "the dining room": a buffet table just inside the door was set with pizzas, hamburgers, condiments, and rolls. There were also Arab dishes: *hummus*, ground chickpeas in oil, and *babaghanouj*, a baked eggplant spread, plus Arab bread and potato chips. Beer and soft drinks were on ice in plastic garbage cans by the table. In the corner to our right, a classic dark wood bar, with brass foot rail and stools, overlooked the living room. Most of the furniture had been removed to make space for a dance floor. Some Marines and their houseboys were tending bar.

There were about twenty guests. Clayton, Maryann, several of the communicators, Will Dawkins and his smart, pretty Lebanese wife, the Kirbys, and of course Pete Valiant. The Marines had dates—about two or three apiece, it seemed. Ah, youth! Some older Americans were there. I guessed they'd be ex-Marines. Kapecka was at the bar with his back toward us. On the bar's mirror hung a poster in red and gold lettering: "Welcome DCM/Lieutenant and Mrs. Chamberlain—*Semper Fi!*" From the drink bins, I picked out a diet Coke for Marj and an Amstel beer for myself.

My eyes widened. Easing up to the buffet table—a battleship coming into dock—was the ovoid but powerful-looking bulk of Frank Greer. And next to him, a pilot ship? I thought of Botticelli, and of Olive Oyl and Brutus—the disproportions were about the same. Marj and I walked over. The girl was laughing. Curly dark brown hair, a creamy, golden brown complexion. Her white tank top and white culottes seemed too large for her. From a distance she looked preadolescent; up closer, a slim and elegant nineteen.

I introduced myself and Marj. Frank seemed at a loss for words. The girl answered: "I am Aminat al-Furi; I am here from Hajar al-Salayah, visiting family friends." Her English came out fluently, a little British-sounding.

"I've heard of the town," I said evenly, looking at Frank. "Is that where you met?"

"Yes," she answered. "I met Frank when you sent him to represent the ambassador. My father used to be the area's . . . head man?

He's not living now. We were all impressed that the ambassador should have sent his first deputy to represent him. (Frank avoided my look). Then Frank is such an athlete and a scholar—after Frank's show no one would have been interested in the Nuban wrestlers. And he has even memorized parts of the Koran."

I looked straight at Greer. Rather defensively he asserted: "I *have*, really."

Aminat finished: "So when I came to see friends and visit the sisters at Camboni College where I studied, Frank invited me to come tonight. It is wonderful for me to be practicing English again. At home it's mostly Furi and Arabic. And not many parties, either." Aminat laughed—a well-tuned, silvery laugh.

I looked at Frank. His face was turned toward Aminat; I thought of a plaster saint contemplating the Sacred Heart of Jesus. On an impulse, I asked: "What were you laughing about when I came over?"

Aminat giggled. After a look at Frank she explained: "I am helping Frank with his French. And he wanted to say: 'I was left behind.' It came out: '*J'ai été gauche derrière*!' " She touched his arm: "But we will continue. Frank is serious and works hard; we'll do better." Frank nodded, watching her. This time I thought of Ferdinand the Bull, just smelling the flowers.

The gunny came over to greet us. "Hope we'll see you often here, sir," he said, "and Mrs. Chamberlain, too."

"We're at home here, Gunny," Marj answered. "Three years as a Marine Corps wife, and fifteen years in the Foreign Service. We've seen a lot of Marine houses—and a lot of wonderful birthday balls. I'm looking forward to this year's. But this is a very attractive house. Perhaps sometime you could show us around?"

I could tell the gunny was pleased. "You bet, ma'am. As soon as you get back from Juba, maybe the DCM and you could come over for a breakfast. And if the DCM would ever like to run with us (he smiled), why, it's most mornings at 0430."

"No thanks, Gunny. It's fine to be second to the ambassador in the office. But not on the road at 0430."

These were our last audible words. The strobe globe went on, the dry-ice machine began to breathe fog, and the music hit us. The volume was just a little lower than that of the 106s the previous day. For a moment, the gunny looked to be lip-synching to a song he didn't know. Then he shrugged. He asked Marj to dance. I asked Clayton. Others came out with us.

Good music. Fast. Soon the floor was full. The ambassador was right. People *had* needed to let off some steam. A few more dances, and I could see Marj was finishing a *real* drink—looked like something "south of the border." A *margarita?* A *piña colada?* Unusual for her. Then she was back on the floor. Marj had never liked sports, but she was well-coordinated and a very good dancer. She looked flushed and happy. The next song was a slow one. I asked her to dance.

"Having a good time?"

"Oh, yes! The Marines are so nice. Like our own family. Almost our own children. They make me feel so welcome. It feels good to dance again, too. We never do it in Washington. And then there're memories." She smiled. "Remember when we won the Charleston contest at 'The Basic School Ball?' Your commanding officer gave me an orchid."

It was a nice song. I knew the melody. I'd heard it from Sally's room the evening before. I began to listen to the lyrics:

A cool evening dance,
Listen to the blue grass band,
Take the chill from the air,
Till they play the last song . . .

Over Marj's shoulder I saw Sally and Sa'eed al-Masri dancing. I hadn't seen them come in. Sally wore a light-blue cotton dress, with a close-fitting bodice and thin straps going over her shoulders. Cut low in the back. Pleated panels gave the skirt a simple, yet elegant look. She and Sa'eed moved well. They were smooth, well-coordinated. Nothing fancy—but they looked as if they had a lot of moves and style in reserve. "Close, but not intimate," I said to myself. I glanced at Sa'eed. The strobe light gave his face an African mask quality. I looked—then looked again—at his hand, black, splayed out against Sally's bare back.

Another Marine asked Marj to dance. I went to look the buffet over. Sa'eed excused himself from Sally and came over to me. Together, we moved to the door to talk and for the fresh air.

I wasn't prepared for Sa'eed's opening remark. Jabbing a bony finger back toward the dance floor, he asked with asperity: "What's *she* doing there? Why is she with your embassy officer?" I explained. Sa'eed had heard of the weight-lifting episode.

"Do you know her?" I asked.

"A cousin—from the other branch of the Furi clan. Her father and mine . . . didn't always see eye to eye. A little like Somalia, you might say." Sa'eed seemed to shake off a thought.

In a more neutral tone he went on: "But my dear Mr. Chamberlain, *I'd* hoped to give one of the first Khartoum parties in your and Mrs. Chamberlain's honor. Still, this is a happy *faute de mieux*, wouldn't you say? From the poster over the bar—terrible posters one sees these days, no?—I gather you were yourself a Marine? Were you a Marine Guard, too, by any chance?"

"No such luck—or luxury," I replied. "I was a platoon leader first and then executive officer to a rifle company in the Mojave Desert in California—a little like Khartoum in the summer. And afterwards, I was sitting somewhere below the waterline of the *Okinawa*, a helicopter carrier, in the Pacific. I had a good time, though. Good experience. And these men deserve what they've got. They've worked hard. They're the best."

"I'm sorry to hear from my friend, Sally," Sa'eed broke in, "that you'll both be going to Juba. Miss Tolson will be missed. She's most attractive, wouldn't you say? So fresh, so . . . American! She admires you a great deal. You've served in Latin America? You should know that Latin Americans are like us Muslims in many ways. Our young women are always chaperoned. Mrs. Chamberlain is going along, too? You take my point? Ha, ha! Only joking, of course."

Sa'eed went on: "Where will you stay? The Equatoria Inn has an interesting floor show, but the rooms!"

I explained that we'd be staying at the A.I.D. compound.

Sa'eed nodded his approbation: "A fine place, I've heard. All the comforts of Southern California. A good tennis court. Maybe the best in Sudan, except, of course, that of Mr. Bogosian himself. We must go and play there someday? At Mr. Bogosian's, I mean. Such a fine gentleman! Everyone knows and likes him.

"And I also want you and Mrs. Chamberlain to visit my home town. It's near Jabal Marrah. You know, I am not only a simple protocol officer. When my father died—may God preserve him—*I* became paramount shaykh of the Fur people. Paramount shaykh at only twenty-two! Sounds romantic and important? I assure you, the reality is the reverse. All the time my people they come to see me, at home, in the office. Marriage, inheritance, land squabbles. I tell you, Josh—may I call you that?—applying ancient customs, *'urf*, we call it, to a transitional people in the modern world is most difficult."

I interrupted Sa'eed's breezy monologue: "Sa'eed, I gather Ambassador Farnsworth and the acting foreign minister did not see eye to eye during their meeting today?"

"Quite so. Nose-to-nose would be more like it, as American football fans say. Mr. Ambassador was very strong. I can't blame him. But he must believe—your government must believe—we are doing everything to find those behind the deaths of Mr. Hilverding and Minister Deng. And then maybe we will also find who writes those evil notices that our papers publish."

"Come on Sa'eed. You could stop these articles. Self-censorship, and all that; but the editors know the rules."

"No, no. The articles are bad. But only to a little degree. And why blame us poor Sudanese—when the mighty BBC tells the world all about the unhappy events in our country? But hardly a word about the race riots in Birmingham! Isn't the 'British disease' hypocrisy? Or masochism? Or homosexuality? Maybe now AIDS? Or mad cow disease? Maybe all of them together? Yes! Yes! All of them! That would be very nice! Ha ha!" Sa'eed laughed merrily at his own humor.

"Sa'eed," I asked, "since you know so well the manners and customs of your people, can you explain something that's been puzzling us?"

"One more question, yes, Joshua. Then I must go and ask Mrs. Chamberlain to dance. She has rhythm, I think," I looked over and saw Marj and Pete Valiant dancing a fast number. I thought how music seemed to draw Marj out. You could right away tell that she knew what she was doing—whether it was rock or regular ballroom dancing.

Next to them, Frank Greer and Aminat were dancing. Frank's shirt looked as if he'd been swimming in it. He was rising from a rock-and-roll crouch—the strobe lights seemed to interrupt drops of sweat in their trajectory, as he shook his big head, like a sperm whale breaching, I thought. Would a geyser of steam and water suddenly issue from a blowhole at his forehead? Aminat was dancing in a merry, abandoned way.

I said to Sa'eed: "At the embassy we can't figure out for the life of us what the writer in *al-Buq* was referring to when he said something called 'the Red Wind' would come and get us."

I thought Sa'eed hadn't heard. He seemed engrossed in watching the dancers. Then he turned to me. "The 'red wind,' you say? I know *The Red Barn*—a fine, scary story and play. But no, I've never heard of this 'red wind.' Wait—I know—maybe they mean the *hubuub*, the forty-day sandstorms our Egyptian brothers send us in exchange for the water from our Nile. No, Joshua," Sa'eed put his hand on my arm, "you just watch out for people who may not like you. Let anthropologists worry about 'red winds.' But the song is ending. Maybe you should see Shaykh al-Mughraibiy. Now there's a thought! Ha Ha! *If* he'd see you."

"You think this al-Mughraibiy would know?"

"Know? As I've learned to say from your Marines: 'Does a bear shit in the woods?' A wonderful expression, no? He understands all that old stuff."

"Can you tell me something about this al-Mughraibiy? I've heard he's in the Parliament."

"Joshua. I promised you one more question. One more answer. That is all. Mrs. Chamberlain will be impatient. She will think I do not know protocol. Duty and pleasure call. Ask your Mr. Kirby. Maybe *he* can go see him. Or, 'maybe a monkey will jump out of my butt!' Another great expression I learned here at your Marine House." Giggles this time.

He danced well with Marj, too. And I could tell she enjoyed dancing with him. A slow number. A fast one. I like dancing myself—but Sa'eed, I had to admit, was in another, higher, class.

I walked over to Sally to discuss our going to Juba the next day. She asked was I ready to start serving my "internal exile." I said a week or so in Equatoria sounded interesting—for sure a pleasant change. She asked was I bringing my tennis racquet. Phil Collins began to sing "One More Night."

"Dance with me," Sally whispered with sudden urgency. Taking my hand, she led me toward an open space on the dance floor. Behind us, at the edge of the floor, stood Kapecka. His mouth was half open. He looked frustrated. Like a special effect from *Jaws* that had just run aground.

"I turned him down a couple of times the last time the Marines had a party," Sally was saying. "He was pretty drunk. He wouldn't take 'no' for an answer. Finally, he sort of pulled me onto the floor. And one doesn't want to make a scene. So, hands like an octopus. Broke a hook off my dress. But I'd feel like a fool claiming 'sexual harassment' against a bottom-feeder like Kapecka. So thanks again, Galahad."

"Wasn't he the pure of heart one?" I asked.

We stopped talking and got into the rhythm of the song. It drew to an end. Several calls for "Encore!" One of the Marines rewound the tape.

"Again?" I asked Sally.

"*You're* asking this time?"

"You betcha."

Her palm was hard—I could feel the structure of her hand. Strong. Bones and tendons. I took her hand firmly in mine. She put her arm over my shoulder and stepped in closer to me. I was conscious of my other hand on her bare back. Smooth and firm. Of her hair against my cheek. Of her cheek against mine. Through the thin cloth of my sport shirt and slacks, it seemed I could feel the whole length of her body against mine. The inner faces of her thighs. The music continued. I became a little embarrassed. I swallowed. Backed off a little. The music ended. My breath was a little short.

"Thanks for the dance," Sally said in a flat tone, without looking up at me.

We were standing next to Frank and Aminat when Marj and Sa'eed came over. I began to make introductions when Sa'eed—breaking into some other language—shot a question to Aminat. Almost defiantly, she answered in English: "I am staying with the Bogosians and visiting the sisters, and the family approved the trip."

Sa'eed seemed to drop the subject. "Time to go!" he told Sally. "Can you believe it? Chiefs of protocol still have work to do tonight. But may I pick you up in the morning, and take you to the airport?"

"That's OK, Sa'eed," I replied: "Marj and I can pick Sally up— it's on the way. You know, chaperons, and all that."

He looked over at Sally. "Fine?

Sa'eed turned to Marj: "It was such a pleasure to meet you. And in the fall, as the weather cools, I can promise you more dances in the diplomatic community. You'll find Juba a pleasant change. You'll be amused by the Equatoria Inn. Watch over Josh carefully!" These were his last words to us. He took Sally's hand, and, ignoring Frank and Aminat, went to say goodnight to Sergeant Poe.

Marj watched him go. She turned to me: "He seems a Sudanese blithe spirit. But Aminat," she said to the younger woman, "what was that all about?"

Aminat said only: "Sa'eed's father and mine never were good friends—they were cousins of a sort. It's all very tribal and complicated." Her tone precluded any follow-up. Then she turned to me: "Mr. and Mrs. Bogosian said I might meet you tonight. They had a message for you. They hoped to meet you soon, perhaps for an afternoon of tennis."

"Accepted with pleasure—perhaps when we return from Juba? But how is it you know the Bogosians?"

"Mr. Bogosian used to do business with my father—hides, gum arabic, things like that. Then when my parents sent me to the sisters' school, I'd spend weekends often at the Bogosians'. They are wonderful. Like parents."

Frank and Aminat said goodnight. One more dance and we, too, said good-bye to Sergeant Poe.

TO FLY

13

I got up quietly and early for breakfast. Marj was sleeping well. She'd been happier last night than I'd seen her in a long time. We didn't have to go to the airport till nine, and I wanted to give her as long as possible. Also, I wanted a private talk with Mustafa.

As usual, he brought me a pot of tea and a smaller pot of hot milk. Also, two pieces of whole wheat toast. (Marj would laugh at the amount of peanut butter I loaded onto the bread surface. Said I looked like a hod carrier!) As Mustafa was turning to go back into the kitchen, I called him back.

"Mustafa," I asked, "do you remember the . . . the talisman . . . the amulet you gave me?" I put my hand to my neck and made a knotting motion. "And you said something about 'Red Wind'? Mustafa, *what is* the Red Wind? It's important. They speak about Red Wind in newspapers yesterday." (I hated it when I heard myself slipping into special English. Someone else speaking with my voice. No wonder, I thought, that American women who marry foreigners can end up sounding like Cassette No. 1, in a teaching-of-English-as-a-foreign-language course.)

Mustafa smiled and nodded. "Yes," he said, "*Ta'widh* important. We call it *tilasm*, too—like you do. But Red Wind very dangerous. Blow near Your Excellency. I look—and pray—and see still is blowing. Be careful still. Carry all time? Must *carry!*" he added almost urgently.

He's been talking to Pete Valiant, I thought.

"You know, Mustafa, I *do* carry it with me. I really do. It hasn't hurt me yet. I'll take my luck wherever I can get it. But what *is* the Red Wind? What does it do? Where does it come from? Would you want to speak to a translator? Someone from the embassy who speaks Arabic well? Mr. Dawkins?"

Mustafa shook his head emphatically. "Not language. Not speak of Red Wind. It hear and maybe come nearer. Just wear or take *ta'widh*. Soon, very important. Maybe I speak with someone. *Al-murshid al 'am*, he Sayyid al-Mughraibiy. I will ask. Maybe he tell. He know—know it all."

A bell rang in my mind. "Mustafa, is Sayyid al-Mughraibiy a member of Parliament?"

Mustafa seemed to smile. "He many things. Big man. He sometime in Parliament. But Parliament not matter, he more." Mustafa made an expansive gesture. Then after a moment added: "Shaykh al-Mughraibiy—he head of *al-Ikhwan al-Muslimiin*, Muslim Brothers you say? People afraid, but mistake. He good man."

Try as I might, I got no more from Mustafa on the Red Wind, nor would he say anything else about al-Mughraibiy. My hopes of a political—intelligence?—scoop, would have to wait. About this time, the ambassador and Sally and Marj joined me at breakfast. We began to speak of that morning's trip to Juba. It would be Sally's first as well.

After flying over the Atlantic, at night, at 38,000 feet, what a change to fly over central Africa, in the morning, at 8,000! The three of us sat in A.I.D.'s charter Cessna. Behind us, in the General Aviation hangar, we'd left 212 pounds of provisions and office supplies. But we still had food and drink enough for a month, I guessed.

George, the pilot, a Greek expatriate, was tough on overweight. He'd have been hell at a health spa, Sally had remarked. Each of us had been weighed. Then our luggage. Even my tennis kit. Then the supplies. The pilot had said—as the excess was trucked back to the warehouse, "We could actually carry more—maybe even all the supplies. But then we would have to land at every small strip along the Nile to refuel. And at one of these stops, maybe someone from Mr. Garang's organization—or one of the rival factions—would show up and say to me, 'Gee, thanks, for the picnic supplies. How about you and your friends joining us on a nice stroll to Uganda?'"

The air currents had not yet been stirred up by the sun. For the first few minutes after takeoff, as we gathered speed and elevation to fly south, the experience—the immediacy of it—was more like riding a car. The neighborhoods we'd left could be clearly made out. Even individual houses. As we crossed the Blue Nile, Sally called out: "Look! There's the Bogosians' compound! See? Past the Khartoum North bridge."

With my eyes, I crossed the bridge, and—following directions—turned right. Between the road and the river stood an institutional block of buildings. "That's the al-Kober political prison," Sally said. "Look further up, to the left." One couldn't miss it: from two thousand feet, the Bogosian compound looked like a small emerald. Inside it was a still smaller one. "That's their pool," explained Sally. "Maybe you can even see their grass court. Wait till you play on it. You'll never want to go back to clay or asphalt." But the compound was already out of sight. Khartoum was falling behind. The White Nile—with Juba at the other end—was just ahead.

The White Nile looked almost animate. You half expected to see the landscape convulse, as the river, with a twist of its coils, moved another million gallons of water northward. Sixty miles south of Khartoum, we overflew the Gezira project—the world's largest cotton plantation. More than a million hectares of irrigated land.

The pilot called out to us: "From up here it looks good, but down there—too much pesticide over the years, means a very bad environment; mosquitoes have developed a resistance to everything—bionic bugs—and so has the white fly. It makes the cotton sticky. Clogs up the cotton gins. The soil is waterlogged now, and the government has no money for the tile drainage needed."

From time to time we'd see a small town along the river. But as we flew further south, the plane swung briefly inland. "Don't want to get too close to Malakal," the pilot explained. "There are southern rebel troops down there. They've been moving across this area to the Nuba Mountains in South Kordofan—good guerilla territory. They want to get there before the rains end in November. Once the rains end, the tactical advantage shifts to the army. The rebels could take a shot at the plane. They've done it to small planes like ours in the past. Why? Maybe they're serious—the way they go after the river barges—want to disrupt north-south communications. Or maybe we're more in range than commercial planes are. They fly too high. Or maybe the rebels are just bored. Like a boy throwing a stone at a bird. But soon, we'll be able to drop down. Then I'll show you something interesting. Start watching out the left side in about ten minutes."

Marj and Sally were across the aisle—facing each other on the shady right-hand side of the plane, to be cooler on the flight down. If any of us were tired from the night before, it didn't show. No one wanted to nap. We were cheerful, exhilarated. We'd left Khartoum and its problems behind.

Marj took out her dramamine—she'd forgotten to take it at the house. I heard Sally ask, "Uppers or downers?" We all laughed. It seemed irresistibly humorous.

"Look down there," came the pilot's voice, "about eleven o'clock ahead of us."

Across the middle of a savannah there ran . . . a trace? It was as straight as if drawn with a ruler. It ended just below us. George made a slow descending arc. "See the digger?" he asked. At the end of the trace, an enormous piece of machinery stood—maybe two hundred feet high. Its base was swamped by vegetation. Near ground level, a conveyor arm projected to the side.

The pilot explained: "That machine is—was—the largest and most complicated earthmover of all time. The brontosaurus of all earthmoving machines. The French built it to dig a 300-kilometer canal across the Sudd—that's the marshland of Upper Nile Province. The canal was supposed to drain an area about as big as England, or larger. Results? More water for Lake Nasser, and more farmland for Upper Nile. That conveyor arm you see used to move the earth from the canal to an embankment along its top. For a road . . . "

"Why did the work stop?" asked Marj.

"A couple of reasons. The government didn't consult the local people. So they got scared. They thought the government was planning to steal their water, or that their rangeland would be reduced. They had a point there. The company didn't design the canal with any crossing points for animals. Also, the rebels—the S.P.L.A.—thought it was going to be a strategic weapon against them. You know, a big moat? So one day they came and shot the machine up and kidnapped the French work crews. After six months, they released them in Ethiopia. But no one wanted to come back here. Now the machine's just the world's biggest, most expensive trellis."

"It doesn't look like a swamp down there," said Sally, "more like grassland."

"It's the angle you look down from," answered the pilot. "Look out of the other side—where Mr. Chamberlain sits."

Sally unbuckled her seat belt and half rose to look through my window. I felt her hand touch my bare forearm as she reached to brace herself. Her blouse pushed taut just before me.

"Why, it's all shiny and wet down there."

"That's right. From Mr. Chamberlain's side you can see the sun reflecting off of the water between the reeds. It is almost solid swamp down there now. A contradiction in terms, maybe?" The pilot added: "Since the insurgency began, river traffic's down. The channels are filling in with water hyacinth, papyrus, and elephant grass."

There wasn't much conversation for the next two hours. The cabin started to get warm—and the air was getting bumpy. The pilot opened a cooler of Pepsis and offered them to us, taking one for himself. "There's also tea and coffee," he said. We all declined. I was beginning to regret my second cup of breakfast tea. I read for awhile—Gore Vidal's *Lincoln*. I napped.

12:30 P.M. We came upon Juba, just beyond two largish, cone-shaped hills. King Solomon's Mines country? I asked myself. The town did not look at all like Khartoum. Khartoum was an Arab desert city; Juba, an equatorial African town? village? Round, thatched dwellings, farmland all around—we could see some plots were being cultivated well inside the city limits. Not much urban-looking architecture. Some paved roads—but most were dirt, bulldozed through a hard-packed, reddish, laterite soil. I saw an obvious government complex toward the edge of town.

The pilot lined us up and brought the little plane tripping in on its toes. The runway was damp. Pools of water stood about.

When he popped the door, Africa welcomed us. After the valley-of-dry-bones air of northern Sudan, Juba's was overpowering. First, the moisture. You wanted to reach for a snorkel and face mask. Then, the green, vegetal, flowering odors. I thought of Washington's Botanical Gardens. Of vegetable markets. And there were other odors. Human ones. No doubt about it, there was life in Juba. Nothing like the thin, dry, Mars-like environment of Khartoum.

Rob McAndrew, an international development intern for A.I.D. met us. A former Peace Corps Volunteer in Chad, Rob was the first direct-hire American to return to the South after the rebel siege of Juba was lifted. His colloquial Chadian Arabic was easily understood here.

Also at planeside was the governorate's director of protocol—stocky, muscular. I missed his name, I was so distracted. There was his color, first of all. *Black*. The sort of total blackness that must have preceded the Lord's command in Gen. 1:3. Then his smile: his central and lateral incisors were filed to needle points. Had Bram Stoker come to Juba?

The protocol director was saying: " . . . and our governor, Lieutenant General Abdul Aziz bin Shakir, will receive you this evening at six o'clock. Then tomorrow morning, one of our development ministers will escort you on a field trip to Yei. Tomorrow evening, at 8 P.M., Lieutenant General bin Shakir will host a dinner in your honor at the Equatoria Inn. Welcome again to Juba. We wish you and your ladies a happy sojourn." His handshake was strong—like a workman's.

"Well done," I said to McAndrew as we drove out the airport gate, past some dug-in tanks, and headed for the A.I.D. compound. "You've put together a good program, fast."

McAndrew laughed. "You ought to see what I've rejected! Let me tell you, it's a buyer's market for aid donors in Equatoria. The government runs on it. So do all the local people—except for some Arab merchants and the subsistence farmers. The siege is over—but Juba's still pretty cut off to the north by land or water. And economic links with Kenya, Uganda, and the C.A.R. don't make up. You can get the luxuries, especially beer. But other cargoes don't offer enough profit for truckers to run the rebel blockade. So our payrolls, our residual projects, some help from the UNDP, the Swedes, the Norwegians, and especially the Kuwaitis keep it all going. Here's the compound. I'm really proud of it."

We stopped by the gate. Soldiers at a guardhouse rose to their feet and stood at attention. They'd been lying on the ground just inside the chain link fence, enjoying the shade of a flowering mimosa. All were Equatorian, or at least south Sudanese. A few had that Giacommetti, elongated look of Nilotics. Others were shorter, stockier, more the Central African, Bantu type. One had a string of protruding, cone-shaped scars across his forehead that, I recalled, identified him as a Nuer. A corporal presented arms, British-style, stamped his feet as if to warm them. "Welcome to Juba, *sah!*" He slapped the stock of his bolt action weapon. A Lee-Enfield! Had I seen its mate in the Presidential Palace?

I returned his salute: "Thanks for the military courtesy, corporal. At ease." A moment later, I looked back. Had I cast a spell? The guards looked asleep!

Inside the compound, it was as much greener than the rest of Juba as Juba was greener than Khartoum. Four ranch-style houses with high, generous screened porches occupied the compound's "high ground." Downhill was a recreation complex: pool, clubhouse, and tennis courts. McAndrew pointed out the compound's water treatment plant and generator shed.

"We're responsible for our own fuel, power, water. Like a space station. A kind of Biosphere. Our offices are across the road," he went on, "with the motor pool and workshops. The Foreign Service Nationals, the FSNs, would like to meet you. Maybe tomorrow? They're good people. Stuck with us even when several were killed by the former military governor on trumped-up charges of helping the rebels.

"I've put you all in one house, if that's OK. It used to be the director's. The other houses are vacant. Had all the furniture moved out. You're in the master bedroom—it has its own bath; the two other bedrooms share a bath. I've put Miss Tolson in the front bedroom. There's food and soft drinks and beer in the ice box. Why don't I leave you alone now? Your baggage is here.

"The houseboy will serve a light lunch, then you can nap, swim, play tennis? I didn't book you for dinner tonight, either. From what I've heard about Khartoum, I think you've earned a day's rest. I'll be back around five-thirty for the call on the governor. Dress is informal. Coat and tie, that is. I'll get out my suit—if the white ants have spared it."

Sally didn't play at tennis. She *played* tennis. I suppose I should have expected it. We warmed up briefly—she kept the ball nicely in play. Low and flat over the net. Not extending herself. Never rushing to get into position—she was always *there*. Never straining. Only connecting just right, with an easy, open, relaxed motion. The ball seemed to come back to me as if willed—as if on an elastic cord, like the paddle game. She *looked* good, too—white tennis skirt, sleeveless white blouse, hair tucked back under a visored cap. (Maybe you've been too tough on Kapecka, Chamberlain, I thought. Extenuating circumstances?) She won the toss.

"These are good," she said, stepping to the service line.

My mind must have wandered. A fragment of space debris hit just inside the center line. It was her serve. I stabbed with my backhand. An airball. Her next serve, into the ad court, cut the angle sharply. And out.

I stopped and called over the net: "Sally, serve just a little harder? Then we'll have nuclear winter and the end of vertebrate life on Earth." She didn't respond. Just walked to the service line, reloaded, and fired again. I got something on her third serve—but not enough. One more service; a love game.

Easy there, Josh, I said to myself, get into the rhythm. You've not played in two months. Remember Bobby Riggs and Margaret Court Smith? Unfortunately, I also remembered Bobby Riggs and Billie Jean King. It's a friendly game. Don't try to overpower her. Remember: form, position, follow-through.

I still lost the second game.

The trouble was that for Sally it *wasn't* a friendly game. It was competition. And she was out to win. Her expression was stony. She looked intent. Pitiless. Gray-eyed Pallas Athena.

But I hadn't stayed near the top of Bates's tennis ladder by gracefully deferring to competitors—even ladies. *I* didn't want to lose either.

Get with it Chamberlain. Rush the net . . . women players prefer the baseline . . . try some aggressive approach shots . . . angle your volleys . . . you can apologize *later* for those big serves. I pulled the set out, 7–5; the second set, 6–4. By then, a blister on my right thumb had burst and was bleeding. The soles of my feet? Those of an apprentice Samoan fire-walker. Somehow, Sally still looked strong. Quit while you're ahead, I told myself. While you're alive, I added.

"A swim?" I suggested.

In a bathing suit, Sally's shoulders looked broader than they did in office or tennis clothes. The suit was just short of immodest. Metallic red in color and cut high on her hips. Its material was just a little heavier than that of racing Speedos. Wet, it clung to her body as if sprayed on. I thought, Suspension in water seems to round out a woman's body. As we stood in the pool talking, I had to keep bringing my eyes back to Sally's face. Later, I did a few laps with her—but swimming was never one of my sports. When I left the pool, Sally was still at it. She swam the way she played tennis. Hard, stylish, continuous strokes.

We drove to the governor's office in Rob McAndrew's Chevy Blazer. The building was one of those I'd seen from the air. Two stories high, it stood by itself, on a hill, with bare, hard-packed earth all about. No roads led up to the Governorate. You simply drove straight toward the entrance—from wherever you came in sight of it.

"Not a bad building," said McAndrew, "built with EEC aid—but by a local contractor. That explains the one little drawback: no bathrooms. After inauguration they had to contract separately for a line of privies in back. Don't know what the governor does, though. I can't imagine the great bin Shakir lugging all his medals over to a four-holer. Do you suppose governors rate carryout service?" To this Rob quickly added, "Excuse me." We all laughed.

Our protocol friend was waiting. His name, I learned, was Yedol Furj. How ever to remember *that*? I wondered. He seemed pleased—relieved?—we were on time.

"So good of you to be here at just six o'clock. So good we can always count on our American friends." He tapped the face of his watch. "General bin Shakir is, after all, a military man. A most distinguished Arab, er, Sudanese general." He smiled. Yes, my memory was correct. His four front teeth were very white, and very pointed. Were his eyes on my throat?

We waited ten minutes in General bin Shakir's outer office. Furj worked hard to make conversation: no, he did not come from Juba, but from the Zande country far to the west. He'd been to England but not the United States. Someday he hoped. His master's degree. A friend had traveled on an A.I.D. grant to Washington, D.C. A most beautiful city. Furj kept glancing at his watch.

A light bulb came on over the general's door. Furj quickly rose. A young functionary came out. A southerner, about eighteen, smooth-faced, almost feminine-looking. Furj introduced him as the governor's P.A. "Personal assistant," he explained.

Bin Shakir was fiftyish. Light-complected for a Sudanese. Short-cropped, graying hair. A military bearing. Fit-looking. McAndrew was right: bin Shakir wore several rows of decorations, plus some honest-to-goodness metal ones. I noticed something else: on each side of his face, two deep scars ran diagonally from the cheekbone to the corner of his jaw.

"You are welcome to Equatoria, Excellency. If we had had more advance notice, I could have come myself to the airport to meet you. We had a very good visit with Ambassador Farnsworth last year. We gave him several copies of our development plan. You have studied it, naturally?" (I lied, said yes.)

"Good. It is all there, what we need. The number of scholarships, the number of Jeep Cherokees, all that. There are many other development issues that my regional ministers are eager to follow up with you. I told them that, for certain, the American minister-counselor would be bringing answers to the questions that we presented last year to the United States government."

I answered it was fortunate, thanks to Mr. McAndrew's office, that the exchange of information was so open and continuous between our embassy and the provincial government in Juba. To change the subject, I asked for his assessment of the security situation.

"Security?" The general replied: "Perfect. The siege of Juba that your papers spoke of was much exaggerated. Anyhow it ended when the dry season came. There are maybe still some small difficulties in remote southern regions, whose governors have been not so successful to win the hearts and minds of their people. But mostly the rebels also fight among themselves: the so-called General John Garang against the so-called General Riek Mechar!"

Sally asked: "Excellency, as a soldier you must have known Garang for many years. What do you think of him?"

General bin Shakir did not acknowledge Sally's presence. Looking at me, he answered: "Garang was a smart young officer. But no discipline. No respect. Spoiled by foreign military advisors. An Arab officer do well? Colonel Fields—he was senior British instructor at the Academy—say, 'Not bad. You get maybe a passing grade.' John Garang write his name on the paper, and Colonel Fields read the paper to the class. You think Alexander the Great—Julius Caesar—write the paper! My brother was in 'Colonel' Garang's class at the Academy.

"And when Garang he get back from the United States (the general's voice rose), what he need a Ph.D. for? His head was as big as a *gu gu*—that is a grain storage jar; you will see many tomorrow on the way to Yei. You hear maybe Arabs saying Israel is the *rabiibat* of the United States? The 'spoiled child' of America? John Garang, too, is *rabiibat* of the United States. And maybe the two *rabiibat* get together and plot against our Arab nation? Maybe with others' help, too—Egypt? Zambia? Eritrea? That would not surprise me at all. Same like in 1955 to 1972, during the first part of civil war."

Under pressure, it seemed as if General bin Shakir's English was losing some of its polish. There was real grievance in his voice. He was saying: "America and Britain do much for Sudan. But they love the southerners too much. Why do you not make justice for *your* southerners, then come to talk about south Sudan. All time your Carter Center, or your World Council of Churches, or Archbishop of Canterbury try to mediate or set up religious schools. We Sudanese do not need foreigners to tell us how to worship God. We Sudanese have the Qur'an. Why does the Pope come to Sudan? When Italy is still full of Communists? *We* have no Communists. President Numeiry shot them all! (Bin Shakir gave a sort of chuckle.) And why doesn't Canterbury get people to go to church in *his* country. In England no one pray. I go there, and I see. But *I* pray five times a day."

As—rather somberly—we took our leave, I asked the governor what the large, framed piece of calligraphy over his desk said. He replied: "That is the *shahhada*, the article of faith for all True Believers: '*Laa ilaaha illa-laahu, wa muhammada-rrasulu llah,*' That is to say, 'There is no god but God, and Muhammad is *the* Prophet of God.' "

Driving back to the compound, I said to McAndrew, "The general must be a real hit with his Equatorian clients."

"You might say," answered Rob dryly. "Once he told me Equatorians, men and women alike, were good for only one thing—you can imagine what that was. But he at least practices what he preaches. He's got two young Equatorian wives here, and an Arab wife in Khartoum. She never comes to Juba. And did you see his *ephebe*? The tender, androgynous P.A.?"

We lay in bed, Marj and I. Khartoum seemed much further than seven hundred miles away. We'd turned off the air conditioner. An occasional breeze through the open, screened windows seemed to bring with it—from the south—the scents and sounds of a dark continent. A touch of verbena? The tree frogs kept up their chattering. One could barely discern the muffled thump of the generator. On the roof, I heard the sounds of soft rain falling. Light from the perimeter security lamps and from those at the recreation site filtered into the room.

I rose up on my elbow and turned toward Marj. I put a hand on her forehead, stroked it. I kissed her, softly, then more firmly. Stroked the hair back from her forehead.

"A nice day, sweetheart?" I asked. My fingers slid down toward the neckline of her nightgown.

She took my hand and kissed it, then said: "It *was* a nice day, Josh. But I have a terrible headache, really. I hope I'll feel better tomorrow." I opened my mouth to say something. Thought better of it. I sighed. I kissed her goodnight. She snuggled up close to me, but it was a long time before I slept.

THEIR HEARTS AND MINDS

14

I went running at 0600 the next morning. The air was cool and fresh. Out past the gate—no salute this time. Some guards were asleep. Those awake reclined around a teapot. They smiled and waved. They looked . . . amused? entertained? I left the road and took a slight down-hill gradient south, through open countryside. I thought: It's Africa in front of me, all the way to Capetown. The plain was crisscrossed by footpaths and cattle trails. There was no chance of getting lost—the A.I.D. compound and its American flag could be seen from miles away.

A smoky tang was in the air as I passed a tribal enclosure. It came from many small fires over which discs of unleavened Arab bread were baking. Peaked thatched roofs showed over the enclosure's mat and mud wall. I passed women foraging for kindling, boys and girls driving cattle to the day's grazing. As I passed groups of workmen, I gave them a thumbs-up and pointed to their T-shirts—"Chicago Bulls," "USA World Cup 1994," and a faded "Washington Redskins Superbowl 1992." America's number one export to Africa was not machine tools, or air-craft, or automobiles—it was second-hand clothing! I wondered: did Washington realize that used clothes were our most successful effort in public diplomacy?

I heard the children laugh and shout *"khawajah!"* as I ran by. Sudan's great basketball player, Manute Bol, I reflected, was once asked what *"khawajah"* meant. After a moment's reflection, he hit it on the head: *"White dude,"* he replied.

Everyone appeared happy to see me. It's human nature, I thought, to feel amusedly superior to the village idiot. In Russia, he's "The Fool of the World"; in Africa? "the Western jogger." By 0715, as I sprinted the last 200 yards into the compound, my U.S.M.C. sweatshirt showed signs of a good workout. I felt better. I also felt, somehow, that Juba now belonged more to me.

I felt good all through breakfast. A merry occasion. Rob had invited us to his house. His wife, a pretty Vietnamese whom he'd met in Washington, D.C., had prepared almost a logging camp's bill of fare: Ham. Fried eggs. Bacon. Pancakes. Syrup. French fries. Cheese, jam, margarine, butter ("real butter," she called it), and peanut butter. Also tropical fruit salad: mangoes, pineapples, grapefruit, papayas. Plus tea, coffee, and fresh orange juice.

Marj sat at one end of the table and I at the other. Sally was at my left. We travelers were still in the grip of a post-Khartoum high. Both women looked so pretty, and fresh, and happy. How nice just to look over at Sally—to follow the changing expressions on her face as she spoke and laughed with our hostess. I thought: *Verweile doch, du bist so schön!*

We were still at the breakfast table at eight-thirty when Yedol Furj came to take us to Yei. With him was the regional minister of development, Mr. William Aru Bol, and Dr. Hasid Vinnd, the UNDP's resident expert for agriculture and animal husbandry. Bol was tall and massive; Dr. Vinnd, a foot shorter, looked intense, high-strung.

Minister Bol, I quickly learned, had been sent by U.S.A.I.D. to "the Florida State University in Gainesville" for a master's degree. He'd studied entomology and pest control and was "keen" to return for his Ph.D. He had an application—and with these words he half presented me with a manila folder. Perhaps U.S.A.I.D. had a grant?

Dr. Vinnd looked annoyed. He had received his *doctorate* in Bombay. He'd been hoping the U.S.A.I.D. would enable him to continue study in "the United States of America at the *post*-doctoral level." He had written to "the Office of the Dean, the Louisiana State University"; he was particularly interested in sugar cane . . . first-class letters of recommendation . . . he, too, had with him a well-documented application. I took both files, promising to study them later.

Wouldn't they both sit down, I asked. Have some breakfast with us? Yedol Furj looked at his watch and shook his head. He suggested we had better be on our way, so as to reach Yei before noon.

Sally and Marj and I excused ourselves to go get ready. From the porch, I could hear Dr. Vinnd's quavery Indian accent: "Of course, *I* will ride with His Excellency. He and I are both diplomats. I represent the secretary-general of the United Nations, and my doctorate of philosophy . . ." I paused to listen.

Aru Bol's deeper voice cut in, "But you must not forget, *Mr.* Vinnd, *I* represent the prime minister of Sudan; and *I* am a minister. Please correct me if I am wrong, Mr. Furj? You are our protocol expert (this last in a comradely tone)." Silence from Furj.

Dr. Vinnd's voice (higher-pitched, more quavery than before): "*Mister* Aru Bol, Mister Furj, I have no self-respect for you both."

I walked out on the lawn. Marj and Sally were admiring the lush plantings around the McAndrew house. It was then I noticed Furj and his experts hadn't come alone: two Army Land Rovers stood in front of our house. (No, I said to myself, change that to "weapons carriers.") The Land Rovers were the stretched model. In the flatbed of each, twinned .50-caliber machine guns stood mounted on a universal pivot.

Troopers were buttoning up tarps over the barrels and trigger mechanisms. Rob McAndrew was talking to a lieutenant in crisp, well-pressed camouflage fatigues. His paratroop boots were spit-shined. He was no southerner. Nor were the ten equally well-turned-out men he had with him.

"I've explained to the lieutenant," said Rob, "we appreciate the governor's sending a squad from his own guard. But we don't need a military escort for Yei. In the bad times, the rebels would even penetrate into Juba. But for weeks there's not been so much as an incident on the roads. The governor's been saying the road's clear; this time I believe him."

"I do not wish to inconvenience," the lieutenant said, turning to me, "but orders are orders. Would His Excellency wish himself to call General Bin Shakir? The general says we are here for your greater comfort and security." (He's been listening to the airlines too much—but not bad English, I thought.)

Rob tried to call. Of course, the phone lines didn't work. Yedol Furj was relieved. He clearly hadn't wanted, even at second hand, to seem to question a Bin Shakir order. "We should really be off," he said, nervously tapping his watch face again.

In the Foreign Service you develop empathy for your fellow bureaucrat. Furj was in a jam. I took pity on him. "Let's just go," I said to McAndrew.

We took two A.I.D. Blazers. I was interested to see Yedol Furj had put me, Rob McAndrew, Aru Bol, and himself together in one Blazer; in the other, he had placed Marj, Sally, and a downcast Dr. Hasid Vinnd. The lieutenant's Land Rover took the lead. When the lieutenant rolled out the gate, the Equatorian guards, I noted, almost levitated to salute.

Our motorcade turned onto the dirt main road. We accelerated sharply. The lieutenant seemed bent on throwing off aerial pursuit. Through a rooster-tail of dust, I could see the troopers in the back of his vehicle hanging on for their life. Our Blazers followed as best they could. The second Land Rover brought up the rear.

Whenever we reached open country, the cars would execute a sort of World War I naval maneuver: our single file would turn into a rank; fanlike, we'd speed across the savannah, side-by-side. But mostly it was follow-my-leader. We breathed dust from the lead car; Marj, Sally, and Vinnd from both of us. Our "follow-car" was rarely visible.

Halfway to Yei, our "convoy" dropped anchor at Ayood, a Murle village and the site of a training center run by the Episcopal Church, U.S.A. And the site-to-be of my sternest test ever as a Foreign Service officer!

A young American lay volunteer showed us his pupils' work: mimeographed literacy texts in Murle and Ndogo; wood carvings, many of them religious—some nice *creche* figurines; an electrical workshop, a seed-testing site.

"And now there's the inauguration," he added.

"Of what?" I asked.

"Our new hygiene project."

With this he led the way to an old-fashioned-looking outhouse, with separate wings for men and women. The men's wing had a urinal, as well as toilet stalls. A crowd of teenage boys and girls stood on the packed earth in front of the door—on which was stenciled a trousered man's silhouette. As we came up, the student body began to clap and chant over and over: "We-e-elcome USA!"

"You will be the first to use the facility," the lay volunteer explained. "Anyway you wish," he added, perhaps seeing my confusion. The clapping and chanting faltered and stopped. Silence.

What to do? I'd never had excessive personal modesty—it wouldn't in any case have survived the Marine Corps—but I just didn't know if I could manage as nonchalantly as African men. Even on a crowded street, you'd see them turn their back to pedestrians and address the nearest wall.

I addressed the urinal. Not a sound from the crowd. I tried to avoid eye contact with the students facing me just beyond the wire mesh that extended chest-height to the ceiling. A hundred pairs of eyes were fixed on me. I imagined myself alone in the Maine woods. There was an expectant hush. Oh, for some easier challenge! I thought. Why not just die for my country? Maybe the humor helped? Because finally, as patriotism struggled with shame, patriotism won out. As the zinc gutter and drain gave its proof that the inauguration had taken

place, there were cries of approval and applause from the boys, prolonged ululations from the girls.

As I stepped out, I knew I was blushing. To cover up, my embar-
rassment, I loudly announced: "An excellent facility." Then added:
"Fit even for a military governor-general." Rob's translation got a big
laugh. (I saw Furj fasten the points of his little white teeth in his lower
lip. But he succeeded in keeping his face expressionless.)

Finally, we saw the improved *gu-gus*—large earthenware jars used
to store grain. I began to picture John Garang as a sort of revolutionary
"Jack Pumpkinhead." It was explained to us that traditional "M1A1"
gu-gus sat on the ground, or just above it on four short, flimsy legs. The
goats had learned to butt the jars over; rodents climbed in, and storage
losses could be as high as 50 percent. The new "super" gu-gus ("M1A2")
were two or three times as large. They stood on three stout wooden
pilings, waist-high above the ground. Their height and size protected
them from goats. Another improvement: discs, like rat-catchers on ships'
cables, encircled the legs—keeping rats and mice out.

Sally pointed to the gu-gus' legs, and to the steep thatched roof
that protected the gu-gus' sun-baked adobe from the rain. Out loud
she wondered: "Triffids? Planning their comeback?"

We made one more stop. From Ayood, the road began to climb as
we entered the foothills of the Imatong Mountains. An hour out of Yei,
we turned off the dirt road to follow a track uphill. We were to visit a
teak plantation begun with A.I.D. financing twenty years ago. The trees
grew thick and straight and tall up the hillside. Via a series of
switchbacks, we climbed and kept climbing. I looked at Rob, then down
at my watch, then over at Mr. Furj. Rob nodded. "It's worth it," he
replied.

Fifteen minutes more brought us to a clearing near the top. At
the further edge of the clearing, the hill dropped off sharply. We got
out and walked to the edge of the drop-off. The sun was to our backs.
We were maybe four thousand feet above the plain before us. I hadn't
realized how steadily we'd climbed since leaving Juba.

"Yei's there," said Rob, pointing down to the valley ahead. The
rain of the previous night had cleared the air and scrubbed the landscape. The late morning sun drew up moisture from fields and forests.
We overlooked a landscape of green and gold, of luminous, aureal
sfumato. Columns of smoke rose from unseen villages. Silence.

"A nice picnic site," said Rob.

I looked toward Sally. She had on a yellow blouse and a green
skirt. In that light her hair, her clothes, her complexion, the tall slim
trees framing her—their soft matching colors—she seemed part of the

landscape. I half expected to see her suddenly engulfed in bark, leaves, branches—transformed. My mind searched for a term—I got it: *dryad*.

Sally wet her lips. "It has *Tao*," she said in a whisper. She looked at me. Our eyes met. I really *saw* her. My heart sped into a sharp curve, slid into a four-wheel drift.

It was market day in Yei, administrative center for the Equatorian district of the same name. The police commissioner, a colonel, was waiting at a small administrative building. He was in his midforties and was tall and heavy for an Arab. Under his arm he carried a swagger stick, tipped by a 20 mm brass casing.

Rob had urged that we visit the market: "Great local atmosphere," he'd said. When the colonel heard our request, he indifferently agreed. He and some guards, plus our own escort, would accompany us.

It was truly an "African shopping mall." Spread over several acres of hard-packed earth, hundreds of small merchants displayed their wares; thousands of customers looked them over. Occasionally you saw—and heard—a purchase contentiously arrived at. Most items lay spread on the ground—on top of newspapers or display cloths. The sellers were mostly women, who rented one- or two-meter-square market plots from the town. The women squatted on their haunches behind their wares, their arms around their knees. There was a lot of chatter from one stand to the next.

A short walk soon made clear that the marketplace had theme and structure, like an Arab *suq*. Or like a Safeway, for that matter. There were departments, sections, aisles. A grid of wide, dirt paths defined the major shopping areas. Smaller paths divided these into specialized sections and subsections. Some displayed only rusty cooking and eating utensils, or dried, jerked meat, or vegetables and fruits—most of them unknown to me. Some displays consisted solely of transistor batteries, or plastic buckets and laundry cord. There seemed to be nothing you couldn't buy—so long as the item was food from Equatoria, or manufactured in the Peoples' Republic of China, or secondhand. (Rob advised me always to be wary of the batteries. They were used in these parts as a sort of "alternate currency." But what with the heat, and the passage of time, most were dead before ever having been used.)

I turned to ask Rob: "Wouldn't it be a good idea to asphalt the market area? During the rainy season it must be like a buffalo wallow!"

"We already proposed the idea to the police commissioner," Rob answered. "Even had some self-help money for the project. You know what he said? 'They're southerners; they live in the mud. Besides, they're all women.'"

At the end of one heavily traveled lane—what Bloomingdale's would call "driveways" or "power aisles"—we found the basket *suq*. It was part of the greater "Household Wares–Cleaning Supplies" complex. The baskets were striking. They came in various shapes for various uses. In all, though, imaginative geometric designs of black and red and brown were incorporated into tight, stylish weaves. ("Some look like little gu-gus," Sally told Marj.) One woman, in particular, had a good selection. Sally and Marj together picked out ten or twelve baskets—ideal presents, they thought, for friends in Khartoum, or friends and family back home.

"Baskets are some of the authentic folk art in Africa," said Sally. "None of the fakery that's universal with masks. I *mean* universal! And these are about the nicest baskets I've seen anywhere."

"How much?" Marj asked the saleswoman, speaking slowly and pointing to one of the baskets.

"*Talatiin jnaih kul waahid,*" was the reply.

"That's thirty pounds each—about seven dollars. Offer her ten pounds," suggested Rob.

"*'Ashra?*" he said to the woman.

"*Abadan . . . khamsa w'ishriin?*"

"That's twenty-five. We're making progress," he said to Marj and Sally. "Better stick by our offer for one more round, at least. Ten would be fair."

"*'Ashra,*" he repeated firmly.

The colonel walked over and heard Rob's last exchange. He waved his aide-de-camp over (a police lieutenant). Pointing to the baskets he said, "*Ungul al silal hadhuul lissayaaraat*".

"He's telling the lieutenant to take the baskets to the cars," said Rob.

The order was quickly carried out by several enlisted men. The colonel started to walk toward the vehicles; he seemed to be saying the tour was over. Aru Bol, Vinnd, and Furj also headed for the cars.

"Isn't someone going to pay her?" asked Marj. The woman had risen to her feet. Loudly she complained to the other basket-sellers around her. They also began to protest. Voices rose.

The colonel was perhaps forty yards in front of us. He looked to our military escort, then gestured with his swagger stick toward us.

Four of the soldiers walked back to us. They said something abrupt to the woman.

"Too fast, I can't understand," said Rob.

"You don't have to know Arabic," I answered. "I'll translate. They're saying, 'Shut your trap, old biddy, or we'll shut it for you'!"

Whatever it was, the woman wouldn't have it. More shouts. A crowd began to gather. Rob said, "I think it would be prudent for us to follow the colonel. Here." He put two 100-pound notes on the woman's cash box. She looked down, fell silent. But no one else seemed to notice. The shouts grew louder. I heard voices in unison repeating "*Aaarab-kharab.*" Others hissed "*Ruus, ruus*" at us.

"They're calling us 'Russians,' " said Rob.

"They haven't heard the Cold War's over? That Russians are good guys now?" I replied. "But don't tell them it's *Americans* who're stealing their baskets!"

I heard something else. A musical hum was rising from the crowd. The kind of sound that students make when they want to disrupt classroom order, but don't want the teacher to pick them out. I'd heard the tune in Khartoum. Some bolder spirits began to sing the words.

Rob looked at me. "Recognize the song?" he asked quizzically.

"Yes," I replied.

"But do you know what it *really* is?"

"I heard it in Khartoum, and it ain't the Wisconsin Fight Song. Let's get out smartly before John Garang makes a guest appearance to lead the chorus."

We walked quickly toward the car. We could hear and sense the crowd behind us. The colonel was waiting. The singing was quite distinct now. The whole marketplace seemed to be serenading us. "The Robert Shaw Chorale tours Africa," I thought. The colonel watched the crowd without expression. Now and then he'd tap his boot with his swagger stick. With it he motioned that we should mount our Blazers. Furj, Aru Bol, and Vinnd were already in their seats, with baskets piled all around them. They waved, a little frantically, I thought, urging us to get in quickly.

As I looked to the head of our little motorcade, my heart sank, too. The Army Land Rovers were there, side by side. Our military escort had taken the canvas wraps off the twinned .50-caliber machine guns. The weapons were loaded and manned. A paratrooper stood, legs apart, behind each gun, both hands on the grips. The four gun muzzles played negligently over the crowd. As if looking for someone? The lieutenant was smiling. One of the troopers—the ammunition handler—

pointed the index finger of his free hand at the crowd. "Tat-tat-tat-tat-tat!" came from his lips.

We exited the marketplace fast. By some miracle, we left behind only some animal—no human—road kill.

We sat quietly through lunch. The colonel and the lieutenant spoke to each other in fast, Dongolawi-accented Arabic. Even Rob couldn't make out much of what was being said. The colonel seemed pleased, though, with my "hostess present," Robert Cameron's picture book, *Above Washington*. In return, he impassively presented us with some more baskets. A sense of humor? Had they been "liberated," too? I wondered.

The best news came after lunch: Our pilot had flown the Cessna to Yei—Marj, Sally, Rob, and I could return to Juba by air. We were full of apologies to Furj, Aru Bol, and Dr. Vinnd. "Unfortunately the plane is now only configured for four seats . . . "

When the soldiers heard we were flying back to Juba, they mounted their vehicles and immediately drove off. No waiting to escort the others back to Juba. For all the soldiers cared, Furj & Co. could sign up for John Garang's next walking tour of East Africa.

"ET IN ARCADIA EGO"

15

A different set of guards was on duty at the A.I.D. compound. The route-order (sloppy) Nilotics were gone. In their place appeared to be another squad of General bin Shakir's private guard. The same "cammies," the same airborne boots, plus automatic weapons: German G-2s. The salute they gave me as we turned in the gate was the real thing. There was no cookout in progress. The summer campers had been sent home.

"Why the first string?" I asked Rob.

"Beats me," he replied, and went over to talk to the captain in charge. A few minutes of conversation. The captain spoke much less English than our lieutenant of today. He was older. In his thirties. Heavy in the shoulders. A cauliflower ear. There were several medal ribbons sewn over his left breast pocket.

Rob came back: "He keeps on saying that the governor sent him, and no, there is no new threat that he can speak of. 'Everywhere the rebels are in full flight.' The governor sent him, and . . . *da capo*."

"Sounds familiar," I said. "The Germans have an expression for it, '*Befehl ist Befehl*,' 'Orders is orders.' I think I'll wash up, take a nap, then dress for our gala with the governor at the Equatoria Inn. Do you know what the ambassador told me? He said I could buy a bottle of champagne, but mustn't go upstairs."

Rob asked if, in addition to the FSNs, I could also meet that afternoon with some of his local business and government contacts. Several were bureaucrats or agriculturists who had studied in the United States. He said they wanted to talk business, but that I might find their political views interesting, too. I had to agree, even though Sally had suggested tennis. The exasperation I felt at Rob's request surprised me.

Furj got us to the inn at precisely eight o'clock. It was a U-shaped, bungalow-style building, with a courtyard in the middle. A bamboo fence blocked public view of the inn and its courtyard. We parked just inside the gate. Furj showed us to a long "head" table in the courtyard. Thirty smaller tables sat on hard-packed earth, around a cement dance floor. Near the dance floor, some trees were decorated with strings of colored lights. There were only a few customers, mostly Arab-looking men in their shirtsleeves. They were drinking beer. One or two servant girls shuffled about, waiting on tables. It looked more like the end, not the beginning, of an evening.

I wondered if we were overdressed. I'd worn a dark blue suit, white shirt, black shoes, and a Bates College tie. Red, with the round *Academia Batesiana* seal. Marj was fresh and pretty-looking in a lavender dress, high neck, midlength sleeves. The color of the dress favorably set off her milky complexion and light-brown hair.

Sally, I thought, looked tired. I knew she'd taken a swim after we returned from meeting with Rob's local contacts. She wore a simple beige dress, brown pumps (no stockings), and carried a small brown suede handbag. Her only color accent came from a thin gold chain necklace from which hung her name, "Sally," in gold Arabic lettering. Her brown hair—or was it dark blonde?—was parted on the right. Sometimes, I noticed, she parted it in the middle.

By 8:30 P.M., perhaps a quarter of the tables were full. We'd all had a beer or two: Golden Tusker, from Kenya, well-chilled and excellent. By 9:00 P.M., we'd had one or two more. Perhaps half of the tables were full. Many more Equatorians—or at least southerners—had arrived. The unyielding wooden folding chairs on which we sat were beginning to assert themselves: status reports came in from our lumbar areas. At least I'd remembered to use lots of mosquito repellent!

At 9:15 we heard sirens. A motorcade swerved into the Equatoria lot. A cluster of white *thawbs* emerged from the darkness. It made its way toward the head table. Furj made the introductions: the Kuwaiti aid director and his staff and several Arab merchants; with them—mostly in Western clothes—had come a grouping of regional ministers, their deputies, directors general, and commissioners—primary education, veterinary medicine, game management, public sanitation, electric power. I reflected on the size of the government payroll.

Someone had begun to play a tape: Perry Como sang the last bars and lines of "Jingle Bells," then began, "Home for the Holidays." I raised an eyebrow at Marj, who sat to my left, across an empty reserved seat from me (the governor's?). "There's Christmas spirit even in Equatoria?" I asked. Rob explained: "I should have told you. It's always the same beginning tape. We here call it 'Jungle Bells,' and there are always the same lights in the trees."

The music came from speakers set at either end of our table, and in the trees near the courtyard. Real waitresses, in red tube tops and miniskirts, now appeared, and were making their way around the tables. On each they set a bottle of Dewar's White Horse Scotch. *Three* bottles were placed on ours. Also some bottled water, and buckets of ice. Rob said: "Water's OK, but skip the ice." Furj ordered the glasses to be served all around.

Furj excused himself. After a minute he came back to say the governor would arrive "soon."

Nine-thirty P.M. The tables in the courtyard all looked full. By now, about two-thirds of those present, I estimated, were Southerners. The waitresses were already beginning to swap empty bottles of Dewar's for full ones.

Marj thought the chairs were becoming less uncomfortable. I agreed. Added something about not drinking on an empty stomach. Marj and Sally exchanged some confidence. They both laughed. Someone turned the music up.

Nine-forty P.M. More and much louder sirens. The governor this time. He marched out of the dark, in his dress uniform, swagger stick under his arm. Blue jacket, with a high collar, *fourragere* over the left shoulder, frogs and gold braid everywhere. Tight blue trousers with a wide red stripe. Boots and spurs. The display area—his left breast—was shingled with medals and decorations. With him (in service uniforms) came the gendarmerie commander, the garrison commander, and the police commissioner. Arab northerners all. The southern "P.A." brought up the rear. I thought of Chesterton:

> Strong gongs groaning as the guns boom far,
> Don John of Austria is going to the war,
> Stiff flags straining in the night-blasts cold
> In the gloom black-purple, in the glint old gold,
> Torchlight crimson on the copper kettle drums,
> Then the tuckets, then the trumpets, then the cannon, and he comes!

The music stopped. The Sudanese national anthem came over the speakers. Everyone rose. There followed an instrumental version of "The Star Spangled Banner." I wondered how they'd gotten it. I stood at attention, and put my hand over my heart, in the citizen's salute.

"An interesting visit to Yei, I understand, Excellency?" asked the governor, as the food came on the table. "I heard of the display of insolence toward America from my colleague. I regret it—but that is one of penalties of being the only superpower. Do you not agree? Even I may not be popular with some elements in Juba!" The governor laughed good-humoredly at such a preposterous idea. He went on: "My colleague, though, is very able man. He really know his people, how to handle them. These Africans—like children, they only understand firmness. You now see why I gave you my good military escort."

The governor paused for a deep swallow of Dewar's. A little trickled down the corners of his mouth. He wiped it off with the back of a hand and went on: "I, too, have much experience in these parts, believe me! In the first Civil War, I was platoon and company commander right here in Juba. Lieutenant first, then captain. One time I almost captured the rebel leader, General Joseph Lagu. Instead he shoots me (bin Shakir pointed to his side) *here.* Jungle wounds very bad. But I was lucky. Too strong. Years later I see Lagu when he is vice president. I tell Lagu, 'Ha, Ha! Your bullets strong, but my *rih*—that means 'wind'— is stronger.' He agree. He say, 'Only really first-class bullet can kill you, Colonel *Khirtiit.*' That means 'rhinoceros,' that is my *kunya*—what do you say, my . . . "

"Nickname?" I suggested.

"Yes. Nickname. But you and Madame and others must eat now. Please. Then music, and maybe an Equatorian show?" He nudged me playfully.

A waitress brought plates for each of us. Other waitresses brought platters of food. Soon all available space on our table was taken up. Hunks of lamb, halves and quarters of chicken, chunks of . . . beef? The meat was cut up every which way. Were the waitresses serving us the results of a massacre? One waitress tried to place a small roast piglet on the table. Bin Shakir waved it off with a cry of disgust. Cries of "*fazza'a!* (revolting)," and "*haraam!* (forbidden)," rose from the other Arab officers.

Bin Shakir was not a bad host. He urged me to eat. With his own fingers he picked out choice morsels of beef and lamb which he put on my plate. Once he actually fed me a piece. Like a mother bird. But he wasn't much of a conversationalist. He never spoke to Marj or to Sally. And as the dinner wore on, it might have been harder and harder for him to do so. While doctrinally firm on the ritual impurity of pork, bin Shakir evidently viewed alcohol with a more ecumenical eye. I saw him drain glass after glass of Dewar's—only slightly adulterated by water.

I felt the show coming on—it was in the atmosphere. Like a storm. The audience began to look for something—in the reflected light you could see eyes moving, heads turning. From behind us, in the building, came snatches of women's laughter.

During dessert—canned fruit salad—I judged the time had come. I asked: "Excellency, this *riih* you mentioned—the one that saved your life. I have heard of it in Khartoum, also. But what does it do? Is it for everybody?"

"Many *riihs*," bin Shakir answered expansively. "You must make big decision. Need help of a *shaykh*. How strong you think you are. How strong he thinks you are. He must judge. A few people *riih ahmar*. Red spirit, red wind. Sometimes, you even find *riih abyadh*—white. Very hard. I tell you secret; I am strong. But even I not *ahmar*. Too much even for Lieutenant General 'Rhinoceros.' But these are Sudanese things. Must not speak about them. Like military secrets, '*Asraar 'askariyyah*,' says the shaykh. Foreigners think these things are foolish, maybe laugh."

There was no more talk. The speakers opened up at point blank range. The pelvic thud of the base notes vibrated through my body. The hollow of my chest and diaphragm felt like auxiliary speakers. The music was virtually all percussion—an artillery firepower demonstration. I thought of the tanks firing at the university buildings.

Applause. Loud cries. *Les girls*. In a row they snaked out from the side door of the Equatoria Inn. A spotlight followed them. The spotlight operator was standing in one of the trees. Ten dancers and their chorus line leader. The dancers wore red brassieres and short grass skirts (over what looked like men's bathing trunks).

The chorus leader's costume was special: a bouquet of colorful feathers was fastened to the back of her grass skirt, under which she wore tight pants, of the sort women runners wear. Anklets—halfway up her calves—were covered with what looked like horse chestnuts. (Rob explained they were dried kola nuts.) As she led her girls out—a sort of two-steps-forward one-step-backwards dance—the anklets made a crackling staccato with each step. She glittered. Her skin had been oiled, then sprinkled with gold and silver particles.

The governor pointed the lead dancer out to me. "Her name is Francine," he said. "She is very good. Has danced in Khartoum and Wad Madani at big folk festivals."

I found myself enjoying the dances. Better to be here, I reflected, than to have been poor Kapecka and Greer at Hagar al Salaaya! There was nothing special about the choreography, certainly not the costumes. And the dances themselves were more or less what I'd expected. A harvest dance, a hunting dance, ten solid, healthy, perspiring young bodies. But they seemed to enjoy what they were doing. And they had wonderful rhythms. Following the lead of Francine, their "conductor," every move of theirs seemed to produce a sound, not respond to it. Ten solid musical instruments. Yeats had it right:

O body swayed to music, O brightening glance,
How can one tell the dancer from the dance?

The moment came—I knew it would. Francine moved, with many changes of angle and direction, towards us. She turned towards the spectators, not breaking step, raised her arms and looked over at me— as if asking a question. Nods, loud cries of assent (*yallah!*) from the spectators. Bottles and glasses banged on the tables. A stamping of feet. She turned, danced her way behind our table, took my two hands in hers, and moving backwards, led me onto the floor.

There was no point in fighting the problem. I went quietly. But I was soon glad Francine had invited me.

One dances better with a good partner. I'd never had, nor ever will have, one like Francine. Beer, plus several shots of Dewar's, had dispelled any self-consciousness. I felt warm and loose. I took off my coat. (Cheers.) The steps were simple. Francine started some slowly, as if to show me. I imitated her, then did variations of my own. She followed. (Louder cheers.) The beat picked up. She'd dropped her grass skirt. A wonderfully functional, well-constructed body. Not heavy: just solid, harmonious, built to last. Sweat was running down her chest, between her breasts—but she wasn't out of breath. Her spine ran straight and deep between its rounded moldings of muscle on either side. She looked me in the eyes and laughed—good humoredly, not flirtatiously. (She's having a good time! I realized.) I laughed, too.

Again the beat changed, slowed, more insidious. Francine's movements became more fluid. Putting her palms before her, she indicated I should dance in place. A whole courtship followed. Her eyes didn't leave mine, as her movements led me through acquaintance, attraction, courtship. A crescendo of drums. She sank slowly to her knees. In the same motion she pulled down her brassiere—and arched far backwards.

Back at the table. Marj said to Sally: "That's probably how John Smith and Pocahontas hit it off!" They laughed together. I heard Sally say something about "Nureyev"; Marj vigorously shook her head. A short consultation. I heard the name "Twyla Tharp." They laughed. Seemed to agree on "Baryshnikov." Marj look towards me with a wifely smile. She and Sally laughed again.

A brief intermission. Bin Shakir had continued to drink. I began to worry a little about our commandant. His collar was undone. He was now drinking beer laced with whisky. His jacket front was dark with the runoff of beer, whisky, and sweat. He was leaning back in his chair—his hand rested intimately on the thigh of his "P.A.," who'd taken a seat just behind him.

Francine was back—in a G-string, this time. (Body by BMW, I thought.) Three more dances. I half-hoped she'd ask me to dance again. But prudence won out. Several times she looked my way—I could feel Marj's eyes on me—I looked the other way. Then Francine was doing a final number before the governor. His mouth was half-open, eyes were locked onto the hydraulic rhythms of her thighs and buttocks. (Poor John the Baptist, I thought, you never had a chance!)

Francine's G-string came up, like a *tanga*, between the twin hemispheres of her buttocks. During the intermission, she'd oiled and gold-dusted herself again. I heard Marj say, "Close your mouth, Josh, you're drooling." Francine moved closer, aware of the impact she was having. Almost serving them up on our table. It would be like feeling the grapefruits at the Safeway.

The fresh fruit counter was too much for bin Shakir. He half rose, reached out and grabbed from behind at the waistband of Francine's G-string. With a cry of surprise, she pulled forward. Bin Shakir lost his balance. He and the table went over together—Francine's G-string in his hand. Southerners in the audience laughed openly; the Arabs tried, and mostly succeeded, in keeping their faces straight.

Francine stood there, looking shocked, astonished . . . scared? Bin Shakir was up on his knees, his swagger stick still in his left hand. From that position, he gave Francine a sudden, vicious backhand cut across the buttocks. She screamed. Put one hand on the hurt, tried to cover herself with the other. For another instant she stood like that, then turned and ran back into the inn.

The Equatorians in the audience were angered. In unison, I heard voices, "*Aaa-rab kharab.*" The general's paratroopers pelted in, G-2s at the ready. They took their fallen leader away with them. Their lieutenant, one hand on his holster, looked back every few steps. The audience (at least the southerners) continued their chant—"*Aaa-rab kharab.*" The hum of a by-now-familiar tune rose from the crowd.

"Let's amscray," said Rob. No one said goodnight. Our car was one of the first out of the gate. We drove through the mostly dark streets, toward the A.I.D. compound. It stood out from a distance, like an island of light.

Back in our room, I watched Marj take off her dress and hang it up carefully. She moved easily. I thought she was built a little like Francine. Solid. Well-proportioned. She took off her brassiere—reaching behind her back with both hands in that wonderful double-jointed move that women have. Then—still in her panties, she went into the bathroom. As she moved, I watched her breasts from the side: solid, firm. She came out of the bathroom wearing her nightgown and slipped into bed.

When I came out of the bathroom, the lights were out. Marj was lying on her side. I closed the door quietly, crossed the room and sat next to her on the edge of the bed. She half raised her head. I bent over and kissed her. "Surprised?" I asked. I slipped my hand under the covers to enclose her right breast.

Marj rolled to face me. She half sat up. "No, not really," she answered.

I drew the bedclothes back and ran my hand up along her thigh. I liked the firm, solid feel of her body. She had on close-fitting, silky panties. Almost like a panty-girdle. Her nightgown had ridden up. I pulled it up higher. My hand moved up her front. First I cupped, then slowly, carefully, felt her breasts with my fingertips. First the left, then the right. I moved my hand back and forth under her nightgown, brushing her nipples with my palm. They became more pointed, more firm. I kissed her long, slowly. My breath was coming in and out as if I'd just run a fast mile. Her mouth was slack. Her breath was coming fast, too. I tried to ease her backwards. She stiffened. "Josh," came back her voice. Soft, apologetic. "I want you. I really want you. But I've gotten my period. I don't get it that regularly. Maybe the move, and all this worrying . . ."

I opened my mouth to speak, then rose (I think) to the occasion: "You get a hug and kiss anyway."

I lay in the dark. hot and bothered, I suppose, is the right understatement. I couldn't remember having wanted Marj more . . . more passionately . . . more lovingly? Hard to separate the two emotions, I thought. I lay there a long time. At least an hour. Marj—somehow— slept peacefully. I thought of Francine. I thought of the day's trip. I thought of the evening that had not ended the way I'd hoped it would. I tried not to think of Sally, just across the living room.

I was still busy with my reflections (Would a cold shower do some good?) when the generator broke its rhythm, slowed down, coughed, and went dead. The diffuse light of the compound went out.

I listened. After all, in Khartoum, brownouts, blackouts, and power failures were the rule—not the exception. I found I was waiting—as in Khartoum—for the backup generator automatically to cut in. But of course there was no backup generator here. There was no city power at the compound. The compound generator was *the* generator. Who'd fix it? Did A.I.D. have any night duty people who'd know what to do? Who would call them? Was it my business?

I lay awhile longer. Listened. Only African night sounds. Folding back the bedclothes, I got to my feet and went to my tennis bag. My fingers brushed Mustafa's *gris-gris*. I took out my flashlight. It was one of the really useful sizes—five cells and a solid, four-inch-diameter re- flector cone.

I opened the bedroom door and stood there a moment. As I stood listening in the dark, I heard a sound, something . . . stealthy. Some- one going to the generator house? The sound seemed to stop outside the porch. I listened. Only night sounds again. Barking. Then a brief rasping sound. Then silence. Then rasping again.

Feeling a little foolish and indecisive, I tiptoed to the open door of the porch and peered out. There was no moon; the compound was black. But with my night vision intact, out of the corners of my eyes (rods or cones?) I made out a shape—lighter colored, undifferentiated— outside the screen door. (I didn't need glasses and my night vision was good, "like a cat's," Marj sometimes said.) Yet another rasping sound. I recognized the sound: someone was cutting through the screen! The shape moved—the screen door catch slid back. Almost soundlessly, the door opened. (Had someone oiled it that day? I wondered.) I stepped back into the living room.

I counted to sixty slowly. So did whoever was out there. Then I heard a soft sound, cloth on cloth. The slight movements of the intruder's robe. His feet were almost soundless on the tiles. He was coming toward me! (Maybe a repair man to tell me about the power failure? Doesn't want to awaken everyone. Or someone bringing a message, or even Rob McAndrew himself?) Even as these thoughts passed through my mind, they seemed foolish, unconvincing. I took a further step back into the living room and made up my mind. (If he steps inside . . .)

A foot slipped tentatively over the threshold. A silhouette stood vaguely framed in the doorway. Another step. The shape paused. I could discern it was carrying something long in its hand.

I lifted the flashlight and took aim at where head and neck came together. (You might only have one shot, if the flashlight comes apart.) I strained for an ace. The reflector glass shattered. The flashlight held.

A body gasped, slumped to its knees. I struck again—somewhere on the head. And again. I heard a gasp, and felt a body hit the ground. I hit it several more times—feeling for the general area of the head.

From the bedroom I heard Marj's voice: "Josh! Josh! Are you alright?"

"It's OK, Marj—stay where you are."

A light shone from the direction of Sally's room. I heard her voice: "What the hell's going on?" A flashlight beam played on me. The edge of its light illuminated Sally's feet and the hem of the caftan she was wearing.

She exclaimed: "Josh! Are you alright?"

The beam dropped. It touched the prostrate form of a man. He was wearing a *thawb*. From beneath the *thawb* two bare feet projected. A Sudanese turban lay nearby. (Lucky for me, I thought. The first whack must have knocked it off—like a helmet.) The beam moved up the body to the head. It illuminated an Arab face. Pretty battered. He was unconscious, or worse. Blood seeped from a cauliflower ear.

We saw something else: the man had been carrying a broad-headed axe; bright red and black markings ran the length of its handle.

A GENTLEMAN'S GAME?

" . . . and Vindd will get the grant he's been hoping for," Farnsworth was saying. He leaned back in his black leather swivel chair and buzzed Maryann to ask for more coffee.

"He deserves it, Jon," I answered. "Rob took us through the back gate, right to Vindd's house in the UNDP compound across the street. At first, when Vindd heard our story, he thought we'd gone stark raving. You could see it in his face. But he began to get the picture. *A picture anyway.* Maybe he figured that an army officer who had tried to kill some 'American spies' wouldn't blink at killing an Indian international civil servant, and blaming it on John Garang, too. Or that the man's buddies in the Sudanese army wouldn't. You could see the thought dawning: '*Dr. Vindd, you are in plenty of trouble.*' He got scared, but he didn't try to turn us out.

"And he didn't just freeze. He got right into creating a crowd scene for us all. He got his boss, the Swedish UNDP director, to come over. Also one of the Maryknoll fathers. They must have wondered why their Hindu friend was inviting them at such an hour. On the phone Vindd was unspecific, but urgent. Best of all, he got the Kuwaiti aid chief to come over. Mr. Moneybags for all of south Sudan. He has clout— *aldabas*, as they say in Spanish. No one in Sudan wants to anger Kuwait. But Vindd was really worried. He needed still more insurance. As proof, he even called Aru Bol. Who came over, by the way."

"Another grant?"

"What the heck Jon, it's only money. And who knows which of Vindd's guests raised our numbers to the comfort level? One more: Mr.

Furj of Protocol somehow got the word. He came by with several elders of his tribe. Didn't ask for anything. They just sat there—a kind of act of solidarity. Courageous, under the circumstances."

Farnsworth said: "I'll try to put in a useful word for him. Did you know the governor sent me a cable expressing his sincere regret that 'indiscipline and banditry should have marred Mr. Chamberlain's visit to Juba.' He assured me the incident 'was and will remain without parallel.' He extends a personal welcome to any member of the embassy or A.I.D. who comes to Juba. In particular, he hopes that *you* will soon return. Oh! And he wonders when he'll get answers to the requests for scholarships and Jeep Cherokees he made to you!"

I responded: "The S.O.B.! I'd gladly buy him a Jeep Cherokee—and throw in the ignition bomb option! He wants us back to finish the job! I won't be able to prove it, but *no way* the captain went nuts. Or was in the pay of John Garang. Or was a 'common thief,' all straws the governor grasped at when he learned his plans had miscarried. Just trying to throw dust in our eyes."

"Admitted, Josh," responded the ambassador, "but still, *why* this further attempt against you? And in Juba, of all places. How did they know you were there? And put together a plan so fast? That captain you knocked out—what do you bet that he'll do poorly in prison? We'll never get to question him. First 'troubles,' then 'complications'—remember *Ethan Frome?*—then 'poor fellow, we lost him. He just slipped away from us one night,'—*with a pillow over his face*. Wait and see.

"But who was behind *him*? The governor? We assume so, because he would have been the man who ordered the changing of the guard. But that's not proof by itself. The Libyans? Maybe. The PLO? Again, maybe. But it's a little off their beaten track. Far from their *querencia*. Maybe a contract job with Garang? A connection through the Ethiopians? We know Ethiopia is sympathetic to the rebels and has ties with Libya, too. Then there's everyone's favorite, Dr. al-Atrash, who could be linked into several of these groups—and has the military connections. But no answers. Only many questions.

"Poor Jack's stumped. He's getting queried from the White House and the NSC, and his agency's gone pyrotechnic. He's personally betting on al-Atrash. But meanwhile, he's getting nothing from his contacts in the security forces, nothing from the army. Our university sources? You know there are some weird, extreme groups there—but still nothing. The only certainties we have are the AWOL *corpora delicti* you identified from Deng's assassination and the knowledge that *someone* killed Hilverding.

"Meanwhile there's still Abu Nar," the ambassador went on. "Dawkins saw another of his 'open letters' at the university. It speaks of American embassy officers in Juba assaulting members of the armed forces. We're supposed to be in cahoots with John Garang against Arabs and Islam. Then the threat again: something about the wrath of the people—like a 'red wind' about to be unleashed against 'agent authorities,' 'idolaters,' and 'Zionist-imperialist' conspirators. The poster was up the morning after you got back from Juba.

"Someone's watching us. Someone who's able to organize. Jack's not seen anything quite like it in his years in the Middle East. Nor have his people back home. It gives him a creepy feeling, he says, to be surveilled and not even to know where to look for the Judas window or the one-way glass! Could our sources in Tripoli be *that* bad?"

The ambassador involuntarily glanced around. Then he turned his desk radio on loud—and leaning forward said, in a barely audible voice, "Even our liaison with the Israelis has come up with nothing. You know, they've been stepping up their interest in Sudan ever since their agent was hanged. But they're as much in the dark as we are. So we keep looking for 'Factor X.' Sounds like AIDS research.

"But speaking of Factor X," said Farnsworth, "at least Dawkins has got a few groups on the 'Red Wind.' There's a connection with folk religion—what we always assumed. In the early 1880s, when the Mahdi conquered Sudan, he was supposed to be the Red Wind. Or to have invoked the Red Wind to sweep away the British and the Egyptians. Perhaps a Sudanese way of saying, 'Repent, for the end of the world is at hand.' But I'm afraid that our Sudanese contacts aren't very good when it comes to, shall we call it, the 'ecstatic' side of Sudanese Islam? They're too secular. Too much time at USC, or Chico State, or Menlo Park Community College—people like our friend Sa'eed. We should have sent more Sudanese to Bible Belt schools instead.

"But how's Marjorie?" Farnsworth asked. "The department's ordered departure must have been a blow. Not unexpected—I might have recommended it myself soon. But Washington's super cautious these days—the Juba attack on you may have tilted them over the edge. Please tell her we want to do *absolutely anything* we can to be helpful."

I reflected that the State Department hadn't wasted time. No sooner were we back from Juba than State's "crisis arm," the Washington Liaison Group, instructed us to conduct an ordered departure within seventy-two hours. All dependents plus "nonessential personnel" would be evacuated to Washington, D.C. There, I knew, they'd be met by the Family Liaison Office (FLO), which would make hotel reservations and help with onward travel plans, if the evacuees didn't want to stay in Washington. FLO would also provide psychological and 'stress' counseling for family members needing it, and a range of other services.

Evacuations were one of the most painful experiences of Foreign Service life—both for the evacuees and for post morale. Lives, school years, and careers were interrupted, torn up by the roots. What to do with the pets? And after departure—had one's household effects been packed up and shipped? Or looted in the house, or on the docks? Then, back in the States, the obsession with short-term news—were conditions at post getting better? Worse? Could evacuees soon plan to return to post? Or should their assignments be broken and they look elsewhere? *And why doesn't the department ever call me?* The department, I reflected, wasn't always any better in keeping in touch with evacuees than children at boarding school were with their parents . . . or than *I* was sometimes with Marj?

The embassy had made arrangements for a charter company, Falcon Airlines, to move our people out in three days' time. The charter would fly our people to Nairobi—there they'd overnight and take TWA the next day to Washington/Dulles.

Marj's parents had been pleased. Her father called as soon as he'd heard the news. "I could see it coming all along," he honked into the receiver, "anyone could. Sudan's been going to hell for years, and—as usual—your department is the last to wise up. If you people had ever bothered to talk to our bank's Foreign Department. . . . No place for any American anyway, much less my daughter and your wife."

I'd never liked that Back Bay, preppy honk in his voice. It got louder and louder as we talked. Honk! Honk! Honk! But I didn't let him put me on the defensive. In the end, he impatiently hung up. Afterwards, I thought the words "choleric" and "splenetic," had they not already existed, could have been coined for him. A Boston investment banker, he approved of very little in the modern world, least of all the US government, the "goldbricks" who worked for it, and *particularly* the son-in-law who'd taken his only child off to "Bongo-Bongo land."

"Thanks, Jon," I replied, "that's a kind offer, and I'll tell her. She's working closely with the Admin Section and some other wives to organize the departure. We'll set up booths and processing stations at our house; people can gather there, then be bused to the airport when the plane is standing by. Marj'll go straight on to Boston from D.C. and stay with her parents, at least through Thanksgiving and Christmas. I'll try to join her in mid-December. Maybe we'll be able to come back together in January?"

But I knew I was speaking optimistically. Evacuations worked on a ratchet—that is, it was very hard to turn them in reverse. The department—partly to cover its ass—would only let dependents return to an evacuated post for the millennium! Or something nearly as Utopian!

As I came out of the ambassador's office, Sally and Maryann and Clayton were laughing. They stopped when they saw me. There was something mischievous in the way they looked at each other. They burst out laughing again.

"Is it classified?" I asked? "If so, am I cleared for it?"

A pause. Then Maryann asked: "Did the ambassador give you the news?"

"Maryann," I answered, "there are two things you mustn't ever say if you want to stay my friend. The first is, 'Speaking as a friend.' Something disagreeable always follows. The second is, 'Have you heard the news? It puts the listener on tenterhooks—while the speaker smirks at the high cards he's holding. You win. What news?"

"I'll give you a hint," said Maryann. "Can you guess which of our junior officers Sally calls, 'the shark that swims on the land'?"

I smiled. "I expect we're thinking of the same person."

"Well, that shark is headed for colder waters," added Sally.

Maryann explained: "While you were gone, al-Atrash gave a function to try to paper over Sudan's dispute with the Joint Distribution Committee. The government had gotten a *lot* of bad publicity when they seized the committee's transport plane. And Sudan badly wants help from Western donors. The ambassador went and Gray sent Kapecka to represent him. Trouble was, Ward had been drinking. So when our shark got to the reception, he was 'hungry.' He began looking around."

Maryann started to laugh and excused herself. "I know one shouldn't laugh at one's own story—a third thing not to do to stay friends—but I can't help it!"

She continued: "Ward squinted across the room and saw his prey. So to a Sudanese near him, he announces: 'See that gal all in red? I want a piece of that.' But the Sudanese starts to laugh. He calls over Minister al-Atrash and tells him the story. Al-Atrash was in heaven. Watching Farnsworth all the time, he loudly announces that Kapecka must immediately leave the party and Sudan because he'd (a) evidently broken Sudan's laws against drinking alcohol and (b) planned to sexually assault the Cardinal Archbishop of Sudan!"

Maryann added: "The ambassador called from his car just as he and Kapecka left the reception. He told me to come to the Embassy."

When she got there, she said, Farnsworth and Kapecka were in the ambassador's office. The door was closed. It was quiet. Then the ambassador buzzed her to come in.

"The ambassador told me he'd checked with the travel clerk. There was no need to wait for the evacuation. Kapecka would be leaving on Lufthansa at 2100 hours the next day for Frankfurt and the USA. The ambassador's last words to Kapecka at his office door were, 'With luck, Ward, you could be a civilian in a week.' "

Sally broke in: "But another pleasant topic. Will you be playing tennis at the Bogosians' this afternoon? Can you and Marj spare the time?"

I told her I'd gotten a nice note from Mr. Bogosian. I'd written back that I'd give it a try. The evacuation plans were well in hand. But Marj wasn't much of a tennis person. She was planning to go through and air out the winter clothes she'd need, then finish work on our official residence expenses and representational claims.

One couldn't mistake the Bogosian compound from the air *or* from the ground. As you crossed the Khartoum North bridge and turned right (I remembered the directions from our Juba trip), you saw the greenery right ahead of you. A wall of trees. Like the windbreaks the WPA planted out west in Dust Bowl days. A narrow asphalt road led across a sandy, vacant lot to the Bogosians' gate.

Within, all was green and sun-filled and colorful. There were full-grown royal palms, and flowers everywhere. A modern-style house—it would have fit well into a luxury neighborhood of Naples or Nice or Malibu—looked out onto an impeccable lawn. The pool I'd seen from the air was at one end of the garden. At the other, across a profusion of flower beds, was a fenced-in grass tennis court. Beyond that, I made out an orchard of banana and papaya trees, and the Blue Nile itself.

Avo Bogosian and his wife had been sitting on the porch. Aminata was with them. The Bogosians came across the lawn to greet me. He was about my height. Early sixties? Balding, with a tonsure of white hair. He had a good tan and looked very fit. He wore white slacks and a white tennis shirt—the logo read "The San Francisco Cricket Club." Mrs. Bogosian—Solange—was a petite, elegant, blonde Frenchwoman. I guessed she was in her early fifties. Her light-blue silk dress was emphatically *not* tennis gear.

Avo Bogosian spoke first: "Mr. Chamberlain? What a pleasure

finally to meet you. After all we've heard from Sally—and in general."
He laughed.

Back at the porch, Avo said: "You've met our 'other daughter,'
Aminata al-Furi? We saw her often when she and our daughters were
studying at Camboni College together. But you must have had a lot on
your mind since arriving in Sudan. And please, put it all aside today—
and on the many other days when I hope you'll be our guest. While
here, please think only of tennis. Or perhaps lunch. Or perhaps tea.
There's also bird-watching and gardening, that is, if you'll let Solange
show you around her 'mini national park.' "

Mrs. Bogosian laughed. "Avo, you are a fool. Please forgive my
husban', Mr. Chamberlain. He is very *spirituel*—exuberant? My husban'
is sixty-five, but I think sometimes we should subtract the sixty. He is
always this way when he meets a good new tennis player. But his vices
could be worse. Tennis, I can keep my eye on from the house! But join
us on the porch—Sally Tolson and Sa'eed will be here soon. You know
him, I think? Also the Grays from your embassy. But something cold?
Have you tried *karkadeh*?"

I hadn't. As the houseboy, in a red, gold-embroidered *thawb*, poured
me a glass, Mrs. Bogosian explained it was a drink—a *digestif*—made
from the blooms of the hibiscus plant, *karkadeh* in Arabic. The flowers
were soaked in cold water until their coloring was leached out. The
solution could then be dried, leaving behind a fluffy, red powder. Mixed
with water (sugar, too, was sometimes added), *karkadeh* was the color of
red wine. Among the Bogosian firm's many interests was its export of
karkadeh powder (and also dried hibiscus flowers themselves) to France
and Germany. European herbalists believed that teas made with such
a base increased the elasticity of blood vessels and prevented disease.
I liked the taste. Spicy and a little tart. Like cranberry juice.

The other guests arrived almost in a motorcade. The Grays (Chevy
Impala), Will Dawkins (Toyota Corolla), and Frank Greer (something
that looked like a Jeep with a rollbar). Sally and Sa'eed (in his personal
BMW 535) were just a little behind, but closing fast. For a moment I
thought Sa'eed was coming to swim. Solange half rose as he braked
hard, skidded on the gravel and stopped—touching a strip of petunias
just feet from the pool.

As Sa'eed strolled towards me, I reflected he might have been
sponsored by *Le Coq Sportif*. He looked like a tennis pro from Montego
Bay or some other pricey Caribbean resort. The brilliant all-white of
his tennis clothes favorably set off his coloring, I had to admit. He was
well-built. Thin, no excess, and strong-looking. But why did even the
way he walked suggest self-satisfaction? An awareness of the impression

he was making? Why did Carly Simon's lyric to Warren Beatty—"You're so vain"—float through my mind?

Sally was also in tennis clothes. My eyes took in her long, slim legs, her snug tennis skirt and blouse. Greer wore shorts, running shoes, and a short-sleeved Northeastern University sweatshirt. A football rookie come for spring training? He had no racquet, but just the way he looked at Aminata made it clear enough that tennis hadn't brought him to the Bogosians. The Grays wore casual street clothes. They didn't play tennis, "only the market," Bill joked.

Avo had business to talk over with Bill. "So start to play now," he urged. "I'll join you for the second set." At this, Sa'eed turned to Sally and put his hand on her knee. His thumb seemed to stroke the inside of her thigh. He said: "Sally, shall we *warm up*?" (An insinuating, intimate tone, I thought.)

She didn't reply. Just got up, rather quickly, and walked to the tennis court. As we followed her, I could hear Bill Gray intoning: "The IMF team insists that before the Sudanese government can qualify for a bridging loan, it must undertake structural adjustment reforms: devalue the pound, cut the bread and sugar subsidies, privatize the Military-Economic Corporation, and slash the export duties on agricultural products."

Will was only fair. He hit the ball hard, but tended to be wild. His backhand, too, was wobbly, so I had him play the forehand court. Sa'eed and Sally clearly had played a lot of tennis together. They were a team (on and off the court? I asked myself). The first set was brief: 6–2. Afterwards—Avo was still talking with Bill Gray—Dawkins suggested that he and Sally switch. Sally was for it, but Sa'eed held out for their playing a second set together.

Sa'eed wasn't a really powerful player, but he covered the net like a fog. I could often lob him, but almost anything that Will hit he'd fall on like a shark. He wasn't the sort of bad sport who makes opponents dance by aiming shot after shot at their feet. But he'd poach. Once or twice, I saw Sally shake her head and speak quietly to him as they walked back into position. Also, there were his little tennis jokes, at our expense—garbage shots would dink over the net just when you expected a slam. He was agile, quick, and deceptive. He made very few unforced errors. Only he wasn't much fun to play with.

You're just being a bad loser, Chamberlain, I told myself. Concentrate instead on your game. Don't worry about Sa'eed; enjoy this incredible playing surface, resilient, springy; watch the ball. I found myself also watching my female opponent. Some lines went through my mind:

Love–thirty, love–forty, oh! weakness of joy,
The speed of a swallow, the grace of a boy.

Set number two went also to Sally and Sa'eed, 6–1.

Avo joined us toward the end of the second set. He'd changed into tennis shorts. He clearly *was* fit. He looked the way I hoped I'd look at his age. The Grays took their seats on a flagstoned spectators' area. More *karkadeh*, and some icy, fresh lemonade.

I said I thought I'd like to sit out the next set. Could Mrs. Bogosian show me something of her garden? And her birds? As we walked away, Sa'eed called out: "Not finished for the day, I hope, Mr. Chamberlain?" Was there just an edge of challenge to his voice—?

I was in expert hands. Solange spoke about her plantings with the expertise of a professional and the love of an artist/mother. "There is so little beauty," she remarked, "in Khartoum now. Old buildings are *vetustes;* they are collapsing from no maintenance. And new buildings are collapsing, because they are so badly built. The vacant lots everywhere are filled with garbage. Actually, *l'armoirie*, the—what do you call it? ('Coat of arms,' I suggested)—yes, coat of arms for Sudan should not be an eagle. It should be a goat, *rampant*, in a garbage dump, against a wire fence draped with plastic bags. And everywhere the plants are dying."

"You seem especially fond of petunias," I observed.

"My favorite flower, *petunia hybrida.* Forgive me. But we who love flowers can only talk to each ozer in Latin. The national words are all too different. Yes, petunias grow well here. But they are hybrids—as their name says. We must get the seeds every year from Europe. Sometimes Avo gets seeds from California. He goes there much. Our daughters now mostly live there and in Paris. Avo calls the petunias my 'other daughters.'

"Here are some more flowers," Solange went on—the Latin names poured forth. "Hibiscus, we botanists call it *rosa sinensis*, and here is *aloe mitriformis*—I don't know what it is in English. It looks a little like your century plant. Here's my favorite fern, *nephrolepus exaltana.* I especially like my three kinds of *bougainvillea:* Alexandra, Amethyst, and Dania. But come see also our view of the Nile. It is pretty, and many birds in the afternoon and evening. I love birds almost as much as flowers."

We were well above the water level and, just as at the recsite, we stood under rows of acacias running atop the bank. They helped protect against scouring at flood time. Below them, other flood control measures helped shore up the bank: stone-filled wire cages—gabions, willow revetments, and mattresses of wire-linked concrete slabs.

At the water's edge I watched small birds dive-bombing the water to drink. They'd then return in a frantic dash to the safety of the trees. Above us, hawks scouted their evening meal. They looked intent and business-like: interceptor, not reconnaissance models, I thought. Mrs. Bogosian pointed to a goshawk flying fast and low among the trees.

"*Accipiter tachiro*," she said.

I saw it shift directions rapidly. Then a few short wingbeats and a long glide—unseen, unheard—the hawk struck. Poor pigeon! With Abu Nar and his Red Wind hovering over us, I sympathized.

Solange caught my expression. "Poor speckled pigeon!" she said. "Better think of it as a *Columba guinea*!"

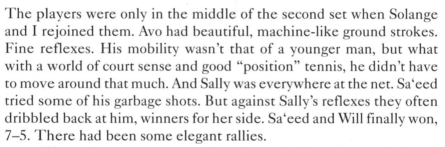

The players were only in the middle of the second set when Solange and I rejoined them. Avo had beautiful, machine-like ground strokes. Fine reflexes. His mobility wasn't that of a younger man, but what with a world of court sense and good "position" tennis, he didn't have to move around that much. And Sally was everywhere at the net. Sa'eed tried some of his garbage shots. But against Sally's reflexes they often dribbled back at him, winners for her side. Sa'eed and Will finally won, 7–5. There had been some elegant rallies.

"How about a quick set of singles, Mr. Chamberlain?" It was Sa'eed, and we were relaxing during the second "intermission" of the afternoon. Again, there was a subtle challenge in the way he said "Mr. Chamberlain."

"I hate for just the two of us to tie up the court when others could play," I answered.

Avo: "On the contrary, you would give us much pleasure. Tennis is also one of the great *spectator* sports. Let's say one set, then tea? There's just time before the light begins to fade."

Sa'eed twirled his racquet. A Dunlop with a maximum oversize head. With raised eyebrows, he'd spoken suggestively to me about "her" large sweet spot. His serve.

I began a little tense and cautious. I didn't think he could blow me away. But I didn't want to look foolish. I figured we were about even as far as being in shape. He was younger. But then my job and lifestyle didn't involve the parties and late nights that his did. He played more than I did, though.

I told myself, keep him back from the net, move him around. If his serve-and-volley game works, don't panic, keep trying to pass him, he'll tire. I usually was a slow starter in any match. But I found myself behind, 3–0. Almost no time seemed to have passed. Sa'eed's serve wasn't overwhelming, but he was at the net in an instant to cut off my returns of service. And he was steady from the baseline. He'd scramble and scramble and scramble, keep the ball coming back at me. Then I'd see—I thought—an easy winner. And I'd hit it into the net. Or out. I started "going" for my second serve. Wrong answer!

Game number four went back and forth on my service. Twice I had the advantage. Twice Sa'eed pulled back to deuce with spectacular, acrobatic saves. One was a lob, the other a passing shot. I let that one go by, praying it would go out. I saw it go wide—just barely. But Sa'eed smoothly called out "deuce!" and moved to receive for the next point.

It got harder to keep an even strain, to say, "good shot!" and smile as if I meant it. The next point: Sa'eed's touch volley hardly seemed to bounce as it wafted over the net onto the surface of the lawn. The applause was deserved. His ad. Next serve: I double faulted. His game, 4–0.

He won the next game, too, a "love game" on his service. 5–0.

He smiled at me across the net: "*Dommage*, as the French say, eh, Mr. Chamberlain?"

I knew I needed to break his rhythm, establish my own. Or else it would be six–zip and Alka Seltzer instead of tea. As we changed sides for game number six, I took a can of fresh balls from my kit. I picked out a different racquet. Toweled off.

"New balls? A new racquet? Almost a new beginning, Mr. Chamberlain? New luck maybe?"

"Luck?" The word jogged something in my mind. On an impulse I went back to my tennis bag and drew out Mustafa's . . . *wanga*? I began to slip it over my head.

"What have you there, Mr. Chamberlain?" Sa'eed's voice came over the net, flat, hard, serious-sounding.

I stepped over to show him the leather sachet with the iridescent white cowrie set in the middle.

"A *suq* purchase?"

"No, actually. A Sudanese . . . friend gave it to me. He said I should keep it on or about me all the time. It's brought me luck this far, you'd have to agree."

Sa'eed wasn't looking at the talisman now. He was looking at me. I couldn't fathom his expression. "Strange," he said. "Silly superstitions, don't you agree? Well, as the expression goes, shall we play ball?"

I felt embarrassed. I hadn't meant the charm to become such a conversation piece. Bill Gray was looking on. The lines of his face looked more disapproving even than normal. He turned to Solange and his wife. I heard the word "gamesmanship." I blushed.

I preferred Frank Greer's loud and blunt (to Aminata): "Gut check time."

But my ploy seemed to be working. Sa'eed's play became erratic. He seemed to have trouble concentrating. He began to make unforced errors. *His* shots were finding their way into the net—or out of the court, *his* return of service became tentative. Meanwhile, my own service, usually the best part of my game, got stronger. I'd loft the ball up with my fingertips. It would seem slowly to revolve, to expand, to hover motionlessly (*2001: A Space Odyssey*), as if suspended for my stroke. And when I served—like pulling a trigger. Wham!

I was astonished. When had I served, or played, so well? The spectators were astonished, too. At first, they'd politely applauded what they took to be my valiant come-from-behind effort. But then, as one ace after another boomed into the opposing court, the applause diminished. Toward the end of the match there was only hushed, prolonged silence. Disapproval? Stupefaction?

Sa'eed had lost seven straight games. I felt disembodied, spent. I hesitated to look over to where the spectators sat. But Greer came to my rescue. To Aminata (in a loud, pleased voice) he said: "DCM sucked it up!"

"You've been hiding something from us, Mr. Chamberlain," said Avo. "Sally told us you were a good player. But you Americans are so modest. I thought you'd be only a 'good player.' But there hasn't been such serving on this court for many a day. Actually, and I am not saying this to flatter you, maybe not since Jaroslav Drobny visited us from Egypt in the early 1960s. Sa'eed, you must watch your ranking now. No more easy victories? Fewer late nights maybe?"

We sat for tea on the lawn. Over us there spread an enormous, orange, lawn umbrella. Solange and the houseboy served homemade jelly roll and an apple *tarte Tattin*. All delicious.

I felt horny, too. Sally was across from me, in a canvas lawn chair, between Solange and Avo. All she'd said after the match was, "Nice play." She sat on a towel, one leg crossed over the other. My eyes followed the smooth, brown line of her thigh up to the shadow of her tennis shorts. Several times, I tried to catch her eye. Impossible.

The sun was setting. But it was not a quiet dusk. One had to speak clearly to be understood. The *muezzin* from the mosque nearby was calling the faithful to sunset prayer. Swallows were settling into the neem trees with chattering choruses of "good night, see you in the morning."

"What are we going to do with you, Mr. Chamberlain?" asked Sa'eed. These were almost his first words off the court. "I must tell you, the prime minister is unhappy with what happened in Juba. And he is not very happy with *you*, I fear."

I looked at Sa'eed unbelievingly. I said: "Does he think that captain broke into our house just to present us with an example of local handicrafts? An axe! In the middle of the night? If something had happened to us . . . And did the captain have just me in mind? With whom would the PM *then* have been unhappy? John Garang?"

"It is all a big mystery," replied Sa'eed. "Thanks God you are well. As for the captain, he is in critical condition. He is now in the military hospital. He has not recovered consciousness. You must have hit him *very* hard." Sa'eed paused. He seemed to eye me reproachfully. He went on: "The doctors fear 'troubles,' even 'complications.' I gather no one saw much.

"I know," Sa'eed raised a hand (it was huge, almost spidery— Marfan's syndrome? I wondered), "you have always acted in self-defense. But consider this: There have been troubling, unexplained events in Sudan. They embarrass the prime minister and his coalition. They deeply . . . displease Minister al-Atrash. Then, this mysterious Abu Nar puts up his posters and bulletins at the university. Even the BBC speaks of him. Who is he? We don't know. Does even your Mr. Kirby know? But the prime minister and Minister al-Atrash *do* know that a certain American diplomat, Mr. Joshua Lawrence Chamberlain (Sa'eed gave each name emphasis), has been involved with many of these events. All of them, even. We have various expressions in Arabic that all mean the same as your 'Don't kill the messenger.' For instance, we say: *'Laa 'alla al-Rasuul, illa al-Balagh.'* That means, 'The messenger is only responsible for *conveying* the bad tidings.' He's not responsible for the tidings themselves—but human nature being what it is . . . do you get my point?"

I nodded.

Sa'eed finished: "So, *verbum sap*, Mr. Chamberlain, as they used to say in jolly old Bean Town. Sally, shall we go?"

I felt lonely, desolate, driving back to the Residence. I didn't like the prospect of Marj leaving. Also, I was worried about what Sa'eed had said. True, when the prime minister criticized me after the Deng killing, the ambassador had stood firm. He'd even said the Sudanese wouldn't dare PNG me. But every situation has its limits. And there were ways in which the Sudanese could indirectly make things so difficult for me and the embassy that the department would have to pull me out.

That would be a career-stopper. No matter how many pages of explanation and qualification Jon added to my last efficiency report, the system would only remember: "Chamberlain went out there recently, yes? Showed real promise, some say. *Something* must have happened. . . . Well, on to the next file. Now *here's* a bright officer . . ." The system, I knew, only wanted—and remembered— results; it was not interested in explanations. What matters is that the family car is back with a dent. Dad doesn't care how it got there!

I found Marj upstairs airing out winter clothes in the guest bedroom. The ambassador was still at the Embassy. Supper—just the two of us—was a quiet affair. Marj seemed absorbed in her preparations. I'd started to tell her about my afternoon at the Bogosians', but she'd listened with only half an ear. Immediately after supper, she went back to her desk work and her sorting and packing.

I was staring blankly at my coffee cup when Mustafa—as he cleared the table—said quietly to me: "*Murshid*, Shaykh al-Mughraibiy, the Supreme Guide, will see Excellency tomorrow night."

THE GRAND INQUISITOR?

17

My host stood in the door. He watched me for a moment, then smiled. "You *will* come in won't you, Mr. Chamberlain? What did you expect to find?" he added, "a bedlamite? 'A reed shaken by the wind'? Come in, please."

I followed Dr. al-Mughraibiy down a short hallway to a book-lined study where he offered me a seat on a couch. He took an upholstered leather easy chair with a telephone at its side.

In front of us was a simple, plain wood coffee table. At one end of the study was a desk covered with papers; a typewriter on a typing stand stood next to the desk. There were even some books piled on the floor by the typing stand.

I mentally kicked myself. I'd not meant for my face to give so much away. But nothing I'd heard about the respected, even feared, "Supreme Guide" of the Muslim Brothers had prepared me for the slim, young homeowner with a well-trimmed beard and moustache, who'd opened the door himself. He couldn't have been much more than thirty-five. Then his clothes: brown slacks, a light blue long-sleeved shirt, open at the neck, well-polished loafers. What with his informal, disarming manner, he could have been an assistant professor in a small college back home.

And the house: I'd expected it to be like that of other Sudanese politicians. Large and disheveled. A warehouse, a storage space for the dignitary's extended family—something that began with wives, sons, and daughters, and shelved off into distant relatives, and finally, slaves. Something at least between "very comfortable" and "palatial." But was al-Mughraibiy's house even middle class? Barely. The neighborhood was marginal, too.

"I don't normally see Westerners," al-Mughraibiy began, "not, as some claim, out of hostility to the West. After all, I hold degrees from two Western schools: a law degree from London and a Ph.D. from the Sorbonne. And the Harvard Law School has been kind enough to offer me library privileges. Someday I must accept. I mean to write a book on the evolution of contemporary Islamic jurisprudence.

"But the fact is," al-Mughraibiy went on, "I have no mission for Westerners; my mission is rather to us Muslims. And you'll notice, please, I just say 'Muslims.' How I dislike the term 'Muslim Brothers'! Every Muslim is a brother to every other Muslim. The phrase 'Muslim Brother' is a tautology—it reflects mainly others' hostility or guilt. They wish to make fellow Muslims appear sectarian. What in America you'd call (he winced) 'Bible Busters.'

"Nor is the term 'Muslim fundamentalists' much better. What is the alternative? Should other Muslims be called 'superficialists'? They may be, actually, but won't admit it. And tell me, Mr. Chamberlain, aren't you Christians urged to love the Lord your God with all your heart and with all your soul and with all your mind?"

Mughraibiy stopped suddenly. He put his palm on his forehead. "Forgive me. My apologies, Mr. Chamberlain. You must think me rude as well as fanatical. Tea or coffee? Pepsi? Some fruit juice?" He rang for a servant girl, who took our requests. She was all in white, her head covered by a coif that let not a hair escape.

The shaikh continued: "As a young man, I used to deplore the distorted view of Islam in the West. But unlike most of my friends, I've come to realize that concern over Western incomprehension, lack of sympathy, is at best a distraction to the good Muslim. At worst, it perpetuates an unhealthy psychological and cultural dependency. Only children want to be loved and understood always.

"And besides, incomprehension and lack of sympathy may sometimes be deserved. We Muslims are not as clear as we should be. Nor are we always sympathetic. We have our demagogues—our Omar Abdurrahmans, our Abdul Hamid Kishks, our Ahmad al-Mahallawiys— I must deal with their like even in Sudan! And you see us at our worst when we try to justify or to apologize for ourselves. Have you noticed? The justification usually takes the form of some just-outdated Western scientific, economic, or sociological theory!"

"You aren't then an Arab nationalist, Dr. al-Mughraiby?" I asked.

He laughed. "Show me someone who is these days. Someone, that is, who is not using 'nationalism' as a theory to justify domination of the majority by his own militarized, ethnic elite. Look at Jordan, Syria, Iraq, even Sudan—no, Mr. Chamberlain. I'm no Arab nationalist. Nationalism is the last and worst joke played on the Islamic world by receding colonialism. The foreign colonialists are gone. In their places at the table we have our domestic variety. But they shout the same orders, and the same people are in the kitchen, only the new customers are harder to please—and they leave no tip at all."

Al-Mughraibiy went on: "Early in Islam, around the year 650 C.E.—Common Era, we Muslims say—our Islamic history and our political history diverged. The state became, first, amoral. Then, immoral. It has never been more so than today. Today it tries to claim the final loyalties of its citizens. But to whom should such loyalty truly be given? Only to God. And what do Christians and Muslims and Jews call a person who gives his final loyalty to some intermediate object? An idolater. A *mushrik*. Someone who places something else in place of, or instead of, God. 'Golden calves,' Mr. Chamberlain."

Our tea arrived. With it, the servant girl brought a tray of dates, Jordan almonds, and peanuts (as always). She also brought a plate of cakes—they looked like shortbreads. Al-Mughraibiy paused: "Cream? Sugar? Try some of these cakes—they were done by my wife. My *only* wife." He looked up with a smile. It made him look even younger.

I asked: "But isn't Prime Minister al-Muntasser a sort of religious leader? Does he stand condemned, too?"

"For want of one just man, Mr. Chamberlain? No, he is not condemned. Only irrelevant. In your stories, you have your frog king? Well, we have our frog prime minister. I tell my followers the prime minister is just a frog. In times past, when it was wet, he sat on his lily pad, snapped up juicy flies and spoke—other frogs said—eloquently. Then the dry times came. A military regime controlled the country. Our frog prime minister burrowed down into the mud for many years. He became dormant. But then the dictator fell. The rains came. Out came also our prime minister. See him there on his lily pad? Still snapping up flies? Still singing the same frog song. He's learned nothing during his dormant years."

Al-Mughraibiy looked directly at me and asked: "To what Christian denomination do you belong?"

"Presbyterian," I responded.

"Excellent!" said al-Mughraibiy: "Because if you are a good Presbyterian, you are almost a Muslim. You know then, the believer stands alone before his God, who loves and judges him. That no chain of beings exists to mediate between him and his Creator. And that his God is one—don't try to explain the Trinity to me, please—One who has revealed Himself in a book, and who continues to manifest Himself in history, until the end of time. Thus history is holy. It trends toward a purpose: the end of the world, and the Second Coming of the Messiah. That, too, we have in common.

"But meanwhile, the sincere believer has, first, this: the obligation, the religious duty, to study and reflect upon God's word. And second: he has a religious duty to exert himself morally, intellectually, *and politically* to help bring God's will to pass. Are you still with me, Mr. Chamberlain?"

Al-Mughraibiy paused. He looked directly at me again and asked, "But tell me. What have you heard about us?"

I hesitated before replying. I looked about the book-lined walls. There were titles in several languages. I saw Weingreen's *Classical Hebrew;* there was the *Oxford Annotated Bible,* too; other shelves—other walls—were solid with Arabic texts, massive multivolume series.

"I've never thought much about Islam," I said. "At school we read about the Crusades. The information wasn't all bad. In Scott's *The Talisman*, Saladin was as admirable as Richard the Lionhearted. But mostly what we hear is bad. Abul Abbas's killing that crippled American, Mr. Klinghoffer? Then throwing the body *and the wheelchair* overboard? There was hardly a word of protest from the Arab world! A lot of Americans see Arab leaders—Muslim leaders? (we tend not to see a difference)—as full of alibis. As demagogues, hypocrites, Jew-haters. We remember the World Trade Center bombing, the murder of schoolgirls by Muslim extremists in Algeria, the suicide bombings by Hamas in Jerusalem. Excuse me. I don't want to seem rude, but I felt somehow you wanted me to be frank."

To my surprise al-Mughraibiy nodded vigorously. "I think maybe I see why my friend Mustafa wanted so much for me to meet you!

"I agree with much of what you have said," al-Mughraibiy went on. "And these character faults are largely the result of not practicing Islam. Instead, we practice what *we* want Islam to be. Not what it is. Not as God has revealed it to us. Because of Islam's early triumphs, it is all too easy for Muslims today to seek power, not righteousness, as the proof of God's favor.

"Oh, believe me, Mr. Chamberlain, I have respect for the Bible. Not all the books—Revelation is too rich for my blood. But Amos! Now, there's a prophet!" Al-Mughraibiy half closed his eyes. In a slightly nasal singsong, he recited: 'But let justice roll down like waters, and righteousness like an ever-flowing stream.' You know we believe the Bible's original, perfect revelation became distorted over the centuries.

First by the Jews, then by the Christians. Accordingly, God revealed the *Qur'an*—the final, 'Authorized Version,' so to speak.

"Let me tell you something more of what we believe, we 'fundamentalists.' Let's use that term, just for discussion. We are not anti-Western, and certainly not anti-Jewish. Palestine concerns us very little. It would be gone as an issue today if Arabs and Muslims had demonstrated just a little charity to those homeless ones, those thrown into our midst over forty years ago. You won't hear Palestinians extolling 'Arab hospitality.' We fundamentalists don't worry so much about Israel, or the moral faults of your society, but about rectifying the moral faults of our *own*.

"And I'd put selective moral vision near the top of the list. Do you recall the Arab furor some years ago when Israel expelled hundreds of Islamic militants to the Lebanese border—and the Arab silence over the *million* Palestinians and Yemenis expelled by Kuwait and Saudi Arabia after your 'Desert Storm'? So we leave to you your own problems—and they are many. We need to work at ours. This means transforming our illegitimate, idolatrous societies into legitimate, religious ones. And when a just Muslim society has been built, even the Jews will convert, and *then* will come the millennium. Or so goes a *hadith*, a saying of the Prophet, 'upon whom be Peace.' Although that *hadith* is not one of those deemed most authentic."

Al-Mughraibiy refilled my teacup. I took some more shortbreads. They were delicious—I thought of Marj's chocolate chip cookies. He continued: "Our true enemies are not Jews nor Western secularists. Rather they are the corrupt, agnostic, pragmatic regimes that serve their own self-indulgence—while they now mouth Islamic slogans. Of course, they *used* to mouth socialist slogans. The folly of the Arabs! To neglect the truth God has revealed and pursue always some foreign light—which always fails!" Al-Mughraiby's voice suddenly dropped a register: "But God will not be mocked!"

More composedly, he continued: "Our leaders, I fear, are not civilized. They are profoundly wild, uncultured, irreligious. In the eighteenth century you had a debate: how would man grow up in a pure state of nature? The Spaniard, Baltazar Gracian, in his *El Criticón*, addressed the question. His book was a translation of an earlier Arabic work. But so much for history. Just look at contemporary Arab politics. Here you have your sorry answer. Hobbes was right."

I interjected: "And what about racial attitudes? In Juba, when I saw how Arabs treated blacks, I thought of Mississippi and South Africa in their worst days!"

Al-Mughraibiy answered: "Again you are right. But again the fault lies not with Muslims. It lies with so-called Muslims. Those whom the Prophet condemned as hypocrites: *munafiqiin*. Whom Christ called Pharisees. We still have them; they may even be a majority."

He went on: "And as for blacks. It is not we Muslims who oppress them or look down on them. There is a strong *hadith* that the faithful should elect as their leader the most upright and pious—even if that person be a Negro slave. We are confident that in the south, as we act justly and seek to do God's will, Islam, God's will, must prevail. The dialectic, you might say, strengthens our hand."

With some force, al-Mughraibiy said: "I am utterly against imposing Islam upon southerners by force. God commands: *La ikraha fidd din*. There is no compulsion in religion! I say give the south time. It's like tectonics: the pagan African plate is being subducted by the higher Islamic one. And where it's happening, we see volanic actions—Wau, Nimule, even Juba. But if we behave with justice and moderation, the Africans will come to Islam. It is the natural African religion. Spread by Africans. It is not colonialist. It is accommodating. It recognizes polygamy, though it does not approve of it; it also recognizes magic, up to a point. Islam is straightforward. Could you translate the Gospel of John into Dinka? Or explain the 'Logos Doctrine' in Zande? Even in English? Forgive me. I know I'm not being fair. But my point is that Islam is simple. Clear. Above all, it is true."

Al-Mughraibiy continued: "These are points I sometimes discuss with your Mustafa. Do you know how fortunate you are to have him? He is a religious leader—a *Sufi*, a mystic—and a credit to his order. You know, I have reservations about the *Sufi* orders. Too often they're the lazy Franciscans of your sixteenth century. But Mustafa refuses to live off of the alms of others.

"He is a sort of Saint Paul to his community. Your Saint Paul made tents. Mustafa is a senior houseboy. He's always worked. And for Americans. He has said he likes Americans as a group. He says you are more honest and unpretentious than Europeans. And he's taken a special liking to you. He's said some strange things about you to me. Some I must disagree with. Some I disapprove of. But enough of my talking. Mustafa's said you'd have some questions for me. His order forbids him to speak of or divulge certain matters. But by a *hiyla*—what your Philadelphia lawyers would call 'an easement'—he thinks I could do so."

I took a breath: "All right. First, since arriving in Sudan, I've been involved in one violent incident after another. I don't know why. Second, an individual or group has published letters over the pen name—

the 'nom de guerre'—of a certain 'Abu Nar.' This party knows a lot about us. We have no idea who he might be. Third, Mustafa—after looking into a bowl of water—has given me a talisman."

Al-Mughraibiy broke in: "A word derived from the Arabic *tilasm*. But go on."

"The talisman contains I don't know what. It has a white cowrie on the outside. Mustafa says I should have it on me or near me always. It's a specific against what he calls the 'Red Wind.' Somehow, it can cause a 'White Wind' to help me. The Red Wind, he says is very dangerous. Whatever it is, I believe him. Also, he says the Red Wind is every day blowing closer to me. Not a consoling thought."

Al-Mughraibiy listened intently: "I can understand your confusion. What does a Connecticut Yankee do when his time machine overshoots King Arthur's court? And he finds himself on the frontiers of magic and animism? But I mustn't be too hard on Mustafa. I think. He feels. And I know his feelings can penetrate further than my thoughts. He's right to remind me sometimes that God accorded Satan some influence over men. You smile? That's right. Some of you Westerners have all but convinced yourselves that Satan never existed. How *he* must be laughing—and not in Hell. But in your hearts. In your 'very neck vein,' to borrow a phrase from the Qur'an. But again, that's a lecture for my people, not yours."

Al-Mughraibiy thought for a moment, then continued: "To address your questions: understand first that what I'm about to say, I don't necessarily believe in or subscribe to. Certainly I don't always approve of it—even if it were true and possible. There *may* be witches—but one shouldn't visit them. Remember poor *Salut*—your King Saul?

"Popular Sudanese belief has it that from time to time, God sends Red Winds, forces of destruction, against the people of Sudan. Our defeat by the Egyptian, Ibrahim Pasha, in the 1820s, was preceded by popular preachers—dervishes—announcing the Red Wind was upon us. They made it sound like a particularly bad sandstorm. It was. And it lasted for sixty years. Then came the Mahdi—another bearer of the Red Wind. I advise you not to mention this to his descendant, the prime minister. But do not believe the myths about the Mahdi's universal popularity. Mostly, he was feared and hated everywhere. Not only for his slave raids in the South."

"Is there a specific against the Red Wind?" I asked.

Al-Mughraibiy replied: "Of course. Magic is like physics. For every action there is a reaction. Here, the supposed opposite force is called the White Wind. But there's a little problem. The Red Wind seems to appeal to what is common, almost universal in man's soul. Greed, violence, lust, cupidity. Thus it finds fertile ground everywhere. It finds leaders and followers. In Ibrahim Pasha and the Mahdi it found strong leaders. Your Mustafa thinks the Red Wind has found itself one such leader in Sudan today. But he doesn't know who. He can't see him. The Red Wind, he says, is obscuring him. It is protecting its own. When he water-divines, he sees only a swirl of sand, and a man's silhouette. That person behind the sandscreen, he believes, is the Abu Nar you speak of. He is 'Abu Nar' or 'the Father of Fire,' also known as the 'Bearer of the Red Cowrie.' "

Al-Mughraibiy asked: "Did you know that Abu Nar was the name the Mahdi chose for himself in the earliest days of his ministry? It's a very little known fact. The name lasted only perhaps weeks. Does it suggest that whoever has taken the name knows our history and is a man of no small ambition?"

He went on: "As for Mustafa's water gazing. It's a form of divining. Lots of dervishes try it, and say they can *do* it. Maybe your Mustafa can. The practice is not *haram*—forbidden—nor exactly *makruuh*—strongly disapproved of. But it's not what a good Muslim—forgive me—it's not what *I* would do. The theory is that by looking into a brass, or copper, or bronze dish of darkened water—some simply add ink—the adept can see past events, future events, and events happening at the same instant elsewhere on earth. A kind of CNN on three channels: past, present, future. Could water-divining be related to the Rorschach ink blot? Could it manifest the inner perceptions of a particularly sensitive personality? Or could it sometimes be phenomenologically true? *Allahu a'lam.* God knows.

"You must wonder," al-Mughraibiy said, "how does one harness the White Wind? Like the Greeks—of course—you put it in a small leather purse. But you must not open it. Ulysses learned his lesson the hard way. Then you seal the wind in place with a white cowrie! The cowrie's been a mark of wealth and power throughout East Africa since time immemorial. It has a place in many cultic practices, even outside Africa and the Middle East."

I asked: "And is the Red Wind harnessed in a similar way? A sachet? With a cowrie?"

"Yes. Its claimant will always have on or about his person a small leather sachet, with a red cowrie affixed to its center."

I reached into my pocket and took out my charm. Al-Mughraibiy regarded it with interest. But he made no move to take it into his hand.

"These are Mustafa's doings, dervish doings," al-Mughraibiy said, "and perhaps, just perhaps, your doings."

"What do you mean by that?" I asked.

"All cultures," he explained, "have their savior myths. You know: the King under the Mountain—Arthur? Frederick Barbarossa? The Second Coming? Sumanguru in Mali? Popular Sudanese culture has one, too. The savior is 'The Bearer of the White Cowrie.' Or as they say in colloquial Arabic, '*kabir al mahara al baida.*' That is, 'The Master of the White Cowrie.' He recurs from time to time in Sudanese history. Always to ward off some peril to the people of Sudan. Not much different from riding a white charger, is it, Mr. Chamberlain?"

I felt stunned. I heard myself asking: "But why would Mustafa think of me? And against what sort of threat am I supposed to be a specific?"

"I suppose," replied al-Mughraibiy, "that not even Mustafa can really answer that question. About the threat, that is. That's one of the problems with magic. Another reason to leave it alone. If it answers one question, it only raises another, even more urgent and ticklish, one. Macbeth should have kept his own counsel."

Al-Mughraibiy explained further: "But the followers of Mustafa's order would say that only a rare and particularly strong person can bear the White Cowrie. Even then, such bearers sometimes fail; they are often distracted. It seems to be harder to bear the White Cowrie, and to use it successfully, than to practice with its red sister. That's the world's way, isn't it? For every hero of good—every Gandhi, or Galahad, or Gawain—how many monsters, witches, warlocks, and other heroes of evil? And always remember: these figures are not fiction—they are the ordinary men and women around us. We feel safer when we make them the exception—and put them in books. But they're really with us everywhere. *All the time.*"

My feeling of numbness persisted. "Do you mean," I managed to say, "that Mustafa sees me as having a potential role in some unfolding morality play in Sudan's current affairs?"

Al-Mughraibiy looked at me impassively. "Perhaps that's just what Mustafa does think. Maybe he thinks you have some talent. Maybe even that you could be a star."

"But this is all madness! I'm a Foreign Service officer of the United States of America. I come from Maine. In the northeast corner of the United States—where no one ever heard of Sudan, or its winds, or its holymen and dervishes. Most insane, though, is this role Mustafa—according to *you*—that Mustafa has in mind for me. Galahad! Great God! Maybe we Presbyterians and Congregationalists aren't 'the Sinners in the Hands of an Angry God' we used to be. But when I look within—even a little bit—I want to drop the seat cover back down. No perfection or perfectibility in here." I touched my chest. "What should I do?"

"There's always diplomatic immunity," said al-Mughraibiy drily. "You can try that. Or you can tell your people this story. You'll get a transfer, on medical grounds, at least. Or you can forget the whole thing. Laugh it off. Or you can keep your eyes open, keep your talisman handy—as Mustafa recommends—and see what happens. Another idea: do you pray Mr. Chamberlain?"

"Well, of course. I say my prayers at church on Sundays, also sometimes when I go to bed."

"I never spoke of '*saying* prayers,' " al-Mughraibiy remarked coldly. "I asked if you *prayed*. There's a difference. Think about it. Try to talk to God. Very difficult. Very humiliating. Everyone would rather 'say prayers.' But try it maybe. Pray."

I asked: "Is there anything else, Dr. al-Mughraibiy—more useful—I mean more practical, maybe—that you could offer or advise?"

Al-Mughraibiy seemed to reflect. Then he nodded slowly. "Your Mustafa," he went on, "is a strange fellow. It's against my judgment. Against my beliefs almost. But I'll agree in a limited way to his request."

"Which was?"

"Tomorrow, take on the 'gardeners' whom I'll send to the residence. They'll cost you nothing. *And* they'll know their . . . jobs. Also, for some of your public functions, let Mustafa continue to provide the servants as he's done in the past. Be sure to hire those he recommends. They, too, will cost you nothing. They may even be of service. And then tell him that if ever he looks into that brass dish of his and sees me, I don't want to hear one single word of it."

"Anything else?"

"Yes. One more. When your embassy people write or speak about 'God' in Islam, don't let them use the word 'Allah.' Please, please, have them say or write just 'God.' Doesn't writing 'Allah' in an English sentence imply that while Westerners worship 'God,' Muslims worship something different? Most likely something primitive, awful, and strange? Depend upon it—our prayers are directed to, and received at, the very same address. They are opened and read by the very same addressee. No culture has a monopoly on intolerance, Mr. Chamberlain."

I replied: "You have a good point there, Dr. al-Mughraibiy."

Mughraibiy gave me another of his sudden, boyish smiles. He extended his hand. "Good night, Mr. Chamberlain," he said. "When you came, I thought I'd soon be saying good-bye. But you never know with these things. Instead I'll say 'so long,' and 'keep your head down,' and 'good luck,' and *Allah ma'ak:* May God be with you."

DOUBLE REVERSE

18

Back at the Residence, Marj was already asleep as I quietly let myself into the bedroom. As I stood for a moment in the dark, a whistle, followed by a rising squeal, pierced through the bedroom. It was a "cell call" and came from the "lunch-pail" radio on our dresser. I turned on the table lamp next to the radio. The time was only 2230.

I always hated the nagging pitch of the sound, the big brother to fingernails across a blackboard. A police chase sound in one's own bedroom! Especially, I hated it each Wednesday morning when the Marines tested the entire system. In bedroom after bedroom, starting at 0600, radios would come to life. Wham! If you were already awake, fine; if not, the cell call took you like a sonic boom through the heart. The Marines, who had been on duty all night, admitted they sometimes punched in with gusto the code for each new call—and especially the calls going to the ambassador and the DCM.

I switched the set to the "send and receive" mode and activated the "push-to-talk" switch: "Hello Base, this is Hickory, over."

The ambassador's voice came in: "Hickory, this is Pine Tree. Go to secure." He went on: "We have a possible hostage situation at PLO headquarters. I'm on my way there now. I should be there in about twenty-five mikes. Ask Valiant to meet me there asap with one of his police contacts. Also, you better call the Presidency, get them onto the matter. But first call the Marine on duty; he knows as much as I do."

I asked: "Is it really wise for you to go there, Pine Tree? Would it be better to go through channels?"

Farnsworth's voice cut back in: "No. By then, 'channels' may be clogged. The best time for a rescue is just after capture. Then, the situation hasn't jelled—the jaws haven't closed. We've got to use maximum pressure right now to see they don't. That means raising all the hell we can and keeping the PLO off balance. My appearance, flag flying, at their gate should give them something to think about."

"Should I join you?" I asked.

Even through the Donald Duck quality of voice transmission, there was something dry in Jon's response: "No. If there's a chance the CO might become 'combat ineffective,' we need at least the exec officer on hand. Have Jack Kirby join you at the Embassy. I'll radio again from the PLO office location. Pine Tree clear."

For the first time I looked over toward Marj. She was sitting up in bed. "Bad news," I explained. "Maybe even a hostage situation. I'll go use the radio downstairs. But don't worry—it doesn't involve *me* this time."

From the study downstairs, I called the Marine on duty, "Post One." On secure voice, the Marine told me he had received a broken transmission on one of the embassy's E&E monitors at 2210. These were set to the radio frequencies used by the nets of American corporations, UN agencies, and the British embassy. We formed a sort of self-help society.

The Marine explained: "This voice suddenly came through—we have it on tape—said, 'This is Mike Gary. Some armed men are stopping me in front of PLO headquarters. Shot up the car . . . they're coming for me . . . do you hear? Get someone . . .' That's where the transmission broke off," the Marine concluded.

Until that moment, I'd half hoped we might be dealing with some sort of false alarm. But what the Marine said sounded serious. Gary was the local manager of the Connel Oil Company (CONNOCO)—they had discovered oil in the south, but what with the insurgency, the oil might as well be on Mars. The company hung on in hopes of better days. Mike Gary was our leading private businessman. He was a personal friend, too, and a good tennis player.

My next call was to Pete Valiant. He said he was on his way and would take with him the police guards stationed at his residence. "They'll at least show the Sudanese flag," he remarked. I contacted Kirby. He said he'd get onto the Interior Ministry, but that if the PLO was involved, we needed help from the Presidency itself.

I called the Presidency. There was no answer at the main switchboard or at the duty officer number. (I thought: How we depend, in Third World capitals, on a miscellany of telephone numbers—often out-of-date or nonworking!) Next, I called Saʻeed's home number—no answer. I tried the numbers we had for al-Atrash; after all, I thought, his office will have to give the orders. No answer. What to do next? An unwelcome thought surfaced. Had I unconsciously been suppressing it? I called Sally on the "land line"—the telephone.

Sally answered. She sounded pleased to hear me. I liked her voice. And how she'd pitch it a little higher, just as she began to speak, then drop into a lower gear, so to speak. "Josh? Hi, how are you? The phones are working! Saʻeed? (A pause) Yes, he's here. I'll put him right on."

I explained to Saʻeed what had happened. Could he help?

"This is a political matter, Josh," he said, "not a protocol one. Not even a Foreign Ministry one. Only the prime minister or the minister for Presidency affairs has the authority. And the prime minister is not in town." I explained I'd already tried but hadn't been able to reach al-Atrash. Did Saʻeed have a number? Or any other suggestions?

"You must know, Josh," he replied, "that Minister al-Atrash would not appreciate my involvement. He is not fond of my association with Americans—(his voice faded for a moment) nothing personal, Sally—he has spoken about it often to the prime minister."

"Saʻeed, this is different." I heard my voice rise, "It could be a matter of life and death, Mike Gary may be in PLO hands, and the ambassador is on his way there by himself. Help us to manage this crisis before it becomes a tragedy."

Saʻeed finally agreed to try to help. He would have an army officer—a relative—drive by PLO headquarters. If the officer saw the car of the American ambassador by the road there, it would be "natural and proper to stop and offer assistance." After considerably more persuasion, Saʻeed gave me a number for al-Atrash. He made me promise to strictly protect the source. "The number," Saʻeed explained, "is to al-Atrash's 'red phone.' It rings in his house and office and is manned around the clock." Saʻeed's last words were: "Remember Mr. Chamberlain, protect the source. This has been a nonconversation."

The number Saʻeed gave me answered on the first ring. The operator obviously did not expect to hear English on this line. "*Ghalat* (Wrong number)," he said in Arabic, and hung up. I called back. Speaking in broken Arabic, I quickly got out that (a) I wanted Dr. al-Atrash, (b) I was from the American embassy, and (c) the matter was "*muhimm jiddan* (very important)." There was the clunk of the receiver being put down, a rustle of papers, voices. One background voice said, "*Mush mumkin* (not possible)." Then into the receiver the same voice said abruptly, "*Allo, naʻam, man inta*? (Hello? Yes, who are you?)."

My interlocutor, it turned out, spoke fair English. Why did I want to speak to the minister? Quickly, I again explained the crisis. A hand went over the receiver. Time passed. The voice came back on the line: No, the minister was not there. No, he had no idea where he was—nor when or where he could be reached. I should try tomorrow in his office, but should go through appropriate Foreign Ministry channels.

A background voice. Another pause. Then a sharp question: How had I gotten this number? I replied that was of no importance. What was important was that the information immediately get to the minister. Could that be done? The reply, "*Insha'allah* (God willing!)," was followed by a dial tone. The time was 2305 hours.

I drove fast to the Embassy and went directly to Jack's office. He was on the phone, a yellow, legal-sized pad of drafting paper lay in front of him. The top sheet was mostly filled with numbers and notations. He looked very serious. "No one here wants to touch the matter, Josh," he explained. "They all say, 'It's a matter for the prime minister or the minister for Presidency affairs.' It sounds like they're reading from little laminated cards in their wallets. Our nonrights. It's the sound of the buck being passed. I've tried but couldn't reach al-Atrash's office director—hardly one of my contacts, though."

Jack was pleased I'd gotten al-Atrash's number. He was even a little reassuring. "Don't worry about your message not getting through! You can bet that piece of work was hanging around the phone! He was probably speaking to you himself the second time. We don't know *what* he'll do. What should *we* do, though? Call Washington? They'll die!"

The phone rang. It was the Marine. I heard Jack say, "They're coming in? Who? *All* of them? You sure? The ambassador *and* Gary *and* Valiant? OOO—Kaaay! (Jack looked up at me questioningly—nodded into the receiver) Yeah, he's here. I'll tell him, just told him. Yeah. Call in the ambassador's secretary, the DCM's too. They'll both be busy. And have the nurse come in, too."

It turned out we didn't really need the nurse. But Maryann and Clayton took dictation in shifts through much of the night.

Excerpt of Mike Gary's Statement: I was driving back to our warehouse in Nasser Extension. There wasn't much traffic. I go by there every day at close of business. It's on the way home. As I got near the "Palestinian Embassy"—until tonight I didn't know what that villa was. Anyway, there were these men by the side of the road. They stepped out as I came by—they were armed. Pointed their guns at me. I tried to go on—that's when they shot the car up, and that's when I made my radio call. They yanked open the door, pulled me out. Took the radio—that got them very excited; it's one of those hand-held Motorolas. They started calling me *jasuus.* I know that means "spy." They hit me a couple of times with their gun butts. (Nurse Peach's comment: "Mr. Gary's head and face showed contusions and abrasions; a concussion, though, was not indicated.")

(Gary again:) They took me into their building, and taped me to a chair. I was in a room on the second floor. It was all inside, no windows, and furnished like an office. The guy who was examining me spoke English. He kept his face covered by one of those red-and-white checked cloths. He said that for several months the Palestinian intelligence—*Rasd* is the name he gave it—had been observing my movements. They and their Sudanese friends had decided it was time to put an end to "imperialist provocations."

Ambassador: The word *rasd* means "monitoring, observation." Did they specifically mention "Sudanese friends"?

Gary: Yes sir. The interrogator was a mean one. He said they wouldn't try to squeeze information out of me; they were in a hurry. But he wanted to thank me for my great services to the Palestinian Revolution and the liberation forces in Sudan—"posthumous services, of course." They brought out a crate and he asked if I recognized what was in it. I said, sure. It's gelignite from our warehouse. Our inventory control numbers were all over the outside. The interrogator took out a folder of papers. They outlined, he said, an imperialist plot against Prime Minister al-Muntasser. The papers would be found on my body, he said, or "what remained of it. People would be astonished that an engineer could have been so careless with explosives, but in this heat . . ."

(Gary continues): The phone call? It really shook them up. It rang in the next room, and someone answered it. The caller talked a few minutes. The PLO guys—all except for one— went to the phone. I heard Mr. Red Dish Cloth speak really fast, excitedly, in Arabic. Then they closed the door.

Ambassador: Was anything said that might give a lead to the caller?

Gary: I don't know. They sounded respectful to whoever was calling. And just before the door closed I heard one of them, I don't know if it was the one on the phone or not, say something about *ad-doktoor.* Right after this, all hell broke loose. A guy came running in shouting, *al-safiir al-amriikiy!* I understand enough Arabic to know that means "American ambassador." But to me, then, it meant Bugles and Saddles, and the Union Cavalry! Then more palaver, more shouting, some gun-waving. In the end one of the guys—Mr. Red Dish Cloth— gave an order, and they took me downstairs. They handed me over to the ambassador. And he smiles a big smile at me, extends his hand, and says, "Mr. Gary, I presume?" Pete Valiant was there, also a Sudanese army officer.

Kirby: About what time was the phone call?

Gary: It was at 2315 by the clock on the office wall.

In the morning we protested to the acting foreign minister. He took our paper and said only that our views would be made known to the prime minister—when he returned from Dongola.

"When would that be?" the ambassador asked. The minister didn't know.

"Soon?"

"Maybe not," came the answer.

Even more discouraging was the reaction from al-Atrash. He had the effrontery to call the ambassador. On the phone he told Farnsworth he was astonished and disturbed to learn from the Palestine Liberation Office that an American had threatened some of their officials the previous night. They had been forced to take him into custody, until he could be handed over to the Sudanese police. The man had a pattern of suspicious behavior—he had frequently been seen driving by and surveilling the PLO office. Last night he had been operating a portable radio—set to American embassy frequencies—when he was apprehended.

The Government of Sudan urgently sought an explanation for such behavior by an American citizen. It was undertaking an investigation. The results would be provided to the prime minister. Meanwhile, the suspect American had best not try to leave Khartoum. No, the Sudanese government did not have anything further on the Hilverding investigation. This question of the ambassador's abruptly ended the conversation.

Later that morning, the PLO organ put out a special edition denouncing the "blatant provocation (*al-tahaddiy al-saafir*)" of the "monopolist authorities (*al-sulutaat al-ihtikaariyyah*)." In its afternoon editions, the more moderate press stayed silent. Jon believed it was either sympathetic to the PLO, bought off, or intimidated. The Libyan mouthpiece, strangely enough, did not chime in against us. There was silence also from Abu Nar.

Dawkins said the Libyans were "sitting this one out" because Qadhaafi hated Arafat and the PLO almost as much as he hated America. The silence from Abu Nar? Dawkins shrugged. "Maybe he's 'on assignment' and has no one to write his column for him?"

Farnsworth was philosophical: "Be glad we got Mike Gary back alive and healthy. Other good men haven't done as well. Cleo Noel. Curt Moore. Spike Dubs. Rodger Davies. But we'll never be able to persuade the Sudanese government the PLO was engaged in terrorism—al-Atrash and the Palestinians have stirred up too much turbidity. But we can now see just how far al-Atrash will go; gives us an insight, though not really a surprise. We must assume it was he calling PLO headquarters, or one of his men."

"But what will we do now?" I asked.

"We'll stay alert, and watchful, and study the options we may have. Renew our travel advisory to Amcits; let's take a still harder look for nonessential staff."

Sally came to me in midafternoon. "I've gotten a strange call from Sa'eed," she said. "He was asking to make sure that you and Jack Kirby had gotten your invitations to the dinner that he and I were putting on at my place tonight at eight o'clock. He repeated the words 'eight o'clock.'" Sally looked a little uncomfortable, and went on: "The point is, we've never given a joint dinner—Sa'eed's just a friend. But what I think is, he wants to talk to the two of you. So I said you'd gotten them and would be there."

The ambassador agreed we should go. "This might be one of those options we spoke of."

I'd never seen Sa'eed *un*-debonair. But, in fact, he appeared worried. Diminished. Like some fluffy lap dog who's gotten wet and looks shrunk to half its normal size.

As Sally served us drinks, Sa'eed was explaining: "Minister al-Atrash summoned me this morning. I have never seen him in such a rage. He is famous for his dirty mouth, but he called me things I have never heard, even in Arabic. Then he cursed me in English and Italian, too. He said he knew I had given his number to the Americans because (Sa'eed hesitated—he looked at Sally) because, let's say, I wanted to find favor with Miss Tolson. He described her in very harsh and unflattering terms. 'Mata Hari' was the least. Also, Sally, he thinks you are too skinny. But he wouldn't let me speak. He shouted he didn't want to hear one word from me. If I even opened my mouth, his guards would throw me out of the office. Finally, he said that when the PM was back from Dongola, he'd make sure my next job would be protocol deputy in Juba—your friend Mr. Furj would be my next boss." Sa'eed raised his hand, as if to ward off a blow. "I left his office—in fact, I did not say one single word."

Sa'eed added mournfully: "The question is now, can you help me?" He looked towards me, but with a certain delicacy—I had to concede him that. He didn't come right out and say we owed him one.

A pause. All three of us found that we were looking at Jack. With his finger, he swirled the ice in his gin and tonic. It made a slight clinking sound.

"Sounds to me, Sa'eed," Kirby said without looking up, "that you have a career-threatening problem." He added: "Juba's no place for a sophisticated, man-of-the world type like you. Why, Josh here told me the people down there still file their teeth to points. They even have some sort of pep rally chant. (Jack's voice and body bounced slightly on the couch as he softly chanted:) 'Whaddoweeat? *Aaarab* meat!' "

Jack looked at Sa'eed for the first time. Sa'eed had fallen back on the couch. He didn't seem to be listening. He was staring blankly into space. Jack put his fingertips together before him in an almost priestly gesture and went on: "The situation is indeed grave. But if you have faith in Uncle Sam, all may not be lost."

Sa'eed looked at Jack warily. "What do you have in mind?" he asked with just a shade of his customary challenge.

"Al-Atrash is no friend of yours," said Jack, "nor of ours. We think he planned to blow up an Amcit and use the scandal to radicalize the government, line it up with Arab radicals. We don't know what he'll try next, or when. So maybe, just maybe, we can help each other."

Jack stopped. Sa'eed was silent. Jack prompted: "What do you say, Sa'eed? Had any better offers lately?"

Sa'eed replied: "I know, 'Mr. Jack,' *who* you are and that what you have in mind is probably against the law, against even my loyalty to Sudan. I know such things are done, but not in my lowly circles. Yes, I will help, but on condition that nothing I do involves killing or injury."

Jack was silent. It was Sa'eed's turn to prompt: "What do you think you can do?"

Jack answered: "We'll talk (pointing to all three of us) to the ambassador; then maybe we'll ask Washington for 'a finding.' I'll stay in touch. I'll let you know when I have something. Meanwhile, be good, and don't get on any Juba flights for a couple of weeks."

Sa'eed smiled uncertainly: "I can stall for a few weeks, I think."

We liked Jack's general plan. The ambassador concurred, and told Washington he'd support a finding. We stressed the issue was time-sensitive. A bureaucratic way of saying "urgent."

At the end of the first week, Sa'eed called us at the office, unusual for him. He wondered if we'd "found" the glasses he forgot at Sally's the week before. We told him: "We were still looking."

The next day Sa'eed came himself to the Residence; he'd received bad news. The prime minister was back, and al-Atrash had wasted no time making good on his threat. A messenger had hand-delivered to Sa'eed orders immediately transferring him to Juba, with instructions to report to his superior, a Mr. Furj! Together with the orders, al-Atrash had enclosed a copy of Alan Moorehead's *White Nile*. Some passages having to do with Equatoria had been underlined in red: Sa'eed read them to us: " . . . the climate was unbearable. . . . To avoid the mosquitoes it was necessary to go to bed before seven in the evening. . . . His brother had already died. . . . Grosvenor was next to go . . . speared in an action against the Bari."

Another panic call from Sa'eed came days later. This time al-Atrash had sent him a copy of Edward Hoagland's *African Calliope;* the sections on "green monkey fever" in Equatoria had been highlighted in yellow. With the book had come a recommendation by al-Atrash's *chef de cabinet* that Sa'eed begin courtesy calls on Khartoum officials with responsibilities for Equatoria. Worst of all, the prime minister's secretary continued to give one reason after another why Sa'eed could not see his boss.

"Had we heard anything from Washington?" Sa'eed concluded in tones that were touched with panic. We hadn't—but would be following up.

Several more days passed. By then Sa'eed was in a bad state. His personal effects had already been shipped south. The leading candidate for his job—a close relative of al-Atrash's—had come by to look at the house. He'd been displeased, almost threatening when he found Sa'eed still in residence. The intercession of various tribal elders had bought Sa'eed another week or ten days, but the Juba assignment stood firm. As Sa'eed remarked: "That al-Atrash is a good hater."

Sa'eed was seen less frequently on the tennis courts or in the foreign community. His protocol duties had mostly been shifted to his deputy. As Sally observed: "Poor Sa'eed, it's only *after* he gets off the social circuit that he looks like he's been up all night." But Jack was still waiting. To myself, I wondered if the delay might be a bit deliberate. Did Jack want to stretch out his man? Not reel him in until good and tired?

One morning, however, Jack came smiling into the front office. "Santa and his reindeer arrived last night," he said. "Better call Sa'eed and give him the news." With the ambassador's approval, we arranged for a meeting at Sally's that night.

Sa'eed was already there when I arrived. He was sitting upright on the edge of a chair. He'd already smoked several cigarettes. Sally said he had declined the offer of a drink. As I made one for myself at the bar, she said in a low voice that Sa'eed seemed tense, hopeful, withdrawn.

I heard the bell ring. The gate opened, and Jack came up the walk, carrying a medium-sized, heavily reinforced cardboard box. It looked like the sturdy packing boxes L.L. Bean sends its merchandise around the world in. Jack set the package down carefully on Sally's coffee table and got right down to business.

"Sa'eed," he began, "we have a situation where perhaps we can help you, and you can help us. I have here a present, a very nice present. I want you to give it to our common friend, Dr. al-Atrash."

Sa'eed looked astonished.

"It comes with some testimonials," said Jack, "that I hope you'll also give—or leave with—Dr. al-Atrash." With this he stood the box on one end, and with a Swiss Army knife began to cut through the fiber-reinforced strapping tape over the top. Looking up, he explained: "This box here is only the innermost casket of the sarcophagus; it took a jumbo pouch to get all this here. There were plastic peanuts everywhere in the office."

Inside the package were more "plastic peanuts," but smaller. *Shelled* plastic peanuts? Sally got a plastic garbage bag from the kitchen. Holding the box carefully, Jack tipped out some of the "peanuts" into the bag. Then, as Sally held the box by its bottom against the table, Jack gingerly, delicately, eased out a tubular object. It was wrapped in bubble plastic and was perhaps two-and-a-half feet tall.

Inside the wrappings stood a clock. An astonishing, multifaced clock, shaped a little like a model of the Chrysler building. The liquid crystal display faces went all around; they were arrayed in six or seven layers, from bottom to top. Jack pressed a button. Soft spectrums of color washed up through the VGA displays. Jack pressed another button. The color show continued, but now the displays showed the names of world capitals and their respective times of day. Jack pressed another button, all went dark again.

"That's just the least of what this gizmo will do," he explained. "It can be programmed to give the times in some fifty world capitals. It can also be switched to the Islamic 'moon' calendar, chime the time for prayers, and give you the dates for Ramadan and the Pilgrimage for the next ten thousand years. The frame and appointments are solid sterling silver," Jack added almost as an afterthought.

"Beautiful. Curious, anyway," Sally remarked. "But how does this address Sa'eed's problem and ours, with al-Atrash?" Jack smiled: "This contraption has another special feature. It explodes."

We all sat bolt upright. "Yes," Jack went on, "it is a masterpiece of the watchmaker's *and* the armorer's art. The two crafts seem related, somehow. The clock came from Czechoslovakia— the Russians sometimes used the craftsmanship of satellite countries for special jobs. It's something that a radical group like the PLO—with some money—could get its hands on these days. Lucky for us—or for one of our friends— the clock never had a chance to do its work. We intercepted the original delivery—on its way to the Gulf. Since then, the clock has been in our inventory, biding its time, just ticking away, in one of Uncle Sam's warehouses—a 'Treasure of the Lost Ark,' so to speak."

Jack showed us the clock's controls, including the one used to set the clock to the bomb mode. At this, Sa'eed spoke up for the first time: "I told you, I think, Mr. Kirby, that I want no part of blowing someone up—not even an enemy like al-Atrash. Not even (he added more slowly) if it involves Juba."

"That's not our purpose either, Sa'eed," responded Jack. "You've not been reading your papers. It's been years since we've been authorized to try assassinations—if ever we were," he quickly added and went on: "No, the purpose of this 'alarm clock' is to awaken the PM's concern about old al-Atrash. You see, the clock also comes with instructions to al-Atrash—for a PLO-backed coup, involving elements of the Presidential Guard as well. The PLO units are to come from the PLO camp in the northeast at Erkowit. Not a bad plan. The paperwork is altogether remarkable—signatures, too. I think you'll find all in order."

Jack took from his breast pocket a clear, sealed plastic envelope and gave it to Sa'eed. Through the clear plastic, I saw variously colored documents, stamps, and Arabic script.

Jack went on: "We'd like you to give the clock to al-Atrash. Give it to him alone. You can do that, can't you? Sneak in with a peace offering, tail between your legs—a bribe or something."

Sa'eed interrupted: "He will not change his mind. He will take the clock, and then insult me more."

Jack cut him off. "Do you want to take a little more abuse and save your job and get some revenge? Or do you want to enter the next dugout canoe race to Juba?" Sa'eed sat back again.

"Like I said," Jack went on, "you give him the clock, then you turn these documents over to the prime minister. Do it yourself?"

Sa'eed objected: "But al-Atrash will simply denounce me. He'll say the clock came from me. That the documents are forged."

"So what?" answered Kirby. "On the clock—can he prove it? Didn't you sneak in, hangdog, some time that no one could see you?"

"That's right," mused Sa'eed.

Jack continued: "And as for the documents, a little secret: they're not forged. They, too, were an intercept. We only had to make a few changes. No one in Sudan could ever spot them!"

Kirby spoke slowly and deliberately: "Sa'eed—intelligence does not have to be precise. It does not have to be 'finely crafted.' Like most government products, it needs only to be adequate. Al-Atrash gets the clock. He gets denounced. He denies any guilt—but then it's *our* turn to muddy the waters. We may not have the contacts that al-Atrash does, or Abu Nar, either. But we have *some* resources.

"Soon al-Atrash will be so busy swatting away mosquitoes and wiping away the mud we'll sling—some moral charges will make juicy reading, too—he'll forget all about you. Or won't dare continue his vendetta. He'll be immobilized politically. Sounds simple? Believe me, the U.S. Army's motto, KISS, has it right: Keep it simple, Stupid."

"NOW THE SERPENT WAS MORE SUBTLE..."

19

I'd just gotten to the Embassy when Jon called me into his office. "The evacuation went as well as any can," he said, adding, "You could say the same of a funeral. But you and the administrative section handled it well. Marjorie, too. She was great in helping to organize the departure, then being the perfect hostess at your house as she and the others were processed to leave. We'll *all* miss her."

I felt flat, empty. I could still see Marj bending down a little in the doorway of the Falcon Airlines Boeing 767 and waving good-bye to me just as the doors were closing. Then takeoff. Jon and I had watched the plane go.

After a few minutes Pete Valiant had turned to us and said, "OK, they're out of range."

"What sort of world do we live in," I'd asked him, "when evacuation flights have to worry about shoulder-held missiles!"

"Today's world."

But the ambassador was right; the evacuation *had* gone well. That was important—first, because you owed no less to your colleagues; and second, because an evacuation that was badly planned or tactlessly handled meant trouble back home for embassy management. My planning with various sections and agencies had paid off: no one appealed the listings I'd worked out with them earlier of "nonessential" personnel. Each household had its vital documents together (including powers of attorney); stateside relatives had been notified—even pets were provided for. Through our network of wardens, we'd notified our dozen

Peace Corps volunteers in Northern Sudan, collected them, and gotten them to the airport in time.

Airports! Foreign Service people have ambivalent feelings about them. We live in them more than most people do. Airports are where congressional and executive branch delegations arrive and depart. Tea ceremonies, arrival statements, destruction-derby motorcades. It's where we ourselves arrive. I thought of our own arrival. Was it only nine or ten weeks ago?

Airports are also where our children come in on vacation— happy event!—and afterwards depart—desolation! How I hated the precise moment when Brian's plane would put its head down and, with a roar, bolt for the end of the runway! I wanted to run after it. Then the receding signal lights, red on the port side, green for starboard. Then just one more flickering star, then the silent drive home—Brian's room still untidy, the bedclothes thrown back. Afterwards, nothing—except very infrequent letters.

"Thanks Jon," I replied. "I'll tell Marj what you said in my next letter. She'll appreciate it—coming from you. Odd," I went on, "to think that she'll be at Logan tomorrow afternoon. Her parents will meet her, and next week she'll visit Brian in Delaware."

"How is he? How has he taken the news he must hear from Sudan?"

"His last letter sounded cheery. And we don't give him *all* the news. I guess Sudan's in another dimension to a young man intent on girls, the Tower Hill game, and his studies—in that order, I'm afraid. He's a starter as defensive end. Scored two touchbacks in his last game. He keeps asking for a car. We keep saying 'no.' He keeps responding: 'But I'm the only boy in the class who . . .' "

Jon laughed: "Parents should have blank forms with just that phrasing. Let their children fill it in. Save a lot of time."

I nodded, and said: "But we've nothing to complain about. He's really a good kid. Happy, athletic, well-adjusted."

The ambassador seemed to have slipped into a reverie. Had he heard my last remark? I tried never to talk about my son. Though I was genuinely interested and sympathetic when others spoke of their children.

"I remember one fall," the ambassador mused, "Ann and I (it was the first time I'd heard Jon mention his late wife's name) went back to the States in November. The Iraqi president and his wife were coming on an official visit. So Ann got to come back with me. Afterwards, we drove to Boston for Thanksgiving with our families.

"We picked Mark up from school in Connecticut—he's now a naturalist for the Woodland Park Zoo in Seattle—and headed north. He'd done alright in his studies, and in sports. Had a lot to tell us as we drove. You know how children are when they first see their parents after an absence? They're sometimes in a talking mood—even confiding. We just let him talk. Were careful not to say anything to check the flow. Scare him off the perch. Stop the singing. I often think of that drive as one of the happiest experiences of my life. Cold dark weather, a nice road, stops for milkshakes on I-95. Inside the car it was warm, a world of our own. . . ."

Jonathan went on: "But while we're on the subject of holidays, it's not too early to think ahead. Sometime soon, let's talk to Maryann and Clayton to see who comes to your house—if you're back in it—and who comes to mine for Thanksgiving and Christmas. So decide who you want, let's talk, and invite early. But whatever happens, it has to be 100 percent."

I must have looked puzzled. Farnsworth explained: "A hundred percent of our people must be accounted for at Thanksgiving and Christmas. To be alone back in the States during our 'High Holy days' is bad enough. It's even worse overseas—especially after an evacuation.

"Then there's the Marine Ball coming up November 10," he added, "the peak event of our Foreign Service social year. Most people don't know the U.S.M.C is a year older than the Republic. I'm glad the Marines can hold this year's ball after all. Decidedly decent of poor Sa'eed al-Masri. Pete Valiant said he used much of his remaining pull to get the rec site secured. I hear al-Masri goes to the Marines' parties."

I nodded. I said: "Even the RSO was impressed with the security arrangements. So was the department. It sounds like half the Sudanese army's going to be there on maneuvers while we dance."

The ambassador looked absent again. "Strange. Ann and I have been—I mean, were—at more Marine birthdays than some of our watchstanders have had birthdays of their own."

Farnsworth sat up straight. He shook his head, as if to clear it. "Enough lucubrations. Let's make the staff meeting happen. Sally! Got the agenda?"

She came in: "On the desk, sir, here."

Today the agenda had only two items: My meeting with Shaikh al-Mughraibiy and preparations for the Marine Corps Birthday Ball.

I said al-Mughraibiy had seemed nonfanatical, sincere, and not so much anti-Western as against the *effect* of Westernization on Muslim society. I left out the eschatology. I also thought it best not to mention his "gardeners." They had, in fact, shown up the next morning. They worked hard, didn't talk much, stuck together. A little to my surprise, the new "gardeners" were all southerners. (Many black southerners, I learned, were Muslim—about 20 percent. Experts guessed another 20 per cent were Christian, and the rest followed traditional African religions.)

The ambassador was very pleased by my contact with al-Mughraibiy. "That's the sort of thing we ought to do more of," he said. "We've tried for a long time to meet him. You never know what works. Your Mustafa is certainly a man of parts. You can count on *that* report making people sit up in Washington, D.C."

Will Dawkins noted that my impressions more or less tracked with what we'd heard of al-Mughraibiy. He wasn't a "screamer." As a *Sudanese* Muslim Brother, or MB, he was seen as more moderate than his counterparts in Lebanon, Syria, and even Egypt. Dawkins reminded us, though, that the Sudanese MBs had some hard men in their ranks, too. The MBs didn't rely just on Qur'anic recitation for their persuading.

I could feel audience interest pick up as the ambassador turned to the Marine Corps Ball. Jack Kirby offered in *recitatif* a few lines from *Kiss Me Kate*:

Three weeks to rehearse and rehearse.
Two weeks and it couldn't be worse.
One week will it ever be right
To pull out of the hat on that opening night!

Laughter. Applause. Speaking over it, Pete and the gunny described the administrative and security arrangements for the ball. A shuttle was available to take embassy people to the rec site; get them home, too (knowing laughter). Bill Gray wanted to bring some business contacts. He guessed his invitation had been misplaced. The ambassador noted it was *the Marines*' ball. It was up to them to invite whomever they chose.

The gunny tactfully remained silent, eyes fixed on one of the leopard skins. (I figured since Gray never invited the Marines to his house, they didn't want to invite *him* or his guests to their party.) Making no reference to Gray, Sergeant Poe began to speak of the ball. "We think it'll be a great ball. A lot of embassy people are gone, but we're inviting a few extra Sudanese and more members of the diplomatic corps—friends we think will dance. And, Mr. Ambassador, we're having our first practice ceremony tomorrow. You know how it goes, but maybe you could join us for a short rehearsal? Fifteen or twenty minutes, max. And maybe the night of the ball, after I read the commandant's message, you could make a few birthday remarks of your own?"

The ambassador smiled, nodded. He added: "I'll be there, and if it all plays well, gets good reviews, we might just bring it back next year." More laughter. The meeting adjourned.

Days later, as I looked over the scene at the Marine Ball, I asked myself: "How could the Marines, even with embassy help, have done all this? Could *I* have invited three hundred and fifty people to a dinner dance, plus ceremonies, when I was nineteen or twenty?"

The lawn was dark green, impeccable. The grass had been carefully tended for weeks—then deliberately not watered for the last two days. Otherwise, chair legs and women's heels would subside into the earth. Row upon row of tables faced the dance floor, each table bright with U.S.M.C. red and gold tablecloths, embossed paper napkins, and U.S.M.C. plastic glasses. Bottles of Paul Masson champagne, like lane dividers, stood down the center of the tables. There was one bottle to every two or three place settings. The tile dance floor was, for the moment, empty. Soft music played, the beginnings of a barbecue aroma in the air. Spotlights illuminated the rec site building itself: an enormous American flag, twenty by twelve feet, was brilliantly displayed against its side wall, facing the entrance.

I took all this in, then went down the reception line, saluting and shaking hands with the Marines.

"Any trouble getting here, sir?" asked the gunny.

"Just the enormous potholes," I replied. "I figure they protect us from armored assault. But I didn't know when they tore down the Berlin Wall, they'd rebuild it here! Armored cars, Jersey barriers, some elite unit or other's all around the place. In cammies. I even saw some flak vests. Pete thought we could have a fashion show."

The gunny smiled. "The security's good, alright. The Sudanese even have a Boston Whaler or a Boghamar standing off the boat landing.

Mr. al-Masri told me he was going all out to help us make this party a real success. A sort of thank-you, he said, for good times at the Marine house. Another thing, we decided to invite Mr. Gray, after all—even if he *never* invites us to *his* functions. Probably not much fun anyway. Here comes the ambassador."

I spoke to Jonathan. Then I got some champagne and began to walk about the garden. The guests were mostly embassy people, so far. There were lots of servants. As in past years, Mustafa had arranged for them. I couldn't tell which might be the *murshid's* "moles." One or two looked like my "gardeners," but what with the lighting, their uniform complexions and robes and turbans, I couldn't be sure.

I felt a little uncomfortable not having mentioned them to Pete. But one thing would have led to another. And how would he have reacted when I told him I was "the Son of the Mahdi, a latter-day King Arthur"? I could just see it: "Yeah, yeah," in a low voice, so as not to excite. Several approbatory nods of the head. The slow backing away.

I walked over to the railing by the Nile. For a time, I watched the river. A great swatch of black, and beyond that a planetary aberration— a line of crescent moons along the horizon, the neon finials of the minarets on the far shore. The evening was cool, dry, and clear. Down by the boat landing I could see the Boston whaler. Three or four soldiers manned a machine gun on the fantail. They were looking up and down the bank. I felt lonely. I heard the music suddenly get louder. I decided to look for Sally and ask her to dance.

Except for the Mike Gary incident, the past few weeks had been quiet—for Khartoum. Our security was tight, but unchallenged. I had played some tennis—and that meant time with Sally. When we played doubles with others, we always won. It wasn't just that we were both good; we simply clicked.

Sa'eed was preoccupied; he had little time to play. Also, I felt a certain distance had sprung up between him and Sally. When Sa'eed did go out, he and Sally were no longer such a "number" in Khartoum's social life.

On tennis afternoons, Sally and I sometimes left the game to others. We'd just sit in the garden and talk. We shared a taste for German writers. We both loved Goethe and Eichendorf; we disagreed over Hermann Hesse (she for, me against). Another common favorite was Don Marquis's *archie and mehitabel*. Sally liked mehitabel, "a strong female character, indomitable spirit! A fighter. At each knockdown, she says only '*toujours gai!*' and keeps coming on. Well ahead of her time."

And so the days had passed. Often in each other's company—in the office, outside of it, and, I confess, at other times with Sally often in my thoughts. But nothing ever said.

Couples were moving onto the dance floor. The music was slow, introductory. I saw the geologic slope of Frank Greer's back and massive forequarters, glimpsed Aminata's smiling face—the sun peering over the edge of a hill! Frank had complained to me she'd had him get evening clothes made, then afterwards told him he looked like a night club bouncer! But he'd complained good-naturedly.

Over by the dance floor, I saw Sally and Sa'eed talking to the Italian ambassador. I looked Sa'eed over. Did *Le Coq Sportif* do evening clothes? What a tuxedo! Double vents, of course; cuffs on his sleeves, edged with a black, finely braided piping. Black patent leather pumps, shaggy with tassels. Nothing extreme about the shirt front, though. Plain white, and pleated. I figured he knew how garish he'd look in band-leader burgundy.

A voice at my elbow said: "Sa'eed is quite a fashion plate off the tennis courts, too, wouldn't you say?" I looked over to see Avo Bogosian. My eye must have wandered past him, because he answered, as if to a question: "Solange is in Paris—but the Marines were nice enough to invite me anyway. It's Aminata they really wanted, but they took me too—part of a package deal. My good fortune!"

Avo turned toward the Nile and rested his arms on the railing. Looking out over the water, he observed idly: "Bill Gray was saying you'd met Dr. al-Mughraibiy. And that afterwards your embassy nurse did not prescribe lab tests or a rabies booster!"

I felt momentary anger. Gray had no business carrying our classified discussion out of the conference room. But I also knew Gray could never resist trying to look important to Avo. So I simply and factually described (most of) my talk with al-Mughraibiy. Avo listened without much apparent interest. But when I finished, he turned and said, "Thank you Josh—I've learned from you." His tone sounded like a friendly dismissal.

I walked over to Sally's group: "Good evening, Mr. Ambassador. Good evening, Sa'eed. Hello, Sally. We're all looking our best tonight." What I said sounded stupid to me. But Sally *did* look good. Very good. Dark gold hair, a soft tan, as usual. Her smile made me feel hot and cold about the heart. I'd asked her once about her smile. "Orthodontia?" "No," she had replied, "Genes." She wore a short-sleeved, fluffy, rose-colored sweater, cut low, and a stylish, straight leather skirt. I looked—too long.

I heard Sa'eed ask, "And how are your researches into folk anthropology going, Mr. Chamberlain? Any good winds blowing your way? Ha Ha! Any chance of catching cold? Do you take Vitamin C, as Dr. Pauling recommended?—6,000 Units a day, I hear. Or do you carry a charm? Ha Ha!" He unbuttoned his jacket. I got a flash of red paisley lining.

"Nice threads, Sa'eed," I remarked.

"Marks and Sparks," he replied, "their best."

I regretted my behavior at the tennis court. In fact, I still had the charm—it was in my right coat pocket. Earlier in the evening, before Mustafa left for the rec site with the other servants, he'd come to see me: "His Excellency must carry *ta'wiidh*. 'Red Wind' here. Outside window, door, inside house. Blowing all around. I look—only red sand." Mustafa had rotated his arm over his head to imitate a whirlwind.

Sa'eed asked again: "You don't *really* still carry that thing?"

I tried to respond offhandedly: "Sa'eed, that's classified information. Would you ask a lady or a gentleman what they're wearing under their clothes?"

"It would depend," Sa'eed replied evenly, "upon my degree of interest in a particular lady. I might not ask, but I might do my best to find out." At these last words, the note of banter was entirely gone from Sa'eed's voice. We were all silent momentarily, the three of us: Sa'eed and I, Sally in the middle. The Italian ambassador looked on, a little puzzled but aware he'd missed some sort of an exchange.

I broke the silence: "Sally, would you like to dance?"

I liked the nonthinking part of dancing. Letting your body take over, and sending your mind on vacation. At least the office part of the mind. It was nice to feel the music going through you. Nice, too, to watch Sally's moves as Whitney Houston urgently asked:

How will I know if he really loves me,
I'll say a prayer in every heartbeat,
I fall in love whenever we meet,
I tried to call but I feel weak . . .

Without a break, the D.J. spliced into a slow number. Alison Moyet, I recognized, began to sing:

But I just don't want to be lonely, night and day,
But as I look around me, I just feel that way, for you only.

As I took Sally's hand and put my right hand on the small of her back, she placed herself right against me. We stood that way for a moment. Then began to dance. A confusion of feelings poured in. The tensions of the past weeks. Thoughts of Juba. The beautiful evening. The feel of Sally—the length of her, the strength of her—against me. I was aroused. I intertwined my fingers with hers. We continued dancing—was Sally even closer? Stomach, knee to knee, the inside of her thigh. My right hand moved down, to the beginning of a curve. I felt a fine ridge of elastic under her skirt. I splayed my fingers downwards. Sally didn't pull back. Didn't seem to mind. Alison, please, *keep singing* . . . After a time, the music slowed, ended.

Sally slid her arm down from around my neck and placed her right hand lightly against my chest. She looked up at me. In a serious, even tone she said, "You know, I like you better than I should."

We stood there briefly, looking at each other. Couples were beginning to clear the floor. The Marines moved about—passing word the ceremony was about to begin. They moved a lectern and an American flag to the middle of the dance floor. I escorted Sally back to her table. We didn't speak. I didn't trust my vocal cords. Then I joined the ambassador at the head table in the front row.

My thoughts were all in a muddle. I felt as if I'd knocked on a door that I half hoped would remain closed. But as I watched, it was slowly opening. The door to what? My heart? I pushed the thought away. Focused more practically: "Don't look foolish," I said to myself, "think of your pride. Don't let down those who need your leadership and look to you for it."

Except for belief in the Easter Bunny, I knew the dumbest thing a Foreign Service officer could believe was that he could play around at post without everyone writing home about it in the first twenty-four hours. Some senior officers tried to fool themselves. They imagined the public eye would not pierce their veil of discretion! They were fools. Then there were others—with careers often at an end—who didn't worry about a bad corridor reputation, or forfeiting the moral dimension of leadership. Napoleon, I reflected had it right, when he warned his ambassadors not to become intoxicated by either sex or status. "Remember," he advised, "they're alike: the pleasure is fleeting, and the position ridiculous."

But a welcome distraction was unfolding before me.

I confess to a weakness for ceremony. And no one does ceremony better in our route-order society than the U.S.M.C. We rose to sing the first verse of the National Anthem. The ambassador and I faced toward the flag and put our right hands over our hearts.

Then the Marine detachment marched forward as the Marine Corps band—on tape—played the Marine Corps Hymn. One reads about "a heart swelling with pride"? That's what my heart did. Even Sergeant Poe's reading of the commandant's message was only slightly anticlimactic. No one expects an NCOIC to sound like an anchor man.

It came time for the ambassador to speak. I always looked forward to hearing him. When he spoke, it was always personal, appropriate, and to the point. Once he'd told me, "Josh, embassy people and other Americans *want* to feel good about their ambassador. He is, after all, a sort of priestly figure in their midst. So at congregational situations, when he must officiate, he should try to do it well. With a little style. He should try to look good. And to sound entertaining, maybe even a little original."

Looking at Farnsworth at the lectern, I thought he looked the way an ambassador should. He was the only one present whom I'd have matched, by way of elegance, with our friend Sa'eed. Farnsworth's was an altogether different approach to the subject, though. There was no attempt at contemporary style. Nor was the tuxedo new. It just seemed to fit the man. Naturally, gracefully. No effort seemed needed or expended to make a statement by way of clothes.

The ambassador took out a sheet of paper. Glancing at it, he laid it down upon the lectern, then spoke directly to us: "Sergeant Poe, members of the detachment, Excellencies, friends of the Marines. How does one salute heroes present and properly remember those past? You've heard it said on many solemn occasions: 'Words aren't enough.' That saying is right, too. Which is why for this evening I've added some music. You'll recognize it—the great Cole Porter's 'You're the Top'; but the words—and the voice, I'm afraid—are my own."

A familiar tune began to play over the stereo loudspeakers. At this the ambassador turned to the Marines and, in a clear, well-tuned tenor voice, sang:

> You're the Corps
> You're all Patriot rockets
> And what's more
> Haiti's in your pocket
> You're Okinawa, plus Arnold's power on stream
> You're all much too good, you're Belleau Wood
> You're our Gyrenes!
>
> You're a crack
> Force, you're jump jet Harriers
> In the rack
> Or upon a carrier
> First you're Parris I., then 8th and I's your beat
> You're Palms twenty-nine, you age like wine
> You're Willy Pete!

You're the Corps,
You're Tom Clancy heroes,
Spend your days
Saving the Emirates
On the coldest nights Saddam sweats with fright I think,
Dreams he's at the table, with Noriega,
in a U.S.clink!

You're so fine!
Centuries of winning
Two-one-nine's
Just a good beginning
Tho' daybreak comes too soon, the hit tunes won't ever stop!
So raise your glasses high! say Semper Fi!
You're still the top!

The last words were lost in applause. I saw the gunny bring the ambassador a glass of champagne. Then Farnsworth turned back to us saying: "Ladies and gentlemen: please rise and join me in a toast to the United States Marine Corps: Semper Fi!"

The ambassador had just regained his seat when Sa'eed crossed the dance floor and headed for the microphone. "What's this?" I wondered. I couldn't remember the program providing for a statement by the host government. A message from the PM or the like? Something else Sa'eed had cooked up for the occasion? The applause faded uncertainly. We looked at each other. Sa'eed waited until it was quiet. He looked very self-assured, I thought.

Then he spoke: "Excellencies, friends of the Marines, I have two brief but very important announcements. The first is entirely in line with Mr. Ambassador's witty and elegant statement. Please listen." Sa'eed looked at his watch. He took out a pocket transistor radio, turned it on, and raised it to the microphone.

We heard martial music being played. Then it was broken by a voice, speaking in Arabic. The voice was exhorting its listeners. It sounded familiar, then I recognized it. Dr. al-Atrash! In a moment, Dawkins hurried forward. Dropping to one knee, he leaned over to the ambassador and me saying: "It's something political—a new government—or worse."

Just then, from the transistor radio there emerged a roar. A broken, growling, jagged sound. The transmission abruptly ceased. Sa'eed held the radio near the microphone for another few seconds. Complete silence. He smiled radiantly at us. We sat immobile . . . transfixed.

Sa'eed bent over the microphone. "Delete one possible room-mate for Mr. Noriega. I refer to Dr. al-Atrash. The doctor should have stuck to small girls, or to biology, or to the Ministry for Presidential Affairs. Instead, alas, he aspired to something higher—with the help of that fat renegade Yasir Arafat and his Palestinians. Sorry, Dr. Al-Atrash, Good try—good-bye."

Sa'eed went on: "Now to my second point. I ask you to look around you. And then to be perfectly still and stay calm. There is no need for excitement. There is not the slightest reason for alarm."

We looked. While Sa'eed had been speaking, soldiers had quietly been entering the rec site. They stood all about the inner wall, automatic weapons pointing at the ground. A captain and several noncommissioned officers came up on the dance floor and joined Sa'eed. There was a sort of family resemblance between them all. Color, build; most, like him, had vertical tribal markings on their cheeks. Sa'eed repeated: "Please stay perfectly calm, enjoy your drinks, and listen to a few more announcements—not as eloquent as Mr. Ambassador's, or the late doctor's, but listen carefully anyway."

I heard a shot. One of the soldiers near the railing along the Nile collapsed. Several more shots. Another soldier fell. Then a third. I saw some waiters with sidearms in their hands. They were shooting slowly, methodically, all using a two-handed grip. The soldiers were slow to react. They'd not expected any resistance. Besides, their commanders were up at the lectern with Sa'eed.

"*Uqtilhum! Utliquun-nar!* (Shoot! Kill them!)," Sa'eed screamed into the microphone. A pistol round narrowly missed him—the bullet shattered the picture window of the clubhouse. The captain next to Sa'eed fell back, wounded. The soldiers began reacting. The sound of M16s on automatic, at first mingling with, then drowning out, the sharper punctuation of the handguns. Guests were screaming, throwing themselves down, under the tables.

It was an unequal contest. In all, the shooting couldn't have lasted more than a minute. Five or six of the waiters had been armed—they were all dead. Why in creation's name had they tried to take on infantry regulars carrying automatic weapons? The number of bodies told me that not only the Muslim Brother waiters had been killed. When the troops began shooting, any waiter in traditional Sudanese dress was—had been—fair game. Perhaps half had been killed or wounded. With relief, I saw Mustafa rising to his feet. I couldn't tell if any guests had been hit.

Sa'eed had lost much of his cool. "Get back up on your seats again!" he shouted at the microphone. "And you all listen and watch! Mr.

Ambassador (Sa'eed pointed), Ambassador Farnsworth, I mean, come forward! (The Spanish ambassador, who was sitting near Jon, looked so relieved he almost smiled). Also you, Mr. Chamberlain!"

Jon and I looked at one another. "Let's do as the man says, Josh, he's got the guns." Farnsworth rose to his feet and walked over to Sa'eed. I followed.

We stood in the middle of the dance floor, in a circle of light. All around us were Sa'eed's troops.

"Sa'eed," the ambassador began, "I don't know what you've told your troops. But there can be no explanation or excuse for tonight. You are finished. But if you immediately lay down your weapons, I promise to try to see you get as fair a trial as your country's laws allow."

"No, Mr. Ambassador," Sa'eed interrupted, "*you* will be silent, and *I* will do the talking. And it is your presence that will assure Sudan of a brilliant new foreign policy, allied to Libya, and with myself at its head. Not that fool, al-Atrash. Soon, Libyan troops will be landing at the airport—they will occupy all strategic government centers. And unlike the failed Libyan coup of 1976, this time, Egypt and the United States will not interfere.

"Why? Because we have the American ambassador to Khartoum and his deputy chief of mission in our hands. And your Egyptian lap dogs won't stir against us without the nod of Washington. So you see we really want you alive and not dead—at least one or the other of you." As Sa'eed spoke, he began to look and sound more like his old self again. He looked at his watch.

"Oh dear! I can't be late, as Alice or that White Rabbit may have said. Which brings us to the concluding portion of this evening's entertainment." Sa'eed looked toward me: "Please understand Mr. Chamberlain, this next little *divertissement* is not meant for you Westerners. It's for my soldiers. Poor credulous fellows. None speak English. But soon I'll do all the talking for us Sudanese. You have your *ta'wiidh*, I'm sure? Give it here."

As I took it from my pocket, Sa'eed reached into his. He took out and slipped over his head a charm that was the very twin of mine. No. Not quite. For in its center was a dark red—a blood-colored—cowrie. It hung, like an obscene order or decoration, just in the middle of his chest. Sa'eed yanked my charm from my hand. At this, the soldiers, I noticed, shuffled their feet and looked a little uneasily from him to me.

"You've troubled me a long time, Mr. Chamberlain. Among those susceptible to superstition, you've even acquired a kind of credibility. That will cease. Observe!"

Looking at the soldiers around him, he threw my charm to the ground. Then with his right hand holding his own, red, cowrie, he stamped down on my charm. There was a crunch. I heard a nearby voice—Mustafa's—cry out: "*La'nat allah 'alayk*!" (May God curse you!)

Sa'eed spun around. He motioned to the captain, who with an upward swing of his gun butt dropped Mustafa to the ground.

"You son-of-a bitch!" I shouted. I lunged for Sa'eed. A soldier clipped me across the back of the head with *his* gun butt. I fell. From the ground I looked up into the muzzles of several M16s.

"Temper, temper, Mr. Chamberlain," said Sa'eed. "Shall we practice a little more self-control? Remember, I only really need *one* of you!"

In the meantime, Frank Greer had been sidling closer to the dance floor. At these last words from Sa'eed, Greer pounced. A blur of speed. Several guardsmen went sprawling. With one arm Greer swept Sa'eed off his feet, and in two steps stood against the rec center wall—pinioning Sa'eed against him as a human shield.

"Drop those guns!" Greer shouted. Effortlessly, Greer seemed to hold the struggling Sa'eed locked in his left arm. Long black legs scissored the air. Spiderish. Sa'eed's fingers raked at Greer's biceps and forearm—about as large and immovable as the Marine house bollards!

"Now! Or I'll snap his fucking head right off!"

Sa'eed's head and neck were held back at a sharp angle. His face was hidden in Greer's hand—about the size of a catcher's mitt. Sa'eed's voice box protruded, outlined by the taut, shiny skin of his neck.

The soldiers were at a loss.

"Tell them to drop their guns, Sa'eed!" Frank ordered, as he gave the captive head an inch or so of slack.

In a language—not Arabic or English—Sa'eed barked out an order.

We weren't prepared for what happened next.

Two soldiers seized Aminata and brought her forward. One held her, while the other drew a knife and, with both hands on the handle, put it low against her stomach. He applied pressure. Aminata cried out, as a small bloody spot appeared on her white gown.

I heard Sa'eed: "Let me go or you'll see your sweetheart's guts on the dance floor!"

The soldier with the knife kept his eyes fixed on Sa'eed. He pushed again, harder. A stifled moan.

Farnsworth's voice cut in: "Frank, let him go. That's a direct order."

Greer seemed paralyzed. "Now!" Farnsworth added. His last word came out like a whiplash.

Greer dropped his arms.

As Sa'eed rejoined his men, he motioned them to release Aminata. Greer hurried to her side and held her. I could see a line of tears on his face.

Sa'eed had regained much of his composure.

To Greer he said: "For a moment I thought of shooting you both. Your misfortune; because I have an even better idea. I swear by (Sa'eed looked down to his chest) this red cowrie that tomorrow night Aminata will be given in marriage to the first Nuban wrestler we can find. And Mr. Greer can live happily ever after, thinking that his true love is cooking with cow flop, and washing her children in buffalo piss."

Looking now to us, Sa'eed continued: "But soon I must leave you. Please listen for Mr. Abu Nar's next communiqué. It will not be seen only at the university. Nor will it be in Mr. Abu Nar's name. I think we are finished with him. 'Mr. President' sounds better, wouldn't you all agree? You will hear him—me—broadcasting from the People's Palace. I may even invite Your Excellencies to hear the speech. Check perhaps with Palace Protocol? Ha Ha!"

Sa'eed looked at the ambassador and me. "Just one more little thing," he said, "for the road. We couldn't have either of you trying to escape! Oh no! But my Libyan friends are foresightful." From his breast pocket he took out a small plastic case. In it was a full hypodermic.

"*Massiko* (hold him)," he said to two of the soldiers, and pointed to Farnsworth. Holding up the needle he explained: "The full hypodermic contains a two-person dose. Half the dose, should render Mr. Ambassador unconscious for a few hours. Plenty of time for our purposes.

"But hear this, Mr. Chamberlain. I think you like your boss. If you try to escape—if you succeed in escaping—know that I will inflict grievous injury on the ambassador. I will not kill him. But you and he will be sorry always that you ever escaped. He will be sorry that he ever lived. We Furis have much practice—use your imagination? *That* should hold you better than chains!"

With this, Sa'eed jabbed the needle through the jacket into Farnsworth's right arm, just below the shoulder. He pushed the plunger in about halfway. In moments, the ambassador sagged.

"And now we leave you charming ladies and gentlemen," Sa'eed announced. Then, to the Marines: "I may also have you Marines someday to the Palace, maybe as my honor guard?"

"Get fucked, asshole!" I heard Sergeant Poe say.

Sa'eed only replied: "Tsk! Tsk! But apropos of that, Sally, Ms. Tolson, you come, too. Who knows (Sa'eed spoke as if to himself), maybe the toothsome Miss Tolson will 'come across' better for a president-to-be than for a simple functionary in Protocol?"

"RED WIND"

20

Sa'eed couldn't resist one last touch of drama. At the edge of the dance floor, he stopped and turned abruptly to face the guests. I caught another flash of red paisley.

"I don't mean to seem inhospitable. Please go on with the ball. You might consider it even my *inaugural* ball. Ha!" He looked at the disk jockey: "After those 'joy shots' we better have the music resume—immediately! Continue your reveling. My soldiers will see you aren't disturbed. The party *will* last until dawn. After that, I promise you, you will all be free to go. Then you may spread as much confusion as you wish. Also a tip: don't miss tomorrow's 7 A.M. BBC broadcast. It may be of unusual interest. Hardly your usual little diplomatic rat turds, I'd say!"

To his guards: *"Yalla!"* (Move it!)

In the street, Sa'eed looked over the row of ambassadors' limousines. I thought he'd take Farnsworth's. Instead, he walked over to my armored car. "People would find it strange if you drove the ambassador's car, Mr. Chamberlain. But it's known you often drive your own. Actually, I look forward to you chauffeuring me in this magnificent armored vehicle. What with my guard, and you, a respected diplomat, at the wheel, plus—as a last resort—the 450 horses under your hood, we should have no trouble reaching our rendezvous point.

"We'll put Miss Tolson, the ambassador, and one of our guards in the back. Here, the ambassador goes in the right-hand seat. He can be napping. Would look odd if he weren't in the place of honor, eh? We protocol experts are always on the job! Then our guard next to him.

202

Miss Tolson, I must ask you to keep your head down in the well. Sorry. But we can't have you making any eye signals to drivers on the way. Their imaginations—their interest—so easily inflamed."

I got behind the wheel. Sa'eed took the bucket seat to my right. An automatic pistol in his lap pointed in my general direction. The ambassador was slumped in the back seat, a soldier to his left. Sally couldn't be seen in the rearview mirror. We pulled away from the rec site, a follow car with several soldiers close behind. The guards moved the barriers aside, then closed them after us.

"Where are you taking us?" Sally's voice came muffled from down near the drive shaft.

"Be quiet, please! Absolutely no talking. We mustn't distract Mr. Chamberlain. Any more comments, you'll be severely chastised." To the guard: "*Idha tatkallam kamaan, iskitha*" (If she talks, shut her up).

"Easy does it, Mr. Chamberlain," remarked Sa'eed. "Drive defensively, both hands on the wheel, eyes on the road. No funny business at all. Follow the Wad Madani Road to the south. I remind you: if our progress is checked—if something goes wrong—your ambassador and Miss Tolson will be the first to pay. I mean business, I think you know."

Sa'eed became aware of my tennis bag on the front seat. "But what is this?" he said, speaking as if to himself. "A tennis bag? Your briefcase? I often wondered why you seemed to use this for business as well as pleasure. I prefer Mark Cross myself." Sa'eed unzipped the bag and with one hand rummaged inside.

"And what have I here!" Sa'eed announced, self-satisfaction in his voice. "A gun, or cannon, maybe. A replacement for the .45 which we have as evidence in the Deng killing? A twin of the weapon maybe that killed my friend 'Umayyir?"

I felt the urgent need to distract al-Masri: "You call *him* a friend? 'Umayyir?"

"Well, not exactly a friend. He may have thought he was *my* friend. He and I had some good times in Rome. But crude. Rough with the ladies, no finesse. He put all that into his work. But even there—limited, immature, no managerial talent. Imagine insisting on doing poor Deng himself. His apprentices were quite up to the job. But, oh, no! he says, 'I want to show them how it is to be done.' He was overconfident, they were offended. The survivor's taken 'Umayyir's 'martyrdom' rather well. Promotion is welcome, whatever the means, I suppose."

"Was it your idea to kill Deng?" I asked.

"Yes, indeed," Sa'eed answered. "A masterstroke. We'd hoped the riots would topple our 'balancing rock' of a government off its perch.

Not quite. But they left it weak and more vulnerable, circling the drain, you might say."

"And I suppose your people killed Hilverding?" I asked.

"Right again," answered Sa'eed, "and also Hilverding's killers. *They* were from our 'slave auxiliaries.' They'd hoped for full tribal status, but (he sighed) they had to settle for martyrdom. We must all serve as best we can."

"And Juba?" I asked.

"Easily planned," answered al-Masri. "Bin Shakir is, of course, a close relative. My tribesmen are found in most places in the army. Though the late captain was not a Furi, he just had his orders. Your . . . passing . . . might have been just the nudge the government needed. And cleared the way for me with Sally. I was doing alright until you came." This last with another mock sigh.

Sa'eed continued: "Juba gave me a problem, though. That was your third escape. Some of my people began to talk about another 'cowrie.'

"As for al-Atrash, he knew all along that *someone* else was also plotting. He knew *someone* else was making trouble for the government—bidding for Libyan support. That's one of the reasons we were both at the airport when Qadhaafi's man, 'Umayyir, arrived. And when you happened to arrive, too, Al-Atrash thought his 'rival' might show. He did—but al-Atrash never knew it.

"Then later, your Juba escape made him and his PLO friends speed up their plans. The PLO was getting very nervous. The incident of your Mr. Gary. It was a race against time, Mr. Chamberlain, and you might call this my victory lap."

With a laugh, Sa'eed mocked: "Someone must tell Mr. Kirby how much al-Atrash liked your clock. So much that he decided to use it to time his first address to the nation. A simple, but eloquent declaratory statement, wouldn't you say?"

I wanted to keep him talking. So I broke in: "Sa'eed, isn't your scheme—whatever it is—clearly hare-brained? How can you and your tribesmen, and a few Libyans, I guess, take over Sudan? The country's as large as the eastern U.S.! And who else is on your side? And how were you able to keep word of your plot from leaking? How did al-Atrash not find everything out?"

There was a superior, almost complacent tone to Sa'eed's reply: "One answer at a time on this quiz show, Mr. Chamberlain, and keep your eyes on the road. First, about our small numbers: Remember the story about the Texas ranger getting off at the train station to quell a riot? The sheriff asks, 'There's only one of you?' And the reply: 'There's only one riot, isn't there?' That's Sudan today. A mob, maybe a riot."

Speaking in a schoolmaster's tone, Sa'eed went on: "Tell me, Mr. Chamberlain, what are the bases for power in the world today? I suppose you'd mention patriotism, nationalism, ideology? I've studied them all at your schools. None work here. Does a Syrian, or a Lebanese, feel he's part of something called Syria, or Lebanon? An entity he's prepared to work for, even die for? Or are these names just shadings on a map? Something for passport covers? And even if there once was content to the names, what's left after forty years of independence? Forty years of selfish, destructive administration? I'll tell you: damned little. Not *even* 'Tribes with Flags.' "

He continued: "When I came back from the United States, I used to hear my friends talk politics: Arab nationalism, communism, even liberalism and democracy. But the 1967 war showed the hollowness of Arab nationalism! Capitalism was already out. Communism had a good system of control—we can learn something there. But it has no resources for us, and with the end of the Cold War its ideological appeal is zero. All that remains is the memory of deep snow, and beatings for Arabs who dared date Russian girls."

Sa'eed's voice rose a notch: "What was the result of all this? I'll tell you: cynicism and contempt—we now see the ideologies of East and West as just so many imported fashions. Hems above the knee, hems below the knee, hems at the knee."

Sa'eed reached into the back seat with his left hand and felt around: "Did you guess, Sally, that I, myself, am a no-hems person? A no-skirt person? Is that your thigh there, Sally? What is *that*—and *that?*" He kept his eyes and gun fixed steadily on me. He took a few deep breaths and swallowed.

Then he smiled: "I am not smart, but I may have a bit of genius. I saw something my overeducated friends did not. I saw the rubble of our political landscape. I saw ideology dead. I saw the political parties fragmented. I saw the army discredited—after all, had it not ruined the economy under President Nimeiry and some successors? And then blundered back into the swamp of another civil war? I recognized the mess that was Sudan, and decided to exploit it.

"I went back to my origins. Back to the one structure that has remained firm here and elsewhere. I returned to my *tribe*. My friends could not believe it. Tribes were old-fashioned, provincial, *vieux jeu*. Some even despised their tribes and themselves. They went to surgeons to have *these* removed (he pointed to the scarifications on his cheek). Why, they wanted to look like you, Mr. Chamberlain. They'd have given their souls to have been born WASPS. Many *did* give their souls. A lot of good it did them!

"I saw my tribesmen neglected, bitter, and forgotten. I worked to change all that. I've stayed in my job more than a decade. I've passed on bribes and promotions to friends, who are now in high positions. I've done especially well with the army, as you've seen. My close relatives now command several well-trained, well-armed tribal units. The urban middle classes, you see, don't want their boys doing something as plebeian as military service. They're happy when some simple tribesman drills and trains and maybe dies.

"Well, Mr. Chamberlain, Sudan is about to experience a kind of airplane hijacking. It's been done by Hafiz al-Asad in Syria, and by Saddam Husain in Iraq, and I'm doing it here. Al-Atrash despised me as a playboy, but *I* had the sort of base the Libyans wanted. This is Africa, Mr. Chamberlain, and 'the tribes are restless.' They *will* come into their own."

Sa'eed reflected for a moment: "Strange, but in all of this the only person who had some notion of 'where we were coming from' was poor Deng. Deng, too, you see, had kept in touch with his tribal roots. He was getting warm—*he* was beginning to guess from which way the wind was blowing."

We'd reached the city limits and were driving north on *Shari' al Mahatta*, Railroad Street. We'd skirted the airport and had left the suburb of *Bahr al-abyad* (Mediterranean Sea) and the last street lamps behind. Traffic was getting light. We saw fewer and fewer passenger cars and not many lorries. The site of Omdurman battlefield—now in darkness—was just ahead.

Sa'eed warned: "Steady as she goes, Mr. Chamberlain, eyes on the road, please. Let's not run into any stone cairns my idiot countrymen might have left behind after propping up an axle to change a tire. And make no swerves or sudden stops. I have my seat belt on, too, you see. You may be quick, but remember, the bullets in this gun are quicker. And don't forget those 'fates worse than death' for your friends in the back."

"Don't worry, Sa'eed," I replied. "You've got all the high cards—a guard, the guns, your men in the follow car. But you didn't really answer the security question. And the mechanics of a takeover. And can you trust Qadhaafi?"

"Ever the diplomat, eh, Mr. Chamberlain? You are hoping for an exclusive?"

"Something like that, Sa'eed. It's not every day an FSO gets a preview of things to come." (It was important to distract him, to keep him talking, to play to his ego.)

"Alright, Mr. Chamberlain. You see, security was the least of our problems. We Furis are only semiarabized. We speak our own Hamitic language among ourselves. No tribesman would inform on another, especially not to a Westerner. That's an idea your Mr. Kirby could not grasp. But he's not to be blamed. Not even al-Atrash—that Italianized town Arab—understood the Arab tribal bond. I had people watching him, but he had no one near me!

"But back to Mr. Kirby. How I'd laugh to see him running about town with his bundles of money and his meetings with agents! And all the time 'Abu Nar' was before him. I'd see Mr. Kirby excusing himself from official functions to go to some midnight meeting, and each time . . . nothing. You see, he—all you Americans—only worked with enfeebled, deracinate town Arabs. For ten dollars any one of them would sell his sister. His mother? Maybe he'd start at twenty dollars, but soon come down!

"You asked about Qadhaafi? Of course. You Americans have a thing about him, don't you? You're all masochists, and he's been buggering you for decades. You've got a real taste for him by now. A kind of homoerotic attraction, for sure. Watch out for AIDS! Ha Ha! I'll *use* Qadhaafi. We western Sudanese know Libyans well. And with him on the scene, you will all pant after me.

"Sudan holds the strategic balance of the Middle East. A radical takeover in Khartoum? Guess who *then* controls the Nile, which now barely provides enough water for Egypt's sixty millions? And see the Saudis quiver! Eight hundred miles of radical shore front to contemplate, as they cower in their palaces and holy shrines! No, you Americans will give me development projects and food, the Saudis oil for free, and the Libyans all the arms I want, also for free. The world's well arranged, wouldn't you say?"

"Isn't there something you've forgotten, Sa'eed?"

I could see the muzzle of the gun rise slightly. Sa'eed tensed in his seat. His eyes flickered over the road. To the rearview mirror. "What do you mean, please? Answer quickly!"

"Don't press the panic button, Sa'eed." I paused for an instant, then repeated slowly and clearly: "Don't *press the panic button*. I refer to organized religion. Yeah, maybe your political parties aren't what they used to be. That's even true in the U.S. But I read everywhere about Muslim fundamentalism. How much it worries some Arab regimes. Will Sudan's Muslim fundamentalists be happy with your neotribalism? Will they go along? Wouldn't they object to your bringing back an un-Islamic, or pre-Islamic, power base? The tribe, that is?"

"I congratulate you, Mr. Chamberlain. And thank you sincerely also. Your question is good. And the answer is already taken care of.

Here (Sa'eed tapped his chest) is a list. Guess who heads the list? No. Not the prime minister. I may keep him as a speech writer. Maybe even put him in Protocol. Ha! He'd thank me. He'd be happiest there. No, at the very top of my *hit* parade! (al-Masri laughed and repeated 'my *hit* parade!') is Dr. Al-Mughraibiy. Then come many, many of his followers.

"Brother Qadhaafi has promised to lend a hand. He doesn't like the Muslim Brothers either. We'll fly them all to Libya. 'Expediters' will meet them at the airport to facilitate their onward travel—to join the late, great Shiite leader, the Imam Musa Sadr. So sad. He left his hotel in Tripoli to catch a flight back to Lebanon. He never made it. Brother Qadhaafi had booked him on another one—to heaven! Ha!"

"But why did you thank me, Sa'eed?"

"Because a little birdie is telling me that your embassy and Dr. al-Mughraibiy have been fooling around together. Maybe your resourceful Mr. Kirby arranged it? He's no dope at all, I hope you know. That beard, those boots, that bluff manner. But watch out for his piggy little eyes. They don't miss much. As you see, I try not to underestimate you Americans. Naive? Yes. But also inventive, forceful, resourceful. Brother Qadhaafi underestimated you. Poor man! He hasn't had a formed stool since Desert Shield and Desert Storm!

"Yes, yes, I'm sure I'm right," Sa'eed continued, almost to himself. "I don't suppose you'd wish to confirm my hunch? Maybe Kirby wouldn't let you know. But that would explain those crazy waiters at the ball. And why they shot so well." Sa'eed resumed in a louder voice: "Yes, the Brothers could be a little problem. But in a revolution, between two armed groups, the one with the heavier weapons wins. Armies always defeat National Guards. We'll beat the Muslim Brothers." Sa'eed laughed, adding: "And afterwards, I'll see about borrowing their best religious lines. We Furis will sing as loudly in the choir as anyone. Paris is worth a Mass!"

He went on: "Still, how *did* the Brothers and you meet? Was it Kirby? (Pause) Or did Mustafa, your houseboy, maybe lend a hand? You know, don't you, he is a minor religious leader in his own right? Actually, I'm a little bit sorry about striking him. His mystics are no threat to us. But it was a tense moment—even for me. And I could see my men looking at that cowrie of yours. Certainly Mustafa gave it to you.

"I won't bore you with the fable—maybe you know it—but these cowries are supposed to confer powers upon their bearers. For me, those of the white cowrie were useless. No interest. They're passive, a sort of specific against the activity of the red cowrie. The Mahdi carried a red cowrie. Then the so-called 'Red Wind' bore him to power. No white cowrie bearer around then? Maybe Lord Kitchener had it all along. Ha! Did you know he had a big collection of porcelain and glazes? So maybe there really was something there. Anyway, I heard about the Abu Nar fable while living with my tribe. They really believed. Right away, I saw how the superstition could help."

I glanced over. Sa'eed still wore the cowrie charm. What with his white shirt front, it looked like a bloody hole in the middle of his chest.

We drove on in silence for another ten minutes. No lights in view. Nothing on the road. My heart sank as Sa'eed broke the silence with "I have a sudden hunch! Did I look at everything in your bag? Any 'backup' as your police shows say?"

He pawed again through the tennis bag: "Clothes, papers, pens, a *heavy* can of tennis balls. TENNIS BALLS?" Out of the can he rolled an M1A1 fragmentation grenade. The gunny's parting gift. Sa'eed's self-satisfaction was boundless and unrestrained. "My luck is clearly running strong, Mr. Chamberlain! And yours seems to be in pieces, back on the dance floor.

"Go slower," said Sa'eed, in a more serious voice. "Watch now— high beams, please." Ahead of us on the right, I could make out a sign. I drew up to it slowly. Out loud, I read, "Mannesmans Baugeschaft." A well-scraped dirt road led off into the darkness. "Turn here," ordered Sa'eed.

The road wound its way through low dunes. We passed scrub acacia trees. Nothing else was visible. After a quarter-mile, we came to a gate in a chain-link fence. A soldier, in camouflage dress, stepped out of the dark. He was heavily armed: submachine gun, extra clips in a bandolier, sidearm, bayonet, flak jacket, poncho, plus some sort of field radio, too. As he approached the car, I could see a single, deep, vertical scar on each cheek.

Irrelevantly, I wondered why the first thing Third World armies learn from the West is to overload the foot soldier. Was there ever an army that kept the foot soldier's pack to the one-third of body weight we've known for a hundred years was best? At 'Twenty-Nine Palms' we wished headquarters types—who designed our loads—had to carry them first. Then in Grenada and the Gulf, we'd had radiomen going ashore with *160 pounds!* A good load—on the Moon, maybe.

The soldier asked a question. I heard him clearly—his voice was picked up by the exterior mike. Sa'eed didn't know how to use the hand mike to talk outside the car. And the bulletproof windows were sealed. So Sa'eed opened the door. Again, he didn't use Arabic. Furi? The news seemed good. Sa'eed nodded. The soldier said something into his radio. He unlocked the gate and swung it open. We drove slowly past him.

In our headlights, we picked up some prefab office buildings, a bunkhouse, a water tower, and what looked like a generating plant.

"Around and behind the buildings, one of our rallying points," said Sa'eed, "but slowly. Let's not startle anyone."

There were lights—flares—on the ground behind the generator plant (if that's what it was). They marked out a landing site, in the middle of which sat a small troop helicopter. British? French? I didn't recognize the make.

Peremptory orders from Sa'eed: "Pull up near the helicopter—not too close. Stop! All right. You will wait here. Miss Tolson, you may come up for air now! I will take the keys. Please keep the door closed. No scampering away across the desert. You may keep the lights on. I won't be a minute. Should we put some money in the meter? A 'no standing' zone? 'Kiss 'n Ride'? Something from the Safeway, Mr. Chamberlain? Miss Tolson? Ha!" Sa'eed sounded drunk.

The pilot had climbed down from his helicopter. He wasn't Sudanese. Nor was his uniform. A Libyan, I guessed. He and Sa'eed began to speak. They talked fast—the sounds came clearly through the mike. The pilot bent down, looked toward us. I saw him shake his head. He said something more to Sa'eed, then turned and climbed back into his machine. Sa'eed handed his pistol to the guard. He took the man's submachine gun. In a moment, Sa'eed and the guard came back to our car.

"I have good news and bad news, Mr. Chamberlain," he called from the outside. "The good news is our flight is ready for boarding. It will take us to the airport to meet our Libyan delegation. My last protocol action! I'll meet two companies of paratroops. My own forces are linking up with us there. Then we must begin our calls. But there I go, still speaking like a protocol officer. Habits die hard, wouldn't you say?

"Which brings us to the bad news: Our flight is fully booked—and there is no later flight, at least not for *you*. Do you take my drift, Mr. Chamberlain? You will please step out. Slowly, with your hands on top of your head."

Instead, I reached over and locked the car doors. Through the bulletproof glass, I could see Sa'eed's face. It was tightly drawn. He looked feral, hungry. His eyes seemed to shine in the light of the flares—wild animals' eyes, like what you'd see from your campfire, as you looked toward the dark.

"Mr. Chamberlain," Sa'eed's voice came plaintively through the mike, "be reasonable. I'm giving you a chance to be a hero. You know that bulletproof glass won't stand up to concentrated fire. Think of your boss. Think of Miss Tolson—think of the upholstery!"

I felt Sally's hand press on my shoulder. Urgently, she said, "Don't go out, Josh. He means to kill you.!"

Sa'eed went on: " 'I have a rendezvous to keep,' Mr. Chamberlain. I give you twenty seconds, then I'll huff and I'll puff and I'll blow your house down! No fooling. One . . . two . . ."

Do fear and confusion paralyze the mind? Certainly. Can they cost one one's life? Often. Did that red cowrie somehow cloud my vision? Before my eyes, in my mind, a fog, a reddish mist. Why did my arms and legs sluggishly stir—as if of their own volition—toward opening the door and getting out?

What al-Mughraibiy had said about prayer went through my mind. Did I pray? Did I concentrate all my being in a kind of appeal, a plea for help, for guidance? A lighter, opalescent spot showed through the fog, beckoning me. A thought seemed to break free in my brain. My fingers relaxed on the door handle.

The count went on: "fifteen . . . sixteen . . ." I saw Sa'eed pull back the slide on his weapon, cocking it.

I called out: "OK, Sa'eed. You win. I'm coming out. But please let me just write a short note to my family." I picked up my kit bag and put it on the seat.

"I am not an animal, Mr. Chamberlain. You may have all of two minutes. But I warn you, no funny business. Two minutes, no more—one . . . two . . . three . . . four . . ."

I rummaged in the bag. Paper, pencil—on a piece of paper I scrawled a few nonsense lines. My mind was elsewhere, thinking hard. I recalled my unarmed-combat instructor saying, "You always have a weapon handy—if you can recognize it and know how to use it." Into the bag again—nothing.

"Write fast, Mr. Chamberlain," came Sa'eed's voice through the mike. "In thirty seconds you turn in your Blue Book! Ha!"

I reached into my pocket—and blessed my school days. And Mustafa. And Dr. al-Mughraibiy.

Outside the count went on: "One hundred eleven . . . one hundred twelve . . ."

"What are you going to do?" Sally whispered.

"*Toujours gai*, kid!" I answered. And began to open the door.

21

Sa'eed was waiting, submachine gun at the ready. He was breathing heavily. He had a hard-on. I felt a little sick.

He said: "Move out smartly now, please. We wouldn't want to cut a sorry figure before Miss Tolson, would we? Tell me, where do you want to take it, Mr. Chamberlain? In the front or the back?—a question later maybe for Ms. Tolson, yes? I begin to think that my friend 'Umayyir had something. He always claimed fucking was the *second* greatest thrill. Afterwards, Ms. Tolson will help me find out if he was right. Come now! Step lively!"

Sa'eed was talking fast, excitedly. I let him talk as I stepped out. In a conversational tone, I said: "Sa'eed, I'm sorry but *I'm* going to have to shoot *you*."

Sa'eed actually goggled at me. He glanced over to his guard. He maybe thought I'd lost my mind. But as he uncomprehendingly stared, I raised my right hand and pointed my index finger at him. Still no movement from the dumbfounded Sa'eed.

"Bang!" I said. And with that I let fly the heavy rubber band I'd found in my coat pocket, using a trick I'd learned at school. The rubber band slapped across Sa'eed's eyes. He flinched, the gun muzzle wavered, and I administered a terrific kick in the balls.

Sa'eed went down. My .45 fell from his pocket. I saw the grenade, too, roll on the ground. I dived for the .45 and brought it up just as the soldier tried a shot from Sa'eed's pistol. He missed. Quickly, I shot him twice in the chest.

A round zinged overhead. It came from the door of the helicopter. The pilot was standing there trying to draw a bead on me. I picked up the grenade, ducked behind the car, and pulled the pin. ("One . . . two . . .") A quick glance through the car windows, then I rose from my crouch just enough to throw the grenade—hard—at the open door of the helicopter. I remembered a Marine instructor shouting "Goddamn it, throw that grenade with authority! You *want* it to bounce all around— an onside kick. So the other guys make their last fumble, their last error—ever—if they try to grab it and throw it back." I exposed only a flash of arm and shoulder. Another bullet ricocheted off the top of the car. Close.

A giant clap. Iron fingernails beating a quick tattoo against the armor panels on the far side of the car. The helicopter swayed on its skids. The pilot was in the air, arms extended, knees bent backward. Free-falling? Or trying a broad jump over the car? He didn't make it. He landed face down, five feet from his machine. No movement. The helicopter started to burn.

I stood up to catch my breath. I felt tired. Disoriented. It almost cost me my life.

Out of the corner of my eye I caught a movement: Sa'eed was dragging himself past the edge of the car. The grenade blast that had taken out the helicopter had also sprayed shrapnel over his legs. They looked broken and tattered. Muddy with blood. He still had his Kalashnikov—but he needed both hands to pull himself along. That saved me.

As Sa'eed brought his weapon around, I switched the .45 to my right hand and snapped my shot off first. It missed, but was close enough to throw Sa'eed's aim off. His shots went wild. My second round took him in the shoulder. It flipped him on his side, facing me.

For an instant our eyes met. Nothing foppish about his looks now. Vulpine, carnivorous. Through his bared teeth, I heard him breathing out, "*Rih abyad, Rih abyad . . .*" He tried to raise his gun again. This time, I easily had the drop on him. I aimed carefully and shot him once, twice, in the middle of his chest. The shots drowned out my voice: "Hilverding, Deng . . ."

Sa'eed had fallen over onto his back. A quiver in the legs. Then— nothing. I looked down at the body. His lips were still drawn back in a wolfish rictus. The shirt front showed three dark spots—the cowrie and two others.

I heard voices shouting to each other in Arabic. There were muzzle flashes from the dark as bullets kicked up lines of dirt near the car.

Less than a minute had passed since I'd stepped out the door. Now the perimeter guards were closing in. I rolled back into the front seat of the car, pulling the door shut. Small arms fire raked the outside.

Sally's voice: "Josh! Are you wounded?"

"No," I replied, "but I'm afraid we're all out of contingency plans." Turning back in the seat I looked at Sally. "To tell the truth, Sally, I'm beginning to think this story might not have a happy ending."

Several shapes approached the car, weapons at the ready. Libyan soldiers. Through the mike, I could hear their voices, but couldn't understand what they were saying. Then I caught a word: "Blasteek."

Sally caught her breath. "You heard it too?" I asked.

One of the soldiers—he looked like a senior NCO—had taken the pack from one of the other Libyans. He took out a watertight, shiny-looking package. Carefully extracting the contents, he began "caulking" the door-handle recess with what looked like modeling clay. Once, he looked up at the window, and I caught a glimpse of teeth below his moustache. Concentration? Anger? Was he smiling?

I heard Sally saying: "It looks bad, doesn't it? I mean *really* bad?"

I didn't answer. My eyes were on our "plumber," as he busily continued his work. He was unwrapping another, much smaller package. A fuse-timer?

Sally's voice came over the back seat. Firm and steady. "I love you, Josh. I love you. I've not said that since I was in my middle teens. And I *really* mean it now—for the first time in my life."

I turned, reached a hand over the seat, and drew Sally's face to mine. Her eyes closed at the last minute as I kissed her. Her lips felt surprisingly soft and full. A voice—my own?—said "I love you too." It added: "I'm glad I lived long enough to feel this way, and to tell you."

Outside the NCO stepped back to look his work over. He nodded, as if to himself.

I thought: Should I jump out and take some of them with me? It seemed a low percentage move, though, because the soldiers kept their weapons carefully trained on the car doors. But to be smoked out like a badger in his den!

The car mike brought us the sound of hedge clippers. Heavy-duty hedge clippers—5.56 mm hedge clippers, to be exact.

The NCO fell forward against the car door, and then slid to the ground. A dark smear showed on the bulletproof glass. Two of the other guards went down. There were heavy, tearing sounds against the car door. The remaining Libyans, four or five of them, were confused. They began area-firing into the dark.

I could see flashes of light moving in toward us—first from one direction, then another.

Someone, I thought, is running his squad damn well. The last of the Libyans fell.

I strained my eyes looking into the dark. The firing had stopped. Silence. A shape was coming toward me. Several of them. The helicopter fire picked up a flash of scarlet—It was our Marine security detachment! Still in their dress blues!

A knock on the window. Sergeant Poe looked in. I heard his voice: "Get the ambassador out of there pronto, Sir. The chopper may blow anytime!"

Sally and I needed no urging. With the help of two Marines, we lifted the still-unconscious Farnsworth from the car and half walked, half ran in the direction Poe had indicated. We didn't even stop to say thanks. Before us were two Marine Land Rovers. Also a third car, which I didn't recognize. From where he stood near my car, I heard Sergeant Poe shout back to his men: "Get the ambassador, the lieutenant, and Miss Tolson into the Land Rovers! Keep 'em there!"

Sally asked me: "Is he going to move the wounded Libyans to safety in case the helicopter blows up?"

I looked toward Sergeant Poe. I could see he had drawn his .357 Magnum. As I watched, I saw him bend solicitously over one Libyan, then move on. When he came to the second, he turned his back to us. I heard the deep bark of his handgun. Then again when he came to the third and fourth downed soldier.

In a voice full of shock and disbelief, Sally exclaimed: "Josh, I think he's killing the wounded. Stop him! Stop it!"

Poe was already on his way back to us. He was walking slowly and easily. His weapon was again in its holster. The helicopter fire seemed to be dying out.

Poe opened our Land Rover's door and looked in. "Maybe the bird won't blow after all" was all he said.

I held out my hand. "Thanks, Gunny," I said. "Thanks a lot."

Sergeant Poe ignored my hand. Instead he saluted. *"Semper Fi!* sir!"

Sally asked: "Gunny, how could you shoot those wounded men? I can't believe . . ."

"Just policing up the battlefield, Miss Tolson," Poe replied. "You've got to understand. This wasn't a battle. These men weren't soldiers. They were terrorists. If something were to go wrong in Khartoum, and some survived, why, they'd swear on a stack of Korans that you kidnapped and attacked them. Then *big trouble*. Believe me. Much simpler this way. No hostile witnesses. No hostile investigation."

Movement by the third car caught my eye. The driver's door opened, and out stepped—Avo Bogosian! From the other doors came three young men. I recognized one of them: Avo's *maître d'hotel!* Avo's embrace was almost paternal. "And we're all alright!" he said. "But first introductions."

The three men with Avo were Israeli commandos. The *"maître d'hotel,"* an Israeli of Egyptian origin, explained: "After the hanging, Jerusalem sent us to deal with al-Atrash. The Government of Israel has long known and respected Mr. Bogosian. We call him a *zaddik*, you'd maybe say 'a righteous Gentile'? Tonight our mission was 'overtaken by events,' but you can't say our trip to Sudan was useless."

Avo broke in: "After Sa'eed took you and the ambassador away, I had a quick decision to make. If I did nothing, Sa'eed—with Libyan help—would probably head a new government of Sudan. But I knew I had the means, *maybe*, to tilt things in another direction, toward the al-Mughraibiy forces. Six of one? But then I thought of what you had told me of your talk with al-Mughraibiy. So I used my beeper, and *they* came." He pointed to the three commandos.

Avo went on: "It took them no time to dispose of the guards Sa'eed had left behind. Then the Marines heard where you were, and we came along."

My mind still seemed to be working at half speed. All I could think to say was: "But you all stayed in the car during . . .?"

It was the *maître d'* who answered. "Mr. Bogosian's orders. He said: 'This is the Americans' job.' As it was, you didn't need backup."

There was a groan from behind us. We looked into the Land Rover's back seat. The ambassador's eyes were open. He was looking at Sally and me. "Children," I heard him say in a blurry voice.

"How are you feeling, sir?" I asked.

"The way one shouldn't—but often does—after a Marine Corps ball. Really thirsty, too."

"Don't try to get up right away, Mr. Ambassador," said Sally. "We'll get you some water, then Josh and I will give you a hand in walking around."

With one hand on Sally's shoulder, the ambassador walked slowly and silently around the cars, the helicopter, the bodies. He stopped often. I described the events since our arrival at the Mannesman compound. Farnsworth listened carefully.

He thanked the gunny and each Marine. To them he said: "When I finish my report to the commandant, you just may see another Iwo

Jima Memorial go up here in the desert! And I promise you all some of the finest custom-tailored dress blues! Plus another stripe or two on each arm!"

Farnsworth then shook the hand of each Israeli. He took Avo's hand in both of his, saying: "Quebec has a motto, '*Je me souviens*, I'll remember.' Right now, it's my country's motto, too. Shalom!"

"Shalom, shalom," the Israelis replied smiling.

Farnsworth turned to us: "I'm sorry this happened to you both. To the extent I was a cause—even indirectly—I'm not worth it. Not worth what you had to go through, that is. But I'm glad *they're* there (he pointed toward the helicopter) and *you're* here. And I'm impressed—No, I'm overwhelmed."

With this he put one arm around Sally's shoulders and the other around mine and, for a moment, held us. In a muffled, unsteady voice he quickly said: "I do sincerely and always will thank God that you two survived!"

In a changed voice Farnsworth said to the gunny: "Let's go home. Call base on the radio. Tell them I'm coming in to the Embassy—Nurse Peach will insist on looking me over. We'll drop the DCM and Miss Tolson at the Residence to clean up. They'll have a long day ahead."

Sally and I entered the residence compound from a side gate. Two of the Marines came with us. The ambassador and the others went on to the Chancery. We were to join him there later in the morning. It was a little before sunrise, and the garden and house seemed quietly asleep. I sent the servants back to bed. Mustafa, I learned, had been taken to the embassy health unit. The Marines set up a foot patrol about the Residence.

Sally and I walked up the split staircase of the Residence to the second floor. At the top was a landing that opened onto an upstairs living room. Its wall was decorated by a large, blue tapestry, on which was appliqued a phrase from the Koran. Bedroom suites opened onto each side of the landing.

We paused at the living room entrance. "Happy New Year," I said, as with my right hand I tilted Sally's face upwards. Sally looked at me quizzically. "I never thought I'd live to see another," I explained. I bent my head and kissed her.

We were holding onto one another. My legs felt unsteady. A current seemed to run through me, like the vibrations of a power line. A thought, a chorus of thoughts, told me I was alive! I was alive!

Sally leaned into me, rising slightly on her toes. She kissed me back.

I'm alive! I'm alive! I'm alive! kept echoing through my mind, and my heart.

I put my right hand on her sweater, cupping her breast through the loose wool. I kissed her again. My hand moved to the bottom of her sweater and came up inside. I felt her breast through her brassiere. I got out the words, "Be my lover!"

Sally pulled my hand away. "That's enough," she breathed.

But I didn't stop. Not taking my hand off her body, I slid my palm—just above her waistline—around behind her back. What a delicate rib cage for such an athletic girl! With the thumb and forefingers of my right hand, I unsnapped her bra. My mouth was dry.

I kissed her again. And brought my hand forward under her sweater—brushing aside the straps of her bra. I felt her bare breasts. Her nipples were small, hard, sharply pointed.

"Oh God." Whose voice was that? Mine? Sally's?

With both hands, I began to draw up her skirt. It came up in handfuls, easily moving over her slip. Like reefing a sail, I thought. I drew her slip up next. My hands slid down inside her pants. I filled my hands with her firm buttocks.

In my ear, I heard Sally breathe: "I've got to hold onto myself . . . mustn't let myself go . . ." Inside her pants, I drew my right hand toward me over her hip. Across a flat, hard stomach, then down. I fastened on her crotch. Soft, springy flesh. A pad of silky fibers.

My coat was on the floor. Sally's skirt was coming off. I lowered her to the carpet. Seemingly no bones—there was no power in her. I was on her. Then *in* her.

Then I heard her say, "I love you." And a deeper, louder voice—mine?—said, "I love you too," and, "I like having you in my arms." Sally's voice: "It can be for the rest of your life." The talking stopped.

Standing on the balcony looking east, we held a sunrise ceremony. My arm around Sally's waist, her head on my shoulder, we waited for the sun to come up. The horizon was lightening in the distance over Omdurman battlefield. The time was just a little after 6 A.M.

"What will we do now?" Sally asked.

"I don't know." I replied.

Sally went on: "I used to think of you at first as a challenge, maybe a distraction. I liked your bright blue eyes and the way you talked. Though there haven't been many men in my life"—Sally glanced up at me—"never Sa'eed.

"Then my feelings changed. They developed. Was it after Deng's garden? I don't know. Around that time. I started thinking about you a lot. When I'd think of you I'd feel happy. Happy you were in the world. And when I'd look at you it was like a light shining through me. I felt so transparent. Translucent? Look (she held her arm out from her side), even in this light, I still cast a shadow. It shouldn't be there—not the way you make me feel." She laughed softly. "What do you like about me?"

I answered: "I like the way you play tennis. Though I don't like the way you serve (laughing together). I like the way you feel. Firm, good muscle tone. I love your legs. Most of all though, I love your face. The ambassador was right. He said you lived more inside yourself than many people did. I love that quality of enigma, of mystery, about you. Then you smile—and light up the world. Like the sun. Watch now! Here it comes!"

Up through our two-dimensional plane, the sun's rim ascended. Red, glowing, but an alive, clean, purging red, I thought, not that clotted blood of Sa'eed's cowrie . . . and his shirt.

I turned Sally's face up toward me. "It's your turn now," I said.

"What do you mean?"

"Why, it's *your* turn to smile. See? I knew there'd be no contest. Now, if that sun had any sense, he'd hide his face in shame. He'd just sink down below the horizon again!"

"You ass!"

"No. It's true! And your full smile? Pow! A violation of the Nuclear Test Ban Treaty! A supernova! A cosmic event! Why, in fifteen billion years, astronomers across the universe will pick it up on their instruments and wonder what might have happened just now in our galaxy. A new quasar perhaps?"

We kissed again. And again. My hand slid up to her breasts. "Did I say I loved the feel of you a moment ago? Well, I told the truth." My mouth felt like the desert floor. I needed a drink of water. I needed oxygen. I knew what asthma must be like. Sally's face looked rapt, withdrawn. Her eyes were closed. I started drawing the sweater upwards . . .

The phone rang. It was the ambassador. "Josh," he said. "I hate to bother you but Kirby says the BBC's got a special broadcast coming in a few minutes. You'll want to hear it." I thanked the ambassador, sort of.

We turned on the radio, and sure enough it was Pippa on the air, in her perfect Emma Thompson voice: " . . . to bring you a special news bulletin from Khartoum, Sudan."

To Sally I remarked: "Finally, number one on the charts!"

Pippa went on: "There are preliminary reports that a pro-Libyan coup attempt may have failed last night. Libyan transport aircraft were observed circling Khartoum's international airport for an hour before veering off toward Tripoli. The planes entered Sudan air space minutes before the bombing death of a senior Sudanese minister who appeared himself to be claiming power. Pro-Libyan army units are being disarmed by units loyal to Prime Minister al-Muntasser. Rebel soldiers are said briefly to have held several Western ambassadors hostage at a diplomatic function last night . . ."

"You ought to write to Pippa, Josh," Sally remarked. "Or better yet, she ought to write *you*. Aren't you her single most productive source of news? Why, without you these past months, they'd have had to furlough half the BBC! She should make you the BBC Man of the Year." Sally paused. "No," she said, "she should make *us* BBC's Man and Woman of the Year."

THE WHITE KNIGHT

22

The next week—a blur. I was busy. The embassy was busy. Sudan turned out to be busy, too.

The BBC's broadcast of the attempted coup was only the beginning. The story grew in scope and juicy detail. But I avoided the public eye. There were several calls by foreign correspondents who'd heard some American, an embassy American even, had been in on The Great Desert Massacre—*Al-madhbaha al-sahrawiyyah*, the local press called it. London tabloids wrote of "the Second Battle of Omdurman."

The hardest call to deflect was from BBC's Washington representative, Semaan Habib Semaan. I wavered. I felt as if I owed him—the BBC—something. But embassy and U.S. official spokesmen in Washington would only say, "the abducted American diplomats were rescued by the courage and quick thinking of Sudan's Security Forces. The United States government is most grateful." And *da capo*.

A few days more and the calls dropped off. The GOS refused to give visas to foreign newsmen. It wanted to avoid any public disagreements with Libya. Ever the Arab way! And correspondents (except for the *New York Times*'s Howard French) could not maintain a steady focus—Africa's crises appeared to be merging in a gigantic political-demographic-ecological-economic firestorm; the news from Rwanda, Burundi, Liberia, and their neighbors was so uniformly bad that correspondents and readers alike could hardly distinguish between the megatragedy and its individual parts. Like focusing on a single house afire amidst a burning block! Meanwhile the Balkans and the Soviet successor states were also spinning further out of control. Human rights violations everywhere. (What had ever happened, I wondered, to the serviceable, old-fashioned word *atrocities*?)

TDY orders also helped keep my profile low. Thirty-six hours after the Marine Corps Ball, I was on my way to Cairo via the defense attaché's C-12. Our assistant secretary was there and needed to be briefed. A separate interagency intelligence team was coming to Khartoum to debrief the ambassador and Sally. Before I left, the ambassador asked me to see the Marines. "It would mean a lot to them," he said, "your stock is high."

I knew what Jon was referring to. Somehow, photographs from the desert site had made their way to the Marine House. Large, glossy color prints, 8"x 12"—some even larger. Jack admitted his people had taken the photos ("a legitimate intelligence interest"), but both he and Pete disclaimed any knowledge of how they'd come into the Marines' hands. Pete I believed; but there was a suspicious pro-forma blandness about Jack's denials.

"So a photo goes astray," he had shrugged. "Doesn't show you standing over the bodies with a smoking gun, does it? I could show you pictures from Vietnam, or Desert Storm, or the Balkans." At this Jack took a photo from a stack on his desk, studied it carefully, then handed it to me saying: "Now that Sa'eed fellow. You know, I take it all back— he really *is* photogenic."

I looked at the photo: a close-up of the dead Sa'eed. Jack's photographer had gotten to the scene in the early-to-mid-morning. But even at that hour, the intense sunlight seemed to flatten out, to bleach, the photo subject. There was a taut, waxy, artificial look to the skin— and the teeth! I excused myself and left.

When he wanted to, Jack could laugh horribly.

Valiant, too, urged me not to worry about the photos. "Won't hurt your career, you know, just means you'll probably never get that protocol job you've pined for. No passing the cucumber sandwiches at Blair House. But as for the Marines, you know them. It's the biggest thing in their lives, their getting to the Mannesman compound just in time to back up a fellow Marine! They'd rather have an autographed photo with you than with the late J. Christ of biblical fame!"

So we went through the group and individual photo ceremonies, plus autographs and inscriptions. And when I'd walk into the Embassy lobby, the Marine at Post One would react as if Chesty Puller himself were coming aboard!

The second day after the ball, Jon held a staff meeting for all direct-hire (meaning security-cleared) Americans. He described the meeting to me as "really an EOD—Explosive Ordnance Disposal—project." I asked why. He responded: "Because if we don't have it soon, half the embassy will explode from pent-up curiosity."

Farnsworth began the meeting with an admonition: "Whoever leaks anything said here to outsiders (did his eyes wander toward Bill Gray?) serves his country next at McMurdo Sound, on the South Polar ice cap. Don't distract the Sudanese. Let the Libyan scare work its way through their politics—through their gut, like an emetic. Just what they need. Clear up that wishy-washy political complexion of theirs. And, we're saying a lot to the Sudanese in private."

At the meeting I touched only briefly on the abduction. After all, the embassy people had been at the rec site, too. But I felt I had to come clean about Mustafa and the Muslim Brothers' guards.

This angered Bill Gray. He said my actions "had put the whole community at risk."

I didn't argue. I said: "It was a judgment call, and maybe I was wrong." I didn't mention the broader significance of the cowrie charms. Just that Mustafa had given me mine for good luck, and I'd thought it was pretty. "Did it's job, too," I remarked.

I gave a summary version of the drive to the Mannesman compound, and the shootings. Sally made a few supplementary remarks. I'd also dictated a *fairly* complete account for the record. So the facts were there—those, at least, that U.S. officialdom needed to know. But embassy colleagues, for once, had lots of questions at staff meeting. I thought the questioning would never stop. Bill Gray was the most indefatigable:

Q. Did you ever think of trying to snatch the gun away from Sa'eed as you drove, Josh?
A. Sounds unimaginative, Bill, but no.
Q. Why didn't you crash the car into a tree or something?
A. Because we might have gotten hurt in the accident, or Sa'eed or his guard might have shot us.
Q. When did you think about tipping Sally off to "the panic button"?
A. Good question. Too late. Not until Sa'eed got nervous when I asked him about the Muslim Brothers. But Sally'd thought about it as soon

as they put her in the car. Right away she hit the button—and asked where Sa'eed was taking us. That's when the security transmitter in the back started broadcasting back to Post One. She deserves a world of credit.

Q. You must have been in a kind of fog.

A. Yes, that's exactly right.

Q. Even after you mentioned "panic button" to Sally, why didn't you say something that would have tipped the Marines off about where you were?

A. I was afraid Sa'eed would've smelled a rat. He was smart and suspicious. I figured I had to make my comment a good one. Then I saw the Mannesman sign! As the psychologists say, that was my 'Aha!' moment.

Q. You were very lucky that al-Masri said something early on about the Wad Madani Road, and that Sally had the presence of mind to activate the transmitter button right away. Otherwise the Marines wouldn't have known where to go. Or they wouldn't have gotten there in time. She saved your life!

A. Yes. I was very lucky. She saved my life . . . maybe Sudan too!

Q. Were you convinced that Sa'eed would have shot you? *You*, an American diplomat!

A. That's what the man said. It's on the tape. In a word, yes.

Q. (Bill's last question) Josh, do you feel at all that maybe your actions, and those of the Marines, were not entirely proportionate? There were ten dead at the site, after all. And how come no wounded?

A. (The gunny) Good, straight Marine shooting, sir.

Q. (Bill) And the papers all talk about the "Great Desert Massacre." I know you were under great pressure, but one thinks of police in situations of urban violence, how they handle threats to their person. It might be useful, don't you think, Mr. Ambassador, for some sort of guidelines to be available at this post—maybe even other posts—as to when use of a weapon is called for and when not? When deadly force is appropriate and when it isn't? What do you think, Mr. Ambassador? What do we say about *ourselves* in this year's Human Rights Report? And maybe we should review our weapons inventory! I, for one, never imagined the NCOIC was allowed to stock such a quantity and range of weapons. And maybe we should get some of those modern 'other-than-lethal' weapons?

A. (The ambassador) I think you've an interesting idea there, Bill.

Q. (Bill again) And Josh, what do you think?

A. I agree with the ambassador, Bill.

After the meeting Pete Valiant asked to see me. "Poor Gray. Can't get mad at him, though. It's kind of sad when a man tries to get at other people and always ends up hurting himself most. And his timing! You can't go for little cheap shots in a community like ours. People will freeze you out. Or be mean back. And then what? Ulcers on ulcers. Bio feedback. All Bill can eat, you know, is different kinds of mush. The Marines left a Gerber's baby food jar on his desk. Strained prunes, I think it was. He got really upset. 'I demand an investigation. There may be fingerprints. . . . No respect. Number Three on the diplomatic list, chargé d'affaires in the absence of the ambassador and Mr. Chamberlain!'

"Anyway, I told the gunny to have his men cut it out. 'Don't pick on the poor old guy,' I said, 'or he'll go out as a head case.' "

"You did a nice thing, Pete," I said. "You can't get mad at someone like Bill. You look at him. You feel a little sad, a little scared, too. You wonder what disappointments *he's* known. You wonder what *you'll* be like when you get older. Will you end up bitter, too, like Bill, when—if—your career somewhere comes to a dead end?"

Pete looked at me quizzically. "Nice way to look at things. Won't happen to you, though. Not to our 'White Knight.' "

"What's that?"

"Yeah. Your nickname. I don't know who started it. Or when exactly. Maybe the Marines. Most of the good and *all* the bad names start with them. That's what embassy people call you now. Don't sweat it. I've heard worse."

He went on: "But talking about hearing things. I've got something for you. It's about to go to Washington by courier—but there's one for you, too. Can I use your cassette player?"

From his pocket, Pete took out a cassette tape. The ninety-minute kind. Opening the cassette, he loaded the tape into my radio-cassette player. I kept one on a low cupboard behind my desk. Several times a day, I'd listen to the BBC and local news on it. VOA's signals were never clearly audible. He set the counter to zero, and pressed "Play."

When our USG electronics work, I said to myself, they work. The car mike (a Motorola product) was supposed to pick up sound clearly over a forty-foot radius. It did. The recording had voice recognition quality, even on my small Panasonic RX-410. The sound track began in midsentence with Sally's ". . . taking us?" And Sa'eed's reply, "Be quiet, please! Absolutely no talking. We mustn't distract Mr. Chamberlain."

Pete fast forwarded the tape. He checked the counter. Still watching, he said, "The equipment at Post One is voice-activated. You get a lot of talk on tape." He stopped the tape and made an adjustment: "Here's a good part. Kirby will like it, too."

Sa'eed's voice: ". . . your resourceful Mr. Kirby, inventive, forceful. Brother Qadhaafi underestimated you Americans. Poor man! He hasn't had a formed stool since Desert Storm!"

Fast forward again. Pete said, "Listen. Here he starts to get serious."

Sa'eed's voice came in again: ". . . How do you want to take it Mr. Chamberlain? From the front or the back? A question later for Miss Tolson . . ."

Pete snapped the tape off. He took it out of the machine and loaded it back into its box. He paused. "We're near the end. You can play a little more; there are some great sound effects. Like the sound track from *Patton* or *The Longest Day*—amplified! Then some talk about 'Blasteek,' and then"—Pete looked right at me—"a malfunction. I talked to the Marines on duty. They'd no explanation. Just the blank tape."

I looked back at Pete. He put the cassette on my desk. "Thanks," I said.

That night, after I arrived in Cairo, I called Marj and Brian in Boston at Marj's parents. It was Saturday evening my time, late morning theirs. I knew it was one of Brian's long weekends from St. Andrew's. Marj's father answered. He sounded—I racked my mind—like Bill Gray! He must have been eavesdropping at the staff meeting, I decided. He even asked some of the same questions. Said the deputy secretary had called. He'd pretty much given Marj and her parents the facts.

Marj was next on the line. Her voice was unsteady: "I am so happy you're alright, the happiest in my life, maybe. I'm so glad you're alive and well! I'm so proud! We're fine; everything's the same. Mom and Dad, too. Come home soon!" A pause. Her last words: "Keep your head down for us. I love you, Lieutenant!"

In fairy tales, the hardest test, the dénouement, is always the third one. Brian got on the phone: "Dad, this is Brian."

"Yeah, Brian, this is your dad. I remember you. How are things? Studies? Get my letter? The one with the check and advice about a Bruce Hornsby tape? How was football?"

"Everything's fine. Dad, we won the state championship for the first time in twenty-two years! Beat Tatnall 34–0 in the last game. I played a couple of quarters! The coach says I'll start next year!"

Then Brian's voice changed gears: "Dad, I was at home this morning when the secretary-of-something called. I picked up the phone. I guess he's really important, isn't he? When he found out who I was, right away he said, 'You should be really proud of your father!' Then he asked for Mom. I went and listened on the upstairs phone.

"Dad . . . (the connection seemed to get worse), I'm so proud of you . . . I'm so glad you're alive. You're the best, the bravest father any boy could ever have. If anything'd happened to you, I'd have killed those guys——" A stifled sob. Pause. Brian's voice again. Shaky. "Sorry, Dad, guess I lost it . . . but come home soon when you can. I guess they're all counting on you over there. But we love you. Mom needs you . . . better hang up now . . . love you . . . hugs. God bless . . . 'bye." A dial tone.

My eyes were streaming. I sat by the phone a long time. Then got up to wash my face and change for the ambassador's dinner for the assistant secretary. I was in Cairo four days, the phone conversations always on my mind.

I got back to Khartoum Thursday night. The next day was Friday, the Muslim Sabbath—or "Sunday" for U.S. embassies in the Middle East. The ambassador asked me out for a drive in the desert. The next morning, Saturday, I got to the office late, just a little before staff meeting.

Sally was in the office. She'd been at work a couple of hours, I knew. She was always early, but Saturdays were special. The department liked to clear its desks on Friday afternoons. So our Saturday A.M. "take" might equal *all* the incoming traffic of the week before.

"Morning, Josh, how was Cairo?" she asked. There was little expression in her face or voice.

"Busy, crowded," I answered. "A million more Egyptians every nine months. And it looked as if they were all in Cairo, in front of our hotel."

She said, "I'd like to see you after staff meeting."

THE TIME MACHINE

23

8:30 A.M. The ambassador began the staff meeting. I noticed no agenda had been distributed. I learned why.

Looking about the room, Farnsworth said: "Prime Minister al-Muntasser would agree that this has been the week that was. So would Dr. al-Mughraibiy, our new prime minister-designate." We looked at Farnsworth with astonishment.

"That's right," he went on. "Al-Muntasser resigned last night. Immediately afterwards, leaders of the different political parties met to discuss next steps. They were really in a hurry. The coup attempts scared them, and they didn't want to leave any vacuums for some military officer to fill. It seems they've agreed al-Mughraibiy should be the man. That's what Jack told me last night.

"Then, very early this morning, Dr. al-Mughraibiy himself called me at the Residence. He wants me to come see him today at three. You're to come, too, Josh. He said he attaches particular importance to his relationship with the United States. He wants to talk with us about reconciliation with the South—you knew his views, he said. Let's see. What exactly did al-Mughraibiy say to me?"

The ambassador leafed through some notes. "Always keep pencil and paper next to each telephone," he counseled. "Someday, it will save you a lot of shouting and panicky emptying of drawers. Here it is: 'There is no place in my program for imposing Islam by force upon the southern Nilotics and Equatorians. There is no compulsion in Islam.'

228

Al-Mughraibiy says he wants the U.S. to help get this message across to southerners. As an earnest of his good intentions, he'd have an announcement of interest for us this morning, at 8:30 A.M. Right about now, that is. Will, you've got one of your people on it?"

"Yessir, just as you asked," said Dawkins. "One of the FSNs is taping it. He'll call the front office if anything's important."

A knock on the door. Maryann entered. She gave the ambassador a note. He read it carefully, then looked up: "Ladies and gentlemen, Dr. al-Mughraibiy, or should I say Prime Minister al-Mughraibiy, has told the Chamber of Deputies that effective today Sudan has broken relations with Libya. The cause is Libya's 'blatant' and 'unacceptable' interference in the internal affairs of Sudan. He also calls on the leaders of the southern insurgency to meet him under safe-conduct in Khartoum, or any capital of their choice, maybe Nairobi."

Applause. Cheers. After a moment, the ambassador continued: "Not a bad week's work? Ms. Tolson and Mr. Chamberlain are back safe" (applause). I heard a voice: "Cheers for the White Knight" (laughter . . . more applause). The ambassador paused, then resumed: "The Libyans are out. We've all got work to do. Let's adjourn while we're ahead, shall we?" The clapping went on as he rose; together, we left the room.

I was at my desk when Sally came in. She closed the door behind her, came over and took the chair in front of the desk. She sat straight up in the chair as she always did, knees and ankles together. "I thought you might call yesterday," she said. There was little expression in her voice. Her features? Grave? Impassive?

I replied, "The ambassador called early. He wondered if I'd want to go out for a desert drive, have a picnic with him. We didn't get back until late afternoon . . ."

Sally broke in: "While at home, I made a snowball."

"A snowball? In Sudan?"

Sally shook her head. "It's not what you're thinking, not from an icebox freezer. Here." She pushed a sheet of paper across the desk. It said:

SNOWBALL

I
in
the
dark
hours
forget
manners
overcome
obstacles
dissolving
inhibitions
breathlessly
relinquishing
justifications
heartbreakingly
incontrovertibly
hyperventilating
unquestionably
intoxicatingly
soulshakingly
surrendering
concealment
abandoning
restraint
morality
neglect
wisdom
blurt
love
you
do
?

"I don't know what to say," I replied. "I've never seen anything like this—It's beautiful."

"You don't have to say anything," Sally cut in, "just listen. That night in the desert. It wasn't just fear. It was love. And later at the residence I asked you, 'What do we do now?' And you said, 'I don't know.' But *I* know. Could we have an affair? But that's not what I want with you. It's not your way, either. I love you. So you see, I want to marry you. I want you to marry me."

She looked up; I couldn't meet her eyes.

Sally went on: "Do you think this is sudden? That I'm being impulsive? Josh, this is the real world, not an English Department at some Eastern school. One month of Khartoum is ten in Foggy Bottom. Khartoum's no ordinary post—it's a time machine. But I'm not impulsive or casual in my affections. There haven't been many men in my life. I'm no *femme fatale*. But we have a lot to share. I'm talking about our lifetimes."

Sally continued: "I think I've read your feelings, and I don't mind speaking up. That's what love partly is—a free-will gift—nothing demanded in return; a willingness to be vulnerable—without being a wimp, or a victim. A dope," Sally added, with a lightening of her voice and expression.

I was staring at Sally's poem. Silence.

"Do you think I'm being serious? sincere?" she asked.

My mouth was dry. My lips and tongue felt stiff, unpracticed. They began to say: "I believe you're serious and sincere. I'm honored you feel that way about me—"

Sally broke in: "Josh! This isn't one of your awards ceremonies, no 'grip and grin.' "

I thought of the fairy tale in which the wicked stepmother's words turned to toads and jumped from her mouth as she spoke.

My voice went on: "There haven't been many women in my life either. There's never really been anyone but Marj. Maybe if we'd met earlier——I'm married——I have a family——a nice boy. (Pause.) I love Marj very much. I just don't feel about you that way——"

Sally: "One can't argue over love. It's not a case you can win in court. There's no appeals system. But I don't think you're giving me a chance. I don't think you're giving yourself a chance, either. I think you *do* care for me. You're not being fair to us both."

With a touch of anger in her voice, Sally added: "I may sound selfish, but I don't care. I deserve you more than . . . others do. More than someone who always defers to you, always at your elbow, like a pretty music box figurine, a marionette, pulled along on a string! There's so much you and I have to share, and it's not at all just sex. It's the lifetime I have to share with you——and you with me."

I looked her in the face. Why did looking full in her face—why did that particular combination of features move me so? My mind said "regular, pleasant," but as I looked at her, my heart said "poignant—— unforgettable."

This time my words came like stones: "Sally. It's not doing you any good. It's not going to *change* anything. Marj needs me. Brian needs me. I'm married. Twenty years ago I made a promise. I'm not that kind of person——" My mouth was desert-dry; I badly needed a glass of water.

Sally put her hands on the arms of her chair. She leaned forward. "Do you think Marj will ever leave you?" she asked.

"How do I know what will happen to us," I replied, "or who she'll meet. There are parts of Foreign Service life she doesn't like—we've had our ups and downs, most couples have. Right now it's hard, the troubles of the last couple of months . . ."

She sat for a minute more. Then stood up: "Somewhere I read that asking for love is the saddest plea in the world. If you have to ask, the answer is too painful to hear. But I've had the chance to say what I wanted to say, what needed to be said. I'm glad I did it——I'm such a fool——I wish I were dead." She left the room, walking quickly.

As she reached the door, I called out, "Sally, always remember what a wonderful person you are!" She paused, without looking back, then opened the door and left.

I sat at my desk for a time. The morning sun came through. I raised my hand—a clearly outlined, dark claw shape, deformed, stood out against my blotter. "No transparency there," I thought. "Just the old Adam——no, the Old Nick."

Thirty-six hours later, Sally left for the States on a two-week R&R. Maryann and Clayton were surprised. Sally, they said, hadn't planned on taking R&R until Christmas.

Afterwards, the ambassador called me in. "Josh, how was Sally's morale when she left? I thought she'd taken the kidnapping pretty well. But then came her rather sudden request for R&R."

"I agree, Jon. She took it really well. I didn't get the feeling that it shook her up. She's brave, and tough, really steady. That's not exactly what I mean——"

"I take your point, though," the ambassador went on, "that's why I'm surprised. Here, read this." Jon passed a cable over to me. It was addressed to him from the director general. It read:

Subject: Request for Transfer—Tolson, Sally (SSN 126 28 3251)

1. Khartoum's Staff Assistant Tolson called on my Deputy Tuesday Nov 20 to request a direct transfer from Khartoum to Department. Because of the recent terrorist incident, she said she did not believe she could continue to function effectively in Sudan. A change of scene was needed.

2. My Deputy knew about recent events in Khartoum. He told Ms. Tolson she had shown great courage and resourcefulness. We all admired and were proud of her. If she wanted a transfer from Khartoum, he was sure that a transfer to an appropriately good onward job could be arranged. Could Ms. Tolson give him two or three months? Her answer was a firm "No." She asked for an immediate transfer to Washington; she did not wish to return to post. She was not choosy as to the job. Any Washington job would do.

3. I know, Jon, of your interest in your people. Do you have any advice for me? I gather she really *is* a good officer. Her behavior seems uncharacteristic. Certainly, she's not acting in her career best interests.

4. How can I help?

5. Warm regards.

That day, Jon cabled back to the director general:

Subject: Request for Transfer—Tolson, Sally (SSN 126 28 3251)
Ref: DG's cable 181220ZNOV

1. Thank you for the personal attention and consideration your office is showing my staff aide, Ms. Tolson. It is deserved.

2. Even before Ms. Tolson's display of heroism (award recommendation to follow), she was, in my opinion, one of the best junior officers I'd met in years.

3. Personnel is certainly right in advising against immediate curtailment of her tour. Perhaps an extension of her R&R could be suggested? She could delay her return to post until after Christmas or even into the New Year, if she wished.

4. I have discussed Ms. Tolson's case with DCM Chamberlain. He has worked closely with her, and fully shares my high opinion. He concurs proposal para 3.

5. Please advise.

Sometimes, the department goes autistic. But on this occasion, the response was swift. It came to Jon from the director general himself.

Subject: Request for Transfer—Tolson, Sally (SSN 126 28 3251)
Ref: Ambassador's cable 181623ZNOV

1. I have spoken with Ms. Tolson. She is impressive: intelligent, composed, well-spoken. Certainly no case of shell-shock (as we used to call it), or of 'post-traumatic syndrome' (as it's called today). In brief, I'd say she knows what she is doing. And, among other things, that means not returning to post.

2. Why? I don't know.

3. Her request, however, leaves us no alternative. We cannot act otherwise toward an officer who has shown such courage and resourcefulness.

4. Accordingly, Ms. Tolson is being directly reassigned to the Economic Bureau, Division of Tropical Products, Directorate of Fruits, Fibers and Textiles (E/T/FT).

5. This is in no sense a heavily bid position. But at present, the number of good, off-cycle vacancies in the Department is nil.

6. Orders and fiscal data follow septel for Ms. Tolson's transfer and the packing and shipment of HHE.

7. I'll keep an eye on Ms. Tolson; in my book she's still a player. Warm regards.

Jonathan shook his head as he gave me the message. "Poor Sally. 'Fruits, Fibers and Textiles'—also known as 'Fruits and Suits'! Was Khartoum *that* bad?"

THE VIRGINIAN

24

Thanksgiving came. And Christmas. The ambassador and I opened presents together. My R&R had been postponed. And postponed again. A lot was going on in Sudan. The Libyans were not giving up easily, and Prime Minister al-Mughraibiy seemed to value my presence. Once he said—half-jokingly?—he wanted someone lucky, like me, around. Washington was eager to oblige him. The al-Mughraibiy premiership was seen back home as one of the best developments in U.S.-Africa relations in years.

No one had heard from Sally. Maryann and Clayton were puzzled but not sore. They wrote, sent Christmas cards. Then in early January they got Christmas cards from her. Not much text. She'd found an apartment, was beginning to learn about the crops produced around the Equator. We should avoid Iraqi dates—full of insect and rat infestation, also known as "frass." "Fondly, . . ."

What did Clayton and Maryann know? Think? They never spoke about Sally to me. Nor did the ambassador. Was there a message, perhaps, in *that*?

There was no one for me to talk to. No therapeutic conversation. Job needs, fastidiousness, a taste for privacy, all made me keep my mouth shut. Isn't the adult personality independent? Free-standing? And can a boss go about with a long face, clutching at his heart? Comic opera! The constraints of *bella figura* again. The boss—even the number two boss—must be a 'Happy Warrior,' a moon, at least, to the ambassador's ever-radiant sun.

Thank God, I thought, for a sense of humor, of the ridiculous. One day, I laughed to think what the community liaison officer who handled embassy morale would have said if I'd gone to see her. I could hear myself: "Ma'am, I have a problem." Cheerily, she'd answer: "Ye-e-es?"—with a rising inflection. Then I'd drop it on her: "I'm besotted, perishing with love for Sally Tolson. And she for me." Then, the spilled coffee cup. Hell! The overturned coffee urn. This was 16-inch stuff, 42-kiloton gossip.

I clung to a sense of perspective: What could seem less lovable to others, I thought, than a lover? Pained, self-absorbed—a man with an allergy! A hay fever victim!

I had to hand it to the Marines. I'd think often of my advice to myself at the Marine Guard Ball about the foolishness and irresponsibility of playing around at post. But they and Pete could keep a secret. Nary an arch look.

Maybe it was just as well, I decided, that Sally had left. In a crisis environment, embassy people deserved leaders who had their personal problems under control.

Sometimes, also, I wondered why I'd reacted as I had. Loyalty to Marj? Love for Marj? It wouldn't be true to say I *didn't* love her. Was it my love for Brian? Or my reluctance to rock a career boat that was moving ahead well? I knew, though, that what I felt for Sally was more, and different, than what I'd ever felt for any other woman.

Foreign Service people, though, are not deeply introspective. Our analytical skills can be considerable but tend to be focused outwards. We take a situation and tend to get on with it. In real life I've met very few of the tormented, chain-smoking, hard-drinking mavericks of spy novels.

So I worked hard. And I worked out hard. Tennis wasn't intense enough. Every evening, I'd run or, more commonly, swim at the rec site—length after length, a couple of miles sometimes. Exercise manufactures its own pain-killers: endorphins. Momentum will carry a hard-driving mind and body through muddy stretches of self-pity. Even in middle age, the boarding-school formula for peace of mind works! Just don't slow down, I'd tell myself. Don't get sick. Don't get hurt. I got thinner.

There was consolation, too, in reading. Sally had lent me her prized first edition of Owen Wister's *The Virginian*, published in 1902 by Macmillan, New York. "Our first real 'Western,'" she'd said, "and still one of our best." I'd listened tolerantly, but did not begin the book until after she had gone. Sally had been right, though. I copied out and put in my wallet a line from page 146, where our hero (the Virginian) writes to his cold, slim sweetheart: ". . . and bein' busy always keeps me from grievin' too much about you."

Two more weeks passed. Then one quiet Sunday afternoon in January, I returned to the office from lunch. From the door, I could tell the pouch had come in. There was a stack of letters in the middle of my blotter. As always, the bills were at the top. Once I asked Clayton why she arranged my mail that way. She answered: "Bills—bad news—first. But you'll know that good news, personal letters, are probably waiting. Like dessert, see?" It made a kind of sense.

Under the bills was a letter from Marj. And another letter, with no return address. On the envelope was written only "Mr. Joshua Lawrence Chamberlain, U.S. Embassy, APO 09697, New York, New York." It was postmarked "Wash. DC." The letter was unopened, which was strange. Clayton used always to open "anonymous" mail. Usually, it was some schoolchild in New Mexico, asking for a button or a license plate from Sudan, or for help with a school project on Africa. We were glad to try to help; Clayton routinely sent these letters to our consul for action without my ever seeing them. But this letter was still sealed. The handwriting looked familiar to me. I guess it had to Clayton, too.

First, I read Marj's letter. Not much news. Brian was a starter on the St. Andrews JV basketball team. She'd gone down for one of his games. He'd played well. Made some points. She'd had a bad flu. Was still weak. The doctors said she shouldn't travel again for a few weeks. When would I take my R&R, she wondered. In the spring? She was thinking of working part-time for UNICEF, and of taking an adult education course in computers and word-processing. Her parents thought she should try to acquire work skills and experience while she was still young.

I put Marj's letter to one side. I picked the other up. What if it's just my college roommate, I thought, asking for a contribution to the new fieldhouse? I pressed it between my fingers—two, maybe more, sheets of paper. I held the envelope against the light. Opaque. For a second I thought of pressing it against a light bulb—an old intelligence trick. Dope! I said to myself. I opened the envelope carefully. With my letter opener. Not, as I usually did, with my index finger. My heart was beating faster. My mouth felt dry.

It was a handwritten letter from Sally. It read:

Sunday, January 15

Dear Josh,

Soon, it will be two months since I tried to walk away from you. It's been harder than I thought. I honestly didn't ever think I'd feel this way for a man. But falling in love is like sliding off a roof. You lose your purchase on the tiles—next thing, you're over the edge, and the gutters aren't holding. And I also think, too, that you love me—or could, if you let yourself go. Am I wrong? I don't believe so.

But remember also what I said about love being a free-will gift? Something that doesn't require a response? It's true. One of the answers, maybe, to that Zen conundrum about clapping with a single hand. True love of someone else does not need reciprocity. It's not essential to *be* loved. That's thinking of oneself. More important is *loving*, period. And to work a little at remaining lovable. Love doesn't call for quick service. A good customer, it makes no demands.

I wonder: Does this letter evoke nostalgia? Or impatience—as when a bill for a canceled subscription shows up again in the mailbox? And I worry—briefly.

Then I decide I'm a pretty normal, worthwhile, run-of-the-mill sort of person. That my feelings are not abnormal. Only rare. More people should feel as I do; it's too bad they don't.

I conclude, in the immortal words of mehitabel the cat:

> but there's nothing i really regret
> wotthehell wotthehell
> there's a dance in the old dame yet
> *toujours gai toujours gai*

Like mehitabel, I'm not always nice, but I'm likeable.

I love you, my Chevalier.

Sally

I got up and looked out the window. The usual yellow winter dust in the air. Pretty much the same as the spring, summer, and autumn dust, I reflected. The buildings looked fuzzy, cottony—a blurred, indistinct horizon, the world through a yellowish scrim.

I went over to my radio-cassette player. From my attaché case I took out some tāpes Brian had sent me. I loaded one—*On the Beach*, an album by The Cure. I pressed the "Play" button, sat down. The first song was just right—yes—"Boys don't cry." What's next? Pause. I heard the words "killing an Arab. . . ." It's like listening to the BBC, I thought, and shuddered. I pressed the Stop/Eject button. I tried another tape—Robert Dallrey's *Take Me Home.* He sang: "This machine inside my head remembers everything she said. . . ." Stop/Eject again. I opened my middle desk drawer. There was Eric Clapton's "Unplugged." Closed it. Some days you're just a loser, I decided.

I spread Sally's letter on the desk. I reread it. Then put on a safe cassette, Bruce Hornsby: ". . . the tears roll down my face as she turns to go!" I closed my eyes.

"Do you have a moment, Josh?" The ambassador's voice. I looked up. Jon was standing by the desk. "A nice ballad," he added.

"It is, isn't it, please, sit down," I said. He took the chair by the desk. (He couldn't have missed the letter, I thought.)

For a few moments Farnsworth sat there, silently, looking out the window. Then he began to speak, as if to himself.

"You're looking tired, Josh. The ladies, Maryann and Clayton, are worried about you."

He was silent again. Then: "Foreign Service life has many rewards and hardships. The rewards come mainly from our colleagues, the people, the friends we work and live with. The hardships . . . ?" Another silence.

Jon went on: "In time, we learn to enjoy the rewards, and to endure the hardships. As a poet once wrote: 'Bear them we can and if we can, we must.' We bear them, each in our different ways. Some of us endure. Some crumple. Some pray. Strange, the answers that prayer can sometimes provide—not always the ones you're looking for. But should we not listen? Should we not try?"

He continued: "I remember the day of . . . her funeral. It was Teddy Roosevelt's birthday, October 27. His wedding day, too, did you know that? But the end, I thought, of all my hopes. What did I do? That evening, on the plane, I read the *New York Times.* Was it habit? Was it meaningful coincidence? Jung's synchronicity? Was it my answer?

"Because an article caught my attention. It was about an Indian epic, the Mahabharata. The hero, Arjuna, knows the war he is about to fight must end in unspeakable sadness, silence, and desolation. All for no apparent purpose. For no ensuing good. The god Khrishna reveals himself. And Arjuna learns the real purpose of life is not happiness but to link duty and action, even while the consequences seem tragic.

"Bleak words, aren't they?" the ambassador mused. "Duty. Action. Hard words to live by . . . thin air . . ." He turned to look directly at me. He seemed to be baring his teeth. His expression—intense, wolfish—for an instant it reminded me of—— I pushed the thought from my mind. "Thin, dry air," Jon was repeating, "but it will sustain you. It won't let you down. Not throughout a long, interminable life-time." Silence again.

"Older men will maunder," Jonathan said. "Is a transfer of learn-ing possible? We live at untouchable distances from each other. Should one reach out? Is the effort worthwhile? Do we ever succeed? The right answer is: 'Hardly ever.' But who says one has to be right? Or has to succeed? Why shouldn't one sometimes do *something*. Duty, action once more. Why not sometimes try to give something of ourselves to others? And besides, Josh, I like you *all!* "

Jonathan rose to leave. I got up too, saying: "Thanks for taking the time—and for reaching out. I know what you mean, and I under-stand it. As one of Brian's songs would put it:

You gotta take control, you can never stop,
You gotta keep on climbing till you reach the top;
Never givin' up, ain't life a bitch,
You gotta keep on going till you strike it rich!

Jonathan laughed: "Life *is* a bitch, often. And I like that part about 'taking control.' Khartoum is no place to lose it." He nodded several times, and walked out.

I watched him leave. He looked old. I was touched.

THE END OF THE BEGINNING?

25

Two more weeks. The pouch was in again. A letter from Brian. He was fine. School was fine. Sports were fine. I thought, this isn't a letter; it's how a boy back from school answers his parents as he heads for the icebox. Nothing from Marj.

Clayton buzzed me. "Could you step in and see the ambassador?"

"On my way."

Farnsworth came from behind his desk. He had a cable in his hand. Also a sheaf of other documents. From the smudgy blue type, I recognized them as raw CIA reports. "Have a seat, Josh. I've some messages here from our 'sister agency.' And something else. Frankly, none of it surprises me. In a way, I wonder that it took Washington so long. I was beginning to hope it might blow over—on all sides——"

"Blow over, sir?"

"I'll be direct. The department is requesting—no, ordering— your direct transfer home. I first heard about the possibility a few days ago."

"Is it because of the desert business, Jon?" I asked. "Does Washington think I've made too much news——get Chamberlain home, back in the box?"

"Maybe part of it is, Josh. If that were all, we'd just fend them off. Assuming, of course, you wanted to stay. No"—the ambassador raised a hand, cutting off any reply I might have made— "it's not that. What's happened is that the intelligence community is picking up hostile interest in you, Sons-of-'Uumayyir kind of stuff. It looks real. You can see the material yourself.

"I went over the reports myself with Jack Kirby. He made further checks. He likes you, you know. His comment on the intel reports are (the ambassador read a handwritten note appended to the CIA file): 'No bull. If Josh were one of my people—wish he were, wasted at State—I'd get him out of Sudan.' That was Jack's recommendation—put forward, as he has emphatically reminded me, as my 'senior intelligence advisor.' He added that, as your friend, he'd do the same."

Jon continued: "I spoke yesterday by secure phone with the director general. He knows—all the top brass in the department know—what you've done here. I asked him what were the prospects if you *did* leave. I said *how* you left and *where* you went next had to show the Sudanese, and the Foreign Service, that the move was for a job well done. Washington could keep its honor awards, I said, even cash awards—sorry about that—but you know that among FSOs such awards are used too often for special pleading. For arguing with the results of last year's selection boards. For smoothing over the feathers of someone who wasn't promoted—and with whom you'll have to work for another year.

"I'm not cynical, Josh, just realistic. So I put some pressure on our velvety-voiced DG. On the secure phone, he assured me that he and the department were already addressing my concerns. He's personally looked into your next assignment."

As Farnsworth spoke, my mind accelerated. My heart plummeted. Groups of thoughts inserted themselves between his phrases—his words even. I thought: The slow curve—here it comes, watch for the fast break. It's the department's way, let a person down gently. I guess I made too many waves? "Run silent, run deep," the Foreign Service's motto, too? Get ready—here it comes. Keep your expression under control, try to pitch your voice low when answering—or else you'll squeak. Fruits and Suits? Maybe I'll be Sally's boss?

Looking down at his papers, the ambassador remarked: "Perhaps you'll say the DG's done alright." Farnsworth passed over a cable:

To: Ambassador Farnsworth
Fr: Director General
Subj: Off-Cycle Transfer: Chamberlain, Joshua Lawrence (SSN
      638 30 4335)

1. Concur fully in your view that in transferring DCM Chamberlain we must make clear the approval and admiration with which he is regarded by his government. In fact, his performance has been

noted with admiration throughout our intelligence communities, as well as in the NSC and even at the White House.

2. Chamberlain would not ordinarily be eligible for promotion this year. As you know, he was selected by last year's boards for FO-1. Your special interim report on him, however, was brought to the attention of the current promotion boards. In strict confidence, you may extend to him my congratulations. Tell him that he was unanimously selected by the counselor panel (FE-OC) for promotion and selection into the Senior Foreign Service. The boards' results will be announced soon.

3. But we know that a promotion is a reward for past performance. What does the future hold for Chamberlain? I have spoken to the Secretary who authorizes me to extend further congratulations. The Secretary has consulted with the White House and reports that informal White House approval has been granted for Chamberlain to receive a presidential appointment. We are nominating him as our next ambassador to the Republic of Cameroon.

4. The processing time for such appointments is lengthy, usually six to eight months. It includes security, health, and conflict of interest clearances, followed by *agrément* request to host government, formal nomination to White House, White House announcement of nomination, nomination to Senate, Senate hearings and confirmation, attestation by Senate, swearing-in, and oath of office. Because the position is vacant, and because of the Secretary's interest, however, we will try to hasten the processing as much we can.

5. Presidential phone call formalizing assignment will be scheduled following Chamberlain's return to DC.

6. There will be congressional interest in Chamberlain's Sudan experience. Without being crass, we frankly expect his record, "in war and peace," so to speak, to convey a positive—activist—impression of the Foreign Service.

5. Accordingly, we want Chamberlain back in Washington asap. No farewell parties. No foot-dragging. He should call on me when he arrives in Washington. Tell him I remember him from my time with his DCM class. Thought then he'd do well.

6. This represents exceptional preferment for an officer of Chamberlain's age and rank. We think he deserves it and will continue to serve his country well. I am confident he will not let his good fortune go to his head. (We want no "weather-balloon" officers whose heads swell as they rise in the Service.) Advise Mr. Chamberlain that while he has been decisive, brave, able, he has also been very, very *lucky*.

7. In this I am sure even the original (and also very lucky) Joshua Lawrence Chamberlain would agree.

8. Warm regards.

I looked up. The ambassador was observing me, appraising my reaction. His features suggested the beginnings of a smile.

I felt dizzy. I must have looked pale. My heart—a *maître tamborineur*—seemed to break into a syncopated, Caribbean rap. Arrhythmia? I remembered how I'd felt during my first free-fall parachute jump: panic and nauseated disbelief that this was happening to me—panic exceeded only by the fear of admitting fear—and then the wash of triumphant relief as the chute opened with a springy bounce, and I looked up and could see a good, square canopy.

"What should I say, sir?" I finally got out. "How should I feel? Should I be happy? Bewildered? Above all, grateful?"

"You can skip the last one," answered Farnsworth, "but congratulations, Mr. Ambassador-designate." He rose, shook my hand, and continued: "Your flight leaves tomorrow at 11:00 A.M. You'd better get started. See the admin section about packing out. Shall we break the good/bad news of your departure to Clayton and Maryann? Maybe a glass of champagne? Then you'll have work to do. But we'll go to the airport together."

All that afternoon and much of the night I was at my desk, tidying up, dictating into my cassette—letters, efficiency reports, biographic notes. Finally, I was able to seize a moment to reflect on what had happened to me.

"You're going to be an ambassador," I said half-aloud several times to myself. You've done it! I thought, rather smugly. No matter what happens now, assuming you get confirmed, you'll have reached the top of your profession. You've made the summit. Broken through the cloud cover of Foggy Bottom, so to speak. Your *life* will have been successful.

In the next breath I reproached myself: What a careerist you sound like! Despite all the values that religion and a liberal education should have taught? But then: Maybe it's OK, feel as you do—but only briefly.

I had a sense of relief, almost languor. I'd crossed over a professional watershed; after years of competition, I could for a moment catch my breath and purely enjoy the moment.

I mused on: Imagine! You've been chosen by your president to represent your fellow citizens and the United States of America to another sovereign power. That's an honor that no one afterwards can take away from you. And in our republican, egalitarian society, an ambassadorship is one of the few public honors available to a citizen. I'd wondered how I'd do as a DCM—and now this!

My thoughts then turned elsewhere—as they so regularly did. Before I left the office, I took up a pencil and, on a legal-size yellow pad, in large letters, firmly printed out for myself: "I AVOID, AS I WOULD A KNIFE THRUST, RECALLING YOUR SMILE." I ripped off the sheet and put it in my pocket. Then I took a last look about the office, closed my safe, spun the dial for the last time, signed out, and went home to bed.

The end? Not quite. The next morning I packed my sixty-six pounds and said good-bye to my servants. I thought they had liked me, and I liked them. I hoped my successor would keep them on and treat them well. I gave them excellent references. I gave Mustafa an extra bonus. He was fully recovered from the blow he'd taken at the rec site.

Mustafa, though, had a final message for me as I got into the car. He looked serious. He said: "*Rih ahmar* always in world. It not forget. I will pray for you, for Madam, for your son. And you carry this. . . ." He handed me a twin of the white cowrie charm Sa'eed had crushed. I was touched. I smiled and—(maybe) taking the words out of his mouth—said: "I know, arm, pocket good, neck better!"

I made a final call at the Marine house. The Marines gave me a detachment plaque and an "Amembassy Khartoum/USMC" T-shirt. I kept the T-shirt; the plaque would follow by pouch. Next a walk-through and more handshakes at the Chancery. Clayton and Maryann offered Moët & Chandon champagne.

Maryann (always well-informed?) whispered: "I'll be glad to work with you again." (Ambassadors in the Foreign Service are allowed to choose their own secretaries.) I gave her a kiss on each cheek. "You'll hear from me," I said.

Then the drive to the airport, with the ambassador and Pete Galant. Bill Gray sent regrets. He had "a crucial meeting with the minister of finance."

The airport hadn't changed; only the weather, a little. I felt like a character in a video movie that was being played on rewind.

Jack Kirby was there to say good-bye. So was Frank Greer—in an obviously custom-tailored dark blue suit. Nice material, two-button jacket, white shirt of long-staple cotton, a solid burgundy tie. The haircut was *styled!* I looked him over.

"Old wine, new bottle?" I asked.

He laughed: "All a gift from Aminata. She made me promise to wear it today. And she herself gave me this—(Frank hesitated, then pointed upwards with his finger)—'layer cut.' (Did he blush?) And she sends her (Frank hesitated again) *love* (yes, a blush)."

We shook hands—I felt the piston starting its descent. I braced myself. Then the movement abruptly stopped. The needle fell back to zero.

Frank stepped away and smiled, "Good luck!"

The expeditor had checked me in and brought me my baggage checks and boarding pass. I'd been upgraded to first class as far as Frankfurt. The Lufthansa manager and his wife were there to help. I could board any time.

We were at planeside. I could see Jack Kirby looking toward the diplomatic gate. His eyes were following a maroon Mercedes 300 that had just come onto the field and was speeding toward us. "The new chief of Foreign Ministry and Presidency protocol," Jack remarked.

When I saw who stepped out of the Mercedes, I couldn't hold back a full South American *abrazo*: "Take good care of all of my friends," I said. "Good luck, and God bless you, Yedol Furj!"

THE RETURN TO ITHAKA

26

How good—how wonderful!—to get back to the United States of America. It was midafternoon Friday when our United Air Lines 747 began its approach to Washington. We were still in sunshine, but from the south a storm front was moving in. Looking out toward Leesburg, Poolesville, and White's Ferry, I thought again, as I always did on coming home: What a green, peaceful, and blessed land.

Soon, at an improbable angle, I glimpsed l'Enfant's familiar urban design. Then the landmarks—I easily picked them out: the Capitol, the Washington Monument, the bridges, the Potomac. Light rain dashed horizontal lines across the windows. The plane stabilized as the pilot lined up his approach to Dulles. With the asthmatic wheeze of the undercarriage going down, I thought back to another landing—long ago?—to a much younger man. A slight shock, a skid. The roar and pressure of reverse thrust. Then, inwardly, the sudden inrush of homecoming! Coming *home* always made me feel so privileged, so incredibly, undeservedly fortunate! To most of mankind, America was heaven. And I was one of its angels. A sort of "guardian angel" even?

A lawyer friend once asked: "Isn't it quite a letdown, after your exciting, cosmopolitan life abroad, servants at your beck and call, to be back in 'WASHDC'? To have to mow your lawn? Rake the leaves? Haul out the trash Sunday night?" He was wrong.

How could he appreciate the pleasure we took in having, again, a private life after years of circling around in the diplomatic goldfish bowl! *His* chores were—in the title of the hymn—*our* "Simple Pleasures." Even the leaves and the trash. And he was wrong more basically, too:

the closer a Foreign Service person comes to truly understanding a foreign culture, the more clearly he sees the distance that will always separate him from that culture. Zeno's Achilles and the tortoise.

That was, I reflected, why some of our very best area specialists were among my least "cosmopolitan" friends; their very expertise made them more aware, and more appreciative, of being *Americans*. They knew you were only truly at home when you were *at home*.

Mobile lounges brought us to the main terminal. Walking fast through the "cattle chutes" I was one of the first passengers at immigration. The inspector looked briefly at my passport. She handed it back: "Welcome home, sir." I thought: St. Peter is black—and a woman!

With only carry-on luggage (my garment and tennis bags), I was also one of the first through customs: "Nothing to declare." I walked through the double doors into the USA.

Marj and Brian were standing in the crowd, against the line of bollards, near the passenger exit door.

I've never been very good at handling such situations with "Yankee" composure. I didn't try now. Marj looked familiar, pretty . . . desirable. She'd had her shoulder-length hair gently permed. Under her camel's-hair coat, open in the front, she wore a simple, blue knit dress that suggested rather than emphasized her figure.

It felt good and familiar to put my arms around her and kiss her. She wore my favorite perfume, "Beautiful."

"Missed you, Marj."

"Me, too. So glad you're home!"

"You're looking great!"

I hugged Brian, and we kissed on both cheeks. I was surprised by his appearance. He'd had a growth spurt. He was my height now, though still a few pounds lighter. He wore blue jeans, docksiders, and one of my old Oxford-cloth shirts. He looked—I admitted candidly—like a handsome variation of myself. But he wasn't wearing socks!

"Won't you catch cold?" I asked.

Brian laughed: "I told Mom you'd say something like that. I bet Columbus said something like that when *he* got home to his family. The hero vanishes!—plain old Dad again. I told Mom that if you said something like that, then I'd regress too. The way State Department psychiatrists say we Foreign Service children often do, after each move? Now I'm supposed to ask: 'What did you bring me?' "

We both laughed. "That's OK," Brian added, "you can bug me this one afternoon."

Brian did most of the talking as we drove in a friend's car from Dulles to the Guest Quarters residential hotel, off Virginia Avenue near the State Department. Remembering Jon's comment, I listened.

I heard an almost play-by-play replay of the last St. Andrews basketball game against Tower Hill. Brian had scored sixteen points; the coach was going to move him up to the varsity. He clearly was having a good experience at the *Dead Poets' Society* school. "And the winter dance was really nice," he went on. "A live band! They even played music by Glenn Miller and some Lester Lanin arrangements, music from *your* days, Dad."

I interrupted: "From the K-T Boundary, Brian? By the King Tut Trio?" I corrected him: "Glenn Miller was *my father's* generation. But did you dance?"

"Yes."

"Do you have a girl friend?"

"Dad, I remember you once told me never to talk about my girls. You said the talkers are never the doers. And that besides, it's not considerate."

I nodded in agreement, smiled.

I wondered if Foreign Service people who proudly told of sending their children to fancy Swiss boarding schools knew how bad the Swiss thought most of these schools were. One Swiss friend described them to me as "just extended daycare centers for the castoffs of broken marriages, children of the third-world rich, and the demimonde, backward schools for forward boys, and girls!" Most of Brian's schooling up to the ninth grade had been at international community schools in South America. The schools taught a basically American curriculum. They were academically solid, even conservative, but also provided good intercultural experiences: excellent instruction in the local language, and the company of students from many different nations.

At high school time, though, we'd unhesitatingly made one of our hardest decisions ever. We sent Brian back to the USA, to St. Andrews— my own preparatory school—for an "all-American" education. That way, we thought, as he grew through adolescence and looked for identity beyond our family, he'd know who he was as an *American*. We wanted Brian to be open, curious, self-confident, well-balanced—and *American*. Not a rootless cosmopolitan. Citizenship of the world could come later.

We'd pulled off the Dulles access road and were headed for Washington via the George Washington Memorial Parkway. The homebound rush-hour traffic had begun; but on the lanes going *into* town, the traffic was light. On our left, just before the Key Bridge, my eye followed the jagged "Flemish Gothic" spires of Georgetown University as they walked stilt-legged across the skyline.

Listening to Brian and Marj, I completely missed the turn-off for the Theodore Roosevelt Bridge. No matter. A few minutes more and we were crossing the Potomac on the Memorial Bridge—one of my favorites. Its arches seemed to carry it across the river in just a few long, smooth strides, like the movement of good infantry on the march. No bounces. I also loved its exuberant, colossal, Hellenistic horses and riders. Quite fittingly, a gift of the Italian government! Then the incomparable monument to Father Abraham, and the Vietnam Wall!

Always, as I walked down its gentle sloping path to the Underworld, as its black, marbled waters closed over my head, I thought: This, for us Americans, is the true "Valley of the Shadow of Death."

I tried not to spoil the moment by looking up toward C Street, where lay the two city blocks of the State Department, as whitely massive and shapeless as a glacier. I thought of Farnsworth's comments on the building, and the link between form and function!

Marj was saying: ". . . Brian isn't staying at the Guest Quarters. He's going on to the home of a school friend who's also down for the weekend. But he'll join us tomorrow at breakfast before he has to go back."

Just before Brian left us, a thought came to me: "Wait," I said, "I *do* have a present for you." From my pocket I took Mustafa's white cowrie charm. "A good luck charm," I explained. "Never open it. Keep it on your person. It's never let me down. What with midterms, basketball season, you never know—it might be useful."

That night at the Riverview Restaurant in the Watergate, a photographer offered to take our picture. I agreed. As the Polaroid photo was returned to us, I laughed to see the wolfish gleam in my eye, as Marj smiled at the camera and I smiled at her.

The Riverview has a famous French chef. Also famously intimidating French waiters. But tonight their *hauteur* was lost on me. Confidently, I charged through the menu's linguistic obstacle course: swinging over *le soufflé aux écrevisses, aromatisées de coriande (pour deux)*, I quickly climbed *le halibut poché au vinaigrette chaude le Bernardin*, jumped down from *la cotelette de veau grillée, avec courgettes au romarin*, and sprinted across the *mousse au chocolat* finish line. But even overseas, I've always served American wine. I asked the sommelier for a bottle of my favorite chardonnay, a Covey Run from Washington State.

Through the picture window we looked out onto the Potomac, a dark, opalescent corridor separating the District from Virginia beyond. I thought of the dining room table at the Khartoum residence. Irregular points of light marked the Roslyn office complexes, in the depressed real estate market many of them now "see-throughs"; merciful darkness obscured the recyclable plastic architecture. The outside temperatures were in the thirties, and no stars were out. The wind, a stressed-out, pushy Washington wind, ran the red light past the Kennedy Center access road, hooted angrily as it shouldered past cars, people, trees, and buildings in its way, then sped on toward the Tidal Basin.

The wine came. We clinked glasses: I said: "To you Marj, to you and Brian—to us."

I set my glass down, and went on: "Marj, I have some news for us. Before I left Khartoum, I heard from the director general about our next assignment."

"Is it overseas?"

"Yes."

Marj thought a moment. "I frankly wouldn't have minded something back home. I thought we'd had enough excitement to last us awhile. We could be near Brian. Maybe take him to visit some colleges. But after Khartoum, it won't be another hardship post, at least. Josh, you're quiet. Don't tell me it *is* another hardship assignment!"

"Well, yes and no . . ."

To my surprise, Marj smiled and took my hand. She looked me right in the face. "Don't beat around the bush with me, Lieutenant. Just tell me what beach the Chamberlains will be storming next. Inchon? Mogadishu? Cap Haitien? Sarajevo?"

Watching her carefully, I answered: "We're going to Cameroon, *Madame l'Ambassadrice.*"

Marj's French was excellent, far better than mine. A minor at college, plus a year at Angers in a curriculum for *French*—not international—students. She understood the words right away. But it took a moment for their meaning to sink in.

"What you say isn't possible, but even in your unique, franco-hispanic dialect—Catalan?—I can guess what you're trying to say. You *are* serious?" I handed Marj a copy of the director general's cable.

As she read, I could tell from her expression that she felt a little as *I* had on receiving the news. She looked happy and excited as she looked up.

"We've done it, dear," I said. "We're there. And whatever else may happen, we'll always have been there. And we got there *together*. Can we handle a second bottle of wine? Perhaps some champagne for you, Ms. Tenzig Norkay? Some Schramsberger?"

"Let's go for it, Sir Edmund!"

Marj liked what I could tell her about Cameroon. The capital Yaoundé, was inland, set in a range of hills at about 2200 feet. The weather was good. The Residence was one of the best in Africa, with its own pool and tennis court. The economy had potential, with a strong agricultural and petroleum base. The government was pro-West, although moves toward democratization and privatization looked badly stalled. There was also tension between the anglophone Cameroonians in the northwest and the francophone majority. We talked. And talked. I thought: So much of the fun of a good assignment is the anticipation, the preparation, talking it over.

We'd almost finished dessert when Marj changed the subject. Turning her head to look out toward the river, she began speaking softly, almost as if to herself: "I missed you more than I thought I would, these last months at home with Mom and Dad. Everything was so bland . . . and always the little digs at you. I don't mind criticizing you—you often deserve it, you know—but I didn't like them doing it. I finally told them to stop it, or I'd have to move out. Mostly it *did* stop.

"Then there was Mom's underhanded little campaign—was it unconscious?—always to include at her dinner parties a few of Boston's so-called 'eligible bachelors.' (Marj mimicked:) '. . . and this is my daughter Marjorie. Her husband's off in Africa, and I'm afraid she's finding Boston dull with just me and her father about!' Ugh! What a pack of losers! Pasty, unformed, youngish men, with receding hairlines and soft, comfy little stomachs resting on their belts. Their idea of hitting on a girl was to whisper in my ear: 'The Nasdaq Composite is holding steady,' while they tried to grope my thigh. Ward Kapeckas, just better dressed!"

Marj added: "If only Men's Furnishings at Brooks Brothers sold balls! You have your many faults, Josh. Underneath your nice manners, you're egocentric, you know, and you're driven. But you're not a wimp."

She laughed: "These months, I've felt a little like that Greek heroine, Penelope. And when you got off that plane, I thought of another great traveler! The patron deity of Foreign Service people—Hercules?—when he showed up with his club to polish off all the suitors?"

"It was Odysseus," I said, "and he used a bronze bow, not a club. And his son gave him a hand."

Marj laughed: "Whatever."

She took a sip of her wine, reached over for my hand, and went on: "But—but I did make a—friend. He was the squash coach at Harvard. About your age. A widower. Shy, but with a quiet sense of humor. He sat through one of my parents' dinners and hardly said a word. But the next day he telephoned and asked me out—to the Arnold Arboretum! If he'd said dinner, I'd of course have said no. Then he offered to give me some squash lessons. He moved so precisely, grace-fully, around the court. We'd take walks together. Another time it was a movie. Then we had dinner at Chez Françoise off Mass. Ave; it was near his apartment, so afterwards we went there for some coffee and liqueur." She paused.

"Josh, nothing happened. I *almost* wanted it to. I've missed you *that* way, too. And it was flattering that a really nice, gentlemanly, at-tractive man was attracted to me. You'd have liked him yourself. But I couldn't do it. I just couldn't. I felt awful, felt I'd led him on just a little. I felt cheap and confused. He didn't argue or push, though. Just drove me home. He didn't even try to kiss me. He just put his arms around me and said call him if I ever wanted to walk, or talk, or play a game of squash. Afterwards, he called the house once or twice. Mom was reproachful. But I never spoke to him or saw him again. And *that* is *that*," Marj concluded in a tone of finality.

We didn't linger over coffee.

Back in our room, I hung out the "Do not disturb" sign, locked the door, and told the operator to hold all calls. I turned out the ceiling lights, but left the bedside table lamp on. Marj was sitting on the bed taking off her shoes. I sat down beside her and reached over to undo the buttons at the back of her blouse. She sat still while, carefully, I drew it out of her skirt and dropped it on the floor. Then she stood up and, from behind, I unhooked and unzipped her skirt and let it fall. I drew her slip off, over her head. I unsnapped her bra. Marj brought her shoulders together as I slid the straps off.

"Hold my breasts," she said. I slid my hands under her arms and took one breast in each hand. They were full, substantial. I could feel her nipples stiffen under my fingertips. Dropping to one knee, I peeled off her panty hose and underpants last.

Tonight there was none of that restraint about her that so often preceded our lovemaking. With Marj, there was sometimes a threshold of inhibition to be overcome. But tonight she seemed to enjoy showing off her good body in the light, moving about, having me touch her.

Then the feel of her body beneath me—fucking Marj was a transfiguration. A relief. The tensions of past months forgotten. Drained from me by making love to a generous, familiar, giving body. Later in the night we made love again.

Monday morning I called on the director general. He seemed the model of everyone's perfect godfather—including, I'd been told, Mario Puzo's. He said I'd be seeing the secretary. I should avoid the press. There would be hearings (closed) before the Senate Foreign Relations Committee. The senators were eager to hear exactly how "we biffed the Libyans out of Sudan."

"Don't be modest," the DG advised. "These are men and women who only understand hyperbole. Blast out their eardrums. I'll make it easy for you," he smiled. "Just pretend you're giving a rock concert—or a recruiting talk for the USMC! You'll find them well disposed. Attentive. Maybe even respectful. Your friend Kirby had a whole set of color blow-ups of your Omdurman scrap shown to the committee. Legislative history was made: eleven senators all momentarily at a loss for words."

The director general also said to get on with my processing. "You'll be debriefed on Sudan, and you'll want to read up on Cameroon—even before we make an announcement. But *do your paperwork first.* It is massive. Financial disclosure statements, background, personal history. You're going into the USG's equivalent of Jungian psychotherapy. You'll come out a Boddhisatva, with new degrees of astral self-knowledge! Maybe even Nirvana! And the process always takes longer than it should. Our security agents can get pulled off your background check to help with the secretary's protective detail. Also, we mustn't miss the spring session of Congress. This is a presidential election year, and Congress might just not reconvene in the fall. You deserve this nomination, so don't miss the boat. Enough said."

I knew the director general was a fly fisherman. I was almost at the door when his feathered hook settled softly before me.

In a voice that barely reached, I heard him say, "Just one more thing: Sally Tolson struck me as an able officer. You were her supervisor. Can you help me to understand why she so suddenly chose to leave Khartoum?"

I turned to answer. His expression was bland, almost bored. But I wasn't taken in. His eyes seemed to look into me like a sonogram.

I chose my words carefully: "Well, along with everyone else at post, I was surprised that Sally wasn't coming back from R&R. She's a great officer and a friend. No, heck! Much more than that. Twice she saved my life: When the foreign minister was assassinated. Then again when she remembered the 'panic button' and started us broadcasting after we'd been taken hostage. But I guess she has a right to her own reasons."

"A lawyerish answer, Mr. Chamberlain," the DG replied. He went on: "It's been my experience that the human chemistry of posts—under heat and pressure—can quickly take remarkably complex forms, almost in the way early life first appeared on earth. But do you recall that verse in Genesis that goes: 'The sons of God saw that the daughters of men were fair; and they took to wife such of them as they chose'? DCMs, and ambassadors-to-be, and others in authority might ponder that text."

Outside the DG's office, I thought: The old devil can draw blood! I also thought he could have taken his own advice. Madame DG, I knew, was wealthy and beautiful; a fixture in the *Washington Post*'s "Style" section *and* wife number three.

Don Oberdorfer had heard I was in town and wrote an article in the *Post*'s "World News" section about "Khartoum and the Battle of the OK Corral." For a time the story reechoed in the Middle East and Europe. But I continued to avoid the media. The department stuck to "no comment," and again the echoes died.

Weeks passed. My processing moved ahead smoothly. We liked the Guest Quarters and decided to stay on, month-to-month. We took AAA's advice and bought a new Acura Integra—there would be better maintenance, I was told, for a Japanese-made car in Cameroon than for American models. Often we'd drive the 108 miles to St. Andrews to see Brian, or bring him and his friends to DC for a long weekend. Oh! the pleasure of driving on cruise control, on a nice road, in a nice car, with nice music coming from a nice tape deck!

I'd resolved not to try to see or call Sally Tolson. The department is large, and our paths didn't cross. But she was still on my mind. I'd learned she, too, had been promoted and had been reassigned to a first-rate job as special assistant to the under secretary for political affairs. And the door appeared locked from her side of the partition, too. She'd declined a lunch that friends in the Foreign Service Association had given for me.

We finally met one Thursday evening at the Lion d'Or, on Connecticut Avenue across from the Mayflower Hotel. Avo Bogosian had come to town on business and invited Sally, Marj, and me to dinner. Avo and Marj did most of the talking. She told him of our life in DC and our preparations for Cameroon.

He brought us up to date on Khartoum. The news was good. Negotiations between the government and the rebels seemed to be going well. The pope might visit again. On a personal note, Frank and Aminata were secretly engaged. I was able to tell Avo that Frank had been given tenure and promoted, because of his quick-thinking and courage at the Marine Guard Ball. He'd also been commended by the department for a major ethnopolitical study, "Tribes and Clans and Septs of Sudan." We laughed, seeing Aminata's hand in this.

Throughout the evening, I could hardly bring myself to look at Sally. I felt abashed. Maybe she did, too. As we all parted, she extended her arm stiffly to me and said goodnight, as if to ward off even a social kiss. Afterwards, Marj commented: "Sally looked pretty tonight, but tired. Her face is looking lined, older. I don't understand why she doesn't use some makeup. She'll have to start coloring her hair soon, I bet. She seemed even more quiet than usual, too. I like her. She's smart. Why can't she find herself some nice man?"

"She's in one of those twelve-hour-a-day, seven-day-a-week jobs," I responded.

The next day Sally called me around noontime: "How about lunch?" she asked. She was downstairs at the C Street lobby. I hesitated—then said I'd be down.

Instead of taking the 1500 corridor to the first floor cafeteria, Sally took me to the elevators and pressed "B" for the basement parking garage. "I thought we'd eat out somewhere," she said. Lamely, I answered: "I'm not sure this is a good idea," but, obediently, I followed to her little silver-gray BMW 325.

Sally was saying: "I feel like getting out of Foggy Bottom. Practically live in this building. Do you know the Tombs in Georgetown? Don't worry. It's full of faculty and students. No one will know you there."

It was raining lightly in Georgetown as we parked on Prospect Street and walked down the steep wrought-iron stairs to the Tombs. The waiter seated us side-by-side in the "No Smoking" section in a small corner booth. Sally had a vegetable-something-or-other; I ordered a Reuben. We each had a Coors Lite.

Sally talked: ". . . finally bought a house, a very small one, in Vienna, Virginia. On one floor. Two bedrooms, bath, living room, kitchen, and dining wing. A very small front yard. A very small fenced-in backyard. The 'subcompact' model among houses. But I feel like a plantation owner. *Gone with the Wind* makes sense now. And for me, the commute's not bad—I get to work by six or six-thirty and don't usually leave before seven or eight. So I miss most of the traffic. I'll be settling in over the next three or four days. I'm taking some leave."

I hardly listened. I could only look at her. Looking at Sally made me understand how thirsty I'd been for the sight of her. As she spoke, and smiled, and moved, I thought: My hands have been over every part of that tight, well-knit body. In the background Nancy Griffith was singing "Once in a Blue Moon."

"Do you know why I called?" I heard Sally say. Her words seemed to float softly down from a very great height. Like "snow falling on cedars."

"No idea," I answered. Our thighs touched.

"After Khartoum," she said, "I promised myself I'd never call. I may be a modern, assertive career woman, but believe me, pride—old-fashioned modesty?—keep me from pushing where I sense I'm not wanted. To seem a feminine version of that horrible Bob Packwood! And then maybe to be received by you indifferently—or put off with one of your cool Protestant smiles! My flesh crawls!

"My main reason, though, for not calling is that I wanted the TV controls, so to speak, to be in your hands. I wanted *you* to choose for us. Even if it meant you'd turn the set off. Because if you *really* care for someone, then *you* want to do what *they* want to do. *That's the difference between love and selfish obsession*—between love and the desire to control, or some sort of egotistical, psychochemical addiction to oneself!"

Sally took a breath, closed her eyes for a moment, then went on: "So just why did I call today? You know, I'd been telling myself: Are you making a big, dramatic deal out of what to Josh is nothing? Or is it just a bore? Is the phone line between us—so to speak—not just silent, but disconnected? Am I blowing on ashes that I wish were coals?

"But you can blame Stendhal for my lunch call. I'd just reread his *Chartreuse de Parme*. Remember how our hero, Fabrice, has tried and failed to speak to his beloved Clelia for fourteen months? Then he makes one final effort to see her—and this time she agrees. So I said to myself: Why shouldn't I call? Maybe I *am* being objectionable. But why not try ONE LAST TIME? What do I have to lose? Afterwards, we'll be a long time dead.

"Why do I feel this way?" Sally shrugged and smiled: "I've no idea! You see, real love's like faith—either it's given or not. It's like kudzu, too: with hard work you can maybe control it, but you can't ever seem to eradicate it. My feelings? Sorry if I offend; I know how completely wrong they are, but *ten years from now*, I'll still feel the same. I'll love you unconditionally all of each day of my life until I die, and I hope there are moments, too, when you'll be moved to remember me well."

Sally paused. "Do I make any sense at all?" she asked.

Without answering, I leaned forward and slid my hand down onto her knee. My fingers drew back her skirt and touched the inside of her left thigh. She pushed my hand away. Shook her head. "Christ, Josh," she said, "this isn't a bedroom. Let's go."

I tried to replay the scene in the department's garage. "Not here," Sally breathed. "Remember, we both have work to do." All that afternoon I tried to focus on arctic snows, and on the rec site pool waters early on a November morning.

Our airfreight had been delivered that week. Among the boxes littering the apartment was one containing china of Sally's. A note said it had been accidentally left out of her lift van. Could I see it got to her?

I decided to deliver it myself the next morning. C&P information gave me Sally's number, and her address in Vienna. The road map showed her living in a development called Murmuring Pines. Who makes up these names? I wondered. It sounds as if Sally's bought into a memorial park, not a suburb!

As I crossed Chain Bridge and followed Route 123 through McLean and Tysons Corner, I kept asking myself: Are you being prudent? Aren't you being plain dumb? I thought of the director general's advice. But each time I'd accelerate, maybe turn the stereo up a notch—Bruce Hornsby—

On turning left at the last corner, I could tell exactly which was Sally's house. Halfway down the block on the right, at curbside, there rose one of the identifying monuments of Foreign Service life: a cairn of boxes and packing tape; also cartons of books, magazines, and bric-a-brac: items damaged either in transit or while stored with one of the third-rate moving firms that tend to win the State Department's contracts just before going out of business! I also saw a pair of camel saddles—I guessed they didn't look or smell as good in the gray damp of Washington as in dry, sunny Khartoum.

I carried my box to the front door and rang the bell. The inner door opened. Through the glass of the storm door Sally looked at me for a moment. Then smiled and let me in.

"It was open," she said.

"Am I coming at a bad time?"

"Not at all. I can use a break. I've been making 'sheers' for the windows, but don't have the technique quite right. Also, the material's hard to work with. It's Oysternet, a sort of miracle fiber designed by DuPont to irritate the hands. Come in."

Inside was another Foreign Service tableau. Shipping cartons everywhere, pictures on the floor, leaning against the wall, kitchen cabinets and drawers open—and mostly empty. A couch and coffee table stood in the living room bay; some chairs were still wrapped

"I can 'mike' you some coffee," Sally said. "I hope you've already had breakfast."

She brought coffee to where I sat on one end of the couch. She had a cup, too, and sat at the other. I drank some coffee. I made conversation. I seemed to hear a stranger in the room speaking with my voice. After a few minutes, I put the cup down and slid over toward Sally. I took her in my arms and kissed her.

There was a moment of stiffness. "Josh, this doesn't help—doesn't do any good——" I kissed her again, longer. I felt the muscles along her back bend and soften. She kissed me back. We stood up. I took her in my arms and as we kissed, I slid my hands to her buttocks and pulled her close against me. Then we moved down a hallway to her bedroom. With little steps I urged her to the bed; she half fell backwards onto it. I tried to unbutton her jeans. She said: "Let me do it myself."

In my arms Sally's body felt taut and slight, yet soft and strong. As we began making love, she looked up at me and said with a little smile,

"No curtains yet—the neighbors are missing the show." Then a different kind of lovemaking. Urgent, electric, almost competitive.

Afterwards, as I lay spent, half-asleep by Sally's side, the complacent thought occurred: It's like driving a European sports car after an American luxury sedan. Each great, though the ride, the suspension, are very different. Smug, sexist bastard! I told myself.

I came back often to Murmuring Pines. My schedule was flexible. Marj never questioned my late evenings or weekend absences. Once Sally and I spent the night together. I'd told Marj I was off on a classified briefing at the CIA "Farm" near Williamsburg.

In the morning, I asked Sally, "What's going to happen to us?"

She replied: "I've learned from Khartoum. I'm making no demands. The answer is, *anything* you want."

"TO THE HAPPY FEW"

27

But time was passing. The paperwork was done. Cameroon had given *agrément*. The White House had announced my nomination. The Senate hearings had gone very well. At the end, the acting chair, Senator Nancy Kassebaum, put in the record that "the Senate Foreign Relations Committee was privileged today to hear from Ambassador-designate Joshua L. Chamberlain. He has served his country in an exemplary way. We are proud of him, and wish him continued good fortune and success."

Friends in Washington and overseas sent letters and cables of congratulations. I was especially touched by the sincerity and goodwill in a letter from Prime Minister al-Mughraibiy. Its final paragraph, too, caught my eye. Al-Mughraibiy wrote: "Our friend Mustafa, too, sends best wishes. Recently he came to my office to press on me one of his white-cowrie charms. I thanked him, but you, as a good Presbyterian, Josh, understand my feelings on these matters."

Sudan seemed already far away and long ago. More and more on my mind was the knowledge of the real possibility that, in a week or two, I could be sworn in and we'd be traveling to post. The paths of my life and Sally's were still close and converging. But soon they'd separate again.

Life without Sally was unthinkable. But when I tried to imagine myself saying to Marj "I'm leaving you"—— Impossible! Especially because Marj hadn't seemed so relaxed, so radiant, in years. My mind, heart, soul were being tested to the destruction level. Such tensile strength, my mind kept thinking. We must be all carbon fiber inside.

One night, though, as Sally and I lay naked next to one another, I started to say something. I don't know what I had in mind, but inside me something strained and parted. The words that came out of my mouth—unwilled—were: "Will you marry me?" Maybe Dr. Freud would have had an explanation! But Sally rose on an elbow and leaned her upper body on my chest. She kissed me. "I'll marry you in a minute," she said. We made love.

Sally never referred to Marj then, or at any other time. Nor did she ever again advert to my marriage proposal. One day, I awkwardly tried to return to the subject: "You know what I asked awhile ago. I know I haven't made it easy for you——"

Sally cut me off. "I'm relaxed," she answered. "It's in your hands, now. Remember? *I* want what *you* want."

But my emotional life was staggering—imploding—under multiples of atmosphere and gravity.

In the end, I resolved to break the news to Marj at the worst, but only possible, time: after the swearing-in. "If you're going to be the complete bastard," I told myself, "then *be* one—and head for the border."

I'd have to go to post alone, but eventually, once the legalities were done, Sally would join me. What I was doing was not so unheard of in the Foreign Service today. Selfishly, I told myself that my professional stock was high; at this point, my career would not particularly suffer. The decision, though, and my rationalizations, brought no peace of mind. I did not share my plans with Sally.

Marj noticed my mood. "You're so tense these days, Josh. This should be a time for us to relax, enjoy Washington, our Foreign Service friends. I know your briefing schedule's been very heavy, but why don't we take a few days off, to Williamsburg, or Charlottesville? And make plans maybe for some leave in France on our way to post? We could visit some of the Loire Valley chateaux? I could show you the one at Angers. Josh?"

The day of my swearing-in arrived. The ceremony was set for 11:00 A.M. I'd lain awake almost all night, listening to Marj's even breathing, shaping the words in my mouth, imaging the scenes to follow. The alarm clock finally announced what should have been the sunlit peak of my Service life. I was about to be "knighted."

I prayed: "Dear God, I'd give up anything, yes, anything for some way out—just as long as it didn't mean I had to leave Sally Tolson." And instantly I reproached myself for such an unworthy, even monstrous, wish. *The Monkey's Paw?* I thought.

I couldn't eat breakfast. My sense of unworth was choking me, as I sat at the table and listened to Marj and Brian's happy conversation. Brian was with us—he'd come from school the night before. He'd be driven back after the reception. Marj's parents were coming from Boston. Some 150 of our friends would come to the State Department's Benjamin Franklin Room for the swearing-in and a champagne reception afterwards. Marj was speaking of a very pretty, very expensive dress she'd bought for the occasion. "It will give me something special always to remember the day by."

I excused myself and out of habit went to the TV and turned on CNN. (Back in the U.S., I could hardly read too many newspapers or watch too much TV; Marj spoke of my 'infomania.') Bernard Shaw was speaking: "We now take you live to Peter Arnett." I grasped the familiar scene almost before I took in Shaw's words. A camera panned over a townscape. A reddish dust was in the air; far away, columns of smoke were rising from along the bend in a river. It was Khartoum. The smoke was coming from the Palace area.

Arnett's flat New Zealand voice was saying: "Authorities confirm that Prime Minister al-Mughraibiy has been killed following the seizure of power by a military junta headed by Major Hassan Omar al-Furi. Heavy casualties are reported as fighting continues in Sudan's capital, Khartoum, between Arab elements, led by the junta, and Khartoum's black African population. The new prime minister, Lieutenant General Abdul Aziz bin Shakir, announces that the Libyan *Jamahiriyyah* . . ." I turned the set off. I couldn't bear any more. Besides, it was time to get dressed.

Later, at the apartment door I got out: "Marj, I have something important to say when we get back."

She looked over, smiled: "I guess what I have to say can wait until then, too."

The Benjamin Franklin Room on the eighth floor of the Department of State is no Hall of Mirrors, but it is just what such a room should be for a republic. And its magnificently decorated and tastefully furnished reception areas are in no sense museumlike. None of the chairs—genuine antiques—have cords blocking the seat. One can sit and pen a note to friends at the very desk on which Thomas Jefferson and our other Peace Commissioners signed the Treaty of Paris in 1783. All the furnishings are intended for *use* in what some call "our nation's living room."

The rooms open onto one of the great panoramas of the world. From the balcony, looking east, one sees the Washington and Jefferson monuments and the Capitol itself; to the West, the Lincoln Memorial, the Memorial Bridge, the Lee mansion, and Arlington National Cemetery. A number of crews are always visible on the Potomac—their pointed shapes waterbugging up and downstream.

We were early, but the director general was waiting for us when we arrived on the eighth floor via a reserved bank of elevators. His appearance was diplomatic perfection.

The DG looked first at Marj, his eyes lingering, a kiss on her cheek. Then he turned (perfunctorily) to me: "A happy day for the beautiful Mrs. Chamberlain! And her hero husband! A pity though about Sudan, eh? You've heard? Those Arabs! A genius for self-destruction! But what a lovely dress! It scarcely does you justice!" Marj blushed and smiled.

Turning his back to me, the DG directed Marj into the room—with his hand moving to her hip. With his other hand, he indicated she should stand near the podium. My thoughts went to Sa'eed al-Masri.

We made small talk as the guests arrived. "It sounds as if the Cameroonians plan to be here on time," he said. "They called my office at least twice yesterday to be very sure of the date and time of your swearing-in." He was right. The Cameroonian ambassador, his wife, and his counselor of embassy, came in almost as we spoke.

With the director general standing by, the chief of protocol, a distinguished and attractive presidential appointee, administered the oath of office. I concentrated on speaking slowly and clearly. As Marj held the family Bible, I repeated after the chief of protocol: "I, Joshua Lawrence Chamberlain IV, do solemnly swear, that I will support and defend the Constitution of the United States . . . so help me God." To my relief I didn't stumble.

Then the DG came to the microphone. He read a message to me from Ambassador Farnsworth. Laughter and applause; but I wasn't really paying attention. Then came a surprise. "Ambassador Farnsworth has a message for Mrs. Chamberlain, too," the DG announced.

At this, one of the special assistants came forward and presented Marj with a long box. Within were (of course!) a dozen, long-stemmed yellow roses. The note read: "It may all seem far away and long ago, but Abbas, Mustafa, and I and all your other Khartoum friends wish we could, again, present these in person! Most affectionately, Jon"

The DG's own brief address followed. I half heard these remarks, too ("... in real terms we are sending our best"). But from more laughter and occasional applause I knew another polished, professional performance was under way.

Marj had the roses cradled in her arm. She looked attentive and, I realized, beautiful! Something from a John Singer Sargent painting. But all the time my eyes were wandering over the audience, looking, searching. They found Sally in the back of the room. She gave me a quick smile—a flashbulb going off!

Then amidst louder applause, I knew it was my turn to speak. I'd written out my statement and had rehearsed it often enough to deliver it without notes. I recalled Ambassador Farnsworth's advice about public speaking.

First I greeted the Cameroonians, the director general, Marj's parents, and some special friends. Next, I turned to my audience. I began on a light note: "One of you asked me, when I spoke to you today, if I'd say something about how it felt to be going as ambassador to the Republic of Cameroon. I'll try to oblige. When the president asked me to be his representative, I felt honored and grateful. It is always an honor for an American to represent and serve his country, any place, anytime.

"After that, I felt lucky. I felt as if I had won the Thanksgiving Turkey, as if Vanna White had just stepped back from the 'Answer Board'—and there it was! My parking problems over for the next few years!" I spoke of people and favorite sights and places that I'd miss. I mentioned the Tombs in Georgetown. I looked over—that flashbulb again——

The rest of the talk was more serious. But it seemed to go well. Applause. I stepped down from the podium to sign my commission. Photos followed, single and group. The waiters immediately began to pass champagne and light refreshments. Then, moving counterclockwise, our friends and well-wishers filed by to shake hands and offer congratulations. When it was Sally's turn, she looked cheerful and completely at ease. "You were great. Thanks for the reference," she murmured as she kissed my cheek.

At the end of the hour, the DG was one of the last to go. He kissed Marj on both cheeks, and said: "I must leave you now—but as with all things you both have done in your lives, your swearing-in ceremony was first-rate."

Brian, Marj, and I took the elevator down. Marj asked, "Josh? You're looking awfully pale. Is it the news from Sudan? Have you picked up a bug or something?"

I couldn't answer. I was thinking of what lay beyond. I knew how Abraham felt as he led the unsuspecting Isaac up the sacrificial mountain. I thought: Brian's ride was to leave directly from the department's diplomatic entrance. Marj's parents would go back to Boston that night. Should I break the news to Marj tonight? Wait until morning? Or? Or?

Almost sleepwalking, I made my way past security, through the diplomatic entrance's heavy, bulletproof glass doors and out onto C Street. The air, a finely spun cotton candy—a ruddy, blurred aerogel— seemed to cling to my arms and legs, to resist my progress. My peripheral vision was constricting to a single blurry point. An attack of "panic disorder"? I felt chest pains, a frantic heartbeat. I half sat on one of the red granite crash barriers by the entrance. Shook my head. Closed my eyes.

I heard Brian: "Mom, I think something's wrong with Dad." Then I heard Marj's worried voice: "Josh, we'll take a taxi right home. You must have a temperature. You're going to bed. Taxi!"

A taxi pulled up. Marj asked the driver: "Can you please give me a hand? I think my husband is sick."

The taxi door opened, and the driver came toward me around the rear of his car.

I watched him come. Medium height. Mustache. Mediterranean-looking. He held a rolled-up newspaper in his right hand. He *limped.*

Something stirred in my mind as the newspaper fell away from a silenced, small-caliber, long-barreled revolver. The revolver swung upwards. I was in a waking nightmare. One of those dreams where the danger is upon you, and you're frozen—you just watch it happen.

Brian had the reflexes and reactions of a young athlete. He dived. Knocked the man back against the side of his taxi. The assassin slammed the butt of his revolver down against Brian's head. Brian crumpled to the pavement. The man quickly aimed at me. The gun coughed.

Marj threw herself in front of me. She flinched as the bullet struck her. But she held onto me, keeping herself between me and the shooter. I felt her breath on my cheek, caught the aroma of Beautiful, heard a hard scrabble as the heels of her shoes scraped for purchase on the smooth pavement. The gunman fired into her again.

A loud report. The driver spun to his right. One of the department security guards stood at the entrance, his service .38 extended in both hands. Off-balance, the shooter fired at me a third time. Two simultaneous reports. There was a flash——then darkness.

The doctors and nurses at Georgetown University Hospital were very kind. More than twenty-four hours had passed. Brian was fine. He could return to school anytime. I would recover fully. It had been a grazing shot. No signs of a heart attack, but they liked to keep an eye on head wounds. I'd be hospitalized two or three more days.

Marj's operation had been a success. Her condition had been upgraded to good. "She's young," the doctors said, "and the chances of a good recovery are excellent."

That afternoon, I was taken in my wheelchair to her room. She was sleeping, so they left me by the side of her bed. She looked older, wan. Her skin, always pale, looked translucent. I took her hand. She opened her eyes.

"They tell me you'll be alright," I said. "You're looking good," I lied.

Marj half smiled. Shook her head. "I've seen myself in a mirror."

Then her mood suddenly changed. Her eyes filled with tears. "Josh, do you remember the important news I was going to have for you after the ceremony?" I nodded. She went on: "I was going to tell you we were going to have another baby. I'd decided to try after you got back. I wasn't too old."

She paused: "But our baby——I lost him——the shooting. And now, after the operation, the doctors don't think——" Marj couldn't go on.

I tried helplessly, uselessly, to console her. After a time she asked: "And your news for me?"

"Nothing at all, Marj. Let's talk about Angers."

What more is there to tell? The assassin was dead. Jack had a probable fit with a Palestinian terrorist who had arrived in Sudan the previous summer. I *knew* Jack was right. Several different terrorist groups, however, claimed credit for "the heroic blow struck in the very heart of the oppressor-capital." I made the BBC again—by name this time. Our friends and the department couldn't have been more supportive. The DG assured us we'd still be going out to Cameroon.

One thing more. While I was in the hospital a book came from Sally Tolson. It was the Flammarion edition of *La Chartreuse de Parme*. Clipped to the cover was a note from Sally: "See p. 509."

There, on the last page of the book, she'd written: "Love, and Good-bye—and *toujours gai!*" just below Stendhal's English-language dedication

"TO THE HAPPY FEW"

AFTERWORD

Hume Horan, a career Foreign Service officer, was United States Ambassador to Côte d'Ivoire from 1992 to 1995. He has also served as ambassador to Cameroon, Equatorial Guinea, Sudan, and Saudi Arabia. In 1991–92 Horan was president of the American Foreign Service Association, following two years teaching foreign affairs and history at Georgetown University. Other assignments have included Iraq, Libya, Jordan, and an earlier tour in Saudi Arabia (1972–77).

Ambassador Horan is a graduate of Harvard College (A.B. *cum laude* 1958, American history, A.M. 1963, Middle Eastern studies). He has also studied independently at the University of Baghdad, the University of Jordan, and the Islamic University of Baida (Libya). He speaks French, Spanish, German, and Arabic. His publications include translations from Arabic of a novel by Egyptian author Mahmoud Teymour and a number of Sudanese short stories.

Horan enjoyed his 1983–1986 assignment as ambassador to Khartoum, Sudan, the principal setting for this novel. His ambassadorship there was an active one: he supervised the extraction of Ethiopian Jews from Sudan to Israel, which he had helped negotiate; Sudan's North-South civil war broke out again; Muslim canon law was imposed; and a revolution overthrew the seventeen-year dictatorship of General Jaafar al-Nimeiry.

Readers should not take literally all details of the narrative. The real and fictional Sudan *do* share common traits. But the theme of the "Red Wind," for instance, while part of Sudanese folk religion, has in the book been given a higher purpose. In actual Sudanese folk religion, the "Red Wind" and the "White Wind" are types of spirit possession. The role of the cowries is the author's invention. In addition, certain liberties have been taken with the precise location of some ethnic groups (notably, the Fur) and of some geographical features (Omdurman battlefield would have been at a sharp angle from where Sally and Josh stood on the Residence balcony).

Those who want to learn more about one of Africa's and the Arab world's most interesting countries cannot do better than to begin with Alan Moorehead's *The White Nile* (Harper, 1961, available in paperback). The best history is by P. M. Holt and M. W. Daly, *A History of the Sudan* (Longman, 1988). The murder of Cleo Noel and Curt Moore is the subject of a truly superb book by Ambassador David A. Korn, *Assassination in Khartoum* (Indiana University Press, 1993).